Jigglyspot and the Zero Intellect

PD Alleva

Chamber Door Publishing, LLC
Boca Raton, Florida

ISBN (Digital): 978-1-7351686-3-0
ISBN (Hardcover): 979-8-218-17788-1
ISBN (Paperback): 979-8-218-15140-9

Cover: Cherie Foxley (cheriefox.com)
Editor: Chamber Door Publishing, LLC
Interior design: Nancy Fraser

Printed in the USA

Trigger Warning: **https://pdalleva.com/jigglyspot-graphic-content**

Dedication

For those who love horror the most and the reader who understands that horror is so much more than just blood and gore. Although, we love those too.

“Haven't you ever heard of the healing power of laughter?”

~ The Joker (*Batman 1989*)

Part I
Casting Call

1

6:34 A.M.
Friday June 7, 2019
Brooklyn, NY
Jigglyspot

Jigglyspot stood in the middle of a barren living room holding a mop handle. Morning arrived not five minutes before and now gleamed through the windows. He took a deep breath. The smell of bleach burned his nostrils, a fragrance Jiggly had come to admire over the past few decades. He was proud of his work, noticing how the sunlight reflected on the light brown wood floor and across the beige walls in the empty brownstone. He'd done well. Not a spot of blood remained from last night's carnage and mayhem. Jiggly would know. His eyesight was 20/20 and he could spot a pimple on a falcon if falcons ever had pimples.

He itched his stubbly cheek. White flecks from makeup crinkled by sweat-the cost of last night's labor-flaked across his thick fingers. He'd gone with the traditional frowning clown last night. A red frown with large black circles around the eyes. All else was white. Jiggly enjoyed the clown style, always had. And why not? Gacy was a god in Jiggly's mind. Plus, the clown style reminded him of home. People love clowns, and being a clown was never a problem. Nope, not at all. Jiggly's problem was with humanity, a species he despised more than he could fathom. Why? Because they have half a brain. At least to Jigglyspot, who always stared down on human beings as having not half a brain, but less than half, especially when compared to a Warlock, a fact Jigglyspot took with pride.

Jiggly always knew he was a Warlock, his Nana had said so. And it was Nana who coined the name Jigglyspot; a reference to the white spot of hair on the right side of Jiggly's occipital lobe and his always round stomach. It was the white spot that Nana said proved he came from the Warlocks, their signature trademark for any human who carried the Warlock gene which, according to Nana at least, meant that Jigglyspot was half human and half warlock, a reality that Jiggly also despised considering his contempt for humanity. Too bad Nana had abandoned him at the young age of eight. Double bad that the Warlocks had perished into the void millenniums ago, leaving Jigglyspot with no real connection to his heritage. Although, he was more than grateful for the otherworldly species that adopted him-something about their ancestors' connection to the Warlocks prompted the decision-because it was through their kindness that Jigglyspot fell in love with the clown style. When they first arrived to gather Jiggly into their circle, they did so wearing clown outfits for the simple reason that little kids love clowns-also because their true features would cause one large ruckus should they have revealed themselves in the open. Nevertheless, Jiggly's obsession with the clown style took hold on that very day.

But back to the humans. Stupid Human Scum is how Jiggly referred to them. The SHS or the Zero Intellect, whichever you choose is fine. He enjoyed looking down on them; inferior species deserve to be looked down on. Although Jiggly couldn't look down on too many people, not with that pudgy five-foot frame. Not at all. Jiggly looked down on people because on the inside he was large, with an energy larger than life, affording him a stature that crept through his eyes, those emerald blues, with just a touch more blue than green, when he stared his victims down. Made one feel hypnotized, circling, spiraling. Gone.

Jiggly laughed. Started laughing at least, pinching the bridge of his nose with his free hand. His heavy husky voice bounced off the walls like an echo toppling over on itself as he laughed out loud. Then a sigh, followed by a deep breath. His nostrils burned with bleach and a hint of sulfur that filled his eyes with tears.

Or was he crying?

Couldn't be. Warlocks don't cry.

And he had to tidy up; there was no time for tears. Finish what he started and be gone and leave the rest for the police. Of course, they'll find nothing. Jigglyspot had been cleaning up body parts and discarding evidence for so long the process came naturally. He was proficient and meticulous, always had been. Even in the beginning when fear controlled the obsession to not get caught. Well, with one exception, his very first clean up.

But *they* always praised Jiggly for his expertise in cover up.

They held him in the highest regard, knew his potential, and encouraged Jiggly's desires. Not that any human could ever see the rising stock of Jigglyspot. All he ever received from humans was a quick disregard, dismissing him and all because of his size. Little did they know what lurked beneath the surface, the true Jiggly. But he learned to accept their dismissive nature, which, over time, became his greatest asset. Humans have been underestimating Jiggly since he was born, giving him the upper hand every time he identified his next victim. Half a brain, remember?

Less than half by far.

And Jiggly couldn't wait to hear the praise. He knew *they* would send the accolades soon.

2

Minutes Before 4:00 A.M
Beverly Hills, California
Tyler Reese

Tyler set his gun down on the table. He was tired and wanted to stretch. His victim—one James Reilly-was strapped to a chair across the table from Tyler. Bound by duct tape, James eyeballed the Glock 9 with attached silencer as if his eyes could pick up the weapon. Tyler yawned, closed his eyes for just a second and James jumped in his chair. Not that he could jump too far. Tyler was good with duct tape. He was certain there was no way James could free himself. This being Tyler's first kill, he had to go the extra mile. One never knew what to expect. All he'd seen on television and in movies could have gotten it wrong; perhaps there is a way to wiggle free from duct tape. So, Tyler used all of it, just to be sure. No one needed a screaming James Reilly disturbing the neighbors at this early hour. Not in this neighborhood.

Tyler fixed his eyes on James. He definitely used an amusing amount of tape. The thought—and of course seeing James exactly where he wanted him—brought a smile to Tyler's lips.

Now he was just staring. Silent. And James muttered, "Fuck you," his voice muffled by duct tape. Tyler ran his hand through his hair-those thick dark locks kept falling in front of his green eyes-then gripped the gun and pointed the barrel at James, who cringed and shuddered.

Tyler's original plan was another mass shooting, but after careful consideration, he decided all those types of shooters were pussies. Plain and simple. Killing innocent people when they should have the balls to stare down their victim, the one who caused so much trouble. Whose bullied torture over the years molded the killer like a sculptor chips away at clay to reveal the true masterpiece that exists within.

No, mass shooters had no balls, according to Tyler.

Nonetheless, what Tyler was struggling with was what to say. Of course, James knew why he was duct taped to a chair in front of his kitchen table in his parents' Beverly Hills home. He'd always been one of those preppy little creeps, thinking he was better than everyone and whose parents' success served as a free ticket to treat others like shit. It's called rich privilege, and Tyler was tired of all those rich pricks sitting up on high while the rest of the population scrambled and clawed at each other over the scraps from their tables. Divided when they should take up arms together and celebrate their differences while sending all those rich shits to the hell they deserve. Reilly's parents were a part of the three percent of the population that controlled all the money in the world. Although they hadn't graduated into the one percent who owned even more of the world's wealth than the other two percent who were in their rich little circle.

If Tyler had done even close to any of the dastardly deeds James Reilly got away with, they'd throw him in prison and forget about him. Too poor to give out bribes to the powers that be and too much of a nobody for anyone to care. Tyler would play the pawn in their little game of rich versus poor, an example that they were doing all they could to keep thugs off the street while allowing true criminals to walk out the door into freedom. And that's all it took, a large bribe and an unsaid favor and all those rich motherfuckers got away with bloody fuckin murder. James Reilly knew this fact all too well, and in return he got away with everything, no matter what it was. And Tyler refused to allow it to continue, not if he could help it. James would be his first, and likely, his last victim. Of course, he could go on a murdering rampage and shoot all of them, but he knew he wouldn't have to; the others will heed the warning. Everyone knew James was an asshole and his death is justified. But there was another side to the coin; if Tyler went around shooting everyone who ever bullied him, he'd get caught. The police aren't that stupid and there are school records they would look into. Any detective with half a brain could add, and two plus two was still four.

No, James had been as ass all his school career and Tyler had checked the school records. Twenty-two separate incidents and those were the ones on record. Tyler knew of at least a dozen more bullied rampages he'd witnessed with his own eyes. After all, they did grow up together.

Back to the problem at hand. Whether or not to speak? And then another question popped into Tyler's mind. Should he shoot James between the eyes and be done with it, or straight through the heart and watch him gasp his last painful breath?

He elected the latter. And what he said was very modest.

"You're an asshole, James, plain and simple." Then shot him in the chest, remembering the ridicule since sixth grade, mostly about the white spot, the circle of white hair on the left side of Tyler's head. The gunshot whistled like a dart. Bullet impact slammed James back in his chair and for a second Tyler was sure he'd tumble over. But he didn't. The duct tape held strong.

James was breathing, wheezing, like sucking air through a straw. Wet gurgles now, Tyler assumed it was blood in the back of James' throat. His body bobbed back and forth. Blood, pouring from the gunshot wound, saturated his shirt, spilling down and across his pants, droplets squeezing beneath the duct tape to the floor.

"Look at me," Tyler ordered. He wanted to see his eyes; wanted to watch life leap from Reilly's baby browns to reveal the darkness where James was going. Tyler stood, the 9MM scraping across the table as he did. And then he screamed, "*LOOK*, AT ME."

And the wheezing, gurgling, dying James did just that, giving Tyler what he wanted. Perhaps it was James' last plea for life, still not believing he could die, but die he did. Strapped in the chair he'd had breakfast in since childhood, by the table he'd eaten said breakfast on, James closed his eyes and died at the very moment when the grandfather clock in the living room let out its gong to signal the top of the hour.

Tyler's only regret as he quietly and meticulously left the house was the thought that James' mother would find him when his parents return from Monte Carlo later this morning. Their flight was scheduled to arrive just after nine.

"She'll get over it," he said to himself.

Especially when she discovers how truly horrible James had been. Just look in his room, find the bags of pills hidden beneath his mattress. How many lives had he ruined already? Bullying was one thing, addiction was another, and getting people addicted was even more of an asshole's pride, and James had befriended some sketchy people in the last few years. Everyone knew it too, even school faculty, especially when the cartel arrived to confront James last Tuesday. Tyler had watched while teachers and guidance counselors stood by and did nothing. Rich privilege indeed.

But what Tyler was looking forward to was the response. The response from teachers, students, and counselors after James is found. Tyler expected for the response to spread like wildfire by the day's end. Probably around sixth period. Tyler will be strapping on his gym gear at that moment, getting ready to run miles for an hour. The school year was coming to a close and would end with a bang. Literally a bang.

Senior year will be historic.

3

9:00 AM
Brooklyn, New York
Jigglyspot

Now Jiggly completed his masterful cover up with one exception: he had to lock the door from the inside then slip out unnoticed. This posed a problem for Jiggly since people were walking outside, looking to catch the subway to work. But there was a simple answer, thanks to his compact frame.

He'll squeeze through the window in the basement after having locked the doors and windows. This particular window, Jiggly had noticed, locked in place when slamming it shut with just enough force to not break said window. The mop and bucket—having been cleaned thoroughly—should be smoldering at this very moment, mere seconds away from burning. Of course, the smoke will trigger the smoke detectors, but not before the mop and bucket raged with fire, quickly extinguished once the sprinkler system does its job.

Which will bring the fire department. Who will call the police. Arriving police will call the FBI and the FBI will send SAC John Mills. Jiggly knew this to be true. A sure bet if there ever was one.

Now Jigglyspot, having cleaned off his face—most people wouldn't notice someone walking in the street, but most would take a second glance at someone wearing clown makeup so early in the morning—slammed the window shut and yes it locked in place, and waited for the praise he knew was coming. It always did, every single time once the job was complete. He surveyed his surroundings from the alley he'd just crawled into between two Brooklyn brownstones. Yes, there were people on the sidewalk. A few passed by, phones to their ears. It was when Jiggly stood—wearing twelve-inch platform shoes so if anyone spotted him in the corner of their eye they would say that he was tall, just over six feet—that the praise arrived. The first was from Kera; usually the last was from her too, the others paying him less mind than his beloved. Although Jiggly hadn't seen Kera in a day's age, she always chimed in to thank him for his service.

Thank you Jiggly.

Another great night.

You did well as always.

See you at solstice.

Jiggly took a quick glance at the window on the second floor, seeing fire and smoke. Satisfied, he strolled to the sidewalk, a sense of pride in his step.

I'll see you soon Jiggly.

That last one was Kera, always the first and the last. Jiggly smiled, thinking of her. He'll see her again soon, real soon. Definitely before the others. Summer solstice was two weeks away, the biggest feast and celebration of the year. But he knew he would see Kera before solstice. Kera couldn't resist, never had been able to, and Jiggly enjoyed her indulgent tastes. Enjoyed indulging as much as he did.

Jiggly took the steps up to the subway platform, walking carefully. He had to focus when wearing platform shoes. Sometimes he misjudged the height and would catch the shoe on the steps. He held the rail for support, all the way up to where the train was pulling in, then hobbled in those tall shoes across the platform where the train stopped. A familiar ding followed by the doors opening and Jiggly stepped onto the train within a deep thicket of people. He gripped the hanging handrail to brace himself for when the train raced out of the station. Normally he'd have to sit or lean against the subway, gripping a metal rail by the seat to steady himself. Normally, Jiggly wasn't tall enough for the hanging handrails. Thank man for platforms. Jiggly was admiring his tall reflection in the train's door window when another voice chimed in from the center of his brain-that's how the voices came through-but this time there would be no praise, not from Emmanuelle, who was in charge of the solstice celebration. A certain hurried anxiety in her voice.

　Jigglyspot, she said, *We have a problem.*

4

7:00 AM
Hollywood, CA
Sharon Mable

Sharon Mable had her dreams like everyone else. And like so many others, those dreams grew further out of reach the older she became. Not that Sharon was old, but in this town the new rage required youth and Sharon was about to see her thirtieth birthday, now just a month away.

So, when the alarm on her phone started buzzing and Sharon jumped out of bed, she felt confident about today's casting call and her ability to speak the truth: she was still in her twenties. Still young enough to capture the hearts of millions, hopefully on the big screen playing a minor role that would land a weekly television show or another movie. Sharon did not like to lie; the truth was always the better choice since the truth always comes out anyway. There was no reason to be caught in a lie, which to some was worse than lying, but not to Sharon. To Sharon, lying was the problem. She hated liars.

Sharon walked to the kitchen, yawning as she strolled across the living room in the two-bedroom apartment. Muffled music in the bathroom. Sharon's roommate and best friend, Cassandra LaRue, had to be at work by nine and she already made coffee. Sharon was grateful as she poured herself a cup, stretching her eyelids to wake up those tired eyes. Get some air in the eyeballs. She took her cup and phone to the living room and sat cross-legged on the couch. A quick sip as she checked her phone. Text messages first, always first. A small smile as she read Kevin's message: **I've got great news. I'll tell you tonight. Let's get some dinner. Around seven, OK?**

Sharon met Kevin Johnson six months ago during a casting call for a potential pilot episode. Kevin was on his way up. He played a minor role in last year's sleeper hit and was receiving more than a few accolades from the Hollywood community. He got the part on the pilot too. Although the project was cancelled last month, Kevin's agent had called the day after with surprising news: Kevin landed a supporting actor role in a teenage drama. His star was definitely on the rise. Filming was set to begin in early July in Atlanta and Kevin was tying up loose ends. Sharon wondered, more than a few times, if she was one of those loose ends. In this town, relationships take a back seat to career, at least until you made it. Then maybe some lucky person would take center stage, although that never lasted long, either. Sharon knew it was difficult to maintain a solid relationship in the Hollywood industry, although many couples enjoyed the limelight and the familial relationships, but those were the exception, not the norm.

She texted him back: **Seven is perfect.**

Bathroom door opened, music cut off and Cassandra, looking pristine and ready for the day's labor, strolled into the living room. Cassandra was an assistant for a talent agency. The receptionist, really. Cassandra was the person everyone and anyone who wanted entrance had to charm to gain admittance. Not that anyone could charm Cassandra. She saw straight through bullshit, loved her job, and wasn't about to risk employment for some schmuck with a dream.

Sharon sent another message in a hurry: **Where?**

"What time is the audition?" asked Cassandra, fixing herself a cup of coffee. She looked good and Sharon wondered why Cassandra had settled for a receptionist position. She would definitely make it on the big screen with those blonde locks and crystal shimmering blue eyes. But Cassandra always told Sharon the real money was in talent agencies. The money was abundant and there were no paparazzi camping out in a tree outside your bedroom window.

Sharon looked up from her phone. No response from Kevin. He must be sleeping. Sharon slipped her phone onto the glass coffee table. Arched her back, cup still in hand.

"Ten," she said.

Cassandra sat on a plush chair opposite the couch.

"Perfect, you'll be out before five."

Sharon remembered then, she had made plans with Cassandra for tonight. A girl's night out. She bit her lip; a common nervous tick she knew Cassandra recognized immediately. Shoulders slumped, coffee mug nested between folded hands on her lap.

"You forgot, didn't you?"

"No, not at all. Kevin's got big news..." she said. "Great news about his career and he wants to celebrate."

Cassandra rolled her eyes. "So you're not coming?"

"No, I'll be there. Little late but I'll be there."

Cassandra eyed Sharon. "Don't lie Sharon, you're not good at it."

"Fact," Sharon shouted, an enormous smile graced her lips. "But I'll be there, I promise."

Cassandra sat quietly, took a sip of coffee, staring out the window.

Sharon took advantage of the silence. "Why don't you like him?"

Cassandra met Sharon's stare. "It's not that I don't like him. I..." her voice trailed off. "I just don't trust him."

But did she trust anyone with a shaft between their legs?

5

12:32 PM
Brooklyn, New York
SAC John Mills

Twenty years. Same M.O. People disappeared all the time, sometimes entire families at a time. Those who were good at it were never found. But then again, some people didn't want to be found, while others yearned to be discovered. The problem was that they couldn't speak, at least not in this dimension. Couldn't utter one word, not that they wouldn't, if they could, but being dead posed many problems for those who wanted to be found. And in the last twenty years SAC John Mills had seen more than his share of the dead but never had he recovered anyone who'd disappeared with the mop bucket M.O. There was never even a true crime detected, except for the very first mop bucket incident. Nonetheless, Mills believed in intuition, the gut reaction, pure instinct, and he understood there was something waiting behind the mop bucket. And whoever was doing it had been taunting Mills for over two decades.

Six foot three inches tall, rough around the edges, dark hair turning gray and a stubble of a beard, John Mills stretched a pair of latex gloves over his hands and crouched down by the mop bucket, charred and burned to a near crisp. A swarm of firefighters, uniformed police, and agents watching him work. Mop handle on the floor beside the bucket; the mop had been burnt to a crisp prior to the sprinkler system working its magic.

"Did you dust the handle for prints?"

He asked this question to no one in particular and received no answer. They all shared perplexed stares. To them, there was no crime other than arson, and why the FBI had to be called was beyond everyone in the room. If anything, it was neighborhood kids taking advantage of an empty home.

But Mills knew differently. Something sinister had happened in this very room, just like it did in all the rooms he'd seen with the mop bucket in the center. Twenty years and at least twenty mop buckets in that time. Maybe more. Some people just saw no need to call it in. To them, it was a drop in the bucket, no pun intended. Some dumb kid liked to light fires and there were a ton of them to be accounted for.

But patterns emerged over the last twenty years. The mop bucket scene might appear like an isolated incident to the norm, but to Mills, it meant something more. His senses were tingling. His nose like a bloodhound, picked up on something. Bleach, the faintest smell of bleach and...

He touched the floor, still wet from the sprinkler. Put his fingers to his nose. Sulfur. Behind the bleach was sulfur, as if the bleach was used to cover up the smell. Same as in all the others. Always sulfur, followed by a bleach clean up. Always an abandoned, charred bucket in the center of the room. Mills stood and eyeballed the detective who was watching him.

"Were all the doors and windows locked when the fire department arrived?"

The detective looked perplexed, and Mills shook his head.

"Go and check. I need to know."

That was another part of the mop bucket enigma; all the doors and windows were locked as if whoever started the fire had disappeared into thin air. Not that someone couldn't leave through the front door, or any door, and lock it prior to leaving. The dead bolts would be the problem, unless said person had a key. But how strange would that be? Same MO and what were the odds that the same incident always involved some dumb neighborhood derelict with a key to an abandoned house? Sure, it was possible. Possible but unlikely.

The detective went to check the doors and windows, and Mills eyed a uniformed officer. "What's your name?"

The officer stepped forward. "Weaver," he said.

Mills pointed at him. "Officer Weaver, you're on door to door, so start knocking. See if anyone witnessed something strange over the last few days. Anything at all, especially last night."

"Sir, yes sir." Weaver just about saluted Mills before taking his task outside. Mills liked that; respect for your elders was a virtue going by the wayside in today's youth.

Now Mills was observing, staring, searching. Eyes roaming. Other than the charred bucket and mop, the fire had caused no additional damage except the ceiling, just above the bucket, where a black circle stained the ceiling. Quite obvious to Mills, the fire licked the ceiling prior to the sprinklers doing their job. Said sprinklers causing more damage than the fire. Water damage was always the worst. But there was something else, like all the others, there was something else. He could hear screams and feel pain, however faint and mute they were.

There were three floors to the brownstone. The first floor was a large basement, while the second floor served as the main floor with the front door and a stoop outside the front door with stairs that led down to the sidewalk. The second floor had two bedrooms, a kitchen and full bath with a staircase that led to the basement, and a small narrow hallway that led to a second flight of stairs to the third floor, and the living room where Mills stood now. A large living room too, with three windows, two facing the street and the third looked over the driveway in between two brownstones. The third floor was a loft.

Mills was sure all eyes were on him. Not that he paid them any mind. Mills was well aware how ridiculous he seemed, but he had no time for ridicule or impressions. What these officers couldn't hear, see, or taste was the crime that took place between these walls. But Mills did. He always boasted a keen eye, a bloodhound nose, and an uncanny knack to see beyond what was in front of him.

Beginning at his very first mop bucket scene.

6

10:04 A.M.
Los Angeles, California
Delilah Hempstead (Goes by Lilly not Lilah)

Lilly had no time this morning. Everything was on fast-forward from the minute she opened her eyes, a full hour after her phone alarm attempted to wake her. Not that the alarm didn't try. It did its job sounding off at six, although Lilly never heard that all too familiar screech. One of her children-she was sure it had to be Sam-must have turned down the volume prior to meeting the pillow. Those damn games again. Sam was infatuated with games, and he was only six. What kind of future would that hold?

Anyhow, waking up an hour late resulted in a rash of get dressed quick and eat in the car on the way to school. Lilly's coffee in the cup holder all the way. She'd thought about adding one of her morning pick me ups, would have done it to if Christopher-Lilly's first born—hadn't been bitching up a storm on their way to the car. That boy couldn't find an elephant in a barn without his mother. Always losing things and this morning it was his earth science homework. Of course, it wasn't where he said it should be and of course the blame game—that would be Chris blaming Sam—escalated with Sam protesting he'd had nothing to do with the missing homework.

Lilly made a mental note to give the babysitter a good talking to the next time she walked through the door. That girl's about as useless as an elevator in a port-a-potty. Was she babysitting or on her phone the entire time? Lilly had given explicit instructions to make sure Christopher's homework was put in his folder and the folder placed in his backpack, which Chris had assured her he had done. The optimal reason for the missing earth science homework was Sam, with his tricky little fingers. Said homework had never been recovered despite Christopher's protest that his science teacher—one Ms. Finicky—would more than likely provide a bit of ridicule over the missing homework. Of course, this would happen in front of his classmates, none of whom Christopher cared much about with one exception: Jenny Crawford, who, according to Chris, was the most beautiful girl the world had ever seen. That being said, Chris wished to avoid a scolding from Ms. Finicky.

Lilly played the world's smallest violin, her forefinger moving across the tip of her thumb as they waited in the car line at Christopher's school. Those blue eyes narrow as she watched her son's reaction in the rearview mirror.

"Do you know what this is?" Lilly asked. Chris eyeballed her and Lilly could see he was sucking it up, swallowing the tears and over-emotional entanglement.

"Don't I?" Chris said. "The world's smallest violin playing just for me. I know. You play it all the time."

Lilly shrugged and looked at Chris. "Well, stop losing your homework."

Chris went to speak but stopped before the words dripped off his tongue.

"What?" she said.

Chris said nothing. He looked out the window.

Lilly shook her head. "You're not the first student to lose homework and you won't be the last. Tell Finicky to lighten up. Take that stick out of her ass."

Which made Chris smile. Just in time, too, he jumped out of the car like he was sitting on a spring. Lilly saw why. Jenny Crawford was walking into school ahead of him.

Lilly didn't like Jenny, especially for her son. She knew Jenny's mother. Knew her enough to form an opinion that was for sure. They were part of the same book club; a passion Lilly was more than fond of; she even had a popular book review blog. She loved blasting an indie author. The way she saw it, everyone had a dream, but Lilly didn't have to stand for someone else's dream. If they wanted to be popular, then write a damn good book. No reason to fill it up with personal points of view, especially if those views were counterproductive to the rest of society, or, at least, Lilly's society. And Lilly had no use for metaphors. The way she saw it, that writing style went out with Hemingway. But Jenny's mother, Kathy, never saw it that way. She enjoyed a different perspective. After all, according to Mrs. Crawford, that's what separated the human race, our ability to go against the norm and offer a wide lens with a fresh perspective. Lilly would cringe every time Kathy's turn to share arrived. Lilly always gave a headshake prior to Kathy's turn. Kind of a *'here we go'* gesture. Rolled her eyes too, but that gesture came in the middle or at the end of Kathy's review. Lilly otherwise remained quiet, waiting for her turn to speak and paying Kathy no mind. *You either agree with me or you don't and if you don't, then there's no use for you,* was Lilly's mantra. Always dealing in absolutes was Lilly; there was no gray area. She'd bash and tear down any alternate point of view if she could. Cancel that culture immediately. If it were up to Lilly, she'd have them all burned at the stake like heretics, if you believed in that sort of thing. Then again, if you believed in anything that wasn't right in front of your face, you were already on the side of the foolish.

And that's what burned Lilly. That Jenny girl was still on her mind when she powered up her laptop, ready to provide her opinion for another book on another blog. *She'll grow up to be just like her mother.*

Lilly punched in her password then cupped her coffee mug and took a sip. This time the pick me up was included. The glow of her laptop, home screen cluttered with so many file folders, the picture of Sam and Chris could hardly be seen. Her desk was piled high with books, mostly older books from a few decades prior. Lilly adored her e-reader and since then, print books had gone by the wayside. Nevertheless, she enjoyed the pile of books.

Still holding her coffee mug in her left hand, Lilly double clicked on the most recent file folder dated June 2019. Double clicked on the latest blog, the one from last week, then highlighted the text with a quick Alt-A and hit delete, then performed a save as and typed today's date and, as she was typing the new book title and author, she heard footsteps on the stairs, circling down to the living room. Soft, subtle little creaks on the carpet.

Lilly's husband, Tad, owned his own construction company. He had to be in Beverly Hills by noon for a formal meeting on a reconstruction project. Lilly watched him, now standing in the living room, fumbling with a button on his cuff. Tad was just under six feet tall, well fit, with thick dark hair and brown eyes. His hair slicked back, and his Armani suit fit him like a glove. Black jacket hung over his left arm.

"Need some help?"

Tad turned to her. "Yes. I hate these damn cuffs."

Lilly bounced off the chair, shuffling across the Italian tile. "Why don't you use your cuff links? You've got over twenty pairs."

Tad rolled his eyes.

"Guess not." Lilly buttoned his cuff, then met his eyes with hers and ran her hands across his shoulders.

Tad stretched the jacket across his shoulders and squeezed his arms through the sleeves. She tried to meet his eyes, but he looked away. He's distracted again, thought Lilly, wondering why the distraction. He's been short too. Last night's cocktail party was proof positive he had something on his mind. He barely paid her any attention.

"You look good," she said, but received no response.

Instead, Tad said, "You're being too tough on Chris. Give him a break every once in a while. Take his side. Let him know you've got his back. It's tough out there."

"That's why I'm hard on him, so he can be strong. He's hypersensitive, you know that. We shouldn't placate him," Lilly said, more matter of fact than defensive, as if Tad was a passive observer who required no detailed explanation for why things were happening as they were.

Tad stretched his arms inside his jacket and went into the kitchen. Lilly followed. "He's not one of your book reviews. You're always passing judgment on the kid like he's doing everything wrong." He took the coffeepot and poured the black liquid into the cup Lilly had left him.

Lilly stretched her eyelids. She's heard this before; the same conversation came around every so often. Most people were like a broken record, always on repeat, with the same conversation, same complaint, and same catastrophe, but with different names, places, or faces. But Lilly knew her husband, aware that Tad would forget the conversation by the time he reached his car, so there was no reason to continue. Best to placate Tad and push it aside. Besides, she was still trying to put a finger on his real distraction.

A change in subject was required. "So, Beverly Hills today? How long will the meeting last? Can you meet for lunch after?"

Tad had the fridge open, his head moving left and right, searching. He was looking for the creamer. Funny, thought Lilly, how men can't see what's right in front of them. She walked over, grabbed the creamer from the door, and handed it to him. Tad took it.

"Not sure. Mrs. Reilly likes to occupy time, and she refuses to meet with anyone other than the owner. We've worked with her before." He added the creamer to his coffee. Just a splash. "Now that was a lesson in hostility."

He put the creamer in the fridge—not on the door though, instead he squeezed the container between milk and eggs, popping it behind them so he couldn't find it later—when Lilly's phone buzzed.

Her eyes went wide when she read the notification. Jaw kept dropping the longer she read.

"Lilly?" Tad's voice dropped.

"I don't think your appointment's happening today." She scrolled across her phone.

"Why? What is it?"

Lilly looked up from her phone. "James Reilly," she said, "They found him dead this morning."

7

1:30 PM
Westchester, NY
Jigglyspot

Jiggly received bad news from Emmanuelle. A problem indeed, and he'll need to puzzle it out, but he already had a plan. Well, the start of a plan at least. In his line of work, a contingency plan was a required commodity, a lesson Jiggly learned a long time ago because, as Jiggly will tell you, *'It's a poor mouse who only has one hole to run to.'*

He kicked off his platform shoes when he entered the door to his stately Westchester home. One of the many safe houses available to Jiggly across the globe, all of them owned by a shell company of a shell company of a shell company that was opened before appropriate records were kept. Try tracing that one to any living human being and you'll lose your mind.

Considering this new debacle, Jiggly had to drop dead weight. He stomped over to the basement door where he slipped on his sneakers, followed by the plastic bags he tied around his ankles. The old wood floors creaked beneath his transfer of weight from one foot to the other and Jiggly wished he'd not cleaned off his clown makeup. He preferred staring down on his victims through the veil of clown.

Plus, the makeup covered the pockmarks and gin blossoms Jiggly despised. His face was filled with pockmarks, his nose covered in so many gin blossoms it looked like rotting meat with a tinge of purple added to the skin. Jiggly leaned against the wall, listening. Not for grunts, cries, or whimpers from the basement. Not for the police or FBI nor agent John Mills, but for *them*, possibly listening and watching from beneath the folds of time and space.

He'd been in the house for the better part of a month. The secluded location offered plenty of time for Jiggly to have his way with Mr. Zachary Lovelace, some heroin addict Jiggly abducted in the parking lot after the carnival closed for the night. Jiggly understood he took a risk grabbing the kid. He wasn't supposed to bring unwanted attention. At least not this kind of unwanted attention, grabbing Mr. Lovelace the way he did, in the wide open; although selling heroin, coke and meth as a means to gather victims was not only allowed, it was encouraged, although in safe and secluded locations only. Those victims were too fucked up to see straight, let alone understand when they were being abducted. Easy Pickens is how Jiggly referred to them. But the torture and… yeah, Zach Lovelace gone missing could definitely bring unwanted attention and Jiggly was told many times to keep it to a minimum, but he just couldn't help himself. He was always forgiven.

Zach had pissed his pants that first night. Jiggly smiled when the thought crossed his mind. That stink, stank and stunk should be all too sweet this far along. He allowed the thought to pass, didn't want it floating into the universe. He remained quiet, listening. When he was sure no one was on to him—because they had bigger fish to fry right now—he opened the basement door and that stank tore out of the basement with a vengeance burning Jiggly's nostrils. He took the steps one at a time, slowly; the weathered wooden steps creaked beneath his small frame. He enjoyed the slow, dramatic descent. That fat stub rack of fingers, nails grown long and sharp, scraped the banister on the way down.

Whimpers, muffled cries, and whines graced his ears.

He knew he had little time. There was so much to do and disintegrating a human body in a bathtub of acid required more time than most people know. Plus, he had to be at the carnival by six because skipping out tonight was not in his best interest. Leaving abruptly was one thing, leaving under suspicious pretense was another, and Jiggly had learned not to raise too much suspicion. But Jiggly was angry now. The job ahead of him would prove difficult to pull off, and he had to blow off steam.

Mr. Lovelace was that steam.

At the bottom of the stairs resting against the wall was Jiggly's prized walking stick—well, a cane to anyone else, but to someone Jiggly's height, definitely a walking stick. Thick and red with a smooth golden round handle, the cane was made from old wood with gnarls that cascaded down the cane that looked like lost souls in the throes of a painful, torturous scream. The cane was important to Jiggly. The walking stick was a present from the master of all masters, Mr. West, and Jiggly was all too grateful for the acknowledgement of a good deed. Jiggly himself had discovered Mr. West's cane a few years after it had gone missing in the nineties after the Sleepy Hollow incident. Mr. West had presented the cane to Jiggly a short time after the finding, which also gave Jiggly a rise in power within Mr. West's circle of depravity.

When he reached the bottom of the steps, he gripped his cane with a gentle hand, like holding a baby, and turned to meet Zach's eyes. He always savored the moment, standing a few feet from Zach, hand on his walking stick and Zach grunted through his gag, a red bandanna squeezed into his mouth and held in place by duct tape. The same duct tape that bound young Zach to the metal chair he was sitting on. A red baseball cap covered his head.

Jiggly took his clown nose from his cargo pants pocket and fixed it over his nose, covering those gin blossoms. Zach narrowed his eyes and cringed.

Jiggly began to speak, his raspy thick voice bellowed from the back of his throat. He stood tall, like all skilled performers do. "For today's entertainment, we have a host of games and prizes, all at your disposal. Everyone is a winner today, dear audience." He leaned in closer to Zach, a glint in his eye. "And such games we have... for our wonderful audience."

He turned his head up. "What? What games do we have?" He placed both hands on his cane, craned his head towards Zach. "So glad you asked," he said and a sickly grin revealing rotted, yellow teeth graced his lips. He raised his voice, "For Zach, we have a wonderful game we call... *extraction.*" Jiggly lowered his voice with the word extraction, bowing with closed eyes when he said it. He turned, tapped his cane, then raised his arms. As if speaking to someone, he said, "Is that all we have for good ol' Zach?" He placed his free hand on his chin. "Of course not. We have so much more to offer, Mr. Lovelace, and why is that? Because Zach, in order to extract appropriately, we must first create a plethora of fear and madness."

Zach seemed to recede into himself, his skin so pale, his eyes swollen with dark baggage beneath the eyes. Streams of dried blood cascaded from beneath the baseball cap and down across his face, crusted and dried on the duct tape across his mouth.

"And how do we cause fear and madness?" That grin again. "Zach knows," he hollered again, staring at the ceiling as if addressing a phantom in the room. He dipped his head to the left. A wide grin. "Don't you Zach." And he sighed, started twirling around the room, dancing with his cane. Jiggly loved to dance. He stopped behind Zach; a plastic tube snaked beneath Zach's baseball cap, grimy and stained with a dark yellowish liquid inside the tube that stuck out between cap and strap.

Jiggly gently removed the baseball cap. Zach's skull had been removed, his brain exposed. The tube inserted into his brain, directly in the top center. Jiggly lifted the tube and a spittle of fluid moved inside the tube. He gritted his teeth, snarled, and grunted.

"Not enough," he whined. "Zero Intellect." He leaned in close to Zach's ear. "Is it you Zach? Are you really that low on the IQ or is it just your generation?" He laughed at this statement. Laughed at himself. "How unfortunate for you, Zach."

Jiggly paused while listening to the subtle muffled whines from Zach before he took Zach's chin in his hand and forced his eyes to look at him. Zach was trembling and Jiggly saw himself in those eyes, Zach's pupils large with fear. "No need to worry, Mr. Lovelace. I'll just have to put in a little overtime on that ass." Zach seemed to freeze up at that moment. Perhaps he wanted death, Jiggly thought. Who could blame him? Perhaps he was second-guessing his choice to do heroin. Didn't matter, not to Jigglyspot, whose erection pulsed beneath his cargo pants.

And there was so much to do. He'll have to go buck wild to produce the needed extraction. Jigglyspot was dying of thirst, and he couldn't stand another second living with those gin blossoms.

8

1:45 PM
Brooklyn, NY
SAC John Mills

Detective Tim Sims, a stout and overweight gentleman who Mills knew wanted to be somewhere else right now and not checking every door and window, led Mills to the basement. The room was open and wide, barren and stuffy, not a single box or forgotten tool remained. Afternoon light beamed through the windows.

"It's over here," Sims said, walking over to the window on their right. "Every other door and window are locked. This one too."

Mills dropped his head, frustrated. "Then why are we down here?"

Sims let the statement pass. "I opened and closed all windows and doors in case there were discrepancies." He reached up to the window, unlocked it and pushed the window open, let it hang for a moment, then released the window, which closed with a thud and bang, and the lock snapped shut. "This window locks in place."

Mills cocked his head, eyes narrow. "So, if someone climbed through from the inside, the window will lock in place." He said this to himself as if the window were the key to his enigma.

"Exactly," Sims said. "Although, it would have to be a kid no more than twelve with the way kids grow these days. No adult can fit through this window."

"Unless it's a small adult."

Sims pulled his gloves off. "That would be a very small adult."

"Detective?"

Mills turned to the voice. Weaver, the uniformed officer he'd sent door to door, was standing on the stairs about halfway up, chewing on a toothpick.

"What did you find?" said Mills.

Weaver looked at the notebook. "The lady next door said she saw a white male, dressed in a long overcoat, about six feet tall, this morning just before nine. Said he must have come from here. Watched him from the front window while drinking her tea. She said he seemed strange to her, like he was walking funny and his body didn't fit the frame."

"Body didn't fit the frame?" Sims repeated.

"Her words, not mine."

"What does that mean?" Mills asked.

Weaver looked at him, a certain tinge of pride in his voice. "Well, I asked that same question and she said..." He looked at his notes. "Like a golf ball on a tee." Weaver smiled then continued. "She thought he was wearing platform shoes, possibly to look taller."

Mills grunted in his throat, thinking. "How does she know he came from this direction?"

"Ok, well, per her statement, she's a people watcher. Loves watching 'the people,'" Weaver performed an air quote with his free hand, "on their way to work. Said it's her morning ritual while drinking her morning tea. She said he was out of place, and that she'd never seen him in the neighborhood before, and he just appeared. One second he wasn't there, the next he was. She would have seen him walking from down the street if he had come from that direction."

Mills registered Weaver's information. It made sense, considering the window and the platform shoes. Small guy squeezes himself through the window, then puts on platforms to disguise his height and walks away, slipping into the morning void as if he belongs. "Anything else?"

"Yes. As a matter of fact, there is."

"I'm brimming with excitement," Sims said, and Mills shot him a disturbed shut up stare.

Weaver laughed. "Gin blossoms," he said.

"Gin blossoms?" Mills repeated.

"Yeah, those things on the nose that alcoholics get from drinking too much gin."

"I know what gin blossoms are," said Mills.

"Gotcha. Anyway, she said it was the worst case of gin blossoms she'd ever seen. Said his nose looked like, and I quote, 'rancid meat that's been nipped at by rats for decades.'" He flipped his notebook closed.

Sims interjected, "There you go. You're looking for a midget with a severe case of gin blossoms and a taste for alcohol. Whoever he is shouldn't be hard to find. Start checking every carnival in the tri-state area. Start in Coney Island, then check every bar in the area. Keep going from there. Maybe contact cleaning companies to see if they've got a midget on staff who likes to set mop buckets on fire and drink gin." He laughed out loud, and Mills turned his head, eyes narrow. Sims cleared his throat. "Sorry."

But he was right, wasn't he?

"Thank you, officer. Keep knocking, see if anyone else saw the same."

"Yes, sir." He turned on his heels, gripped the banister and took the steps two at a time.

Mills watched as he did so.

Sims said, "I don't get it. There's no crime here. Why are we wasting valuable manpower following up on leads for no crime? It's just kids lighting fires."

Mills turned to him. "Last I knew, arson is a crime."

To that Sims shut the pie hole, shook his head, and said under his breath, "We've got bigger fish to fry."

Mills ignored the comment and stepped to the window, looking it over before addressing Sims. "Get forensics to dust for prints on the window."

Sims rolled his eyes.

"And on the mop handle, too."

9

11:00 AM
Beverly Hills Private School
Tyler

It wasn't sixth period when news of James Reilly's demise spread through the school like a fire hopped up on speed; it was third period English. Apparently, the Reillys' flight from Monte Carlo arrived early.

Tyler noticed a buzz coming from the hallway as he sat at his desk. Mrs. Finnegan's lecture on the end-of-year exam was swallowed by the buzz and slowly erupting chatter. Tyler wasn't sure what to expect, and he sure as shit didn't know how to act. Just be you, he thought, placing his pencil inside his notebook. He was done taking notes. Felt his face flush red, a reaction he had not accounted for. And his throat closed. He had to force himself to breathe, to swallow air down his gullet into his lungs. Three seats up in the row to his right, he noticed Pam Glazier looking at her phone. He'd always liked Pam, had known her since sixth grade. Pam was the second student who received a scholarship for outstanding scholastic achievement in fifth grade, which transferred to a full ride at Beverly Hills Private School where grades six through twelve were housed in two buildings.

He felt her contract, her bones stiff. He couldn't see her face from where he sat, but he knew. Knew she was aware of Reilly's demise. Knew her jaw hung open, either reading or watching a newscast about James. That made sense to Tyler. James Reilly's parents were high society with notoriety. James' dad, Seth Reilly, was a major film producer and his mother, Lizbeth Reilly—or Liz— was an actress but not a very good one. Although she married well and landed bit parts here and there, which Tyler was more than certain directly resulted from Seth's power.

"Phones *down*," Mrs. Finnegan said, her voice scolding. She wasn't afraid to tell the rich kids where to go. Her eyes were on Pam, and if looks could kill Pam would not just be dead right now, she'd be looking worse than James Reilly.

Tyler saw James' eyes then, staring at him from his empty seat in the next row. All black, no iris, no pupil, no white, just all black, as if black glass had replaced his eyeballs. His jaw hung open and Tyler noticed then how James' lips curled into a grin. Blood on his shirt where Tyler shot him, and the gunshot, the hole in his chest kept pouring blood as if a river had broken through a dam. Blood pooled on his lap, confined by duct tape, although the tape could not hold this pounding river of red. It seeped, then spilled from under his shirt. A river of blood pooled on the floor. Tyler looked down to his feet, couldn't see them, the blood river engulfed them and was crawling up his ankles to his knees.

And James laughed, loud and feverish. Thick streams of blood like veins crept up Tyler's legs and squeezed. He felt pain. Pain that followed the blood stream up across his groin, pelvis and kept going, squeezing and restricting, all the way to his neck, choking the air from his throat. Tyler saw his eyes then, as black as James'. Suffocating, windpipe closing and narrow. His hands trembling, body shuddered, trying, forcing, fearful, strangling across his throat until all he could do was draw in a deep wallop of forced air into his lungs like a drowning victim once they propelled out of water.

"It's ok Tyler," Mrs. Finnegan again, her tone now compassionate.

Tyler noticed some students were crying. Embracing each other. Pam caught his eye. That face, so soft, innocent blue eyes filled with tears.

Mrs. Finnegan was standing over him. She took his hand in hers.

"It's gonna be ok," she said.

Tyler looked away. Turned to Pam. Heard voices, students calling for bloody revenge, hell and damnation. Mrs. Finnegan crouched in front of Tyler's desk. He turned to face her, not seeing her, looking past the short dark hair and sympathetic brown eyes. Past the care worn skin. His jaw hung open. Finnegan patted his hand, smoothed her hand over his arm.

"It's ok," she repeated. "I know you got close to him this year."

10

11:30 AM
Hollywood, California
Cassandra LaRue

Cassandra popped a breath mint between her cheeks as she closed the door to the office she'd been in. She hated the salty, thin, and milky taste on her tongue. Had to get rid of it as soon as possible, because once the taste is gone, Cassandra can trick herself into believing the last twenty minutes never happened. Because forgetting was better than facing the reality that she was being played.

And with the memory stuffed inside a box in her mind and forgotten, she can go back to the receptionist's desk and focus on her work, dreaming of getting the hell out of the office and spending time with the girls later. Dream about leaving this damn agency and starting her own. She touched her forehead and wiped beads of sweat off her brow as she looked over the office. Busy as ever, and she was sure no one noticed, or, at least, no one suspected anything perverted had happened behind the closed door. The #metoo movement had changed little, if anything at all, in the typical day-to-day operations of the entertainment industry. Those predators just found more creative ways to be assholes like wining and dining and building a pseudo-relationship under the guise that they cared, actually cared for the victim.

Ira Monteforte, Cassandra's boss, was one of those assholes. They started dating a few months after Cassandra was hired. His ingenuity, drive, and passion had intrigued her. Fell for it hook, line, and sinker. She thought she was special, but as time went on, she tricked herself into believing the relationship was real, even though no one knew about it, not in the office anyway. Ira had said not to tell anyone because the staff would be jealous and would treat Cassandra differently, their clients and prospects too. And then it became something different, always resigned to a fling behind the closed door to Ira's office. At first it was exciting, a Hollywood love affair, and she caught feelings for him, at least she thought she did. Perhaps that was another trick on reality; Cassandra wanted it to be real, so she fooled herself and took on the role as the dutiful pawn.

And now she was knee deep in it, no pun intended. She wondered if she was sweating from anxiety or the extra work she had to do to get Ira off. At least he wasn't on pills this morning–just a little cocaine, according to Ira–because those pills were relentless and useless with helping the end result happen faster. Cassandra put on a smile as she walked to the receptionist's desk. She looked at the young man sitting in the waiting room and cleared her throat.

"Mr. Montgomery," she said, and he turned to her with a certain excitement. "Mr. Monteforte will see you now." He jumped up from his seat. "Last office down the hall on the right."

Montgomery straightened his tie, standing tall. "Thank you." His grin ear to ear.

"Good luck." Cassandra watched as he walked to the door, waiting for a reply, but he never responded, kept walking as if she didn't exist. Cassandra rolled her eyes. Her jaw tight. Another stuck up prick, she thought, he'll do just fine in this industry. The phone was ringing, but she had no desire to answer it. She was about to take her seat when Sharon burst through the front door, sunglasses on, head down, and tears streaming from beneath her sunglasses. Quite obvious to Cassandra, the casting call did not go well.

And Cassandra thought, Maybe we should get this weekend started early.

11

12:00 PM
Los Angeles, California
Lilly

This day was going to shit, that was for sure. Started off on the wrong foot and kept spiraling into a deeper pile of cow dung and now she had to deal with Christopher. She was so angry with him she could beat him with a stick until he begged for mercy.

"Take that stick out of your ass."

That's what Chris said to Ms. Finicky, prompting a call to the principal's office. The result was a parent conference and a three-day suspension. She couldn't even look at him. Her blood was boiling so fast to her brain she thought her head was going to explode. She needed this like she needed a hole in the head. Driving home, Chris sat in the backseat, quiet as a mouse. He was too quiet, as if he was proud of what he said.

"Why?" Lilly had asked, shaking her head. "Why did you say that when you knew you'd be in trouble?"

Chris eyeballed her from the backseat, glaring into the rearview mirror. "You said it."

Lilly rolled her eyes and shook her head again. "I said it to you, not her, and it was a joke."

Now Chris shook his head and looked out the window.

"I asked you *WHY*?"

Chris turned his head to meet Lilly's stare. "Because she's a bitch."

"Watch your mouth."

"She is, and you know it. Embarrass me like that over homework. What right does she have?"

"The right to give you a failing grade and a suspension. Which will go on your permanent record, by the way. Try getting into an Ivy League school with that on your report."

"I don't care about an Ivy League school. Nothing but stuck-up assholes go to those schools."

"My God, I can't even talk to you right now. You're not my son. You're an imposter. My son doesn't act like that. What's gotten into you?"

She knew what it was, that Jenny Crawford.

The ride home turned quiet, and Lilly preferred it that way. It was obvious she wouldn't be making any headway with Chris today; not in his current mood, and not that she wanted to, either. Not now anyway. She told Chris to stay in his room for the rest of the day after they arrived home. She didn't want to see him. Tad will deal with him later; he'd gone to the office to go over some issues.

Issues?

What issues? She wasn't aware there were issues, but she was confident in Tad's ability to deal with them. Marriage was built on trust and she trusted Tad despite that nagging sensation that something was wrong. Whatever those issues are, Lilly was certain they would see the light of day, and soon. Tad operated like that: hold it in for a while, then open up. Although this time was different, Tad was holding on to those issues for more than a few days. Seemed like months had gone by, which told Lilly he'd be opening up any day now. She thought he was on the verge of talking after the Reilly murder this morning. Thought he was about to say something when she received the phone call from Christopher's school. Instead, he told her to take the call and that they would talk when he returned home.

She typed a quick text: **Chris told his teacher to take a stick out of her ass. Three-day suspension on his permanent record. I need you to talk to him, please.**

Lilly hit send, put her phone on the kitchen counter and opened the fridge where she located the bottle of white wine, thought better of it and closed the door. Opened the freezer, grabbed the bottle of lemon-flavored vodka and fixed herself a drink, a much needed drink.

The day started off on the wrong foot and kept looping on a downward spiral and Lilly's anxiety was kicked into overdrive with Christopher's latest debacle. Plus, that nagging, sinking feeling refused to relent. The same sensation that conjured the thought she'd been holding in the back of her mind, hoping it would die: The worst was yet to come.

12

1:30 PM
Beverly Hills Private School
Tyler

He wanted to be alone. His brain was squirming, and he was having difficulty processing all the thoughts that raced through his mind. Tyler walked to the gymnasium and sat at the top of the accordion bleachers, leaning against the wall. Every teacher was in the cafeteria taking part in some psychological pow wow with the rest of the school, or rather, those students who hadn't skipped out after learning the news that one of their classmates was dead. Dead was an understatement. He was tortured and murdered.

Tyler had wondered how he'd feel in the hours, days and months after he killed James Reilly. Truth be told, he felt nothing. And those thoughts running through his head like a conveyor belt on light speed contained no thoughts filled with regret, but streaming thoughts recounting every fine detail of that murder.

He was meticulous by nature, had covered every angle and executed his plan with the precision of a brain surgeon. Took Tyler years to plan and implement, earning the trust of James Reilly being the longest charade he'd ever played. Sometimes, he'd laughed so hard with James he forgot what the true purpose behind the friendship was: a charade to gain trust with Reilly. To any outsider, the matter was simple: teenagers learning to accept each other while forming a bond that could last a lifetime. Of course, in the eyes of his peers, that wasn't the case. James sold drugs and there you had it because Tyler enjoyed toking on a little weed here and there. At least that's what his peers would say if they were questioned.

Reality was, Tyler had no love for weed. His life didn't require an escape plan for the mind; he was free in that respect. Tyler flushed just about every bit of weed he purchased with one exception: he required THC to be in his blood and urine on the off chance he was drug tested to corroborate his story. He did this a few days prior to the murder of James Reilly. Tyler wanted as much weed in his system as possible to reflect a casual user, but with enough time for his brain to relinquish the effects prior to the night in question. On that night, he required a clear head, needed his meticulous nature to be as profound as it ever had been, as if he was born to murder and his nature was a gift, a true gift.

Tyler turned to the large bay windows across the gymnasium wall. Sunlight beamed through those windows, casting streams of golden light into the gym. He squeezed his hand into his pants pocket, pulled out the bracelet he'd purchased a few months ago. Green beads with one red bead in the center. They brought prosperity, good luck, and good fortune. Tyler never liked jewelry, had a strange aversion to the feel of metal against his skin-truth be told it freaked him out-but he made a promise to himself that when the deed was done, he'd wear them as a reminder of the justice he brought to the world. Plus, the beads were wood and not gold or silver, which settled his anxiety.

And he would do it again. If he had to, he would kill again.

The gymnasium door opened and Tyler snapped his head to it. Pam was standing in the doorway, bathed in sunlight. She seemed like an angel. Tyler cleared his throat; made a mental note to not seem so startled if they questioned him. Sadness was one thing, but paranoia was another, and any good detective might pick up on his reaction.

"There you are," said Pam. "I've been looking for you."

Tyler sat up, watching as Pam crossed the gym to the bleachers, her backpack slung over her right shoulder. "I figured you'd find me. No sense in attending that psychobabble group therapy bullshit they got going on."

She stepped across the bleachers that shifted beneath her feet. Dropped the backpack and sat next to him. Tyler hunched over, arms on his knees, his beaded bracelet between his fingers. Pam leaned back, stretched her legs, elbows on the bleacher.

They sat in quiet solitude, neither talking nor glued to their phones. This was the quiet time. A time to reflect. To place events and circumstances into perspective. Pam stretched her tongue and blew a bubble gum bubble over her lips until it popped and deflated across her chin and lips. Tyler glanced back as she sucked that gum back into her mouth.

She smiled at him, then proceeded to chew.

Tyler returned his gaze to the sunbeams.

"Don't look so happy," said Tyler.

He turned to her, staring over his shoulder. Pam cocked her eyebrows then smiled ear to ear. That smile turned to a frown under Tyler's heavy gaze.

"What?" she said. "Nothing left to do but maintain, right?"

"Exactly. But blowing bubbles and grinning isn't a part of maintaining."

"Sorry."

Tyler turned around. Those sunbeams were gone, nothing left to look at anymore. He stretched his bracelet around his wrist and stood.

"Besides," Tyler said, offering his hand to Pam, "We're not out of the woods yet."

13

4:45 PM
FBI Office
Manhattan, New York
SAC John Mills

Mills had a gut instinct. Those gin blossoms kept ringing in his mind, looping back and forth like a smack to his face.

Short guy with a severe case of gin blossoms.

He was searching through known criminals in the FBI database, looking at pictures both new and old. There weren't many short men with gin blossoms. In fact, gin blossoms weren't searchable criteria. He had to enter criteria for anyone between five and five and a half feet tall, which resulted in thousands of entrants. And he had to examine every picture, zooming into the nose.

And his nose kept twitching, still burning with the bleach tinged with sulfur scent. Not chlorine-based bleach either. Oxygen-based bleach was used in the mop bucket murders. Oxygen-based bleach destroys traces of hemoglobin, destroying DNA evidence. Of course, Mills had forensics black out the windows in the apartment and use an infrared light on the floor and walls. But the bleach had done its job: they found no traces of blood.

Twenty years, Mills thought. Twenty years of murder, conspiracy, and dead ends. Mills often wondered why he continued on this path while under scrutiny from his fellow agents. And in that time, he'd gone through two divorces and had an estranged child living in Colorado whom he never talked to except on holidays and birthdays. And now he was going through a third divorce. Why he was assigned to the case was another mystery. Just like Sims had said, there was no crime other than arson, and the FBI shouldn't be tasked with finding such criminals. If it hadn't been for the very first mop bucket murder, Mills would be like the other special agents in charge, assigned to more promising cases he had a chance solving. But there was a crime with that first discovery twenty years ago. Same oxygen bleach, same sulfur, and the same mop bucket left to burn. But a mistake was made that first time. Perhaps the killer had just forgotten, or maybe whomever this gin blossom midget was, had wanted to be caught. Whatever the reason, leaving a human heart and over ten pounds of human flesh in the refrigerator like the owner of the apartment had paid a visit to the local butcher was either a calling card or a colossal mistake made by a rookie in the murder industry.

From then on, it was only the mop bucket. The first had happened in Florida, the second a year later, this time in Seattle. And when murders cross state lines, the FBI is called. Of course, that second time revealed no ten pounds of flesh nor a human heart or any other trace of a crime and Mills had wondered why he'd been called in, learning later about the Florida murders.

But the same MO was in Seattle as in Florida. A mop bucket soaked in oxygen bleach, a tinge of sulfur, and let's not forget arson. Too coincidental, and in detective work, there's no such thing as coincidence. Whoever was leaving the calling card had learned quickly. The family—recipients of the mop bucket killer—in Florida were a middle-class family. DNA evidence revealed the ten pounds of flesh comprised a mix between the family of four—two parents, two kids ages four and eight. But the heart belonged to another. No match had ever been found. Considering the extent of the murder, the investigative results had landed in the FBI database along with the MO, and red flags were raised every time a similar scene was discovered.

And they were found. One every year, all over the United States. And Mills had knowledge of similar cases in South America, Canada, and Europe, raising the grand total to twenty-eight.

Mills chewed his bottom lip—a common occurrence when he had something on his mind—and his eyes narrowed. The picture on his screen was a young tike taken twenty-five years ago. He was arrested for stabbing his victim with a scalpel outside a local bar.

Four feet nine inches tall, dark hair, blue-green eyes. Served four of a ten-year sentence. Current whereabouts are unknown. He dropped off the radar after being released. Lucky for him, he didn't kill his victim with that scalpel, or he'd still be doing time.

Mills' first thought; could this kid have developed gin blossoms? First break in the twenty-year mystery and all he's got is a short guy with gin blossoms. Mills wasn't even sure how short either. He was about to write the name on a pad on his desk when,

"I got something for you." The voice over his shoulder belonged to Theo Helmsley, a trusted CIA agent Mills had known over the last decade. Well-fit, dark hair and eyes, upper thirties wearing a blue shirt Mills was sure he'd bought at Wal-Mart. Helmsley leaned his arms on the partition.

Mills said, "Hopefully good news."

Helmsley popped a toothpick between his lips that he wedged into the corner of his mouth with a roll of his tongue. "Could be nothing, but I keep thinking, short guy with gin blossoms and we're in the middle of carnival season."

Mills cocked his eyebrows. "Come again?"

"Carnival season," Helmsley repeated. "This time of year, carnivals make their way through the northeast, so I'm thinking, since your guy is always traveling, maybe that's how he does it. He's travelling with the carnival convoy to stay under the radar. And carnivals have at least one short guy involved with their stage act." He raised both hands and cocked his head in a 'could be maybe possibly,' gesture. "Not much but, here's where it gets interesting. I brought my kids to a carnival last weekend and there just so happens to be one of those short guys there. Real creeper too, just didn't sit right with me. Didn't want my kids anywhere near him."

"Why? What did you see?"

He took the toothpick from his lips. "Not see, just a gut instinct. Thought he was a classic pedophile judging by the way he was with the kids, laughing and singing *Ring Around the Rosie.*"

Mills cocked his head. "Isn't that what they're supposed to do?"

"Yeah, I know, but this guy just had that creeper vibe. Like he was enjoying himself a bit too much. Kinda freaked me out. Especially with that voice." He shook his head, eyes down.

"Voice?"

"Yeah, freaky, one of those raspy, thick drone type of voices."

Mills sat back and paused. "Did you see his nose? Any gin blossoms? Did he smell like gin?"

Helmsley shook his head. "Wasn't close enough for the smell test."

"Ok, what about the nose?"

"Couldn't tell, he was dressed like a clown. Had one of those big red clown noses on."

"Clown noses," Mills repeated.

"Clown nose." Helmsley popped the toothpick between his lips, then stuffed his hands in his pockets. "Anyhow, I thought I'd mention it since he fit the description. Might be worth checking out. Carnival leaves Monday morning."

Not a bad idea, Mills thought.

"Thank you, Helms."

Helmsley cocked his eyebrows. "No problemo, if you're headed there, let me know. Maybe I'll come with. There's a pile of paperwork on my desk and I'd be more than ecstatic to leave it right where it is." He tucked his shirt into his pants, gave his belt a quick pull up then walked away.

"Duly noted," Mills whispered, staring at the picture on his computer.

Twenty years and not one lead until today. Twenty years is way too long. The trip to Westchester was worth it, if at the very least to scratch someone off his list. Maybe find another lead, even if this guy doesn't check out.

Mills took his pen, wrote the name of the kid in the picture on his computer on a pad-Milton Worthington-then spun around in his chair like a kid on a carnival ride and called Helmsley back.

When Helmsley confirmed the carnival clown held a strong resemblance to Milton Worthington, a trip to Westchester was indeed forthcoming.

14

5:00 PM
Westchester County, New York
Carnival of Chaos
Jigglyspot

Jiggly was beaming, the effects from the fluid extraction were hypnotizing, awakening his senses and indulgences like a hawk who identified a prize meal in a thick forest, locked in and seething in anticipation of the feast he was about to receive. Mr. Lovelace had served his purpose, a far greater purpose than where he was going. Another junkie that'll cost the public hundreds of thousands in drug treatment, therapies, medicine and more than likely prosecution, since just about every junkie has a criminal record. Jiggly enjoyed the junkies, alcoholics, and addicts; they were always easy prey.

Jiggly had to dig deep into Mr. Lovelace to receive the desired and necessary extraction, but it was well worth it. The sensation will remain with Jiggly for at least a week. Reeling and feeling larger than life, he strode across the shopping mall parking lot towards the Carnival of Chaos. His hearing was on high alert, listening to the carnival sounds as if they made their way to his ears through speakers that were as clear as a bell. Rides and games, laughter, and parents calling after their kids. The early go-getters-as Jiggly referred to them-were people who arrived before sunset to indulge in carnival nostalgia. And then there were the smells, the scents that brought nostalgia with a wave of precious memories: cotton candy, deep-fried sugar-coated breads, sausage, peppers and onions, and ice cream. One can never forget the ice cream. He drew in a deep breath, sensing a thicket filled with excited energy as the sun beamed bright, beginning its descent into night as he entered through the employee entrance behind the wonder wheel.

Jiggly entered the trailer for employees. He had to prepare; his clown makeup and costume were waiting. The trailer, a doublewide, was bustling with employees preparing for their nightly duties. Jiggly looked at the whiteboard on the wall where the night's posts were listed. On his right was a bathroom, door closed. To his left the doublewide opened with a U-shaped couch, tattered from years of use, a coffee table in front of the couch led to the entrance to the second part of the doublewide. A television hung from the wall between the two entrances, forcing most everyone to bend down to enter. Beyond the couch is a small kitchen and beyond that, a bedroom. Music filled the doublewide, the latest EDM. Incoherent chatter beneath the music and the television was stuck on a news channel in silent reverie.

The doublewide was wall to wall filled with employees, and Jiggly wondered if anyone was actually working the carnival. Bodies on the couch, cocaine on the coffee table, and Jiggly recognized how Sandra was giving Kipp a blowjob on the couch.

Heathens, Jiggly thought. He despised that Kipp, the strongman in the carnival, and wondered how long it had been since he'd bathed. Sandra was always giving blowjobs, so that wasn't anything new; perhaps she enjoyed the taste of ball sweat. Typical Friday night for the Carnival of Chaos.

Jiggly spotted his name on the board and smiled. He'll be working the House of Horrors tonight, Jiggly's favorite post, because there's nothing better than scaring the shit out of a bunch of kids, and on a Friday night the teenagers will be in abundance and that was where Jiggly prized himself the most, watching their interactions as they waited in line. He enjoyed finding that one teenage boy who propped himself up to be something larger than he was. Jiggly loved to relieve his frustrations on such a teenager, the perfect target. Hoped they shit their pants, too. He'd give himself extra kudos if he could get one to shit their pants.

"Jiggs, where have you been?"

The voice belonged to Jasmine; she always worked the basketball game. She must have been in the bathroom when Jiggly arrived. Now she stood a foot away, naked except for the black silk underwear. Jasmine was five foot six, with dark hair and dark eyes. Jiggly was eye level with Jasmine's breasts.

"Cat got your tongue," she said and shook her shoulders.

Jiggly broke his concentration. Turned his eyes to Jasmine's.

"My lady," Jiggly said. "I'm always fashionably late." He noticed how her eyes darted over to the couch as if she was missing Kipp's climax.

She returned her eyes to Jiggly. "You got something for me?"

"Of course. Don't I always." He produced a small baggie with three oxycodone pills and Jasmine stepped closer, took the bag in her hand and touched Jiggly's shoulder.

"I'll get you later," she said. "Need to skim off the top tonight." She moved closer and Jiggly thought about stretching his tongue to those breasts they were so close. Although Jiggly's heart belonged to Kera, he wasn't a fool. Everyone has needs, and Kera was not available to fulfill those needs every time Jiggly got a little hot in his pants. He chose to keep his tongue to himself.

"Do what you must, my lady. I'll get with you later." Jiggly knew she was good for it. Plus, those three pills will lose effect before the carnival closes, and she'll be looking for something more. She'll probably skim off a little too much tonight, which was always a common occurrence. Everyone was skimming, but sometimes they took it a bit too far and found themselves abandoned when the time to pick up and move to the next town arrived.

"Thank you, Jiggs. I can always count on you. You look different, by the way." She leaned in and kissed his cheek. Jiggly felt the warmth of her breath and her nipples on his chin.

Jasmine walked over to the couch and joined Sandra with bringing that climax to fruition. Jiggly rolled his eyes. The SHS was in full bloom tonight and Jiggly sensed in his bones it would be a good night. Someone, somewhere, at some point in time, will offer themselves to Jiggly. Not willingly or knowingly either, or at least not consciously. Sometimes a soul requires a challenge and leaps at said challenge without providing knowledge to the conscious mind, much like Mr. Lovelace. Sometimes the subconscious just took over in its primitive reptilian state.

Jiggly went to the back room to prepare, thinking about his transformation into his prize clown makeup. Frown or smiley face? Sad or happy? Devious or gentle? A tear or little stars beneath the eyes? These were the questions on Jiggly's mind. What he knew was that no matter how the makeup looked, he will be prepared. Jiggly patted his right front pocket where a thin round bulge of four inches brought a twinkle to his eye. Jiggly's go to weapon always brought that twinkle.

In his pocket was Jiggly's prize weapon. In his pocket was his trusted, Mr. Scalpel.

15

2:30 PM
Hollywood, California
Sharon

She allowed herself to cry. To shed a few tears in the presence of her friend and confidant, Cassandra. No, she did not get the part, but it was more than just the part. Sharon believed that with the big Three-O right around the corner time was slipping through her fingers like sands through the hourglass. She'd thought by now she would have had some notoriety, some bit part at least, but those dreams were dissipating and in its place a cloud of reality was forming. Sure, she was big around the hips but in today's world, why does that matter? It doesn't. Shouldn't, but still, it does. She convinced herself some years ago that the world was entering a new renaissance and thick around the hips would be seen as it should be, sexy.

Did she just play the fool to her own beliefs? Accepting this reality brought her to tears. The waiter gently placed her second glass of white wine on the table. The alcohol helped numb the solution. Said solution being: put your energy into something else, Sharon. An identity crisis indeed. But what could she do? Sharon was at a loss for the future, and it looked grim, spiraling out of control and she couldn't hold on, couldn't hold on to anything.

"What's the real fear?" asked Cassandra, nursing her first glass of wine, her fingers over the glass like a spider web.

Aside from being Sharon's only real friend, Cassandra offered viable psychological advice. Who needs a therapist when Cassandra has the answers?

To Cassandra's question, Sharon had to suck back the tears. Reality can be such a pain in the ass to accept. Sharon took another sip, savored the dry flavor on her tongue before forcing the fluid down her closing throat. Returned the glass to the table and sucked back a sniffle.

"That I'm not good enough," Sharon answered. This was indeed turning into a therapy session.

Cassandra placed her right hand over her left on the table. "That's a false fear," she said. "In my time, I've seen an abundance of talent who never land a single part. It has nothing to do with talent or the way you look, but whether or not your look is relevant."

This was the part about Cassandra that Sharon despised. Not only did she have it all together, her star on the rise, and Sharon was certain Cassandra will own her own agency in the years or decades to come, but Cassandra also told the truth. Knew the truth and forced the truth down your throat without an inkling of pity or empathy. Kind of a, 'suck it up' bitterness that made your head spin, wanting to ring Cassandra by that thin gullet and squeeze until all your rage and anger were satisfied.

"Relevant to what?" Sharon's voice cracked as she held back her tears. She was tired of crying and frustrated with feeling emotion. Get your head together, she told herself. Maintain some sort of dignity. She sat up, stretched her spine, shoulders back. Sharon was always hunched over. She had to make a conscious effort to keep those shoulders back. Posture was paramount to pride.

"To the latest trends. To what is making money so Hollywood can pump out the same version with new names that capitalize on the trend. Trends are always coming and going so when you've got a new cash cow you milk it for all its worth then wring out the excess, keep it in a bucket hoping the same trend will come back and you'll be ready with a copyright and trademark to spit out and capitalize once again. That's why they're always remaking and reinventing and redistributing." She leaned back in her seat, hands folded on her lap. "People like to remember, to feel the way they did when they were young. Art," she said, "Movies, music, books... they all have their mini resurgence. Sure, there's the artsy fartsy movies that pop in every once in a generation to enthrall the audience with a reminder that movies can be art with a masterful craftsmanship but look around, most of what's on the big screen are regurgitated crap." She looked at her lap, folded her napkin, and Sharon noticed Cassandra's hands had the slightest bit of a tremble.

Cassandra looked out the window, possibly avoiding Sharon's stare. Cassandra sipped her wine, quiet as a mouse.

Sharon broke the silence. "So, what's the new trend?" Cassandra met Sharon's eyes. The look in her eyes revealed a *'how do you not know'* stare. Sharon cleared her throat. "I mean…" she sat forward. "You see what's coming down the pipe, right? What scripts they're pitching. What actors they're looking for. What's the next trend?" She sipped her wine, then arched her back.

"Hard to say." Cassandra shifted in her seat. "I don't see the scripts. I just admit the actors Ira requests."

"Ira." Sharon shook her head. "Still can't get me a meeting with him?"

Cassandra cringed, seemed to melt into the back of her chair. "I told you what he said when I first started."

"I know, I know. *Don't force your friends on me,*" said Sharon, mimicking Ira's firm voice. "But is it possible to find out what scripts he's casting? What actors the studios are requesting? If we know what they're looking for, we can conform to meet those needs. Maybe slip in a new headshot. Ira would never know."

"He's seen you at the office. How could he not?"

"Well, I'm sure we can hedge that bet when we get to it. First things first, though. Find out what they're looking for."

Judging by Cassandra's reaction, the stiff body language and refusal to meet Sharon eye to eye, Sharon was sure Cassandra wanted nothing to do with it. What would it mean to the friendship? Cassandra forcing her friend down her boss' throat. Sneaking around the office for information she was not supposed to have. There were always Non-Disclosure Agreements in the industry and this snooping could mean Cassandra's job. Nonetheless, Sharon knew she would do it. Cassandra was that kind of friend. Even if she knew the relationship would never be the same. How could it, after all? Mutual respect flew out the door once jealously and having something to hold over the other's head existed. But for Sharon, this was the break she needed. Isn't that how it went? Knowing someone who knows someone who has someone else holding something over their head, so they vouch for said person and the next thing you know, a star is born?

Oh Hollywood. Sharon was indeed on her way up.

16

6:30 PM
Westchester County, NY
Carnival of Chaos
SAC John Mills

"Bang, you're dead," said the seven-year-old boy holding two cap guns, one in each hand. He squeezed those triggers and the crack, snap, and pops from both guns spun Mills and Helmsley with a jolt and nervous twitch in his direction. Helmsley drew his weapon, a .38 snub nose, and Mills held his hand on his Glock, still in the holster on his right hip but never drew down. The boy's eyes lit up. Not with fear, mind you, but with a certain intrigue cast from wonder and a desire to explore, seek and discover that only little kids possessed. Smoke drifted from the cap guns, whisked away by the spring breeze, and disappeared.

Mills felt his heart stop. Felt the entire world come to a crashing halt. The scene in a perpetual state of slow motion. God Consciousness, he'd remind himself later. Where time slowed to an aching crawl and within that time, thought processes are as clear as a bell. Mills called to Helmsley to draw down, saw his finger inch over the trigger about to fire a round into the boy. But Mills was quick, on top of Helmsley before he could pull the trigger. One hand on Helmsley's .38, now pointed to the ground, and the other on Helmsley's shoulder. Mills heard himself speak, his voice in Helmsley's ear although he never felt his lips move nor did he feel the voice vibration in his throat, but it was his voice. "Stand down, it's not a real gun."

And then the scene, or time, hopped back on track, caught a rail and was ticking away at normal speed. Mills shook his head.

The boy laughed something awful and sinister, said, "You gonna shoot me, policeman?"

Helmsley holstered his weapon. "Get the hell outta here," he hollered, his face flushed and Mills could feel Helmsley's heart pound in his chest. He missed his holster on his first attempt to put away his weapon.

"Bang, bang, bang," the boy said, firing his caps in rapid succession and with every loud pop Helmsley's body jumped.

"Jesus H. Christ, I said get outta here." Helmsley stepped forward as if to chase the boy who ran and hid beneath the doublewide they were standing in front of. Helmsley kicked the dirt, sending a cloud in the air.

Mills noticed the doublewide window then, the blinds creaked and snapped closed. Someone was watching.

Mills turned to Helmsley, said, "Get a hold of yourself, officer."

Helmsley blurted, "Fucking kids with guns. I thought they stopped selling those things."

"Well, they didn't, so get your act together." Quite obvious to Mills that Helmsley had never seen field action before. He heard the doublewide door open and close.

"Can I help you?" a woman's voice. Mills turned to the voice. A young lady, no more than twenty-five, was on the steps to the front door. She craned her head, searching beneath the doublewide. "Casper," she said. "Leave the officers alone." She wore black pants and a red shirt with the name Carnival of Chaos embroidered on the polo shirt. Hair tied in a bun and pinned to her head by the navy blue hat she wore, also embroidered with Carnival of Chaos.

Mills didn't bother asking how she knew they were officers. Better to let that one go.

Casper shot a few more caps, then went silent.

"Your kid?" said Helmsley.

"That he is. Loves cops too, as you can see."

"Well, put a leash on him. He almost took a few bullets. Real ones too."

"He's just playing around. Maybe you shouldn't be so hyped up, officer."

Mills stepped in, looked at Helmsley, then back to the lady. "We're sorry," he said. "I'm SAC John Mills with the FBI, and this is CIA agent Helmsley." He stepped closer, noticing she didn't give her name. Instead, she stood there, staring, and Mills noticed how her eyes were like pins as if the soul had retreated into darkness. A common occurrence among drug abusers. "And you are?"

"None of your business," she said, one hand on the railing.

"Well, that's not playing nice now, is it?"

She took a moment to consider this. At least, that's what Mills thought she was doing. "Jasmine," she said. "What can I do for you?"

"We're looking for Milton Worthington. Need to have a few words with him."

Jasmine shrugged and Mills could see by her body language that she had no clue who Milton Worthington was.

"Short guy, about five feet tall, early forties, dark hair, blue-green eyes…"

"You mean Jiggs."

"Come again?"

"Jigglyspot, or Jiggs, as we call him. He's the only one here about that height."

"Jigglyspot," Mills repeated.

"That's what I said."

"Can you tell me where he is?"

She considered this for a moment then raised her hand, pointing. "He's in the haunted house, scaring some young ones and parents to all bloody hell." And she laughed as if she was amused by the prospect of Jigglyspot doing what Jigglyspot does best, scare the bejesus out of people, and the FBI were walking into that fate, and that right soon. She seemed very satisfied.

"Any way we can talk to him without roaming the haunted gallows?" said Mills.

The disappointed stare that registered across Jasmine's face was priceless. She shook her head, tight-lipped, that disappointed stare locked on the officers. Mills waited for a response. When none came, "Mam?"

"Hold on, I'll get Hal."

"Hal?" said Helmsley, stepping forward.

Jasmine paused with one hand on the doorknob before she turned to the detectives. "Hal owns the carnival. I think he should handle this." And then she gave a quick curtsey and smiled. "I just work the basketball game," she said, and disappeared through the door.

17

3:45 PM
Beverly Hills, California
Tyler

He was still seeing black eyeballs. But now they weren't reserved to
his visions and daydreams; he saw black eyeballs in everyone he
greeted, met or passed in the hallway, on the street, and in the coffee
shop where he sat now, in the corner by the window so he could
watch and observe with a keen eye all who wandered into the shop
on the off chance he was being followed and had shown up on police
radar. A black coffee between his fingers, which he sipped every so
often. Tyler had no use for coffee, but he went to the cafe to process
his thoughts and he had to order something. He hadn't expected the
black eyeballs. Tyler wondered if a door in his mind had opened.
Some essence of knowledge only murderers could see. Because they
crossed the line between what is human and what is God.

Was he doing God's work?

James Reilly was a good choice for his first victim. What would
Reilly have grown up to be if not a sadist? Getting people hooked on
pills and who knows what else. And Tyler had been waiting months
for the final piece in his puzzle of murder and revenge to land in his
lap and a month ago his moment finally arrived. Tyler had gone to
the Reilly house to pick up a fat ounce of flower. Not that he used
marijuana, but the sale was part of the ploy from the very beginning.
If you want to plan a murder and get away with it, you have to be
patient. It was better to wait, assess, observe, plan, and evaluate,
allowing the plan to unfold on its own. The trick was to take
advantage of the moment and that's exactly what Tyler
accomplished on that night. Acting stupid like high people do, he set
off the house alarm which prompted James to storm out of his

bedroom, rush down the stairs and reset the alarm–punch in the code and provide the password to the alarm company once the phone rang, which was standard protocol. Tyler had played the part without a hitch. James, being preoccupied with returning to his bedroom, talked loud enough for Tyler to pick up on the password: DumbFuck. Tyler found that ironic. As would the rest of the world, irony being a manifestation of one's own arrogance.

Tyler popped on his sunglasses when the sun stretched its beams through the cafe window to squint his eyes. Felt his body temp raise a few notches and a single bead of sweat form above his lip, still watching the street.

Am I acting suspicious?

He looked at his phone because that's what teenagers do nowadays and he needed to act inconspicuous. Notification after notification. Text messages galore. Tyler was part of a group text that was ringing off a few messages at a time within every second.

Still can't believe it.

Cops are at school.

Questioning everyone.

I miss him already.

R.I.P. James Reilly.

Tyler punched in a message, thought better of it, deleted what he'd written, then added something new.

I hope they catch the MOFO who did this. Long Live King James. Miss you, brother.

He put his phone down and turned to the window, coffee cup resting in both hands. His phone started buzzing. One, two, three, four, five.... ten... twenty messages. He had to look. Almost smiled when he read all of them but caught himself before that smile reached from ear to ear. He started a trend.

Long Live King James made up all twenty messages.

Great, he just made James a martyr. He wanted to laugh.

"Another coffee?"

Tyler didn't notice the waitress standing over him until he heard her speak. He looked up from his phone and one of those sunbeams found an opening through the side of his sunglasses. Perfect timing, too. Tyler's eyes were sensitive to the sun, very sensitive indeed. Felt his eye tear up instantly. Normally he would wipe it clean before anyone saw, but, considering the circumstance, he allowed it to fall. Looked like he was crying.

"You ok?" said the waitress, a blonde-haired blue-eyed beauty more than likely working coffee shops while attending one of the nearby colleges.

Tyler cleared his throat. "My friend died this morning," he said, then pretended to suck back his tears. Lips quivered for effect.

"So sorry." Tyler waited for her to say something else, the pause and silence were irritating. "Are you hungry? Let me know what you want. Anything at all. On the house."

"I appreciate it, but no, thank you. I just want to be alone for now."

She forced a sympathetic smile. "Ok," she said, "If you change your mind, just let me know."

"Thank you."

And she walked away, attending to her tables. Tyler watched her, thinking about that night from a month ago and how the waitress resembled the girl James had in his bedroom.

He was a rapist too that James Reilly. No still means no the last time Tyler checked. From bully to drug dealer to rapist, that was James Reilly's progression. The same James Reilly who now materialized inside of the sunlight beaming through the window, sitting across the table from Tyler. Tyler had watched the waitress return to the counter and low and behold, when his vision returned to the sunbeams, James was there. He looked nothing like what Tyler imagined the dead should look. In the sunlight, James appeared almost angelic, sunlight glimmering off the outline of his body. One exception though, his eyeballs were black.

"Death," said James. "It's not so bad."

Tyler noticed then that his mouth was open and made a conscious effort to close it. He snapped his eyes off James, turned his head, looking at the other patrons. Can they see James too?

Reilly shook his head. "They can't see me. Just you."

Tyler locked eyes with James. Noticed there was a wide and round bloodstain on his shirt where Tyler had shot him.

And James smiled. "Pam too, huh? That was a revelation I did not expect."

Tyler crept his sunglasses from his nose to his head. James remained in Tyler's field of vision, looked like he was made from sunbeams, sparkling with a heavy golden glow.

"Surprised I see," said James, a strange grin plastered across his mouth. "Guess I'm locked in on you now." His brow curled, inquisitive. "At least for a while, I guess."

Tyler moved his head back and forth. "Why?" He had to force the question over his lips from his closing throat.

James bobbed to his left, then his right. "Seems that's how this works. I don't know much, but what I've learned so far is that when someone saves your soul, you owe them a debt. Like karma."

"Saved your soul?"

James huffed and grinned. "Crazy right? Yeah, that you did. If I kept going the way I was, yeah…" He stopped speaking, looked out the window, then back to Tyler. "I saw what I would have become. How corrupt and dark. I was already there, already on the path to hell, but you made that right. Gave me a chance for redemption." James rolled his eyes. "Can't believe that's what my parents are doing. It's a sick, sick world, and I was knee deep in it and falling fast. I would have traded my soul for a blow job from Johansen if that option were on the table."

"Doing what?" asked Tyler.

James froze then, those black eyes unmoving and Tyler felt himself cringe, bones stiff, retreating as if he could retreat. James rolled his tongue inside his cheek, turned those eyes to the floor, sat forward, then returned said eyes to Tyler.

"Amazing really. I actually feel bad for you. For what you're about to go through, that is." He craned his head to the right, staring as if he could see inside Tyler's mind. "Certain events that we endure… we don't understand why we go through them when they happen. Not until much later, when reflecting, can we see what the purpose was." He nodded. "You can't kill someone and not expect that energy to come and find you, Tyler. And it is coming, believe you and me. It is coming. And that right soon."

"What is? What's coming?"

James simply smiled at Tyler's question.

"What's coming?" Tyler's voice raised.

Those sunbeams shifted then, and with the shift, James sparkled.

Tyler jumped off his seat. "I said, *what is coming?*" He said this loud too. Not to mention his seat screeched across the linoleum floor and smacked against the wall behind him.

Everyone in the café stopped to look at him. James was gone too. Tyler looked over the café. His body stiff. They all had black eyeballs. Tyler grabbed his phone and made a beeline for the door, barreling onto the sidewalk and rushed through the late afternoon crowd.

James' voice in the back of his mind,

"Tell Pam I said hello."

18

7:00 PM
Westchester County, NY
Carnival of Chaos
Jigglyspot

Jiggly knew SAC Mills very well. Had known him for the better part
of two decades. Not that Mills would recollect any of it, but Jiggly
found it humorous the FBI agent had tracked him down, aided by
Helmsley no doubt, which Jiggly found a bit skeptical, considering
Helmsley was a CIA agent planted by Jiggly's people. Maybe Mills
was getting too close to the truth? But considering current
circumstance, Jiggly was well aware he could use this event to his
benefit. Nevertheless, Jigglyspot prepared himself for a brief, albeit
intense, conversation. Plus, he was still beaming high from the
extraction. Glowing, in fact, was Jigglyspot.

He met with the detectives outside the doublewide, introduced
himself and offered a secluded spot in a trailer courtesy of Hal who,
after informing Jiggly that an FBI and a CIA agent wanted to speak
with him, had warned Jiggly when he said, "Don't bring any shit into
my carnival. I've got enough to deal with." Hal being a sixty-seven-
year-old male who hailed from Alabama, still talked with that thick
southern drawl, and no matter what time of day or year wore the
same clothes with the same stains that seemed to take on a life of
their own. And he always stank like some putrid body odor Jiggly
found rather offensive in every way imaginable. If the SHS had a
president, Hal would make a strong candidate for the position.
Strongman Kipp could be his running mate considering stank and
lack of soap and water was a requirement.

"Have a seat," offered Jiggly, gesturing to the folding table
disguised as a kitchen table where two folding chairs waited for the

officers. Jiggly took a third folding chair from in between the refrigerator and the wall, set it up by the table and sat. Jiggly had to force his eyes away from Mills. Jiggly tried to recount how many nights he had spent with SAC Mills over the last two decades? Had to be close to ten. Good times, Jiggly thought. Good times indeed. Jiggly was fond of the detective's soon to be ex-wife. Lorraine kept in shape, which made those nights so much more entertaining. Jiggly could see her now, her image hovering over Mills' head as he eyeballed Jiggly from across the folding table.

"Do I know you, Mr. Worthington?" asked Mills and Jiggly had to catch and hold on to the chuckle that erupted in the back of his throat.

Jiggly sat back in his chair; put on his best *I'm a happy clown* face and looked at the detective with a soft innocent stare. "Not that I know," he said. "Have you been to many carnivals recently?"

Mills, it seemed to Jiggly, had to force his eyes away. He turned to Helmsley when he said, "Not recently, no," then asked Helmsley to take the first question.

Helmsley took a small notepad from his shirt pocket, pen included. "May we ask your whereabouts yesterday until nine am this morning?"

"Of course," said Jiggly, noticing the detective's noses kept scrunching and whiffing. "Sorry for the smell, detectives. This is Hal's trailer and, as you can tell with Hal, soap and water are not high on his priority list. If cleanliness is next to Godliness than Hal is so deep into hell he can't see straight."

Helmsley allowed his laughter to escape. Mills sat stone faced as if struggling to recollect. Jiggly knew what it was, where had he seen Jiggly before, but that thought would never come to fruition. Not unless he drank from the fruit of extraction.

"To answer your question, detective," said Jiggly, being sure to look up and to his right, a telltale sign of recollection. "Yesterday I came here around four in the afternoon. I worked at the haunted house. We close on Thursdays at ten pm and after that there's always a party. So..." Again, he turned his eyes up and to the right. "I left around midnight, took a nightcap in my trailer, watched some news and drifted off to sleep. Woke up around eight this morning."

"Trailer? Do you share your trailer with anyone?" Mills this time, his hands on the table.

"More than a few people. The regulars, as we call ourselves, move from town to town with the carnival. We always pick up a few locals to help when we get into town, but mostly it's just us." He sat up with a slight bounce. "Tight knit family we all are. Been together for a long time too. Some more than others, like myself. This is my home, my family and friends. Hal is like a father. Sure, he's rough around the edges, but he always looks out for me. For all of us. He's a good man."

"Noted," said Helmsley. "So, who shared the trailer last night?"

"People come in and out all night. Who was there when I woke up? Let's see, Kipp the strongman, Jasmine and her son, I believe you met the boy already. Freda, Jimboy. He works the sausage and peppers stand. Great cook too. You should get yourself some of that before you leave." Jiggly smiled from ear to ear. Felt his clown makeup crack.

"Anyone else?" said Mills.

"Not to my recollection. But like I said, people are coming in and out all night." Jiggly narrowed his eyes. "What is this about, anyway?"

Helmsley shook his head. "We can't comment on an open investigation."

"Oh," said Jiggly and shrugged. He looked at Mills, whose eyes seemed as stiff as a board. Mills seemed so lost, Jiggly almost felt sorry for him.

Helmsley broke the silence. "I'm sure the people you mentioned will verify what you told us?"

Jiggly turned to Helmsley. "Of course." Helmsley wrote in his notebook. Jiggly didn't like him, not one bit. The man was too stiff and-quite obvious to Jiggly-had less than half a brain. "Anything else, detective? I do have a job to do."

It was Mills who answered. "Do you mind taking off the clown nose?"

Jiggly pinched his eyebrows; face scrunched, then lifted his head and smiled an ear-to-ear smile, loving that the detectives were staring at his yellow, rotted teeth. "Strange, but, of course." Jiggly whisked his clown nose away as if he were entertaining a crowd with a big reveal. He posed for the detectives like a nose model in full bloom. Turned left, then right. Noticed how both detectives took a long, hard look at his perfectly smooth nose. Extraction reverses the aging process. His gin blossoms were gone, at least until the extraction effect waned.

The detectives shrunk in their seats, disappointed. Jiggly pressed his clown nose back onto his nose. Fixed his favorite tiny top hat by shifting the piece of plastic to the right side of his head, covering the white spot.

"Anything more, detectives? This has certainly been an entertaining, albeit odd, occurrence, but I do have to return to my post. Can't leave the kiddies waiting now, can we?"

Mills sat still, exploring Jigglyspot. Attempting to recollect, Jiggly was sure. Helmsley answered with the typical, informing Jiggly they'd speak with his coworkers to verify his story. Jiggly escorted them to the door, offered them best wishes and good luck with their investigation, then closed the door. He leaned against the same door, thinking.

His face scrunched in contemplation. He turned to the window and watched the detectives. Hands clenched into fists. Jiggly thought about the time. Soon, the sun will be gone and something had to be done about SAC Mills. Jiggly didn't mind a loose end here and there, but being questioned by the FBI was not one of them. It brought unwanted attention. And what's up with Helmsley? That son of a bitch. Jiggly had said to send someone with more than half a brain. Helmsley obviously did not match the profile considering he brought Mills right into Jiggly's humble abode. So Jiggly thought and then thought some more about Helmsley. Perhaps there was more to the agent than Jiggly suspected? After all, everyone can serve a purpose, even if they have half a brain. And why not, Jiggly thought. Helmsley can serve a purpose too. What beautiful fun Jiggly could have with that one.

Jiggly watched as the two detectives trifled over to the doublewide. *Good luck detectives, the carnival is in full bloom, and all have taken their positions.* Then a thought occurred. Westchester. The Hudson Valley. And by the time the good detectives finish their inquiries, night will have fallen.

Jiggly chuckled at his thought. Started whistling and bobbed over to the refrigerator, thirsty as all bloody hell. The stench in the trailer was nothing compared to the rotting flesh, bones and blood that greeted Jiggly like a tidal wave when he opened the refrigerator. A decapitated head in a mason jar of solvent, one eye closed, the other a faded blue. A rat squeaked and ran across the shelf and jumped into the trailer. A second mason jar on the bottom shelf, no head though. In this Mason jar was an abortion, eyes closed. Next to the abortion, a third, although smaller Mason jar capped at the top, filled with blood. Jiggly took the blood-filled mason jar, twisted the cap, then took a long gulp, being careful not to spill a drop.

He burped, then shivered. Replaced the jar and walked to the window. No detectives. No sign of anyone. Jiggly closed his eyes. It was time to send the necessary information to the people who could implement. Felt his eyeballs move to the back of his skull, eyelids fluttering. Mills' face, Helmsley's too and let's not forget Mills' wife Lorraine, she was sure as anything a firecracker delight. Jiggly's people will thank him for the sweet Lorraine.

His eyes shot open and Jiggly took a deep breath while looking over the trailer. He was feeling ecstatic and made a mental note to be on the lookout for someone special tonight. After nightfall, Jiggly was sure they would arrive. And more than likely around the same time Mills and Helmsley are introduced to a newfound curiosity.

19

6:00 PM
Los Angeles, CA
Lilly

Lilly checked her phone for the billionth time, huddled on the couch with a blanket wrapped around her shoulders, sitting cross-legged with a drink wedged between her legs, television on mute, and the boys upstairs. She'd ordered pizza and let the boys eat in their rooms. She wanted to be alone. Alone in waiting, on the couch and watching, watching for Tad's car to come roaring up the driveway. Still no return calls or text messages from Tad. Lilly passed acute anxiety a few hours ago and was on the verge of contacting law enforcement. Tad always replied or returned her call. Sure, sometimes his response arrived a few hours later but this was going on six hours and because of the extremity of Lilly's last message, Tad should have responded by now.

Issues. He said he had to deal with a few issues.

And the vodka wasn't helping. Lilly's mind kept rolling with sinister thoughts and the anxiety kept circling, spiraling, and raising her blood pressure, her head feeling like a hot balloon. She was drinking to relieve anxiety, but the effect was the exact opposite. Her hands were shaking, and she'd been crying for the last half hour. Slow streaming tears that fell silently without the help of whines, cries or wails as if the tears arrived without conscious knowledge. Frankly speaking, she felt a type of fear she'd never experienced before. After fifteen years of marriage, she never had a doubt about Tad.

Except over the last month. Lilly noticed the change, however slight it had been. Tad was never someone who yelled at the boys and never lost his temper. He was calm, understanding and possessed an uncanny knack to discover the heart inside the concern. Nonetheless, a month ago, he lost his temper over something trivial. The boys were arguing, as siblings often do, and he lost it. Cursed and threw that damn gaming system across the room. Said gaming system being the cause behind the argument.

"I don't slave all day so you two can act like fucking animals."

A loud crash and bang followed Tad's words. Loud crash and bang being the gaming system slamming into the wall with irreparable damage followed by Tad's retreat to his bedroom.

He wasn't the same since that day. Nor was Christopher.

Unhinged. That was the word Lilly used to describe Tad's state of mind. "You're becoming unhinged. What is wrong?"

To which Tad put his head in his hands and said, "Nothing," in a dire and defeated voice.

Lilly let it lie. Now she wished she hadn't. Tad's retreat continued to spiral after the gaming incident. He seemed detached, as if he wanted nothing to do with them. As if he blamed them for existing. And now this, today's events unfolding like they did and Tad's non-response.

Was Chris acting out to earn his father's attention? Definitely possible. Tad barely looked at him anymore. When he was home, that is. He'd been working late every night, weekends too, and he always slept through the alarm. Slept through the hustle and bustle of morning activity. There was one morning when Lilly thought he was pretending to sleep. She let that go too, but she couldn't let go of the feeling, emotion, and sense of dread that something was wrong. It didn't take a rocket scientist to confirm that truth.

Lilly finished her vodka and peeled herself off the couch then went to the kitchen, half stumbling, half shuffling. Wiped the tears from her face. He's cheating, she thought. Has to be. There's no other explanation. Maybe it's that new intern, you know, the one with the pretty green eyes and youthful body. Smart too, Lilly knew. Lilly could see the girl's face when she opened the freezer door. Vodka bottle had one drink left. She emptied the bottle into her glass.

What is her name?

Lilly couldn't remember, as if the name retreated from memory like a child hides from a violent parent. She sucked back tears through a hoarse throat. Screwed on the bottle cap and dropped the empty bottle in the garbage. Looked out the window where the sun now hovered above the horizon.

What the fuck is her name?

She sipped her drink and felt her head spin.

Her phone buzzed in her hand. It was Tad. The message read:

Busy day. Sorry for the silence. Be home soon. I love you. Tell the boys I love them.

Lilly smashed her phone on the kitchen counter. One, two, three times. Crack, smash, total desolation then tossed it across the room. Downed her drink and when she stretched her eyelids, a rush of warm intoxication flooded her brain, her head feeling like a balloon, lightheaded and weary, the room with a slight tilt and spinning. Wet eyes drooping with intoxication. She walked to the stairs and looked up. They seemed to stretch on for miles, more like a mountain than a staircase. Her head drifted. She went to her home office, dropped on the couch, and fell asleep.

Passed out is more like it.

20

6:30 PM
Hollywood, CA
Cassandra

What she didn't want was to get caught looking through Ira's files. Good thing for Cassandra, the office should be empty, considering the time. Most everyone left the office by three on Fridays, either to take out a client or start the weekend early. During the drive to the office, Cassandra kept repeating her reason for being at the office, just in case she was caught, reciting said reason so the words would flow naturally and not seem forced or caught in the throat, as lies often are.

"Just getting a jump on next week," she said in a soft tone, edging her car into a parking spot outside the office, then pushed the gearshift into park, and detached her seatbelt. "Making a list of loose ends for Monday morning. I want the party to end without a hitch." She forced a smile. Practice, just in case. Always best to lead and end with a smile. Cassandra gripped the steering wheel, looking over the office while chewing her bottom lip. The office was too dark to see inside. The building featured blacked-out windows because every afternoon around three pm the sun would beam through the west-facing windows and heat the office like a pot of water on a hot stove. And no one in this town liked to sweat. Never let them see you sweat became the agency's motto over the years. But with the sun still beaming over the state of California, Cassandra couldn't see shit beyond the blacked-out windows.

Anyone could be in there.

Maybe I should come back after dark. I'll be able to see if a light is on in the office and know if someone's in there.

But that would be even more suspicious. Coming back now is

one thing. Coming back after dark on a Friday night is highly unbelievable. And if Ira's in there at that time...

She let the thought drift. Her stomach gurgled, souring from the fourth glass of wine she had at lunch with Sharon. She shook her head, shaking the thought from memory. Plus, she knew Ira's schedule. He should be eating dinner with his client at this very moment. Now was as good a time as any. She cut the engine and got out of the car. Noticed her hands were shaking.

Get it together, Cassandra. Get it together. All you're doing is helping a friend. That's how stars are made. You've got to know someone who knows someone. Plus, if this does work, Sharon will owe Cassandra a favor, one she would no doubt call in when the time was right. Whether or not Sharon was successful after this didn't matter. Cassandra was certain that asshole Kevin Johnson was on his way up which meant that Kevin was on the hook for a starlight tabloid romance with the lead actress being Sharon. Famous for being famous type of thing. Should that be the case, Cassandra would have to call in said favor as quickly as possible. Capitalize on the moment and catapult her career through the roof.

She unlocked the door, then looked over both shoulders and cursed herself for not checking the back parking lot. Forget it, it'll be fine. She slipped through the door; the alarm beeping down the time. Entered the code: 0621, which she realized was the date of the party the agency was funding. The party she was using as an excuse to be in the office.

The alarm clicked off, and Cassandra breathed a sigh of relief. The set alarm meant the office was barren. The last person to leave was responsible for setting the alarm. She looked through the windows, scanning the street. Felt her face flush with heat, listening to her own shallow breathing. No one on the street. She turned around, pulled off her suit jacket while stomping towards her desk, dropped the jacket on her chair, and pushed through the door to the main office.

She knew exactly where she'd left the latest file, on Ira's desk when she was in his office this morning, and she hoped it was still there. Cassandra knew Ira like a book. After a hard climax on cocaine, he didn't do too much other than more cocaine, needing to rev up his engine once again, get the tank full and jump back into the rat race. She hoped that was exactly the case this time out. Her current task would go smoothly if it were.

Cassandra made a beeline towards Ira's office, past the rows of cubicles on her left and the closed-door offices on her right. Ira's was the last office at the end of the hall. She recanted what she had to do. Sharon's headshot and resume were in Ira's office, in the filing cabinet behind his locked closet door. Cassandra had included Sharon's information a few months ago for a minor role in a teen drama for a small, however, up-and-coming network. Sharon was not included on the agency's list of potential candidates, although her headshot and resume were kept for future use. All Cassandra had to do was slip Sharon's headshot in the folder she left on Ira's desk. A folder with headshots and resumes for the top three candidates for a new major role.

But Ira's office was locked.

Should've thought about that. Now what?

Grab the key to the storage room where a locked box contained keys to all offices. Cassandra shook her head, turned around, and stomped across the office to her desk.

The things you do for friends.

21

7:00 PM
Hollywood, California
Sharon

She arrived at the restaurant early, not too early, about ten minutes, and ordered a glass of wine. Her eyes lit up when she saw Kevin stroll into the restaurant like he owned the place. Felt her smile turn to a jealous frown when Kevin made small talk with the hostess who laughed at whatever he said, her eyes shied away a moment later and Kevin ran his hands through his thick black hair, his green eyes seemed to shimmer and sparkle, made even brighter with his wide smile and perfect teeth.

Those emerald eyes found Sharon and Kevin said something to the hostess, who turned and met Sharon's stare from over her shoulder. Now the hostess' smile turned to a frown, her stare betraying what Sharon believed were daggers behind those eyes, sizing up Sharon with little effort. Kevin walked to the table, but Sharon maintained her gaze on the hostess. She felt her heart thump in her chest, her blood curl and her bones tense. Moved her head back and forth and felt her lips curl into a loathsome grin.

"Don't look so jealous," said Kevin. He leaned in and kissed her, then took his seat.

Sharon's lips were stiff with that kiss. The hostess took another glance over her shoulder and Sharon turned her stiff lips into a wide smile, then turned to Kevin.

"Don't trust a woman, either. When they all got their eye on you, there's no telling how far they'll go." Her voice trailed off, hung over their heads, and dissipated.

Kevin cleared his throat and took up his menu, started looking it over. It was obvious he enjoyed the attention. Might as well get used to it. This event was just the beginning and with Kevin's star on the rise, such occurrences will become a daily battle. Sharon sipped her wine, staring at Kevin. He seemed different. There was something about his eyes she couldn't put a finger on. And the way he sat, his demeanor and body language, screamed there was something out of place, some energy that hadn't been there before, as if he were chiseled from stone. Cold and calculated. Calm and arrogant.

Kevin ordered a martini. Sharon another wine. He made small talk with the waitress—another woman who Sharon knew was undressing him with her eyes. Sharon had to inform said waitress she wanted another glass of wine. If she hadn't, Sharon knew the waitress would have moved away from the table as if Sharon were invisible. Kevin seemed untouchable, larger and taller than she had remembered, with an invisible wall surrounding him. A wall Sharon could not penetrate. His demeanor was steady, unwavering, and constant.

The silence between them was maddening. She felt mesmerized. All she could do was stare. Something had indeed changed. Kevin put his menu on the table and looked over the restaurant, scanning every table in quiet solitude. Sharon believed he was ignoring her existence, avoiding any and all questions that may be on her mind. She felt a lump build in her throat, felt her bottom lip quiver. Kevin's eyes roaming, and Sharon cleared her throat.

"So, what's this big news?"

Now his eyes snapped to her, and when their eyes met, a shiver ran through Sharon. Felt herself cringe as if she were shrinking into her chair. He quickly turned away, severed the connection as if he knew what she had seen: the change in his eyes. Kevin didn't look at Sharon with a loving, adoring stare that conjured passion from his soul to his eyes. No, he looked at Sharon as if she were yesterday's dinner.

His grin curled his lips to his ears. Seemed like he was about to laugh. "I'll tell you later. For now, I just want to eat. I'm absolutely famished."

22

10:00 PM
Hudson Valley, NY
SAC Mills

"It's still strange," said Mills, sitting shotgun while Helmsley drove across the winding Taconic Parkway. "The entire time we were with him, I had a sense of déjà vu."

Helmsley was quiet, kept his eyes on the road and grabbed his coffee from the cup holder. Mills turned his gaze to the side of the road, trees cutting across his vision as the car moved forward. The waxing crescent moon hung overhead like an Arabian night. The North Star glimmering to the right of the moon. Mostly clear skies with a few rolling, however sporadic clouds.

"It can't be him, unless he received a ton of plastic surgery to cover up his gin blossoms and he doesn't seem like he can afford such a surgery, not to mention that would have had to have happened sometime today. You saw his nose. It was as smooth as a baby's butt. There's no way he's our guy."

Mills cracked his fingers, one at a time. The fact that Jiggly's nose was as smooth as a baby's butt was indeed strange. When Mills first laid eyes on Jiggly, his stomach clicked; a gut instinct that confirmed Jiggly was the mop bucket killer. The sensation was a combination of relief and shame, knowing that after twenty years the person he'd been searching for all this time was a five-foot tall carnival clown. Not a circus clown, mind you, but one of those carnival sideshows, a freak for all intents and purposes. And the man, this suspect, Mills knew, recognized Mills the moment he saw him. It was like reuniting with an old friend, someone you haven't seen since high school. Mills was embarrassed by the small smile that curled across his lips when he first saw Jiggly. He hoped

Helmsley did not notice. Hoped he didn't notice the haze either. From the moment he saw Jiggly Mills felt like he was in a trance, struggling to speak, respond, and ask questions. Felt like he wasn't in the trailer when they questioned Jiggly. No, those walls seemed to disappear, transporting Mills into a nest of clouds. Perhaps, Mills thought, to allow his thoughts to process, searching, seeking to find the thought hidden behind a host of thoughts, because something sinister existed beneath the folds. A memory long gone, driven so deep into the subconscious the only way to reach it was through death. Or, perhaps, torture.

"Need to take a piss," said Helmsley.

Mills turned to him and gave a quick nod as if he had to acknowledge the fact that Helmsley needed to relieve himself, then returned to his thoughts as the car veered off the Parkway, swallowed by darkness. There were no streetlights to illuminate the path. No cars passing by with headlights to prove the existence of other human beings. The car stopped at a stop sign and Helmsley took a right. Nothing but trees on both sides of the road. Quiet. Mills rolled down his window and closed his eyes when that fresh crisp air graced his skin. So quiet was the night, Mills was sure something sinister existed in the silence.

Helmsley turned left. The back tires caught a hump in the road and the car thumped. Mills looked around. There was nothing to see. Neither gas station nor convenience store. Only darkness bathed in a sliver of moonlight and stars. Helmsley pulled over.

"Here?" said Mills.

"Yeah. Nature calls and well…" Helmsley turned right, then left and shrugged. "All I see is nature."

Mills rolled his eyes as Helmsley got out of the car. Watched him walk to the side of the road, headlights beaming, bathing Helmsley in light.

When Mills looked up, his eyes narrowed, mouth slightly agape. He leaned in closer to the windshield, trying to wrap his head around what he was looking at. There was something in the trees overhead. Looked like a disc hovering in the night sky. And it was spinning. Spinning and moving, moving over treetops. He went to speak, to call for Helmsley, but no words came. His thought was simple, *Helmsley get in the car... now*. His heart raced, breath constricted yet huffing, but his thought refused to bounce off his lips as if some unseen force restricted his vocal cords.

Bright lights now. Light everywhere, beaming through the windshield. He lost sight of the spinning disc but he knew, somehow he knew, the disc was above the car. Understood the light came from this ship. Saw Helmsley, both arms arched over his groin, his head stretched, staring at the light. The car bumped and rocked, but Mills remained still, unmoving. Either he didn't want to move, paralyzed with fear, or he couldn't move, some invisible force wrapped around him, constricting all muscle movement. Mills felt his words in his throat. His stomach jutted in and out. Realized his breathing was the same. Trying to talk. To scream and holler for Helmsley to get back in the car. Watched as Helmsley was lifted off the street and disappeared into the light. Felt the car rock again, then constrict as if an invisible massive hand wrapped around the car and squeezed. The thought never occurred to jump out of the car. Jump out and run. A flood of memories wafted before him. Twenty years of memories. Jigglyspot with a smile leaning on a red cane. In his bedroom, his wife lying next to him on their bed. Unable to move, some invisible force wrapped around his throat, restricting all movement. Could hear his wife panting. He knew those noises that erupted in her throat. Heard the grunts, manly animalistic grunts. His wife's orgasm about to bellow into the night. And in the corner of his eye, he could see the beast on top of his wife. Red eyes watching him as its tongue lapped across her throat.

And then Mills was inside the car. And the car moved. Not forward or backward. The car lifted off the street.

Lifted off the ground and into the light.

23

10:10 PM
Carnival of Chaos
Jigglyspot

Less than an hour before closing and Jiggly had yet to find fresh meat. His hand was itching to use Mr. Scalpel. And the crowd was thinning. No one had entered the haunted house over the last twenty minutes. Jiggly took a seat, a small one-foot-wide bench inside the two-foot square, although six feet high room within the haunted house. A two-way mirror occupied the wall in front of him, providing the ability to see all who were coming down the mirrored hallway bathed in flickering yellow strobe lights. Rock and roll blared from the speakers throughout the haunted house. Eighties hair bands rock and roll, Jiggly's most hated genre. Those damn hair bands hadn't an ounce of talent. He despised the ground they walked on and blamed crack cocaine for the decade's most prominent rock and roll sound. Crack destroyed the brain and Jiggly enjoyed brains. Crack turned extraction into a foul tasting vomit. He could taste it on his tongue now and it drove his mind mad to think about it. During the 80s, Jiggly would wait a week before extracting a victim. Pumped fluids through an IV into his victim's veins and let them piss all over themselves until the crack was drained from their system. And then he would extract, not a moment sooner. Jiggly always said the 80s taught him patience. A virtue indeed.

Jiggly's eyes suddenly rolled to the back of his head. A download of information. He saw Helmsley with a stupid grin plastered across his lips, waving like some damn fool. Saw Mills strapped to a table. They'll plant a rational story in Mills' brain to explain why he left for California. Mills, Jiggly thought. That son of a bitch. All those years he spent with Mills and his wife Lorraine.

Jiggly sighed, thinking about her. She sure was sweet. Jiggly remembered how delectable her flesh was. Felt his erection tighten in his clown pants. A grand smile across his lips as he ran his hand down his pants when his eyes lit up. A male teenager stepped into the haunted house. A female teen, laughing and giddy, bumped into him. The male took her in his arms and she buried her face in his chest. Two more teens behind them, another couple perhaps?

Jiggly stood, eyes wide, watching with bated breath. But they just stood there, as if studying the hall. Jiggly noticed their eyes; mesmerized with wide pupils staring. Reminded Jiggly of those old cartoons when the character was bipped across the head and the eyes rolled and beamed. Jiggly put his ear to the mirror, attempting to hear what the teens were saying over the all too loud hair band guitar. Damn cherry pie was the worst, Jiggly thought. The music irritated him. He'll have to talk to Hal for the hundred billionth time about changing the hair bands over to Jiggly's preferred 90s grunge.

"You go first, I'm beaming. All these lights are mesmerizing, I can't see straight." This was said by the teenager standing behind the one Jiggly could clearly see. The boy looking up and all around.

Beaming?

Jiggly chewed his bottom lip, dug his teeth deep into it, gnawing, staring off to his right, thinking. And then he remembered, beaming, a common term used when on an LSD or mushroom trip. Jiggly felt his lips curl into a grin, held in his laughter, his gut tense, constricted, turned his gaze to the teens as they walked down the hall. The four of them huddled together.

"It's like the entire universe exists in here," said the teen leading the foursome. His head swayed back and forth, now standing, unmoving. The others crowded close behind him.

"All is one in this room. I can feel it," said the female behind the leader. Her head bobbed slightly up and down in unison with her quick breaths. She gestured to the couple behind her. "Can't you feel it?" she said as her eyes drifted, eyelids half closed. "It's like a portal to another dimension. The walls are breathing."

The leader replied, his arms stretched, palms up, "It's the most miraculous place I've ever been in." His head lolled back. Jiggly saw his eyelids flutter.

"It's beautiful," this came from the boy behind the leader, his girl now clinging to him, her head in his chest, her eyes closed.

Jiggly couldn't hold it any longer. That laugh of his bellowed from his stomach to his chest and throat. A thick, sinister laugh belted high into the cosmos that filled the hallway. The foursome looked all around. Jiggly couldn't help himself. He was laughing so hard, so loud he thought the entire universe could hear him.

"What the fuck is that?" said the girl with her head buried in her boyfriend's chest.

"It's God laughing," said the other female.

"It's the devil," the buried head female said. And Jiggly kept laughing. "I need to get out of here." She held her head in her hands. "I've got to go. I need to go." Her hurried feet seemed to have a mind of their own. She raced down the hall, and the others gave chase, pleading with the girl that all was well with the world.

And Jiggly kept laughing. Couldn't help himself, really. Laughed so hard tears rolled down his cheeks, cracking his face paint, he could feel the paint tighten on his flesh. These four beaming teens were a gift, and more than likely from Emmanuelle. She knew Jiggly's task was going to be difficult. Although Jiggly had pulled off a lot harder and more arduous tasks before, Emmanuelle knew appropriate extraction would aid him in his venture. Beaming opened the pineal gland and when the pineal gland was open, extraction never tasted better, and the effect was never more profound.

24

7:30 PM
Hollywood, California
Cassandra

She found the key and opened Ira's office. She wanted to be quick. Switch Sharon's headshot and be gone before there was even a slight chance of being caught. But the file on Ira's desk was not the same file from earlier today. No, not at all. The file she found was thick, about three inches thick, containing pictures of children of various ages, anywhere from a newborn to fourteen. Both males and females. Each picture contained a description of the child. Parents, heritage, location, date of birth, height, weight, ethnicity. She'd never seen the file before, never seen the pictures either. Had no idea who these kids were.

She wasn't sure why, but her heart was thumping with quick, heavy beats. She felt her stomach twist while looking over those pictures. Something about the file gnawed at her instincts. Something was wrong, something seriously, truly wrong with those pictures.

She heard the back door open and the same rapidly beating heart skipped a few beats. Heard feet shuffling across the Italian tile as the door closed with a heavy thud. Cassandra felt her lips purse and her throat constrict. Felt a bead of sweat run down her right temple, across her cheek and bead off her jawline. Cassandra forced a swallow down her closing throat. Felt her eyes grow wide, breath constricted.

Tension released when she saw Ira round the cubicles and stop.

Thank God!

Although he stood unmoving, perplexed, staring at Cassandra, as if he was attempting to understand what he was looking at.

Cassandra could see the cogs turning over in his brain.

Say something.

Speak Cassandra, speak.

Ira started towards her; his pace quickening with every step and Cassandra gently closed the file on the desk with her left hand. She forced a smile.

"Ira, working late tonight?"

That was stupid, she thought.

"What're you doing here?" This was Ira, edging closer to the office door. His right eye twitched something awful, and Cassandra felt her facial muscles tense.

"Getting a start on next week."

Now Ira was standing in the doorway, his presence a gargantuan ball of energy that seemed to leap and wrap Cassandra in an iron grip. She saw him glance at the folder on his desk.

She heard the back door open, and she looked over Ira's shoulder. "You with someone?"

And Ira smiled, his brow curled, and his eyes turned dark as if a sudden shadow crept across his face. Ira asked, "Can you grab the file for the Summer Gala?" then paused, his voice loud as if he wanted whoever was coming to understand he was not alone. "Since you're here." That smile again.

Slow shuffling on the tile ceased. Cassandra looked at the top of the cubicles across the room. Saw a mop of dark hair.

"Cassie?" said Ira with his smug, although grim stare.

Snap out of it, she told herself, noticing her hands were trembling. Jaw tight and quivering. "Of course," she said and now that her ability to speak returned, she could move, sensation returning to her bones and limbs. She stepped to the filing cabinet, felt eyes on her as she opened the drawer, her back to Ira.

Cassandra never heard footsteps, although she could feel how that ball of energy forced itself into her bones with a sudden cringe that erupted from the nape of her neck and shivered down her spine. Felt hot breath on her neck. Blood curled, and her body turned stiff, cringing when she felt a pinch in the side of her neck and a hand

across her mouth. Saw the world turn to a blur. Heavy eyelids.
Darkness.

25

8:00 PM
Hollywood, California
Tyler

He enjoyed the simple fact that the sun was just out of reach, a crescent of flowing yellow above the horizon. Sunset delivered a golden pink and purple sky as if providing a gift to the earth filled with breathtaking colors associated with calm and peace. Tyler watched the sky from the backseat of a sporty BMW. Pam next to him, her hand on his knee. Tyler powered down his window, closing his eyes when the cool, although warm wind graced his skin.

"Hey, shut the window. The wind is ear piercing." This came from Jake Ferris, the driver of said vehicle. Tyler had known Jake throughout his school career, although he'd gotten to know him more over the last year. Jake was the best friend of James Reilly. Sitting shotgun was Jake's better half for over two years, Amber Garner.

The fifth wheel in the vehicle, sitting behind the driver's seat and squeezed between Pam and the door, was Ned Tatty, his hands shaking, itching and scratching his arms. Ned was going through withdrawals. He normally ate a handful of oxy's per day and now, with Mr. Reilly no longer in business, Ned's pain was in full bloom. No one said two words about the demise of James Reilly.

Tyler didn't know where they were going, only that the circle of friends required down time to process the day's events. Perhaps, Tyler thought, to get their story straight once the cops start pounding on doors with questions that will require answers and a streamlined narrative of ignorance and show but don't tell concerning their involvement with James and his drug dealer exploits.

When his friends arrived at Tyler's apartment, the last thing he wanted was to get in the car. Not because he felt threatened by any means necessary. Nope, not at all. The friends he was riding with were innocent; only exception was their desire to get high and act like imbeciles. No, Tyler wanted to be alone and relish in his early morning accomplishment. Plus, he was tired, extremely tired, being up all night with James and then the coffee shop event with his victim playing the supporting role took every bit of energy he had left. He hoped to communicate with James again, even if it was from the netherworld. This murder issue wasn't bad at all. Nothing better than taking a life and having the soul of that person attached to you in some cosmic law most are unaware of.

But what relieved Tyler the most was his decision not to march into school and open fire. He was certain he'd be dead right now if he had. He knew he made the right decision to kill the cause of his discontent through plotting and planning. Assessing and evaluating, planning and reassessing, then a new plan and evaluating that plan. One thing was certain: when you set your mind on something, even if it's murder, things come together as if the universe conspired for your success. You could accomplish just about any task once you put your mind to it.

Tyler closed the window, shut out the wind and with it, those golden hues of pink and purple turned dark and foreboding through the tinted window. Nonetheless, he continued to stare, wondering, contemplating, reliving the timeline in his head. Tyler ran his hand through his dark locks. He couldn't actually feel it, that white spot of hair, but he knew it was there. Years of bullying and torture over the white spot were more than enough to give the spot a life of its own. He hated it. Tyler never needed a bully to point it out. He grew up with it; saw it every morning in the mirror. Sometimes that was all he could see.

During the seventh grade, he dyed his hair. That was a big mistake. James Reilly ran after him on that day, shouting obscenities and declarations over the vanished white spot. Shit, he couldn't even try to look normal, forever doomed and reduced to identify as the white spot. Tyler remembered that day as if it had happened this morning, forever etched in his memory. Why the hell was James Reilly so big? Why the white spot and not the means to defend himself? Why was he made so feeble and James Reilly so large but with the agility to catch up to Tyler, throw him down and laugh at him?

"Bring back the white spot. Bring it back. Bring it back," James had hollered on that day like a political protester wanting vengeance for political gain. Slapping Tyler's head where the white spot had been and yanking Tyler's boxer shorts, attempting to pull those shorts up and over the white spot. Tyler cried that day. Was on the verge of tears now, staring lost out the window. Pam's hand on his and Tyler jumped, startled.

"Chill out, Ty," said Jake, staring at Tyler in the rearview. He must have seen Tyler jump. Or maybe he was referring to the tears Tyler never noticed were streaming from his eyes until that moment. He could feel them on his cheeks, cascading to his jawline. Tyler wiped them with the back of his hand.

Patience, Tyler thought. The intelligent are patient because they know. They know that he who understands time wins the game every time.

"You, ok?" Pam whispered. Now she had Tyler's hand folded in hers.

Yes, she was gentle, but Tyler knew different. What she had to endure over the last year did something to her and that something was not good. Having to pretend the rape never happened. Because what could she do? Pam came from the same part of town as Tyler and with the Reillys' star power there was no way James would receive anything more than a slap on the wrist. She had to put up the façade that all was well and could never be better. Over the last year, she'd lost something in the brain, some part of her that destroyed the last remaining sliver of innocence she once had.

Tyler pursed his lips then swallowed hard. "Yeah," he said and turned to the window. Thoughts returned to middle school, crying in his pillow. The day his plan popped into his thoughts and refused to let go. The plot being set brought a strange relief because knowing all would end one day was paramount and brought a calm to Tyler's heart. Knowing one day James would be dead, his life crashing to a halt at Tyler's hand.

That was the day Tyler decided he would kill James Reilly and put an end to the pain, ridicule, and shame.

All that remained were the consequences. But Tyler was certain he could brush off any karma that was on his way.

26

11:30 PM
Westchester, NY
The Pipeline
Jigglyspot

He followed them from the Carnival of Chaos, always maintaining a stealth distance. Jiggly overheard where they were going, a wooded area the teenagers referred to as the pipeline. A place where teenagers can get high and drunk without the fear of police or nosy neighbors. Engage in fellatio behind a tree, which was Jiggly's preference. Get them separated, drive fear into their hearts and minds and whoever was left standing after Jiggly did his business would be the one he'd extract from. Jiggly could taste the extraction on his tongue. It had been so long since he'd had a pure extraction.

Jiggly had changed from his brightly colored clown outfit into a black and white clown outfit. Better to hide among the trees in the dark. Jiggly bit his bottom lip, watching the beaming teens sitting around a small fire, their eyes glazed over, lost in the flames.

The pipeline is a long desolate stretch of cleared trees in the Westchester woods that begins in the middle of a suburban neighborhood and stretches to the power plant a few miles away. The clearing was made decades ago with the plan to install water pipes that pumped water to the neighborhood and surrounding residential establishments. Oak and maple trees line the path on both sides of the twenty-foot-wide clearing that slithers up an incline towards the power lines. Jiggly hid among the trees, his hand on Mr. Scalpel in his pocket, tapping the metal instrument as if he were petting an attack dog ready to strike.

Soon, he thought. So very soon.

Electronic dance music pumped from a small speaker sitting on top of a rock by the fire. The only thing Jiggly despised more than 80s hair band rock was EDM. No soul, Jiggly would say. Just bleeps and waves like some electronic child's game gone mad and posed as music. A modern day attempt at symphony that missed the mark by miles. The beaming teens were lost in the flames, not speaking, both couples huddled close together, wide eyes or closed eyes, no in between.

One teen, the boy who'd first appeared in the hall in the haunted house, was sitting cross-legged in front of the fire, his girl lying in the leaves behind him, her arm wrapped around his waist and curled in a fetal position, her eyes closed. The boy's arms were outstretched as if he could hug the fire, his eyes wide and black, jaw hung open, mesmerized.

The second couple sat on a rock, the girl with her elbows on her knees as the boyfriend rubbed her back, their heads close together. Jiggly sized them up for extraction and for whom to kill first. Which teen would he allow to live? Whichever teen it was would also be dead by morning. Jiggly had to be in Illinois in a week, offering him a small window to play with these kids.

His eyes kept drifting to the first teen and his girl behind him. Girl or boy didn't matter to Jiggly, he had no preference.

Jiggly noticed how the second boy whispered in the ear of his girl and she nodded, looked at him with a small smile and stood, holding the boy's hand as she stepped behind him.

The boy said, "Tom," although his voice was barely a whisper. "Tom," his voice raised and the teen embracing the fire lifted his head, his arms floating to his lap.

"Yes, Blake Carrington, how may I help you," Tom said, acting studious and well mannered, sarcastic.

Blake laughed. "Jackass," he said, then gestured to the woods.

Tom followed the gesture, then turned back to Blake. "No, Mr. Carrington, I do not wish to have sex with you in the woods."

"Well, that's a relief," said Tom, standing, still holding his girl's hand. "Don't let the fire go out."

"I will not, Mr. Carrington. The fire is safe with me. Go forth with your girl to engage in fellatio and hedonism."

More laughter from Blake and his girl as they walked into the woods. Tom turned to his girlfriend, still lying behind him. Put his hand to the side of her face and her eyes drifted open then closed again.

"You, ok?" he asked, and she nodded. "Just let it take you where you need to go." He returned his gaze to the fire. "It's beautiful. Put your thoughts in your heart. That's the trick." He started bobbing his head and shoulders back and forth as if he were in a rocking chair.

Jiggly looked for the couple in the woods. Like clockwork teens are; always horny as if sex defined a relationship. They travelled far into the woods, away from prying eyes, secluded. Jiggly followed cautiously, his hand tapping his pocket when the couple stopped at a large boulder. Lying on the ground was a blanket, torn and tattered, shriveled, and stained. Jiggly wondered how long the blanket had been in the woods. How many teens saturated the cloth with sweat and bodily fluids? How many lost virginities had this blanket claimed?

Blake wasted little time. He sat the girl down on the boulder and unzipped his jeans. Jiggly turned to the fire couple who remained as before, unmoving. Turned back to Blake, his back to Jiggly. Saw his girl's head bobbing up and down. And Jiggly smiled as he took Mr. Scalpel from his pocket. Took small steps towards Blake, scalpel at the ready.

As he approached, Jiggly shook his head, thinking,

Teenagers, always so predictable.

27

8:45 PM
Los Angeles, California
Sharon

She never knew Kevin was a back door man, but that's where he went almost immediately as if he had no interest in the other entrance. He'd been so cold at dinner, ate so fast, his eyes on her the entire time. He never even allowed her to finish her meal-a thick T-Bone with a side of fresh vegetables and a baked potato that was now sitting in a Styrofoam container on Kevin's kitchen counter.

He said he was horny and couldn't wait. That he needed to relieve some stress. Sharon was willing and able to oblige, but once they were in the bedroom, all Kevin did was flop Sharon on her stomach, raise her hips and went to town. And it hurt like hell, then felt fantastic, but then the pounding started. Kevin like a madman and that hurt even more than when he first broke through that tiny hole. It seemed, to Sharon at least, that he wanted her to feel pain. And there was no connection, not like the other times they'd made love when she felt a connection that filled her mind with splendor and wonder. No, this seemed like he was alone, not connected, disconnected. And he lasted so much longer than normal. Sharon was used to sex lasting a full five minutes with Kevin but this time he went for almost a half hour, as uncomfortable as she was and he slapped her thighs with such a force she was sure there were marks across her skin.

And then he dropped his jizz inside her and went to take a shower, leaving Sharon lying in the bed, hunched over, bleeding and burning. She wanted to cry, although she wasn't sure if she wanted to cry because of the pain, the disconnection, or the thought that she'd been taken advantage of. Her mind swimming in thought when her phone buzzed. She wanted nothing to do with anyone at the moment but required a distraction. Beside her phone on the bedside table was an envelope, the same envelope Kevin had showed her, although he never opened it or provided information on what was in the envelope. Sharon checked her phone, a message from Cassandra.

You're good to go. All is set. I have to fly to Atlanta tonight for a show. I'll be back in a few weeks.

Ok, Sharon responded. **Be safe. See you soon.**

The shower stopped and Sharon dropped the phone and grabbed the envelope, then sat upright against the headboard. Face winced when her ass found the mattress. Kevin was humming *Somewhere Over the Rainbow*, the bathroom door ajar. She opened the envelope. Inside was a card that read: **Special Invitation to Summer Solstice Celebration @ The Prestigious Cannibal Café. Admit One With An Expected Admission Requirement.**

No address, just a date two weeks from today.

Sharon heard about the café. It was in the news lately and on the Internet as fake news, completely debunked. The café was prestigious; known for their prominent guest list and overpriced steaks and chops prepared by the world's leading chefs who flew in from across the world on the rare occasions the café was open.

The invitation was like royalty. It meant Kevin had crossed the line from nobody to rising star. She was indeed jealous. Looked out the window where night had fallen, wishing she was the one who received the invite and hoping, hoping her star was also on the rise. Her career was now in Cassandra's hands, who'd been resistant to helping Sharon over the years, never wanting to put her neck out for a friend. What kind of friend is that? Careers are made through connections. It's not what you know but who you know, and Cassandra was in the perfect position to help a friend. What the two of them could accomplish over the years spent in the spotlight could be historic if given the chance.

Seemed that chance was on its way. If Cassandra did what she agreed to do, Sharon was about to cash in on an opportunity that came along and sparked a career every once in a blue moon. Cassandra had to deliver; their livelihood was on the line.

Come on Cassandra. Get it done.

"What are *you* thinking about?"

Kevin was standing in the bathroom door, a towel wrapped around his waist. Thick, dark, wet locks covered his forehead, and he brushed those strands with his fingertips from his crystal green eyes. A thin frame with a muscular build glistened wet. Sharon's thoughts turned blank, felt Kevin's presence in the room as if he were on top of her. Kevin bent his head, staring.

"You, ok?" His voice sincere and Sharon noticed he glanced at the invitation on her lap. He gestured to it. "Found the invitation? Absolutely spectacular. You know what that means, right?" He was excited, she could tell, as he strolled across the room to the bed.

Sharon wanted to cry. She cleared the frog in her throat as Kevin flopped on the bed. "Yeah, it means you made it. You're one of them now." Her voice a subtle whisper.

Kevin stretched on the bed, his back against the headboard. His eyes roamed over her body. She could feel them on her, desire and intrigue gleamed in his pupils. "You'll come, right?" he asked. "I'd like for you to be there, but it's your decision. You have to agree to be a part of it."

"Invitation mentions one guest and..." She took the invitation and read verbatim, "... only with an expected admission requirement." She forced a smile as her eyes met his. Sharon turned away quickly, feeling his eyes on her as he removed his towel, revealing his erection. Sharon cringed, sensing his smile was ear to ear.

He brushed Sharon's dark hair from her eyes then moved her chin, so her eyes were looking into his. "It's ok. I have permission to invite a guest."

"Really?" Her brow furrowed and Sharon felt a sudden relief.

Kevin just about laughed. "Yeah, of course." His grin was ear to ear. "When they said I can have a guest, you're the first and only person I thought of."

Dumbfounded, speechless. Sharon didn't know he cared for her like that. A moment ago, she was alone, the thought cancelled by glimmering green eyes and sweet words.

"But you have to agree," he said as he looked down, then returned his gaze. "Do you agree?"

Sharon let the bed sheet fall from her body as she edged closer to Kevin, her eyes never leaving his. She took his erection in her hand.

"One hundred percent," she said. "I agree."

Kevin pursed his lips, eyes narrow as he leaned his head against the headboard. "Perfect."

And Sharon said, "Let me show you my appreciation."

28

9:00 PM
Los Angeles, California
Lilly

Her head was pounding, eyes wet. For a moment, she had no idea where she was. Someone was pounding on the front door. She heard footsteps on the stairs. Lilly pushed herself up on the couch and the room spun, dizzy. Her fingertips went to her temples to ward off the spinning sensation.

Again, the door, pounding and knocking, she could feel the vibration as if someone was inside her head and yearning to break free from her thoughts. Chris in the hall now, Sam behind him.

"The cops are here," Chris said, and Lilly snapped her head to him.

Outside the bay window, she could see red and blue lights. Pounding, rapping, thuds at the front door.

"Mrs. Hempstead, can you come to the door, please?" A male voice outside the front door.

"You, ok?" asked Chris as Lilly stood up.

Her legs buckled, weak, and she lost her balance. If it weren't for the couch blocking her legs from tumbling over, she would have fallen. She noticed Sam hiding behind Christopher.

"What's going on?" she said, stomping out of the office.

"They've been knocking for over ten minutes," said Chris as Lilly shuffled past her children. "Is it Dad?"

Lilly stopped, froze is more like it, her mind swimming. She looked at her children, noticed fear in Christopher's eyes. The house was dark except for the blue and red lights that trolled across the walls through the window.

Knock, pound, knock, pound. "Mrs. Hempstead," the officer's voice loud through the door.

She knew she didn't want to answer the door. Had to answer, but with every fiber of her being she knew what was waiting on the other side was horrific. The thought occurred to her then that the world had suddenly changed, and not in her favor. Felt like she was outside of herself, looking in, seeing her children and herself open the door. Felt a waft of warm night air. She never saw the officer, not at first. Her eyes scrunched by the lights, then saw the neighbors standing outside, craning their heads, voyeurs to tragedy.

"Mrs. Hempstead?" the officer asked.

She heard herself answer but would never recall speaking. Her heart dropped into her stomach.

The officer, a thirty-two-year-old husky man by the name of James Ashton, looked at her children, then turned to Lilly. She stood in silence as Officer Ashton delivered the news.

Tad was dead. He shot himself in his office.

And life had indeed taken a turn for the worse.

29

Midnight
The Pipeline
Jigglyspot

The funny thing about beaming is that the effect leads the user into a hole of distractions. The result is a scattered thought process, wild staring eyes, and an ability to stare at one single object for what seems like eternity while the rest of the world melts away like ice from the peripheral. And, as any perpetrator worth a damn will tell you, distraction is the key to a good abduction.

It was easy for Jiggly to sneak up on the unsuspecting beamers. Even the muffled screeches from his victims went unnoticed by Tom, whose psychedelic trip manifested in closed eyes as he sat cross-legged by the fire.

That kid Blake was too easy. Jiggly used Mr. Scalpel to pierce his lung through the back. His girl noticed little of anything except the sudden jerk and Jiggly was sure she had expected something else other than what happened next. Blake dropped like a sack of potatoes and his girl jerked back, puzzled. Jiggly was smart to change into the old black and whites. She never saw him. Her attention focused on Blake until Jiggly plunged Mr. Scalpel into her eyeball. His left hand gripped her throat to soften the scream. Thrust scalpel into her throat a moment later. No more screams after that. Her body jerking and shuddering as blood spouted from her throat.

Of course, Jiggly had to release some of that pent up energy he'd been carrying since the haunted house. And because Mr. Scalpel hadn't seen too much activity over the last week, Jiggly went to town. Slashing, slashing, slashing and always with a grin. He wanted to laugh, but knew the moment required restraint. When he finished, she was a bloodied, bleeding mess, already dead from the blow to the throat. Well, Jiggly thought, maybe she lived long enough to feel the first few cuts from Mr. Scalpel. He hoped so, because if she did the benefit for Jiggly would be substantial. Pain and fear tie the victim to the perpetrator, even in the afterlife.

When he finished, Jiggly heard their souls yelp and rage through the woods. He then eyeballed Tom's girl, lying, probably sleeping, behind Tom. When he had watched them from the woods upon arrival, Jiggly thought she would be the one to accompany him home. But she was so out of it, so sleepy, already giving audience to the dreams in her head. Jiggly used chloroform for his abductions, and considering her current mental state, chloroform may cause excessive sleepiness and sluggishness that could last too long, and time was not on his side. She may be too difficult to arouse and he required his victims to be awake during the extraction process. Jiggly closed his eyes then, closed his eyes to see what would happen if he chose her. Jiggly saw the girl awakening, saw her eyes roll open as he pounded her from the rear. That look of surprise when she finally understood she was no longer free, her neck and wrists bound within the pillory Jiggly kept in the basement. And oh, how he loved his pillory. The wooden device provided the perfect angle for Jiggly to enter and get deep, his victim unable to move. But his vision concluded with her head falling limp, eyes clamped shut, sleeping. No screams, no fear, just a useless blob of limp human meat. Quite obvious to Jiggly, she was not the correct choice, and he turned his attention to Tom.

He snuck up behind him. Enjoyed standing unnoticed. Stood there for a full five minutes before crouching over Tom's girl and with one swift move Jiggly clamped her mouth shut with his left hand and plunged Mr. Scalpel into her throat. Her body tensed and wiggled, flailed like a fish out of water before the body fell limp and dead, her soul yelping and crying, unknowing what happened, confused. Jiggly watched the woods and the girl's soul standing by the fire, her eyeballs black.

Jiggly raised his chin, blew air from between his cheeks and the girl disappeared.

"It's ok," said Tom reaching behind him. His hand patting her head and Jiggly's eyes widened when Tom's hand came within centimeters of her bloodied throat. "It's ok," he repeated. "Just let it take you."

Jiggly rolled his eyes then looked at the back of Tom's skull. He took a deep breath and closed his eyes, listening. The woods were so quiet, the only sound from the crackling fire and Tom's heavy breathing. Jiggly looked at the stars. Those celestial bodies reminded him of home. A shooting star raced across the moonlit sky. Jiggly waved, then returned his gaze to Tom, whose heavy breathing evolved into a chanting, *Ohm.*

Jiggly felt the vibration in Tom's throat. Felt the vibration in his bones, twisting his stomach into knots.

Ohmmmmmmm.

Jiggly gripped the girl's body in his tiny hands.

Ohmmmmmmm.

Rose to his feet, the girl over his head.

Ohmmmmmmm.

Tossed her body into the fire then reached into his pocket with a coy, subtle patience.

"Elsa?" Tom cocked his head, staring at the burning body. The stench of burning, cooking flesh wafted across the woods. Jiggly drenched a cloth with the chloroform he pulled from his pocket. His movements swift, calm.

Perhaps it was Tom's disbelieving awe that caused him to turn around, believing Elsa's burning body was nothing more than a hallucination, but his sudden head turn provided Jiggly with the perfect angle to wrap that cloth across his nose and mouth.

"Time for sleep," said Jiggly, his arms and hands like iron that Tom fought to remove. The chloroform worked fast. Tom's immediate defenses quickly vanished. His arms dropped like anvils. Eyelids heavy, closing, and Jiggly used that last moment of conscious thought to say, "I'll see you soon," in that heavy, raspy voice of his. Jiggly enjoyed adding a seductive edge to his voice when he abducted his victim, watching as they drifted off to Lala

Land. He narrowed his eyes when he spoke and blew Tom a kiss before his eyes closed, drifting back with a slump to the earth. Jiggly tossed the chloroform rag into the fire then sat down, listening to the flames devour Elsa's flesh, loving the sweet fragrance burning flesh reveals. It was hypnotic, put Jiggly in a trance. He remained sitting, watching and listening for a good while before searching Tom's pockets where he found a plastic bag filled with psychedelic mushrooms.

Absolutely perfect, Jiggly thought, wishing he hadn't killed Elsa so quickly. Not with this revelation. And with his discovery, Jiggly knew his trip to Illinois will have to wait another day or two. He can keep Tom alive throughout the weekend with this amount of mushrooms. Nothing conjures fear more than when the victim is beaming, staring at a decapitated head-Jiggly ran out of time before leaving for the carnival and Zach's head was on his mantle-and being pounded from behind as Jiggly drank their extraction, his victim watching Jiggly in the mirror he set up in front of his pillory. Plus, and this simple fact excited Jiggly more than he'd been excited in a long while, after days of beaming the mind cracks, and that's when the fear arrived with a vengeance. The paranoia and detached reality. Now add in a little abduction fear, excruciating pain-think about how much pain is involved when a skull is removed without anesthesia-and the constant devilish projection and rape Jiggly will undoubtedly enjoy, and every ounce of extraction will flow from Tom's pineal gland like a fountain of fine wine. He loved to perform and perform for Tom he will. He'll wear his party mask for the occasion, the one with the horns and rhinestones that formed the figure eight around the eyes. Jiggly laughed at the thought when he caught a large whiff of Elsa. His stomach gurgled, empty. Jiggly hadn't eaten in a few days. He searched the earth. Found Mr. Scalpel on top of a maple leaf and picked it up.

Jiggly knew to never waste an opportunity to eat. And with that flesh searing off the bone, Jiggly had never been so hungry.

30

10:00 PM
Hollywood, California
Tyler

He wanted to come home and had to beg Jake to leave the Hollywood sign. Claimed he felt sick to his stomach with grief. Truth was Tyler wanted to relish the day's events on his own. What a long day it had been. His eyes were tired, salty, and heavy. He'll shave his head tomorrow, he thought. Get rid of the white spot, at least for a while. Thought about dying his hair, but that thought quickly vanished. Stop denying who you are, Tyler. The white spot is a part of him, and he should have no shame in who he is. A warlock is what his research reported, although he had to dig deep to find the answer. Most reports identified the problem as a pigment malady referred to as poliosis, but Tyler scoffed at the explanation. Damn medical industry never got anything right. Ignoring the metaphysical, ethereal, and quantum mechanics of bodily energy doomed modern day science into the dark ages. The exception was quantum physics, which, according to Tyler, was still in its infancy and required so much more learning and theory he wondered just how long it would take for medical science and quantum mechanics to link up. Science, at least in this modern day, held zero answers because it merely scratched the surface of a much larger scientific realm. Therefore, science has its limitations, bound to its own limiting philosophy. Tyler was confident that over the next few centuries, everything we know now will be disproven or take on a completely new context and theory. You can't claim to know when you know nothing because you don't know everything. Truth being a simple acceptance of this fact.

No one knows diddly-squat and to say so with any hint towards absolute fact was primitive in its own right. We might as well continue to burn people for claiming the earth was round. Tyler always believed he was born in the wrong time period. He despised his generation, wished he'd been a teenager in the sixties or at the very least the nineties, although he was sure he had been a child of those generations in another life.

All these thoughts were racing through Tyler's mind as he tiptoed into his apartment. His father in the living room sitting in his favorite recliner, television blaring some news report about James Reilly, an empty beer bottle in his lap, his father slumped in the chair, sleeping. At least he wasn't pounding his chest and throwing his weight around. Tyler was relieved the man was sleeping. He went to his bedroom and flopped on the bed, staring through the window at the moon and the North Star as Tyler thought about appreciation and gratitude.

Appreciate your talents. Be grateful for what you have.

He thought about James then. Saw himself at the Reillys' kitchen table, gun in hand, trigger squeezed, and he heard the pop his bullet made when said bullet tore into the heart of James Reilly. Heard James gasp and try to breathe. Air sucked from his lungs as if the bullet knocked the wind out of him. A spot of blood on his shirt, growing wide then ballooning across his shirt like wildfire. So much blood it pooled on the floor around James' feet. Tyler could hear it now. Each drop slammed against the tile floor like raindrops falling from a gutter to a puddle during the fiercest storm. So much blood it wouldn't stop, as if this storm was everlasting. James attempting to breathe, gasping for life, and his eyes, staring, revealed the horror hell spawned for James Reilly, then flickered when the soul retreated. Turned black and empty, but the blood continued, raining across the floor. Tyler saw himself staring, heard each crimson droplet fall. Trickling down now, the end of the storm, and Tyler's eyes drifted, eyelids slowly closing. Rest. Tyler required rest. Would he dream? he thought. What waited for him on the other side of consciousness? Eyes closed now, shallow breathing. Heard thunder and thought, Good, what we need is a cleansing. Wash away all the death and carnage, sin and chaos, while we sleep, cozy and free, resting our weary minds from the karma of our deeds.

Another loud rolling crash of thunder. Tyler's eyes opened. Lightning outside the window bathed his room in a bluish glow. James standing beside his bed, watching. And Tyler rested easy knowing his Reilly was there.

Part II
A Change In The Script

1

7:11 PM
Friday June 14, 2019
Hadenfield, Illinois
Jigglyspot

Jigglyspot sat in a corner booth in a diner that boasted—like most diners do—a great cup of coffee. Not that Jiggly wanted coffee, nor did he need coffee, not with the weekend's worth of extraction continuing to stimulate the mind. But he had to order something and Jiggly wasn't hungry in the least bit. Extraction suppressed the appetite and unless Ray's Diner offered raw steak—and Jiggly was sure that if Ray did offer raw steak, it would be closer to consuming a grandma meat than a savory young lamb—Jiggly wasn't about to indulge in anything other than coffee. The coffee was a prop, a means to maintain a façade for the patrons and staff. Just a Jigglyspot having coffee while reading the newspaper.

Not that he wasn't watching the family on the other side of Ray's. A father, mother, and two children ages seven and four, one girl and the other a boy. The kids were eating ice cream sundaes, the girl sitting with mom, boy with dad, and the parents were finishing their drinks, a beer for the father, a glass of more than likely cheap red wine for the mother. Jiggly had entered the diner when the family was finishing their entrées. On his way to the booth he noticed the father—one Michael Cummings—looked at him. Jiggly understood that Michael must have experienced a sense of déjà vu. Happened all the time from what Jiggly was told. The information received from the mouths of his victims over years of invested inquiry. Déjà vu is a side effect of the commonality—the potion— given to the victims so they wouldn't, couldn't, remember what had happened to them. Turned the experience into a dream to be scoffed at, tucked inside a subconscious box and forgotten.

Jiggly pretended to read his paper. He could stare at the paper for hours and never actually see the paper or what any one article was about. It was a game Jiggly played, pretending to read when what he was really doing was eavesdropping. The parents made small talk, mostly about work and summer vacations as the kids played silly games with funny faces, squishing ice cream between their cheeks. Michael kept eyeballing Jiggly. *As if he knows what's coming.* Jiggly belted out a sudden laugh, paper held in both hands as he sat close to the table, his feet swinging above the linoleum floor. Seemed the entire diner stopped to observe the odd-looking man in the corner. Jiggly wore a white T-shirt that clung to his compact frame, revealing his slightly round paunch. Cargo pants, relaxed fit, his beard always a stubble hoping to one day become a man. No gin blossoms, his nose as smooth as a baby's butt. Those won't return for at least another month, considering the weekend's extraction and next week's festival. He gripped his paper tight in both hands, easing back into the booth, a continued forever grin plastered across his lips. His belly ached, holding in hysterical laughter. He eyed Michael as if to send a signal, some common sign of knowing. He noticed Michael appeared drawn, his skin pale, his eyes sunken through lack of sleep. Jiggly was sure his wife, Monica, looked the same. They always did, all of them, all the people scattered across the globe who shared a common phantom connection courtesy of Jigglyspot. They'll live all their days without understanding what was truly happening to them, in the dark cover of night, in their very bedrooms.

He couldn't hold the laugh any longer. It caught in his throat, erupting over his lips while staring at the paper, not seeing the paper but laughing at it all the same. His eyes watering he laughed so hard.

The waitress dropped the Cumming's check on their table. Jiggly kept laughing, although he suppressed the out loud bursts. Couldn't help himself. The scene was all too funny. He decided then, as Mr. Cummings paid the check and Monica corralled the children to leave, that he'd paint a big sunny smile on his face tonight. Yes indeed, a big sunny smile, an external representation of what lied within.

More laughter now, in the back of his throat, his stomach jutting in and out, staring at the Cumming's as they opened the door. One of those bells above the door jingled through the diner. The family gone and Michael took a quick glance through the windows. Just a moment and Jiggly laughed even harder.

"May I ask what is so funny?"

The waitress was standing next to Jiggly. He never looked at her. "Just a funny story in the paper."

Jiggly stretched his eyelids and shook his head, warding off the fuzzy sensation laughter often brings. Noticed the headline: Three Teenagers Found Dead in New York, One Missing.

Whoops.

Jiggly turned to the waitress, saw that disgusted stare in her narrow eyes before she walked away. She never even refilled his cup, and Jiggly's smile melted into a grimace. His top teeth bit his inside lip, watching the waitress walking to the counter. He should have been more mindful, now the night will be long. He thought about the time. Just after seven. Diner closed at eleven and he had to meet Kera at two in the morning. His eyes narrowed, thinking. Unfortunately, he'll have to be quick with this waitress, considering he was in a time crunch with Kera's pending arrival.

Jiggly folded the paper inward, covering the headline story, and laid the paper on the table. No more laughter in his throat, instead, Jiggly felt that familiar sensation, the pressure of time and aggravation.

Check that, Jiggly thought, I'll paint a scowl tonight.

2

5:30 PM
Los Angeles, CA
Lilly

The funeral concluded earlier this afternoon. Somber, to say the least. Lilly's mind raced with so many thoughts she felt numb, disturbed, as if she stepped into an alternate universe. So many thoughts with no thought at all. Each thought like a picture in a photo gallery that kept spinning so fast she couldn't see the fine details. She was angry, yes, sad and trembling with fear and grief, unable to think past the next hour. Or the next minute. Sitting on the couch in her home office away from the mourners and supporting cast with intentions to help and understand. The same couch where she'd passed out a week ago, drunk because she couldn't get a hold of Tad. She thought he was cheating, had found a new young lass to indulge in. She hated herself for not seeing the signs, for allowing her thoughts to be consumed with jealousy when she should have spotted the depression and the signs of desperation.

She wanted the sun to go down. Wanted this day over and done with, hoping that when the sun greets her eyes tomorrow morning, the past week will seem like a distant nightmare. And maybe Tad will be by her side. The thought sent a shiver down her spine, thinking of their bed and the empty space where Tad had slept over the past decade. She couldn't stomach it. Seeing his empty space brought a hollow sensation that seemed to pull her down into a pit of hellish thoughts and realities she wasn't ready to accept. She refused to stay there. Started sleeping—when she did sleep—on this very same couch. Immobile, and paralyzed with emotion to the point where she could barely speak, as if her brain couldn't connect her thoughts to her voice box. There was so much she wasn't aware of. So much Tad never told her. She had thought they were fine financially, more than fine, considering. But that was a façade, and every item in her home was a reminder of those financial troubles.

Tad's business plummeted over the last six months. Little did Lilly know that losing the Reilly commission was the straw that broke the camel's back. Tad had been skating their finances through loans with high interest rates that destroyed the business and the loan company was about to take over, liquidate everything they owned. Toss them out on the street in shame. Without the Reilly commission, Tad couldn't pay the loan, and he was already more than a few months behind.

She was still reeling from Tad's choice of suicide. Yes, he shot himself, but that wasn't the half of it. Tad beat his face to a bloody pulp with the butt of his revolver before he used the same gun to put a bullet between his eyes. His face was so mangled and battered, the only means to identify the body was through dental records with the few teeth he had left in his mouth. All these circumstances led to a closed casket, but not seeing the body made this even more unreal. Denial led to unreasonable thoughts that Tad was still alive. His suicide a farce to pull the wool over the lender's eyes. But she knew this wasn't true. What was true? Lilly did not know. Everything around her was a lie, and those lies had become a prison. She spent her days numb to the core and even the simplest decisions she had no answer for. When she attempted to speak, her words regurgitated down her throat, flushed into oblivion.

And what about the boys?

Every time she attempted to think about them, her mind hit a wall. They were in pain. In pain and needed their mother. To tell them all would be fine. To provide a ray of hope, but hope seemed to fade into nothingness with that bullet through Tad's head. She couldn't even look at them, her boys, although she wanted nothing more than to wrap her arms around them, hold them tight and never let go but every time they were in the same room or occupied the same space she avoided them like the plague, as if recognizing their hurt, their pain, their loss, would manifest in acceptance. And Lilly wasn't ready to do that. Couldn't do that.

She looked up from the couch, saw family and friends, and some strangers who'd known Tad, sitting, talking in hushed tones and she felt a tightness in her chest, around her heart. Numb, dry eyes staring, looking up as if she wanted to say something. But what could she say?

When she heard Kathy Crawford conversing with Ms. Finicky, her stomach turned with a hollow pain. Her thoughts went to Chris, up in his room with that damnable Jenny Crawford.

3

6:00 PM
Beverly Hills, CA
Tyler

James Reilly's funeral concluded earlier in the afternoon. More than a hundred attendants said goodbye to James. Family, friends, school personnel, and a host of Hollywood's elite. Three news camera crews, vans included, came to watch the somber event. Police detectives stood by their cars, surveilling the funeral. Tyler was sure they were looking for suspicious activity. Even James was there. To Tyler, that is.

He'd become a little less than fruitful, for lack of a better word. A rotting corpse scavenging his own funeral. Tyler had stood away from the crowd, his circle of friends by his side, Pam next to him, her head on his shoulder, watching, tearful. She held a tissue to wipe the tears from her eyes. And Tyler thought, A performance worthy of nomination, she was so convincing. Even had James second-guessing himself.

"Is she really that broken up?" asked James, standing in front of Tyler and Pam.

Tyler moved his head left than right, eyeballing James through a pair of dark sunglasses. It's not like he could carry on a conversation with a dead man with so many in attendance. Plus, what would the police say? Tyler was certain conversing with no one would send up a red flag or two.

James stared at Tyler. His flesh rotting, decomposing. Tyler could see Reilly's cheekbone through a hole where the skin had completely deteriorated. James cocked his head as if attempting to understand why Tyler was ignoring the question. Tyler gestured to the cemetery where James' coffin awaited a final descent into the earth, a priest anointing the coffin, bible in hand, about to speak. James turned, crossed his arms, and remained silent. A second later Tyler watched James walk through the crowd towards his mother, put a hand on her shoulder as the priest provided procession when a convoy comprising four limousines followed by a line of cars, parked fifty yards from the Reilly funeral.

Tyler watched as the driver opened the back door to the first limo. Watched the driver take the hand of the first passenger, a woman, followed by two boys. They all stood frozen, looking at the Reilly funeral, as if their eyes glimpsed their immediate future. The Reilly priest's words drifted from Tyler's ears into a soft, incoherent mumble. Tyler couldn't take his eyes off the boy who stood close to his mother. Couldn't be over fifteen, Tyler thought. He had this stare, this blank stare that revealed disbelief and shock, perhaps forever engrained in the boy's eyes. Tyler's heart dropped, wondering what had happened, concluding this must be a sudden, unexpected death.

"Suicide," James whispered in Tyler's left ear, something Tyler had grown accustomed to over the last week. Reilly cleared his throat. "Shot himself in his office."

For a brief second, Tyler and the boy locked eyes. Even through sunglasses, Tyler knew the boy felt his stare. The connection broken when Ms. Finicky took the boy's hand, escorting him to the gravesite.

"Finicky," James scoffed. "Forgot about that bitch."

Tyler kept his gaze on the boy, ignoring Reilly, watching as Ms. Finicky escorted him to the gravesite as James laughed one of those hearty, gut-busting laughs. Kept repeating, "That bitch," and laughing. Laughing so hard and so loud, a nest of mourning doves jumped from a tree and crossed over the cemetery.

"Oh, wow," said James. "That's so beautiful. Did I do that?"

Tyler shot James an icy stare, wondering if Reilly's brain was decomposing. The same thought with him now as Tyler took a sip of coffee from the mug in his hand. James was nowhere in sight, but Tyler was sure he'll be waiting for him in his bedroom later tonight, once Tyler removed himself from Amber's house where he was now.

After the funeral, Amber invited every single attendee under the age of twenty-five to her house for what she deemed a 'get together' to talk and process the untimely death of James Reilly. Tyler wanted nothing to do with it, but maintaining appearances was a part of the performance. Act as if all was normal.

Jake cradled a bottle of whiskey. Amber was upstairs quieting her parents. Ned Tatty was in the bathroom, had been there since they arrived and Tyler was sure he'd found a new dealer, his withdrawals a forever staple in his daily functioning as he fought to get high and not just maintain. Pam sat next to Tyler as he leaned his head back against the couch. Tyler wanted to speak with her, but he knew that was not in their best interest. Knew there was a large possibility the police were watching the party, and may even have wire taps hidden everywhere in all their homes, listening to every single word and event James Reilly's closest friends were sharing. And he knew Pam wanted to speak with him. She'd been trying since that very first day, but Tyler kept putting her off.

"When the smoke clears and we're out of the woods," Tyler had said to Pam frequently over the last week. Nonetheless, Pam kept trying. She was anxious, Tyler knew, and her anxiety was getting on Tyler's nerves. He was certain she was hiding something, some truth yet to be revealed, and part of him believed she was full of shit. About what, he had no idea, but he was certain there was more in Pam's mind than just anxiety. Plus, his trust in Pam's ability to keep her mouth shut was dwindling. So, he kept her close, and displayed affection when he believed it was appropriate. An effort to thwart any possible contagious outbreak of second-guessing and regret. Pam may be a part of his diabolical plot, but Tyler is the one who pulled the trigger and that put him smack dab in the middle of a murderous Hollywood scandal that could rock the entire world. Attention Tyler was hoping to avoid. Plus, getting away with murder was even better than becoming famous for it.

Tyler looked at Pam, whose attention was on Jake as he poured whiskey into the crystal glass in Pam's hand. Tyler rubbed her back as she sipped from her glass, turning her head from Tyler's gaze when he surveyed the room. There had to be at least fifty classmates in attendance. Someone turned on EDM and Tyler rolled his eyes. Despised EDM he did, he would have preferred some hard-hitting 90s grunge. Now the smell of marijuana filled the room, and he noticed then how Pam was trembling, her knee bobbing up and down in some nervous, anxiety riddled code of conduct. Tyler craned his head, attempting to see her face, and noticed a tear fall from her jawline.

Tyler sat up, his arm around Pam, who turned and dropped her face against his shoulder. She was trembling indeed. Her cries now muffled whimpers. Tyler saw James in the center of the room, dancing, a gaping hole in his chest where Tyler shot him, his skin flaking off his fingers and face as he danced. Tyler clenched his jaw, holding in the laugh that caught in his throat.

Tyler thought about those birds in the cemetery and Reilly's reaction. And now he did laugh. Pam's head jumped off his shoulder, her eyes on him, filled with tears. Tyler stifled his laugh, eyes narrowed.

And Tyler wondered, Will he need to make Pam disappear?

4

6:30 PM
Somewhere in the dark
Cassandra

She remembered seeing Ira in the office. Remembered the pinch in her neck. How could she not? Her neck was swollen like a balloon and stung something awful every time she touched it; the itch was maddening. But what she couldn't shake was the memory-the presence that accompanied Ira into the office-that refused to relent. The presence she never laid eyes on. That mop of dark hair beyond the cubicles in the office. Said presence was the first on Cassandra's mind when she awakened in a cell in a dark room. The only light coming from a dulled yellow light bulb hanging ten feet high from the cell's ceiling that lost power within inches of the iron bars, as if whatever waited outside the cell had power over the light and no desire to be seen. If there was anyone there, that is.

From the very first day that Cassandra woke up in her cell, she heard footsteps sweeping across the floor, shuffling, scuttling. The same sweeping, shuffling and scuttling arrived every so often, at least three times a day. But no one had ever revealed themselves, or talked, or did anything even remotely human, and Cassandra was beginning to believe that the footsteps were a figment in her imagination. Perhaps her desire to not be alone fueled the delusion. Of course, someone had to put her in this cell, and she was certain Ira was too weak to carry her. He was a pitiful weakling of a man. Which would conclude that the presence who accompanied Ira that evening assisted him in his kidnapping endeavor. She could hear that scuttling now, sweeping footsteps across concrete, beyond the light, out there in the darkness.

Then again, maybe it was another prisoner, a captive in this strange and dreadful predicament. But even that thought was met with resistance. If it is another prisoner, why don't they talk? Or scream? Cassandra spent the first five days screaming and yawping and clambering and crying. Her throat swollen from screaming so much and hurt every time she swallowed. So why don't they scream, unless they've been here longer than Cassandra and had given up on desperate acts a long time ago?

Logical conclusion was that she was alone and whomever her captor was, enjoyed watching Cassandra. She could feel eyes on her, even in the dark, and wondered what evil deeds were behind those eyes. What thoughts about Cassandra swam through their twisted mind? How long were those eyes watching? Was it a simple game? Perhaps they sat and watched for hours as if *Cassandra in a Cell* was a popular viral video. Maybe they sat and waited for her to sleep so they could fill the wooden trough that sat in the corner of the cell, filled with what Cassandra assumed was water. And she got so thirsty she had to drink. Drink or go completely out of her mind. Cassandra noticed that every time she woke up from a nap—was it a nap or actual sleep—there was more water in the trough than before.

Sleep, then drink. Sleep, then drink. Scream. Lose your mind. Scream some more. Let those nightmarish thoughts rule every moment. Perhaps more pacing will help pass the time? She spent a few days pacing, because, well, what else was there to do? She even tried to climb to the top, although that endeavor led nowhere. The bars were too slick and there was no foothold, only vertical bars. Plus, the ceiling had to be at least ten feet high, from what Cassandra could see.

More sweeping now, somewhere in the darkness. Cassandra, sitting and leaning against the bars, her back to the darkness, craned her head around and gripped one of those bars with her left hand, attempting to see what the darkness refused to reveal. Her jaw trembling, felt sweat covering her skin. It was damn hot in the cell.

"Hello," she muttered, and tightened her grip on the bar, forcing a swallow down her chalky throat. "Someone there?" On the verge of tears.

More sweeping, as if someone favored a bad leg that dragged

across the concrete. She heard doors open then close. The sound was faint, but she was sure it was a door. And the sweeping stopped as if it too heard the same. The light turned off. Cassandra bathed in darkness, her eyes adjusting. Cassandra dropped her hand to her lap, and wrapped her arms around her knees.

Started praying, "Dear God, please help me. Get me out of this cell. I want to see my parents. I want to go home. Please God. Please, please, please help me. Get me out of this cell. You're the only one who can help me. I know you will. I don't belong here. Please God, please help me."

She leaned her head against the bars. Started crying and hated herself for crying.

"I just want to go home," she whined. "Just want to go home."

And as her cries echoed into the darkness, Cassandra felt a cold hand brush across her hair.

5

7:00 PM
Hollywood, CA
Sharon

The last week had been hard to handle. Everything seemed to change and changed on a dime, with no recourse to the past and no warning that the change would occur. Things were different, which is to say that everything felt different, although normal to the layman on the outside looking in.

The thoughts she was having, even now, as she squeezed into a pair of designer jeans in front of a long mirror hooked to the back of Cassandra's bedroom door, were fearful, bitter, and angry. Sharon's grandmother had warned her about such thoughts. They breed sin and come back to haunt and terrorize. But she couldn't help it, couldn't stop the thoughts because Sharon had no idea where they came from. Although she could guess their origin, considering the engagement she'd been having with Kevin over the last week. Sharon now referred to Kevin as the back door man. He had no desire to make love, if that was even a term in the man's vocabulary. Sex with Kevin had become what Sharon's grandmother would refer to as sadism. Against the big G-O-D. Not pleasant. Not right. Just evil. And those thoughts arrived with a vengeance, as if she had no power over the thoughts that manifested. As if they were whispered from the darkness and carried on the heels of tainted winds to poison her mind. And the more Kevin went to town, the louder those thoughts became.

Two days ago, Kevin had taken Sharon and bent her over his armoire. Her hands gripped the cherry wood that rocked back and forth. The room bathed in darkness except for a single candle that burned on the table beside Kevin's bed. And the pain arrived.

Something Sharon hoped would have subsided, considering how often Kevin was going to town. But it didn't. The pain had come in full effect.

Pain was one thing. What she saw in the mirror was another.

Kevin's eyes were black. No iris, no pupil, just jet metallic black eyeballs. His mouth open, seething, hissing, and she could have sworn she felt fire burning off his lips as he gripped a handful of Sharon's thick dark curls and forced her head back. His grip so strong, so powerful, she thought Kevin was going to tear those thick locks from Sharon's skull. He seemed to get off on the pain he caused. And only if there was enough pain. Fear too. Like an aphrodisiac that drove Kevin mad. In the mirror, over Kevin's shoulder, she glimpsed dark eyes with fire in the pupils. She saw the outline of arms wrapped around Kevin's chest as if a giant had captured him in its bosom. And the silhouette kept changing, flickering as the mirror shook from Kevin's pounding. She saw teeth, thick jagged yellow teeth bite into Kevin's skull. Then a tongue, long and thin, slithered from its mouth like a snake and lapped the sweat off Kevin's cheek as those arms tensed and squeezed and Sharon dropped her head to the cherry wood. She wanted it over with, but Kevin gripped those dark curls again, yanked her head back exposing her throat as he thrust even harder, faster and bit into her neck when Sharon screamed, her eyes snapped open and that demon—for lack of a better word—over Kevin's shoulder snarled at Sharon and for the first time Sharon could see this demon was pounding Kevin. She thought she'd entered hell, and she forced herself to turn away, to relinquish the demon's eyes from conscious thought and, as she forced her eyes away, she caught her reflection and noticed, her eyes were black too, and that image she'd been unable to wipe clear ever since.

When Kevin finished, he remained inside her, rubbing Sharon's back.

"Are you satisfied?" he asked, although Sharon wasn't sure whom Kevin was talking to. He asked again with ferocity, "Are you satisfied?"

And Sharon yelped, "Yes... yes... I am satisfied." She was on the verge of tears and rested her head on the armoire, grateful her hair covered her eyes. She didn't want Kevin to see her tears. Kevin pulled away and Sharon heard him growl; saw him in the mirror with his arms raised in triumph. Noticed her own eyes had returned, and she watched as Kevin flopped on the bed, his head and back against the headboard. He was watching her, his eyes narrow.

"Come," he ordered.

She didn't want to, but she did. She curled into a ball; Kevin's left arm cradled her against his body. She was trembling, and her neck stung something awful. Noticed how Kevin smelled like sulfur, so odd and peculiar. So many thoughts raced through Sharon's mind that night her brain turned numb.

She hadn't been back since, although Sharon was meeting Kevin for dinner in an hour. Dinner? That was another change. Kevin barely ate, always said he had no appetite and would only eat a small forkful and even that Sharon believed he was spitting into his napkin. But for Sharon, he ordered all the finest food, appetizers, entrée and dessert. Sharon had a fleeting suspicion Kevin was attempting to fatten her up. When he watched her eat, he had this stare, this sinister look in his eyes, like a cattle herder watching his cattle graze.

So many changes, she wondered if she was losing it. All she wanted was to talk to Cassandra, but Cassandra hadn't returned her calls, always responding with a text that she was busy with the new show and working tirelessly on the set. She had not one minute for a full on conversation. Simple texts back and forth were all Sharon received. Frustrating indeed, since Sharon never received the phone call she was expecting. The one from the agency requesting a read through on a new script that would catapult Sharon's career.

Then again, Sharon thought, to hell with Cassandra if she didn't live up to her end of the bargain. She checked her phone again. Nothing from Cassandra, nothing from anyone. It seemed like the world had gone dark, leaving Sharon to fend for herself.

Why can't the bitch just get on the damn phone and talk to me?

Sharon concluded that Cassandra was ignoring her, putting her off until she returned home from Atlanta. And what then? Another excuse? More bullshit explaining why Cassandra couldn't ink the deal, help a friend out, and set them both up for success. Was she destined to be Kevin's plaything, always behind the scenes as some hopeless charity case soon to be scoffed at and thrown to the wolves? She wanted to squeeze Cassandra's throat and suffocate the air from her lungs. Thought about watching Cassandra's eyes bulge from her skull. Saw her hands squeeze and squeeze with relentless rage, tearing life from Cassandra's gullet.

Her phone buzzed. Sharon's eyes darted to the phone on Cassandra's bed. Her heart skipped a beat, body tensed. Sharon surveyed the screen, saw the text was from Cassandra. Relief.

About damn time. Sharon swiped the phone off the bed, opened the text, and her eyes narrowed.

I'll be back next Saturday. I've got great news for you. Bigger than the part you wanted. We're on our way up!!! Just be patient. I'll explain next Saturday. Tell Kevin I said hi.

Sharon chewed her bottom lip, reading the message and thinking. Read again, then thought some more. Twirled her curls in her left hand while staring at the screen and gnawing on her bottom lip. Felt anger growing within. Her body tense, heart racing. This was not good enough. She wanted out and wanted out now. Her hand tight around the phone. She heard it crunch within her palm as she pulled and tugged her hair, heard tearing, felt her face flush with anger and her lips curl into a scowl. She could kill Cassandra right now.

Phone. Message. Read. Bite. Twirl. Tug. Phone. Message. Read. Bite. Twirl. Tug. Phone. Message. Read. Bite. Twirl. Tug. Phone. Message. Crunch. Blood. Pull. Tear. Phone. Message. Crunch. Blood on her tongue. Pull. Tear. Those curls ripped from her skull.

Sharon stared at the bloodied clump of hair in her hand and wondered whose hair it was. Why was she holding a clump of bloody hair? The question answered when she felt a burning sting on her scalp. Touched her head where she felt the burn and saw blood on her fingertips. Her face scrunched in pain and frustration.

"Fuck," she whined, and dropped the phone on the bed then

stomped to the mirror. She ripped a large clump from her skull, a bald spot revealed in the mirror, beads of blood on the skull. Started shaking her head. "Sonofabitch," she muttered and stomped her right foot. A whining cry in the back of her throat. "What the hell is wrong with me?" She clenched her trembling fists, face scrunched in the mirror. Her skull stung something awful, and she would have cried then. Would have cried, but her eyes grew wide when Kevin's demon growled at her in the mirror. Its head swiveled left to right and disappeared. Sharon jumped back and froze.

Many changes were indeed happening, that's for sure.

6

8:00 PM
Amber's House
Tyler

He needed a break, so Tyler found a quiet sitting room in the house. The lights were off, but Tyler enjoyed the darkness, plus there was enough light outside to cast a dull glow in the room. Amber's parents left an hour ago, and the room was quiet except for that damn EDM music pumping from downstairs. Tyler took a seat on a plush white couch in front of a bay window. He couldn't believe how many people arrived. They turned the street into a parking lot with teenagers scattered across the front lawn, on the street, moving in and out of the house. James was still downstairs. Dancing, Tyler assumed. He remembered how James enjoyed dancing; Tyler guessed that even in death, some things never changed. Ironically, it was his party. The night belonged to James. The party was for him; a celebration of his life and friendship.

Friends, Tyler scoffed. What are friends? The person who inflicts trauma all your life suddenly turns into your best friend later in life. Is that friendship or just a misplaced, misdirected stab at wanting to fit in? Let's not fool ourselves, Tyler thought. The fool who garners the attention of their persecutor is without a doubt on a fool's mission. Acceptance and tolerance being a virtue few possessed. To Tyler, everyone harbored resentments, even if those resentments remained to provide some sort of protection. Trust no one, love everyone philosophy.

"Trust no one," Tyler whispered as if he needed to hear the words to make them real; as if he already deterred from this philosophy and required reassurance to get back on track. He leaned his chin on his fist, elbow on the couch, watching the outside, the party continuing to grow, and then a thought dropped into Tyler's mind. This wasn't Reilly's party, it was his party, his creation. No one would be here if it weren't for Tyler. It takes balls to plot a murder, but that was simply an appetizer. He wondered how many people have plotted someone else's demise? Hitmen excluded, of course. That was their job. Tyler was referring to the normal, everyday person. The layman. The pawn. The patsy. He was certain that most people fantasized about murder from time to time. Or, at the very least, entertained, even if for only a second, a fleeting murderous thought. Some may even plan a murder. But they allow their programmed morality to run away with the thought and curse themselves for the impurity. Even less implement and Tyler was sure that when the day of reckoning arrived, they backed out, ran home, and tossed a blanket over their heads while they shook and shuddered with shame. But few, very few, implemented and followed the plan all the way to the end. Tyler was one of them, kind of a 'top of the food chain, pinnacle of the pyramid' person.

He was a killer, a murdering son of a bitch. Kept hearing the gunshot. Kept seeing the bullet pound into Reilly's chest with a force so strong, James came close to falling off the chair to the floor. But he didn't. Too much duct tape, remember? Tyler laughed at himself. That was funny; the amount of duct tape was amusing, but also the sign of a novice. He wondered if the police had picked up on it? Maybe that's why they still hung around, talking with students, finding them in awkward places while they mourned and asked to talk. Of course they talked, that's what teenagers do, they talk about each other to make their lives seem more interesting. Typical for the unintelligent to talk about each other, Tyler thought. They're like pitiful blobs of putty. No balls, Tyler thought. No balls at all. Tyler rolled his eyes, thinking about it.

He started laughing, holding in the bellowing. Can't have anyone see how I'm laughing, he thought. That would send up a red flag. He wiped his hand across his nose and mouth, wiping the smile clean, when he heard screams outside. He jumped off the couch and froze, listening. Seemed the entire world froze with him. Now laughter and giggles from the outside. Another scream but a scream with no fear, only elation. He heard someone jump into the pool. His body relaxed, Tyler bent his head, eyes downtrodden, started shaking his head, then laughed once again. A brief inward laugh.

Saw Reilly's blood pool beneath the shirt he wore. Saw how the blood found its way through the shirt and duct tape, then trickled to the floor with a pat, pat, pat on the tile.

"Did you tell Pam I said hello?"

Tyler turned to see James in the hallway. Bathed in darkness, James was barely visible. Had this strange glow around him like a burning fire emits waves of heat from the flames. Tyler wasn't sure, but he would swear in this moment that maggots were eating James' flesh. He could see them moving, eating, gnawing, slimy slithering. James stepped from the hall into the sitting room. Tyler's brow furrowed, eyes narrow, watching James traverse the room to the back window.

"That looks like fun," said James. "I think I'll miss pools." James paused as if in heavy thought and turned to Tyler. "Yeah, I will miss swimming."

Tyler's eyes widened.

"What?" said James. "The maggots? That's what happens when the dead aren't burned. If my bitch of a mother had incinerated my body, I'd be shining like an angel. No rotting required when the body burns."

"Good tip."

"I'm full of em."

"What do you want, James? I told you I won't talk to you in public anymore. Raises some serious suspicions."

James looked over the room. "But we're the only ones here."

Tyler shook his head. "Anyone can come up those stairs. If they hear me talking to myself, it'll raise red flags."

James scoffed then flopped on the couch, smoothed his hands across the fabric, his eyes downtrodden. "This is where it happened," he said. "Me and Pam." His eyes found Tyler. "Did you tell her I said hello?"

"No."

James shrugged and turned to the bay window. "Lots of people here," he said, his tone soft, close to a whisper.

"Is that all? I'd really like to get back to the party."

James shook his head. "Am I getting on your nerves, Tyler? Is this how you treat your dead?"

Tyler rolled his eyes. "You're dead, James, and the world is better for it."

"And *I'm* here to help *you*? Holy shit, did I get the wrong end of the stick."

"Shouldn't have been such a brutal asshole. Maybe you'd still be living."

"Can't argue with that one, Tyler. You got me dead bang." And he laughed. "Get it, *dead bang.*" Laughed some more, turned his hand into a gun and dropped his thumb.

Tyler shook his head. "Whatever." He walked to the steps.

"Oh, c'mon Tyler. I'm just joking. You're way too sentimental."

Tyler took the stairs.

James raised his voice. "You're gonna need me, Tyler. You're gonna need me big time."

Two steps remained.

"Your day of reckoning is coming, Tyler. And that right soon. You won't ignore me forever. No, Tyler. You won't. Not when it comes. Not when it comes at all."

And Tyler closed the door, shutting out his dead servant.

7

9:00 PM
Somewhere Shiny
SAC John Mills

Strapped to a gurney, SAC John Mills remained perfectly still when the needle drifted down from the ceiling towards his clamped open right eye. Twenty years had gone by since he was first abducted. The needle in the eye had become his favorite and preferred medical exam. It wasn't so bad after all, especially when compared to the alternatives. Those methods of torture John kept to himself. After all, they were listening to his thoughts, always had been and John accepted a long time ago that they always would. Thoughts were easy for them, he surmised, although how they were listening continued to be a mystery.

Here comes the warm liquid, John thought and without a seconds pause he felt liquid like warmth overflow his eye, turning his vision into a gelatinous film. Needle closer now; the machine with the attached needle was humming with a mechanical buzz. Stay still, John told himself. As unmoving as possible. He shuddered when the needle entered his eye and John gripped the bed rails tight in his palms. Noticed how the world on his right side went dark. John felt his feet kick and stretch, felt his muscles tense. It helped to focus on another part of the body rather than the needle in the eye that now turned, spinning towards his brain. He felt his brain squirm, as if the needle sought his memories. He knew they would. The same conclusion had occurred over the last twenty years. On the wall opposite the bed, a television projected those memories. Like watching a movie on fast forward.

What are they looking for? John thought. But even more than what they sought was what they were putting in. John saw images and scenes on the screen he had no recollection of. Simple things, like a trip to Monte Carlo. No wife on that trip, but the women were plentiful. *Is this from another life?*

He felt his throat constrict. Difficult to bring air into his lungs. Suffocated, although John had expected the reaction. Stay calm, he told himself. This will pass. What you have to do is try to remember. Remember that you are here and remember what you're seeing on that screen. Hold on to a memory, any memory. And hopefully, through that focus, the rest of those memories will come flooding back. He felt his heart jump in his chest. Panic? Don't panic, please.

Where are they? Those little grey beings slapping high fives in the observation room behind his head. He was sure of it. Well, maybe not the high fives. His right hand trembled, shaking, as if the hand had a mind of its own.

Why does such an advanced species use such primitive technology?

Are they really from another planet? Had to be. I saw the ship, that God forsaken UFO in the woods. Where's Helmsley? Is he in here too? Somewhere?

Can't take it. Can't take it anymore. John felt the scream erupt in his throat. His left eye darting from one side of the room then the other. Front and back, left and right, circling. Find something, anything, to remember. Do it and focus on it and keep your focus there. Felt his lips part. Something. Anything. Felt his whole body shudder, trembling, shaking, on the brink of eruption with the scream in his throat. SAC John Mills heard his blood-curdling screams before he understood they were coming from him.

Not only did he scream, he pleaded and begged. Begged for them to stop. Clamped his left eye shut and continued to scream, holler, and wail. Shut it out, he told himself. Shut it out and pass out. Pass out please.

Didn't matter if he found a focal point, everything in the room was shiny and looked the same.

8

11:11 PM
Hadenfield, Illinois
Jigglyspot

He was waiting for that damnable waitress, the one who looked at him all cockeyed and suspicious. He didn't want to, but he had to. Can't leave loose ends, not a chance. Not with next week's celebration on the rise and the concerns and issues Emmanuelle had dealt Jiggly. He actually felt bad for the waitress. She will not be coming home tonight. Not tonight, and not ever. He thought she'd make an appropriate pod for the island, a needed commodity at the moment, but Jiggly's intel revealed the woman was infertile. Not that she knew it, not yet anyway. The only solution then was disappearance, and Jiggly was an expert at making people disappear. Had to do it quick though. Kera was waiting, and he had to prepare the Cummings for tonight's festivity.

His thoughts went to Kera. Jiggly hadn't seen Kera in a day's age. Over the last few years, Jiggly's ability to conjure otherworldly beings to the planet had tragically diminished thanks to the newly formed secret task force and a change in power that turned everything Jiggly and his master's had enjoyed for decades on its head. Now they were all scrambling to keep things hidden, operating in secret so things could remain as they were. As a result, Mr. West commanded his subjects to cease otherworldly operations unless he was involved. Jiggly didn't enjoy operating against Mr. West's wishes, but he had his loyalties, especially to Kera, and, of course, Emmanuelle, although his loyalty to the dark goddess was from fear, not admiration. Add it all up and what you got was the fact that Jiggly hadn't seen Kera in over a year. They planned tonight's event months ago, the two of them, all giddy, sending messages to Mrs.

Cummings through her dreams and fantasies; an attempt to create the invitation required for Kera's arrival. It wasn't as if Kera lived around the corner and could come out to play anytime Jiggly wanted. She had to be summoned and brought to the planet. Allowed to enter the earth's atmosphere for one simple reason: she was invited, invited by someone tied and bound to the planet, a human being, that is. In this case, it was Mrs. Cummings who sent the invite. Kera was a guest, and only a full-blooded human could offer such an invitation. It was a part of the cosmic law. But the invitation wasn't required to be a conscious invite. As long as they offered the invitation, even if it was only through the subconscious, then Kera, or any alien species, could come to Earth without causing catastrophic interstellar ethereal war.

He thought about snuggling against her body, her arms wrapped around him. How he loved Kera so. Had loved her for decades and would do anything for her. Not that Kera was in any way possible using Jiggly. Kera didn't operate that way. Sure, she had her sexual desires, but who doesn't? Only the weak suppress their desires. The powerful can control their impulses, and Kera was no exception. For Jiggly, it was a work in progress. He'll get there one day, but for now he could marvel over Kera's unbreakable willpower, hoping someday he will be the same. If he wants to be, that is, because sometimes it was so much more fun to have no control. Although Kera would disagree. Kera can place a thumb on her desires and will them away if she wanted. She'd done it before. There was a decade long pause in Kera's indulgences while she 'worked on herself,' as she so put it. Jiggly remembered how alone he felt during that decade, although he was proud of Kera. Most people never recognize when they're out of balance.

When she emerged from the long decade, she no longer wished to provide everlasting harm. Her purpose during those Jiggly exploits was to leave something wonderful and beautiful in the wake of her indulgence. To help those she loved. And she did, she did every time. Probably why the Cummings had done so well since Kera introduced herself. Although there remained that unknowing stare and that drawn countenance. Really a minor side effect, at least to

Kera. And Jiggly always said that Kera knows best.

It's on the subconscious level, Kera had told him. That part in the brain where the universe exists in all its splendor, the yin and yang flowing effortlessly with all the power and energy in the universe. Kera could tap into the subconscious, and she knew the Cummings were suppressing their desires, those same desires Kera indulged and Jiggly ravaged. So, Kera gave them what they wanted, on the subconscious level, and in the morning their programmed consciousness remained free of shame. In doing so, Kera had told Jiggly, they were free, like a mental block was removed, allowing the Cummings to think with passion and purpose, good thoughts that led to good deeds. By removing the inner desire of the flesh, the conscious mind thought clearly and without interference.

The problem, as Jiggly concluded, was that the conscious programming grew stronger with every success the Cumming's experienced, validating their belief system, and even though the subconscious was free from desire there was still communication between the two minds, resulting in that drawn sensation. Because the Cummings attributed their success to the programming, not to Kera's lifting of the subconscious block. The last time Jiggly met with Kera, he informed her of his theory. She said it was worth it as long as they kept doing good by their species. And Jiggly marveled over Kera's wisdom.

Thinking of Kera, he wanted to kiss those full lips, and run his hand across her skin, her flesh beneath his fingers. Allow Kera's two tentacles to brush across his ear as he lied comfortably in her arms.

Footsteps outside the car now and Jiggly snapped out of his fantasy, listening beneath the blanket he'd wrapped himself in, concealed in the darkness. Heard the car door unlock and then open with a creak. A slight shift when the waitress sat behind the wheel, followed by the door closing with a thud.

Jiggly silently commended himself for shutting off the interior light. The waitress hadn't noticed. He heard the engine start. Mr. Scalpel clenched in his fist as he sat up in the backseat, the blanket falling to his lap. Jiggly saw his painted scowl in the rearview. The waitress caught it too. Her head tilted to the left, staring through narrow eyes, confused, as if she wasn't sure what she was looking at. A clown in the backseat. Jiggly reached his left hand around the headrest, clasped his palm over her mouth and buried Mr. Scalpel in the back of her head. No scream, just a clean, swift and silent movement as her body tensed and flailed. A few gurgling sounds escaped the throat. Blood on Jiggly's hand and the flailing ceased. Jiggly twisted Mr. Scalpel. He enjoyed opening the wound, allowing the blood to flow like a river towards a waterfall. The blood was warm; he felt it pour across his hand, drip drop to the floor and cascade down his arm.

Jiggly pulled Mr. Scalpel from the waitress's head; released her mouth and her body slumped over and to the right. Jiggly licked the blood off his hand then wiped the rest on his clown outfit along with Mr. Scalpel. Sure, the tool was rusty, but dried blood was a bitch to get off. He started whistling. Put Mr. Scalpel in his breast pocket then stretched his arms. His elbows popped and cracked. Interlaced his fingers and cracked those too, followed by a stretch of his neck. That cracked too, but with a quick succession of crack, pop, crack, pop, crack.

Jiggly heaved the body over the seat and dropped the waitress in the back. Still whistling. Whistling and working. Working and whistling. He never looked at the body. Paid the waitress no mind as he climbed into the driver's seat. The pedals were too far for his feet to reach. Jiggly moved the seat closer to the wheel and pedals, continuing to whistle. Jiggly adjusted the mirrors, then scanned the parking lot. There were a few parked cars, but no one was in those cars.

More whistling. Jiggly loved to whistle. Whistle and work, Jiggly. Working and whistling. He caught sight of the camera attached to the building beneath the roof of the diner. Jiggly rolled his eyes, then gave the camera a wave with a big smile. He thought it was funny; Jiggly dismantled the camera an hour ago. He threw the car into drive and headed out. Off to the sanitation department, Jiggly thought. His people were waiting for him. Waiting to run the waitress's bones through the garbage compactor. He whistled all the way there.

9

10:00 PM
Los Angeles, CA
Lilly

She took the steps upstairs. Lilly heard a scream, and she was sure it was Sam. Poor little guy had been having nightmares all week. Aliens. His nightmares were about aliens poking and prodding him, tearing out his insides.

The psychologist Lilly talked with had said nightmares might happen. She said the boys might act out too. Act out? What did that mean? Lilly wished she had asked. She couldn't imagine what the boys were going through. Hell, she was having trouble understanding what *she* was going through. Numb. Robotic. Depressed. Angry. Definitely one hundred percent angry. Resentful too. How could Tad do this to them? To her? Leave them with questions and no answers, no resolution. No closure.

She wanted nothing to do with it. She didn't ask for it, and never agreed to it. Had never thought this type of situation could happen. So far out of left field like she was hit by a freight train and survived, and now she was gathering up the pieces, stuffing her innards back into her body. Only problem was there were so many to claim it turned her mind numb. It was easier to do nothing. Just watch the world go by.

Christopher's light was on. Lilly stood at the top of the stairs. His bedroom door was ajar, and Lilly bent her head to see if he was awake. Another stir from Sam's room; shuffling on the mattress, followed by a moan and a groan.

"It's ok." She heard Christopher's voice. He wasn't in his room. He was in Sam's room.

Lilly bent her head, listening. Took soft, slow steps to the door and waited, listening to her boys. Another groan and Christopher said the same, "It's ok." He started humming, humming nothing in particular, just calming tones with a gentle rhythm. She felt powerless. Lilly wanted to go into the room, but she couldn't. Every time she gathered enough strength to walk in, her feet and legs refused to follow her command.

Wanted to cry, but she couldn't do that either. Instead, Lilly squatted by the door, held her knees to her chest, shivering and wide eyed.

"Everything's gonna be all right."

Christopher's voice was soft, and Lilly could hear the frog in his throat, on the brink of tears. Sam's fussing ceased after a while, and she heard Christopher lie down on the bed. Her children needed her, and she hadn't an ounce of strength to help them. Didn't know what to do or how to do it. She looked at her fingers, her thumb and pointer finger rubbing at the fingertips. She played the smallest violin, just for her.

10

11:00 PM
Hollywood, CA
Sharon

"Would you drink blood?"

Kevin nipped at his fingernail, tearing off the cuticle. Sharon noticed his fingernails were close to nonexistent. He'd been biting his nails with a fever over the last few days. And he looked anxious. All the time anxious, not every once in a while anxious. A nervous wreck.

They were in the same restaurant from the week before. Sharon placed her fork and knife on the plate, gentle and calm, although her stomach wrenched in a knot. She wondered how much more she could take. Kevin's treatment was borderline abuse. Borderline? No, he'd crossed that line already. Now he had this weathered stare. The skin beneath his eyes had turned dark with a shade of purple. She noticed a thick wrinkle within the dark patch under his right eye. Was he not sleeping? Sharon was sleeping, sleeping more than usual over the last few days. Over twelve hours each night. She assumed he was, too. Kevin never exhibited sexual energy like he had over the last week. He had to be exhausted. And he wasn't eating. At first Sharon thought when they went to dinner he wasn't hungry, although, in retrospect, he wasn't eating during the day either. His dinner-sea bass, mashed potatoes and steamed vegetables-was untouched and sat in front of him like a movie prop. He was drinking though, his glass of wine close to finished. Kevin poured himself another from the bottle on the table. Sharon noticed his hand shook while filling his glass to the brim, his eyes staring, devouring Sharon as he cleared his throat, nervously waiting for Sharon's response.

Drink blood? First anal sex, and brutal anal sex at that, and now drinking blood. What's next, eat my flesh?

She sat back; hands folded over the napkin on her lap and glanced at her steak. She'd taken a few bites, but now she lost her appetite. She had no idea what to say. Kevin's inquiry had taken her off guard.

Kevin raised his glass. "Sharon?" he said and sipped his wine. "Would you drink blood?" His voice cracked when he said blood.

"Why?" she asked. "What's the point?"

His hand holding the wine glass trembled, and she noticed how his body seemed to tense. Kevin sipped his wine, then put his glass on the table, folded his hands on his lap the same as Sharon. His eyes seemed to sink beneath his cheekbones, sunken and retreating like a frightened child confronted with the monster in the closet. His eyes were jumpy too; they had this nervous twitch about them, as if Kevin couldn't stare straight ahead.

And Sharon thought, Is he going schizo on me? She gritted her teeth, clenched her jaw, waiting for him to respond.

Kevin bit into his fingernail, at least what remained of a fingernail, and sat up, elbows on the table. "Just asking," he said, then bit down hard on his thumbnail.

No wonder he's not hungry. He's got a couple pounds of nails and flesh in his stomach.

"Where's this all coming from, Kevin? You've changed so much in the last week, and you don't look good. Are you ok? Is there something you're not telling me? You can tell me anything. I'll help you anyway I can, but you have to be honest, there's no shame in anything."

Sharon surmised a day ago that Kevin was buckling under the pressure of success. Happened sometimes, people spend years working hard to accomplish a goal and sometimes, once that goal catches up to them, they tuck tail and hide, fold under the pressure, and implode. Has to do with evolution, said people just aren't evolved enough to handle what they've achieved. Perhaps the anxiety and the pressure of success were weighing on Kevin. Maybe the anxiety is manifesting in nervous delusions.

He didn't answer, kept nipping at his nail.

"Kevin?"

"What?" He dropped his finger from his mouth and a spittle of phlegm stretched from his lip to his nail, broke off and curled across his bottom lip and chin. Sharon cringed. Appetite now completely lost. Kevin wiped his mouth with his palm.

"Are you ok, Kevin?"

"I'm fine," he huffed, then shuddered. "Life couldn't be better."

Sharon looked around the restaurant. Mostly barren, except one other table where an older couple sat, eating quietly in the corner. Restaurant staff was close to nonexistent. Perhaps they were finishing their closing duties, cleaning and mopping the kitchen. The bartender was wiping down glasses and putting them away.

"So, would you?" said Kevin, gnawing on a cuticle.

"What's the point, Kevin?" Her voice an octave below shouting. She noticed the remaining table looked up from their plates.

Kevin tore off another cuticle, and Sharon saw blood stream across his finger. Sharon's eyes narrowed.

"Because," Kevin said, "I hear it's a good way to tap in to the ethereal plane."

And Sharon wondered just how far Kevin was willing to go.

11

1:45 AM
Hadenfield, Illinois
The Cummings Residence
Jigglyspot

Jiggly used his spare key to unlock the front door, his red cane in hand. He stepped in and quickly, although silently, closed the door and locked it, then entered the alarm code. The four-bedroom single family home was dark, but Jiggly could spot a fly on the wall despite the darkness. Extraction did that, took those senses and ramped them into overdrive.

Jiggly strolled into the living room from the front door and stopped, listening. A slight smirk on his lips. A couch and loveseat, recliner chair, television propped on the wall, beneath it a marble stand. In the corner an easel held up a whiteboard with marker drawn stick figures, a sun and flowers. That little one enjoyed drawing, Jiggly knew. On his right was the kitchen and dining room with sliding doors that led outside. On his far right, and behind him, a hall led to three bedrooms. The Cummings turned one bedroom into a home office for Mr. Cummings, the other two were for the children. Jiggly checked on the children and they were as they should be, sleeping sound and peaceful.

Sometimes he locked the kids' bedroom doors. It was for their protection. No child should bear witness to sexual depravity. That wasn't something a child should see. At least not to Jiggly. Despite his sadism and duties as Mister E's—Jiggly referred to him as MysterE, also the right-hand man for the master, Herbert West, or Mr. West as his minions refer to him—curator over the last half a century, he preferred not to personally get involved with the children. Had to do with his past. Jiggly had a soft spot for children.

He'd even been able to block out most of his child type duties that he experienced at the behest of MysterE. Jiggly became so good at suppressing those memories that the sensation in his stomach had gone away. He thought about locking their doors but then thought better of it, remembering the last time he and Kera paid the Cummings a visit when little Lindsey had woken up to a locked door and started screaming. The result was a quick night for Jiggly and Kera.

Jiggly caught his reflection in the hallway mirror and stopped to admire himself. Unfortunately, the mirror was situated a little too high, and he could only admire his makeup. The scowl he painted prior to his dealing with the waitress had cracked from grease and sweat. No hat this time. His skull was smooth and freshly shaved and covered in white paint that made Jiggly look like a ghost. Chin in his hand, he stretched his head to the right, then left, admiring his personal art.

Jiggly took a deep breath and stretched his arms while walking through the house. The Cumming's bedroom door was closed and Jiggly rolled his eyes. He gripped the doorknob. Unlocked, and Jiggly smiled. Closed his eyes and breathed deeply. Gripped a small vial from his shirt pocket and popped the cork, holding his breath. Jiggly placed the vial on the floor close to the crack under the door; open end pointed towards the bedroom.

More than likely they were sleeping, but Jiggly required not one chance for them to wake up and start screaming before Jiggly is able to use the gel he has for them. The gel, when applied across the throat, rendered the recipient incapable of moving, but what Jiggly liked best about this type of gel was the recipient's inability to scream. Although Kera wasn't a fan—because she enjoyed it when they screamed or at the very least taken part—Jiggly couldn't take any chances with an outright holler from the Cummings. He reached down and grabbed the vial, replaced the cork and stuffed the vial in his right pocket.

Jiggly patted his head, once, twice, three times, soft and cautious like, front, top, and then the back of his head. Shallow breathing in the calm quiet. He stretched his arms and his elbows cracked. Stretched his neck too. He had a few minutes before the stars were in proper alignment to summon Kera, so Jiggly opened the door and went inside, quietly locking the door behind him then turning to witness the Cummings' sleeping sound and peaceful. He immediately grinned. It was nice seeing them again. He took the gel vial from his left pocket.

And started whistling as he applied the gel to the Cummings' throats.

12

11:50 PM
Somewhere Shiny
SAC John Mills

He passed out; he was sure of it. His right eye stung something awful. He had to force his eyes open. The right eyelid tugged and then fluttered open. Crusted over, Mills thought. He felt sweat on his skin and his jaw hung open as shallow breaths puffed over his lips.

They had transferred him to a new room, this one as shiny as the last, although the setup was different. No drilling needle machine above him, and the room was cluttered with what Mills surmised were old ventilators and medical equipment. Mills closed his right eye; the pain was too severe, plus the overhead light sought the wounded eye with a vengeance. Mills felt a gag in his lungs and throat. Hard to breathe. He coughed; his chest jumped with each cough. Dry, hacking, and suffocating, he struggled to draw air into his lungs.

Mills flapped on the gurney like a fish out of water. Thought his lungs would collapse if he couldn't turn over. Gagging, choking, and hacking, he turned over on his left side, although his right arm remained secured to the bed rail, twisted behind him. His left arm caught beneath his body. Mills felt his eyes water and cold sweat cascade across his forehead. His mouth opened wide, hacking and gagging trying to force the choke from his lungs and throat. His tongue jutted from his mouth like a stiff erection. He felt saliva drip from his lips and tongue from the back of his throat. He attempted to conjure the spit, opening and closing his mouth, gathering phlegm between his cheeks, which he pooled across his lips and tried to propel from his mouth. But the spittle pooled beneath his chin and on the gurney.

Mills attempted to lift his head, but his right arm and shoulder twisted with a painful sting. He flopped over on his back when he saw the wrinkled grey alien beside him. He would have screamed if he weren't gagging still. The alien worked silently, stretching its long talons and gripped John's chin, forcing his head down and to the left. Two more grey aliens stood on the opposite side of the gurney and Mills jumped, fearful and panicked. The alien holding his head pushed with immense power and John felt his feet and legs flail and pain jolt up his shoulder, attempting to break free. His crusted right eye watched as one of the two aliens on his left gripped his forehead, assisting with holding his head down. John squirmed beneath their firm embrace, right eye wide, watching as the third alien, now holding a petri dish, removed the plastic cap with a quick twist.

John could see what was in the dish, a tiny maggot-like creature, and when the alien used tweezers to lift the maggot from the dish John started screaming. Felt his entire body shudder and twist, saliva dripped off his lips as the alien brought the maggot towards John's head. His screams and hollers reached a fever pitch. Pulling, yanking, he felt his shoulder tear as an alien hand gripped his jaw and shut out John's screams, although muffled hollers whimpered in his throat. He could see this maggot stretch and squirm between the tweezers. Little hairs across its opaque cylindrical body. Muffled whimpers turned to squelched screams when the grey dropped the maggot into John's right ear. He could feel it, feel it move and those tiny hairs tickled his ear as the maggot crept across his ear and John could feel it enter his ear canal, squirming towards his brain.

His head on fire, raging within his skull. Mills never noticed that the grey's released him. He could feel that maggot working itself into his brain and Mills screamed, hollering at the greys that stood idly by. Convulsing, his head slamming against the gurney. And John Mills could feel the maggot gnawing on his brain.

13

2:00 AM
Hadenfield, Illinois
The Cummings Bedroom
Jigglyspot

He enjoyed dancing, arms outstretched as if he held some invisible partner, spinning, swaying back and forth, from the closet into the bedroom. The master bedroom was a spacious room with a large walk-in closet. Jiggly enjoyed the 400 square foot room, it offered plenty of space for Jiggly to move around without concern over bumping into the mahogany four post bed or the furniture–chest of drawers with a sixty-inch television hooked to the wall above, a large armoire that stood in the corner and two nightstands, one on each side of the bed.

He danced and danced, swinging, swaying, and humming. The Cummings watching from their bed, eyes wide open, fearful and panicked. However, unable to move or scream, the gel across their throats pinned their bodies and silenced their voices. Their skin, pale and clammy, dripped cold sweat as Jiggly ceased dancing and took center stage in front of the four-post bed. He cleared his throat as he looked at his audience and grinned. He took up his cane, the red one the master, Herbert West, had given him, which he'd leaned against the bed in anticipation of Kera's arrival. Jiggly leaned on the cane as he addressed his audience.

"Lady and gentleman," he began in that thick and raspy drone of a voice. "Boy and girl, let me introduce to you tonight's entertainment. Mrs. Cummings' favorite subconscious indulgence." Jiggly watched as Mr. Cummings forced his eyes towards his wife. "Keeeerrraa."

Jiggly fell silent, cane in his left hand. He licked his right thumb and held it over his head. Muffled whimpers from the Cummings graced the backdrop. He felt cool air on his wet thumb and closed his eyes. "The air and stars are just right," Jiggly said. He smacked the cane against the wood floor and opened his eyes. With his right hand, he twisted the gold top on the cane, and a swirl of blue and green smoke slithered from the top. Jiggly breathed in the smoke and his body shuddered. He lifted the cane over his head and started swirling the cane in a counterclockwise motion. Seven large circles completed with the cane and the smoke swirled in the air. Jiggly then took from his pocket a small ladle, a short wood stick with a thick and round top. Cane firmly held in his left hand, he smacked the cane with the ladle and the cane vibrated with a high-pitched frequency likened to a crystal bowl. And the air where the smoke swirled changed as if the atoms were constricting; like watching vapor turn to ice.

Another smack against the cane, followed by more vibrating. Five smacks against the cane and his hand hurt from holding the cane with its resonating vibrations. The air around the smoke swirled like a spiraling vortex. Beginning slow, it ramped into overdrive like a hurricane wind. Lightning pumped inside the vortex and thunder rolled across the bedroom.

Jiggly slammed the cane to the floor. Once, twice, three times. Four. Five. A lightning flash and a thunder roll and Kera stood in the vortex. Jiggly felt his face flush red and blush with the arrival of his beloved. Enthralled. Kera stood just under five feet, about an inch or so under Jiggly. Short, dark hair, smooth as silk, cut just below her ears. Her soft pasty skin covered provocatively with leather and lace with a slit down the front, revealing small breasts beneath. Her face so small and round, with lips painted a dark red, and those dark slanted eyes looked on Jiggly with admiration. And those tentacles, the ones attached to her forehead just above and a centimeter away from the temples, lied sleeping within those dark locks.

"Jigs," she said. "The cap."

Startled, Jiggly twisted the cane's top, left, right, then left again. "So sorry, my lady," said Jiggly as the vortex and smoke dissipated. Jiggly bowed to Kera, who watched the Cummings with apt anticipation.

"Been so long, Jigs," said Kera. "Too long."

"Indeed. The last few years have been difficult for all of us, and this last week has been no exception. Seems the chaos has been ramped into overdrive." Jiggly noticed she did not answer. When he raised his head, Kera was already walking towards Monica. Kera's tiny hand removed the blanket and Kera touched Monica's skin, her hand caressing from the leg to the navel, breasts to throat to jaw to lips.

"Have I done well?" asked Jiggly as Kera squatted beside Monica, whose eyes followed Kera, confused at first but quickly her stare changed to admiration.

"Always Jiggly. Always." Kera stood, removing a small parcel from inside her outfit. She tossed it to Jiggly.

"So grateful, Kera. But you know I don't enjoy taking payment from you."

Kera kissed Monica softly on the lips, then looked at Michael as she walked around the bed. She stopped behind Jiggly. "And you know I don't risk a friend's soul without payment." She leaned in to Jiggly's ear. "I've missed you Jiggly," she said. "More than you know." And she kissed him and Jiggly's stomach quivered. He turned to Kera, gripped the back of her neck and pulled her lips to his, lapping his tongue with hers. She wrapped her arms around him and rested her head on his shoulder. Jiggly held her close. Both of them staring at the Cummings.

"Well, Jigs," said Kera, her tentacles playfully stroking Jiggly's right ear and temple with their blue eyes wide and staring adoringly as their long blue eyelashes brushed across his skin. "Which one should we pleasure first?"

14

12:05 AM
Somewhere in the dark
Cassandra

She heard screams. Painful, blood-curdling screams filled with fear, and Cassandra hugged her knees, wondering if those screams would become hers in time.

She had a feeling she wasn't alone. Not that she could see too much of anything beyond her own hand. The room was so dark, drenched in a blanket of black. She'd heard scuttling about an hour ago. Something moving across the cement floor with a heavy, labored breath. And she called out but received nothing in return, no recognition, not even an acknowledgement to confirm she wasn't alone. It wasn't like she wanted someone to be in here with her, but if she was abducted, why would they stop with one person? Cassandra was certain there was someone in this room with her, in the darkness, outside her cell. And she hoped, no, begged to God, that said person was indeed another prisoner. Shared pain is less pain and perhaps they can come up with a plan for escape. Plus, that stream of thought kept an obvious truth at bay: Cassandra was alone and whomever or whatever was watching her was the captor.

Had to be another prisoner. That's where those screams came from.

Unless her abductor was insane, which, considering where she was, made perfect sense. *Ira?* Of course, he had something to do with this. That much was apparent. He was the last person she laid eyes on. There was no doubt Ira was involved. But what did she discover that warranted her current predicament? Couldn't have been what she was doing for Sharon. That deed would get her fired, not abducted. She thought and then thought some more, and all her inquiries reached the same conclusion: the file on Ira's desk. The one with all the profiles and headshots of children. Cassandra first thought Ira landed an account to find child actors, possibly for a new show or movie she was unaware of. But Cassandra knew everything that went on in the office. That was her job, to know everything and have it all under control. She never heard of a new children's show or that Ira was working on a new account. And the profiles were not common to the industry. Not one profile cited previous work or agency. But if they aren't actors, who are they and why does Ira have their profiles? What was the purpose? What are they being used for?

A low guttural grunt erupted from somewhere in the dark and Cassandra's eyes snapped to where the sound originated. Seemed like a growl the stomach makes when hungry. She sat motionless, listening, mindful of her breathing. She scanned the darkness, hoping to see something, find someone moving about. Some voice to tell her why she was here. Nothing. She wondered if perhaps the grunt was hers. She wasn't sure how long she'd been in this cell, but she could assume it was at least a few days and she hadn't an ounce of food in that time. All she could find was the water trough in the cell's corner. Water that tasted salty and thick on her tongue. The thought of that water turned her stomach. She puked the first time she drank from it and tried to avoid it as much as possible, but dying from dehydration wasn't in the cards. She had a constant dull headache she was sure resulted from dehydration. Cassandra had suffered enough hangovers over the years to understand what dehydration felt like. But this was different. It caused her thoughts to restrict, and her brain felt like someone scrambled her neural chemistry with a cleaver.

Cassandra pursed those dry cracked lips, said, "H-hello."

Quiet. Then a shift, a squeak like when someone stands from a chair.

Is that my *breathing?*

She sat, quiet as a mouse, listening to shallow breathing, convinced that someone was indeed in the room with her. When she turned, she saw eyes, red eyes staring. Looking directly at her.

Cassandra jumped back and scrambled across the floor, startled with a scream that erupted from the back of her throat as she slammed against the cell with an iron bang. Her head rocked against the bars when an overhead light turned on from outside the cell sending waves of light into her eyes with a painful sting. Instinctively her eyes clamped shut, but she forced them open, to open as quickly as possible. And what Cassandra saw outside the cell at first brought a confused stare. Confusion quickly replaced by fear. The room her cell was in was gargantuan. If she had more time, she would have scanned every inch of the room, but the overhead light turned off with a pop and fizzle, and the darkness returned.

Cassandra noticed she was screaming. Even though darkness filled her eyes, she could still see the thing outside the cell. Slimy black skin, red eyes and fangs. A large oblong skull and a thin toothpick like frame.

And those screams she'd feared would come arrived with a vengeance as she sank to the floor, hand holding the cell bars as she cried and wailed, wondering what in damnation she had seen.

And what she was being held captive for.

15

1:00 AM
Sharon's Apartment
Sharon

She cut herself across the wrist. Not down the wrist, as Kevin had told her, that method was for suicide. Just a small cut was required, enough to draw blood. Kevin took a pink plastic goblet from the coffee table and held Sharon's wrist over the lip, dripping blood into the cup in thick crimson streams.

Sharon shifted on the couch, rubbing her wrist, applying pressure to the wound. Kevin held the cup in both hands over his head. He was about to speak when Sharon interrupted. "Aren't we supposed to light some candles or something?"

Kevin looked at her with a blank stare. His sunken eyes and drawn, pale skin made Sharon nervous. How unhealthy he appeared, how nervous and jittery. Kevin wasn't the same person he was a week ago. So many changes have occurred and now this blank stare, as if he had to think to comprehend what Sharon had said. As if someone or something was eating his brain.

Where was he going every day? All those hours when he never so much as answered a simple text message. Seemed everyday he lost a little more of himself. He said he was meeting with production and the director, although Kevin couldn't recall any of their names, which sent up more than a few red flags. Kevin had always displayed a vivid memory and recollection. Now it appeared like his brain was deteriorating. Being eaten was more like it. Or something else was going on. Perhaps addiction, so rampant in Sharon's generation, everyone knew at least one addict. Although maybe Kevin was just a terrible liar. Sharon suspected Kevin was lying to her. Lying about so many things, she couldn't find the first lie, the one that started it all.

"Yes," Kevin finally answered. "Can you get one?"

He appeared unsteady, his bottom lip quivered.

"Sure." Sharon sat up and went to the kitchen. She could feel Kevin's eyes on her, roaming, seeking her out, watching her every move. She opened a cabinet and took two candles off the top shelf. Put the candles on the counter by the sink and when she looked up she watched as Kevin drank from the goblet. "Hey, what was that about? You were supposed to wait."

Kevin shrugged while leaning back on the couch, goblet in hand. "Guess I was thirsty."

Sharon cringed; eyes narrowed. "Are you on something?"

Kevin looked over lazily. "Come again."

"Drugs, Kevin. Are you on drugs?"

"Not at all," he said. "I ain't touching that shit."

Sharon shook her head when she opened a drawer where the lighter was.

"You gonna light those?" Kevin, although now his eyes were wide open, he seemed to perk up instantly.

"What's the point? You just drank it all and I'll be damned if I'm gonna cut myself again."

Kevin leaned on his hand, elbow on the couch, his eyes lit up when he cocked his brow. "Indeed, you will."

She cocked her head, staring at him. Kevin laughed, then shook his head as he jumped off the couch. His eyes on her; pinned black pupils that seemed to snarl at Sharon. "What're you doing?"

"Light the candles, Sharon. You know how I like candles."

Sharon forced her eyes away from Kevin. Took up the lighter in quiet desperation and lit the candles. Kevin wrapped his hand around her wrist, the one with the cut still holding the lighter. His eyes looking through her.

"What?" she huffed. Her heart skipped a few beats, then jumped and Sharon's body with it. She took a step back, but Kevin's grip was like iron, holding strong around her wrist. His head drifted to the left, staring at Sharon, hypnotic, as if attempting to see inside her mind. Her hand and arm quivered. His touch was hot; she could feel her blood turn the same.

Kevin craned his head to the right. "May I?" he whispered as he devoured the wound with his eyes.

"What? Didn't get enough?" Her voice a startled response that started strong, ending with a quiet, fearful longing for lies.

No response except the tight-lipped grin across Kevin's lips.

"Why?" Sharon muttered.

"Because," Kevin said, his eyes delighted as he dipped his lips to the wrist that was now pumping blood from the strain of Kevin's squeeze. His tongue lapped across the wrist. Once. Twice. And on the third lick, his tongue slithered up her wrist to her hand, where Kevin spread his hot tongue across her palm, his eyes watching Sharon. Sharon closed her eyes as her body quivered. "I do believe you will find it..." Kevin paused as Sharon opened her eyes. "Rapturous," he hissed and wrapped his lips across her wrist. Nipped at the wound with his teeth, soft although painful. Sharon's wrist constricted, but Kevin held it in place. And he drank, pooling Sharon's blood down his throat.

Sharon's heart fluttered, body shuddered. Eyes rolled behind her eyelids, her blood and skin on fire, jaw tight yet quivering, teeth grinding. Kevin was right, the sensation was immense pleasure.

"Okay," she said, "Where's the goblet?"

16

1:30 AM
Outside Sam's bedroom
Lilly

"Mom, wake up."

She'd fallen asleep in the hallway, her head leaning against the wall. Christopher was nudging her shoulder as she drifted awake. Christopher stood over her, his hands on his knees as if he was surveying some concern or issue that required supreme attention and focus. Lilly shook her head to ward off the cobwebs and static from sleep. Her back ached and cracked when she stretched her spine.

"Christopher," she said. "Why are you still up?"

Chris laughed. "Why are you sleeping on the floor?"

Lilly looked around. She must have fallen asleep listening to Christopher comforting Sam. She hadn't realized how tired she was. Her eyes filled with tears she refused to allow to fall, staring at her son, her boy, now the man of the house. He looked so tired, shot to all bloody hell. Heavy bags beneath his eyes and the nerves in his jaw were clearly visible, like someone who'd experienced a mental breakdown. Nonetheless, Lilly could see he was trying to be strong, a rock in a tidal wave of emotion, for Sam and for Lilly, suppressing the sadness and holding his emotions at bay. But his eyes revealed the truth; they were sunken, dry, and wide. Lilly saw inside of them, to the core, the soul entrenched in loss and sadness, perhaps forever engrained in his heart. His loss would escort him wherever he went for all his days.

And yet she herself felt nothing. Perhaps Christopher felt that too.

"Here, take my hand," he said, offering his help. "Let's get you to bed."

Lilly took his hand, although reluctantly, and stood up. He'd gotten taller, she thought. His eyes were close to meeting hers. Lilly felt dizzy on her feet. She leaned against the wall.

"You, ok?"

"Yeah," Lilly yawned, holding her hand in front of her lips. "Just tired. What time is it?"

"Just after one thirty."

"You should get some sleep," she said, and touched his chin with her fingertip.

Then silence, one of those awkward moments. Lilly felt her throat close with emotion. She could belt out tears and wails right now, but she stuffed them down as she gritted her teeth and clenched her quivering jaw.

"Is Sam, ok?" she said.

"Still having nightmares," said Christopher with a solemn tone.

Lilly craned her head towards Sam's bedroom door. "He'll be all right," she said in a soft hush. "The psychologist said that might happen. You did good Christopher, I'm proud of you."

"You ok mom?"

Lilly snapped her head towards him. She feared her eyes betrayed her thoughts when she said, "Yes, I'm fine." Followed it up with, "I'll be fine."

She couldn't talk about it. Wouldn't talk about it and felt she shouldn't talk about it with Christopher. She had to be strong and besides, what was the point of breaking down in front of a child you're supposed to protect? Why show weakness? She's supposed to coddle and nurture him, not the other way around. Lilly's an adult. She has other means to dump her emotions and thoughts. It's called wine, or vodka, depending on the mood.

"Ok," he said and walked towards his room.

Lilly watched her son, and all she wanted to do was reach out and coddle him with the hope her embrace would take his pain away.

"Christopher," she called, and he turned on his heels. Her eyes welled with tears, her throat swelled with a constricting emotional lump, and her lips quivered as if they had a mind of their own. She had to force the words out. "I love you." She immediately looked away.

"Love you too, mom," he said and there was a small half smile curled in the corner of his mouth.

Lilly raised her head to acknowledge him; she fought back her tears. Looked away once again but Christopher stood, unmoving, in the hallway.

He cleared his throat. "Mom," he said, his voice shaky. "I know this sounds weird... maybe it's not the right time."

Lilly craned her head, staring at her son. "No, it's okay, go ahead." Whatever he wanted to talk about, Lilly thought-despite her own resignation-she was willing and wanting to listen. She could do at least that much.

He hesitated before saying, "It's not important. It's just that, Jenny said there's a carnival next week and she asked me... for us to go with her and her mother."

"Carnival?" said Lilly, brow furrowed. "I don't remember hearing about a carnival next week."

"She said that too, but it must be one of those coming through town and had to stop by type of carnivals. Like a traveling circus or something."

"I don't think those exist anymore."

"Oh!"

"But that doesn't matter. I could be wrong. I'm sure I just missed it with... *with all we've been through.*"

Lilly trailed off, lost in thought.

"Mom?"

Lilly snapped her eyes towards Christopher. She bobbed her head. "Yes," she said. "Yeah, we can go. What day is it?"

"Next Thursday is when it opens. She wants to go that day."

Lilly nodded. "Ok, yes, that's fine. I'll leave Sam with grandma."

Christopher smiled. Lilly was sure he would have jumped for joy on any other day. "Thank you."

"You're welcome. Now get some sleep."

"Okay." Christopher went to his room and closed the door behind him.

Lilly remained in the hall for a few minutes. She went and checked on Sam and tucked his sheets over his little frame. He was sound asleep. No fidgeting, no screams, no restless legs. She kissed him on his forehead then went downstairs. Poured herself a chardonnay and took her glass to the bay window where she sat on the couch watching the moon and the stars. They seemed like distant friends she knew she could confide in.

17

2:00 AM
Amber's House
Tyler

The party was in full bloom. Dancing, loud music, chaos, and chatter found every corner on the property and ballooned like an overstuffed sack ripping at the seams.

Beer, booze, vapes, weed, cocaine, molly, and pills were passed around as if everyone in attendance were a rock star on the brink of a breakdown without a care for the next morning. Someone jumped from the balcony into the pool. Laughter, sometimes a scream or holler, raged across their heads.

Maybe it was getting out of hand, Tyler thought. He was outside by the pool with Pam and Amber. The ladies sat on lounge chairs, cocaine lines on the wood table between them, gibbering and jabbering as if they hadn't seen each other in a day's age. Tyler watched the mayhem while standing in front of the ladies, like a phantom among his prey. It surprised him when Pam agreed to indulge in Amber's cocaine habit. He wondered if she was trying to forget what they'd done. Or what he had done, killing James Reilly the way he had. Although she had been a part of his plot, she wasn't the one who pulled the trigger. If anything, she'd be the one to turn. Pam's current behavior was a deep concern. Tyler believed she was falling apart at the seams. Maybe she was paranoid. She kept looking at Tyler as if her thoughts betrayed their pact and she couldn't allow him to know.

He'll have to keep a watchful eye on her from now on. Study any adverse behaviors to the contrary. Tyler understood there might come a time when he'll have to act and act fast. Because if Pam has a sudden itch of paranoia and decides to spill her guts to the police, he'll have to beat her to the punch and Pam would need to disappear. He didn't want to. He loved Pam. But spending life behind bars was not in the cards. Not for Tyler. Not in the least.

Is he being paranoid was Tyler's next thought, which was always a possibility.

Tyler shook his head, watching as a few friends helped the pool jumper out of the pool, his adventurous tidal wave apparently forgiven. He turned to Pam and Amber and noticed how Pam turned away. Was she watching him? He looked at Amber, whose eyes were steady and looking forward, directly at Pam. Her hands gripping her legs, Tyler could see her knuckles were turning white as she rocked back and forth. Pam leaned in to snort another line and Tyler shook his head again, disappointed when someone crashed into Tyler, close to pummeling him to his knees. Laughter erupted around the pool.

"What the—"

It was Ned Tatty. His eyes half open, stumbling on his feet.

"Ned?" said Tyler.

Ned raised his head and stretched his eyelids. Tyler watched as James Reilly's head snaked out from the back of Ned's skull.

"Not Ned," James shouted with a triumphant pitch. Tyler cringed seeing those maggots eating away at Reilly's blotched, bluish-purple skin.

"What?"

James was giddy, like a child who'd discovered a new toy. "This is amazing, Ty," James said, shaking his head. "Amazing. I can get right in and move him around like a puppet." He laughed out loud, and Tyler could see that it was James holding Ned Tatty on his feet. "It's the drugs, Ty," continued James. "It's like they block out all conscious awareness. I can slip right in and make him do whatever I want."

"What do you want?" Tyler asked.

James froze, eyeballing Tyler. Turned his head to the right as if he were studying Tyler's intentions.

"I told you," James scoffed, and dipped his head into Ned's and

Tyler saw Ned's eyelids lift open with a stretch. "I'm going swimming." Tyler heard a remnant of Reilly's voice, like a faint accent at the edge of every word. Although it was Ned's voice, Tyler knew it was James who said these words.

Tyler's eyes narrowed. "I don't think so. He could drown. What if you can't get him out?"

Ned—no, James—shrugged. Ned-James moved towards the pool, but Tyler caught his arm by his sleeve.

"I said no."

Ned's face changed then, as if Tyler was looking at both James and Ned with Reilly's furrowed, sinister scowl buried beneath Ned's complacent, drawn and weary visage. Snapped his teeth at Tyler and bit into his knuckles. Tyler pulled his hand away.

"What the fuck?" he screamed. Streams of blood pooled across the bite marks.

"I said…" James took a few steps backward. "I'm going swimming."

Tyler stood in awe, head shaking.

"Did he just bite you?" Pam's voice.

Tyler looked from his bloodied hand to Ned.

"What the hell Ned?" Amber this time.

Ned's face lit up with a smile from ear to ear.

"Don't!" Tyler said.

"Bye." And Ned, no James, waved before turning and sprinting towards the pool. Crashed into a group of three dancing teens and they all tumbled into the water. Drinks and vapes went with them.

Tyler rushed to the pool along with a group of teens. The three teens James had slammed into emerged first as laughter and sly comments erupted.

Fucking junkie.

What the hell, Ned.

Get it together.

It's not a party until someone drowns.

They helped one female out of the pool, and she stormed off, cursing and in tears. The other two jumped out of the pool. A friend gave the female a towel. The male stood at the edge of the pool with Tyler, dripping wet. Ned dropped to the pool's bottom like a sack of bricks. Tyler watched as Ned's eyes stretched open and James sprang from the body, water undisturbed as he jumped up and sat on the pool's edge, his legs still in the water although he was completely dry. Tyler looked from James to Ned, then back to James whose stare revealed he was dissatisfied with his exploit as he shook his head and turned to Tyler.

"You were right," said James. "Kid weighs like a thousand pounds."

Someone called over Tyler's shoulder, "He's drowning!"

Tyler jumped in, lifted Ned's dead weight, shifting his body so Tyler could snake his arms under Ned's armpits, and used his feet to propel them both to the edge where the male, dripping wet, helped pull Ned out of the pool along with two other teenagers. Tyler noticed how Ned was convulsing as he lifted himself out. He heard Pam scream, "He's overdosing," in a frantic, panicked yelp.

Tyler's eyes shifted from Ned to James, still sitting on the edge of the pool. James shrugged. "Don't look at me. I didn't do that." Saw a maggot squirm into Reilly's nose.

Tyler moved quickly, started CPR on Ned. Chest compressions and he could see how Ned was turning blue.

"C'mon," Tyler muttered, then breathed into Ned's mouth. Three long breaths and he could see Ned's chest rise. Returned to compressions while everyone else looked on. The music had stopped, seemed to Tyler the entire world froze. More chest compressions, more breaths, the chest still rising but Ned was drifting, turning a darker shade of blue.

"Look out, look out."

Tyler heard the call behind him. It was Jake Ferris. He dropped to his knees beside Tyler and raised his hand, quickly slamming the needle in his hand into Ned's leg. Tyler continued chest compressions.

Another needle and Jake said to Tyler, "Narcan."

But Ned continued to turn, now entering a shade of purple.

Someone screamed to call 9-1-1.

"Not a chance," said Jake and injected Ned with a third Narcan injection when Ned jumped up with a gasp. His skin turned pale and ashen, then turned towards Tyler and heaved a bucket of pool water across Tyler's legs. "There you go," Jake said.

Another wallop of vomited water and Ned drifted, resting his head on his arm. He looked like run over dog shit. The crowd erupted in laughter and applause. Ned coughed and heaved. Tyler put his hand on his back and Ned cringed and jumped as if he'd been electrocuted.

"Leave him be," Jake said. "He's in a shit ton of pain."

Tyler said, "Narcan?"

Jake nodded. "That's right. I got it for this schmuck."

"Smart move," Tyler whispered, looking at Ned, who was now shivering. "Someone grab a towel," he called and through the crowd he could see Pam had taken her seat again with Amber. A second later he was handed a towel, which he wrapped around Ned, still shuddering and shivering.

"Let's get him inside," said Jake. "I've got clothes he can put on."

"Hopefully, he's done with this shit."

They lifted Ned up, and Jake escorted him inside. Tyler watched as they entered the house. Reilly was beside him.

"That's because they're lacing shit with fentanyl. See, Ty, you shouldn't have killed me. I never laced my shit."

Tyler shot him a cold, hard scowl.

"What?" James shrugged. "It's true. It's all coming from China. Blame them not me."

Tyler had no response. What was the point? He wasn't about to have a full-blown argument with a dead man. That would raise some serious red flags.

18

4:30 AM
The Cummings Bedroom
Jigglyspot

They wore the Cummings out. Both husband and wife were sleeping on opposite sides of the bed. A naked Jiggly and Kera on the bed, squeezed between husband and wife, their bodies glistened with sweat. Jiggly's chest hair saturated. Kera leaned against the headboard, a glass of white wine in her hand, those tentacles resting snug, sound, and peaceful within Kera's dark silky hair. Jiggly lying on his back next to Kera, his head against her hip, eyes closed. Jiggly let out a loud, long yawn.

"Tired?" asked Kera with a laugh.

Jiggly stretched his eyelids and turned towards Kera's hip, nestling snug beside her. "Just a bit. Been a long day." And a second later, "Long week too." He yawned a second time.

Kera ran her free hand over Jiggly's head. "I'm not surprised. Seems like the entire galaxy is on edge with all that's going on with Mr. E. I can't believe they turned on him, but it is for the best. Eventually, someone's got to expose the truth."

Jiggly sighed. "Whoever holds power is the one who writes history. There's no more truth in history than there is on the news. It's been written and rewritten so many times most of us have our heads in the sand and know absolutely nothing." He opened his eye, staring at Kera as she sipped her wine.

"Pity," she said. Jiggly caressed her stomach with his fingertips. "How did you handle it? What plan did you come up with?"

She was pressing him, he knew. Kera had always held an alternate belief than Jiggly and those he worked for. "Simple," he said. "I made a last-minute change in the script, so to speak."

"What does that mean?"

"Means we lost a good amount of product, and that product will need to be replenished. Which means fresh meat is required and we need volunteers."

"Volunteers?" said Kera in a whisper. "Is that what you call them? I prefer the word captive, or prisoner, or slave. Take your pick, but *volunteers* seems quite disturbing and contradictory."

Jiggly lifted his head, staring at Kera and the tentacles that were now wide-awake, wide eyes staring angrily at Jiggly. He knew he was in trouble and that it was best not to tell Kera about the smuggling operation he concluded last weekend while sucking on the extraction from his beaming teen.

"What?" she said and crossed her arm over her stomach.

Jiggly squirmed away from her while saying, "This again." He sat on the edge of the bed, his back to Kera.

"Yes, this again. What you're doing is not only wrong it's sadistic, on every level imaginable in the universe. And let's not forget it's against the prime directive and subject to scrutiny and trial by the supreme council."

Jiggly rolled his eyes, put his head in his hands, elbows on his knees. "It's only against the council if there's no permission granted by the host species, Kera. We have that permission. We've always had it."

"No, you don't. How could you have permission when ninety-seven percent of the population isn't even aware of the truth? You even managed to block the subconscious from knowing the truth. How about waking up everyone on this planet to the truth and see if they still give permission? There's still time, Jigs. Still time to put things right with the truth."

Jiggly felt frustration rise in his throat. "Like what you do is any better?"

"Please," she said. "It's not even in the same galaxy. Literally. You know the Cummings gave permission on the subconscious level. They don't want to remember, it's their choice. And you know what we do frees their minds. Those desires they attempt to suppress are satisfied and because we do that, they are free in their conscious lives."

"They're also drawn and weary, Kera. They know something is wrong. They feel it, like a gut instinct they can't put a finger on."

A quick pause and Jiggly was sure she sipped her wine, courtesy of Mrs. Cummings. "Ok then, we stop."

"Sure," Jiggly huffed. "I've heard that before."

"Well, it's tough, you know that. Especially when Mrs. Cummings calls to me from her subconscious. You should see her dreams. She's so repressed it turns my stomach to know she's got to live like that."

"It's her choice."

"Exactly my point."

Jiggly shook his head and sighed.

"Seriously, Jigs, I'd like for you to stop."

"And do what?" He jumped off the bed, standing tall and staring at Kera. "Go where? They're everywhere nowadays. It's not like the old times when they had to hide and scatter. We've become more of the norm and we take in new members every day." He paused, thinking. "We've become the new religion." And he smiled.

Kera rolled her eyes. "That's great, another planet given towards slavery and subjugation." She shook her head. "Last thing this universe needs. Your own people don't even agree with what you're doing."

"My people," Jiggly seethed, spit jutted over his lips. "Are aware of my circumstance and obligation."

"More like black mail and slavery. How long do they expect you to carry on this debt?"

"I don't know Kera."

"You like it. That's the problem, Jiggly. You've always liked it."

"Of course, I like it, the power is immense and these frigin humans..." He pointed at Mr. Cummings. "Are too frigin stupid to realize anything. Always overindulging. Always judging each other. Stupid Human Scum. Zero intellect, that's what it is. They deserve to be subjugated. Petty little vermin they are."

Kera looked at Mr. Cummings, then back to Jiggly. "That's not accurate. You know why they're like that, they've been manipulated for more millennia than we can count. Plus, the damn force field around this planet. For the love of Pete, you know what it takes to break through the barrier, and it gets more difficult as time goes on. That damn frequency keeps tightening, sooner or later it's going to pop and then what? Every human wakes up to see a new dimension. They'll all crack."

"I don't want to talk about this Kera." He dropped his shaking head, breathing shallow.

After a long silence, Kera said, "So, how did you fix Emmanuelle's problem?"

"What do you care, Kera?"

"Because..." She sat up, glass of wine held in both hands, tentacles staring sympathetic and cautious. She swallowed her breath. "I want to make sure you'll be ok?"

Jiggly raised his eyes to her. She seemed sincere, and he understood she cared for him. "I rifled up a carnie. Volunteers will be plentiful." And he cocked his eyebrows when he said, "Dinner served." Then added, "And a few new recruits for conditioning. Once everything on the island calms down, we'll be able to return unscathed. Poor MysterE," he said. "But those are the risks we take and he's had a great run. Better than anyone ever."

"I'm sure he's earned his rightful seat in Xibalba," said Kera sarcastically.

Jiggly remained quiet. He turned around to see his cane leaning against the chest of drawers. He took it up and held it close. "Are you ready to go, Kera? Sun will be up soon and I'm so tired. I just want to get and go. I need sleep."

He heard Kera move off the bed. She reached around him and placed her glass on the chest of drawers, then wrapped her arms around him.

"Yes. I'm ready." Her head resting against his back, tentacles playfully stroking the back of Jiggly's head.

Jiggly hesitated, breathed deeply, then twisted the top of his cane. The effervescent bluish-purple smoke rose to his nostrils.

"Mommy. Daddy." Frantic knocking on the door. "Mommy. Daddy."

"Shit," said Jiggly. "She could wake them."

Kera looked at the door, then back to Jiggly. "Go," she said. "Mesmerize the little one. She won't remember."

"What about you?"

Kera looked at the Cummings. "It'll be ok, I'll get myself back. Just go." She turned to Jiggly. "I hate the idea of leaving a child scared and frightened." Jiggly hesitated. Kera kissed him on the lips, then said, "Go," as she took his cane and breathed in the smoke.

Jiggly went to the door.

"Jigs," Kera called.

He turned, and Kera tossed him his clown suit.

"Mommy. Daddy." Pounding on the door as Jiggly squeezed his legs into his outfit, pushed his arms through and zipped it quickly.

When he opened the door, Lindsey gave him a startled look, but that wasn't an issue for Jiggly.

He said, "Oh, little Lindsey, time for bed." He took her hand.

"It's good to see you again, Jigglyspot," said Lindsey as he led her to her room. He tucked her in and gave her a kiss on the forehead.

Before he left, Lindsey was fast asleep. When he returned to the bedroom, Kera was gone, his cane on the floor. Jiggly picked it up and took the wineglass off the chest of drawers then walked to the kitchen and washed the glass. Quietly and methodically, Jiggly reset the house alarm and locked the door on his way out. Twilight on the horizon. And Jiggly thought, I could use a good extraction!

19

3:30 AM
Tyler's bedroom
Tyler

Before he jumped into bed, worn and tired, Tyler turned to his ghost, and said, "If you ever even attempt to do to me what you did to Ned Tatty, I promise I'll shoot myself and haunt you for eternity."

James raised his hands. "Ok," he said. "Ok."

Tyler eyeballed him before he crawled into bed. "I still don't know why you're here. Maybe you should just go to heaven or hell or wherever ghosts go." He was tired, exhausted really, and quickly drifted off to sleep, but on the brink of passing between conscious awareness and the dream state, Reilly's response followed him.

"Soon, Tyler. Soon you will have all your answers. And I'll be gone."

Part III
Dress Rehearsal

1

12:00 PM
Thursday June 20, 2019
Always in the dark
Cassandra

She'd been hearing loud bangs over the last few days, and what she believed was running or shuffling. Cassandra's pleas went unanswered. How the water trough was replenished she did not know. One day she discovered bread, a full plate of bread tucked in the corner of her cell. Cassandra had stumbled on the plate after a loud bang and what she thought was someone approaching the cell at lightning speed. As if they wanted her to find the bread. She ate like a carnivore, desperate for food. Downed the bread with a gulp from the trough. The water didn't go down easy. There were thick tiny globs in the water, and she wasn't sure what they were.

More loud bangs, like someone using a wooden stick to smack steel. The bangs echoed in the room as Cassandra hugged her knees in the cell corner. Question was, how long would they keep her in this cell? She was sure her parents contacted the police by now, or maybe even Sharon. Hopefully, someone noticed she's been missing over the last few weeks, if it even were that amount of time. Could have been a month for all Cassandra knew. Time moved at a snail's pace here in the dark without an inkling or understanding about time. Was it day or night? Monday or Thursday? Morning or evening? Cassandra was never sure. Even when the pale prince came to her rescue, he never so much as offered the time.

Pale Prince being a figment of Cassandra's imagination. A phantom she conjured to not feel alone. She could never see his face. In her mind's eye, she saw the prince as nothing more than a white blotch, his features smeared across her thoughts. But he was strong and cunning, like a prince should be. And after he carried her outside, she would never so much as leave his side or wander too far knowing the monster, her captor, may have followed them into freedom.

Cassandra heard chanting before she realized the words were her own. "Pale Prince, please come. Help me. Take me out of here and let's be gone. Pale Prince, please come. Take me out of here and let's be done." Her voice soft and low as she rocked back and forth. Her back and spine ached, felt twisted and broken, but still she rocked. Lying to herself that if she continued singing, one day the prince would come, kept convincing herself this wasn't the end and that her destiny would not end in this cell.

She wanted to cry, could have cried if she had any tears left to shed. But those were gone too.

"Pale Prince, please come."

Another loud bang and Cassandra jumped, heard a scream escape her throat. Cassandra's thought process was to cease screaming. She was sure whoever held her captive was listening. Why give them the satisfaction? She held her hand over her mouth to stifle the whining voice that seemed to have a life of its own.

Quiet. Like the silence existed for her alone. She waited before the rocking continued.

"Pale Prince, please come. Help me. Take me out of here and let's be gone."

Shuffling now, lots of shuffling. And she could hear doors opening and closing. For the first time since she'd awakened in this cell, she heard sounds reflecting life outside these walls. Like gates being opened with a fluttering bang. Maybe her time was coming? Maybe someone would present themselves? Something was better than continued silent torture. Cassandra reached for the steel bars, her back and knees cracked and popped. Her legs felt weak as she pulled herself up. More doors opening, more gates, more shuffling.

"Hello." Her voice a whisper. Her breath stuttered across her lips. "H-hello."

Cassandra licked her dry lips. She was sure they were cracked, bleeding too. She'd chewed on them enough to know they were.

"H-hello," she called, the word belting from her throat into the room.

Silence. Quiet. Did she hallucinate those sounds? Cassandra wasn't sure how long she stood holding those cell bars, listening. Hoping those sounds would begin again.

Another loud bang, but not in the distance. This bang came from within the room. That wooden stick hitting steel. Followed by another, then multiple bangs in unison. And she heard hard breaths, chanting in unison with the bangs. "Ahhh. Ahhh. Ahhh." So many bangs, like steel drumbeats, scattered across the large open area she knew existed. Pace quickened, louder bangs, louder chants.

"Ahh. Ahh. Ahh." Bang. Bang. Bang.

Cassandra bowed her head, held her palms over her ears. Started screaming, "Pale Prince, please come. Get me outta here and let's be done. Pale Prince, please come." Her voice carried desperation on its heels.

She wasn't sure when the banging and chanting ceased, but when Cassandra stopped screaming, silence greeted her. Maybe they were watching and in awe over the pitch she squeezed from her throat. Cassandra crossed her arms and returned to her private little corner. Sat down and started rocking, arms wrapped around her knees.

Started singing, "Pale Prince, please come. Take me outta here and let's be gone."

2

1:00 PM
Hollywood, CA
Tyler

Tyler had gone for a run. Had been every morning this week. Running helped curb his anxiety, helped to clear his head, at least in the moment. Plus, Mr. James Reilly never ran with him. He appeared at intermittent periods along Tyler's running path. Watching Tyler, who continued to be angry with James over his treatment of Ned Tatty. James had apologized more times than Tyler could count, but Tyler was over it. Apologies mean nothing if the person doesn't change their behavior. And Tyler suspected James continued to indulge in his new pastime. Reilly wasn't hanging around much since the Ned Tatty experience. And when he was around, he talked to himself in whispers as if there was another person—albeit dead or alive—in the room with them. Not to mention Reilly was deteriorating so fast Tyler found it difficult to look at him.

Tyler was also concerned about Pam. She was falling apart at the seams. Cocaine, perhaps, feeding her paranoia. Tyler's stomach turned every time he thought about Pam's indulgence, and he cursed himself for allowing Pam to be a part of Reilly's demise. At the time, he felt sorry for Pam after she'd endured the sick, narcissistic ego of one James Reilly, but now he regretted his decision to include her in his plans. Tyler was looking forward to his meeting with Pam later today. He needed to assess her level of awareness and understanding. Plus, he needed to know if Pam was going to turn on him. Perhaps guilt had taken over as the leading emotion in Pam's mind.

He'd been following the Reilly case over the last two weeks, and it seemed the police had chalked up Reilly's demise to a bad drug deal. Everyone knew James was selling heroin, pills, and weed and had gotten into bed with some terrible people. And Tyler knew the police questioned Jake and Amber. Jake was Reilly's best friend since grade school and Tyler knew he was broken up about Reilly's death, even if he refused to show his emotions–at least out loud in front of a crowd. Perhaps he confided in Amber instead. Nonetheless, Jake wanted Reilly's murderer to be found, so he provided law enforcement with as much detail as Jake could remember about Reilly's dealing and cohorts in the drug trafficking industry, essentially clearing Tyler of the crime. Tyler had asked Jake if the police were going to question him too, but Jake had no cause to believe they would. According to Jake, "They have enough evidence. I gave them everything and everyone. It's just a matter of time before they find who pulled the trigger."

And Tyler kept thinking about the duct tape. He should have used less, and he wondered if the police had caught his rookie mistake or related it to a kind of torture for the perpetrator to garner information. He could never be certain and had to take Jake's assessment with a grain of salt. Tyler kept a watchful eye for anyone who may be following him. Looked for strange or out-of-place cars and vans. Watched from his bedroom window, standing in the dark so no one could see him, looking for any signs of police activity. He saw none and reminded himself of this fact when he stepped out of the shower after his run. Towel draped around his hips, he wiped the steam from the mirror above the sink and met Reilly's eyes over his shoulder. Tyler jumped when he saw Reilly. Those maggots were in full bloom and had consumed most of Reilly's flesh. Tyler could see the tendons, bones, and cartilage that live beneath the skin. Said skin being a darker shade of decomposed gray. Plus, after the Ned Tatty incident, Tyler didn't want James anywhere near the back of his head.

"I told you not to do that."

James scoffed at Tyler as he stood in the mist of steam that billowed inside the bathroom like a phantom menace.

"Fucking ghost." Tyler shook his head while squeezing toothpaste over his brush.

"White spot's coming back," said James and Tyler caught him in the mirror looking at Tyler's spot of white hair. "You gonna dye it? Makes sense if you do."

"No," Tyler retorted, then started brushing his teeth.

James shrugged. "Whatever," he muttered, then leaned against the bathroom wall to the left of the open bathroom door.

Tyler ceased brushing, spit a wad of toothpaste filled phlegm into the sink and eyeballed James in the mirror. "Do you have nowhere else to go?"

"You want me to leave?" asked James with a tilt of his head. He looked perplexed, as if the concept of leaving was a foreign language.

"Yeah," said Tyler.

James shrugged, then snapped his fingers and disappeared.

Tyler started brushing again when he saw James appear in his mirror.

"I said get the fuck outta here," Tyler screamed.

"Just one thing, Tyler. I forgot to mention, be on your toes tonight. Wouldn't want you to miss an opportunity for redemption."

Over the last two weeks, Tyler wondered if he would kill again, kind of like that serial killer sitcom where the murderer quenches his murderous impulse by killing bad people. But the more James stuck around, the more Tyler thought differently about his newfound career choice. After all, how many dead people can he handle?

James may have been apologetic in the beginning, but now his personality was in full bloom and it sickened Tyler to think that James might be with him for the rest of his days. *There has to be some way I can make him leave?*

"Nope," James said in reply to Tyler's thought. "I'm here to stay."

Tyler shook his head, pulled the toothbrush from his mouth, and said, "That's not what you said, James. You said you'd be gone after... whatever is supposed to happen happens."

James bobbed his head left, then right. "True, true," he said. "You got me on that one." And he started laughing when Tyler punched the mirror with an instant crack. His fist carried streaks of blood across his knuckles. Shards of mirrored glass dropped in the sink. James was in the shower. "You missed me," he taunted. Then James was behind Tyler and Tyler shifted quickly, anger boiling to his temples.

"I said don't do that," Tyler hollered, and James flung backwards through the bathroom door and across the hall. Tyler felt and saw electricity between them, pumping inside of the atoms within the empty space in the hallway. Reilly smacked the back of his decomposed skull against the floor.

"What the hell was that?" Tyler's dad, Frank, called from the living room. Tyler was certain Frank was on his second six-pack for today.

Tyler felt toothpaste drip from his open mouth. James got up from the floor with a confused, although angry, stare.

"Nothing," Tyler answered. "Must be an electrical issue."

No reply from Frank. He must have gone back to his television. Always watching the news, Frank was. Yelling and screaming at the newscast was Frank's favorite pastime next to the bottle. The two went together like peanut butter and jelly.

Tyler shook his head, eyeballing James Reilly who stood in the hall confounded. Tyler closed the door and went back to brushing his teeth.

3

2:00 PM
Hollywood, CA
Sharon

She was changing, she could feel it. She felt strong, stronger than she'd ever been. And centered, as if she hadn't a care in the world. Even Cassandra's blatant disregard for Sharon's text messages didn't bother her. To hell with Cassandra. She'll deal with that self-righteous bitch when she returns this weekend.

Sharon rolled over on her back, lying on her bed. Kevin asleep by her side. She held her right wrist up. Six cuts across her wrist, little scars were forming. She enjoyed the scars, reminded her she was a bad ass who took control and never played the victim's role. She, Sharon Mable, was in control and she loved it. Last night it was Kevin who ached and moaned as she pounded him. She knew he would love the strap-on she bought. Served him right anyway. He wasn't the only person who could inflict pleasure with pain. She smacked his head more than a few times and called him her little boy bitch. Then she dropped on the bed and pleasured herself and forced Kevin—blood trickling down his legs from his ass—to watch with a stare of want and desire.

Now Sharon clenched her fists, staring at Kevin sleeping face down. She turned to the strap-on next to the bed. Got up and pulled it over her groin, the thick erection twelve inches of power. Grabbed the bottle of lube off the armoire, squeezed out a handful, and then stroked the erection with it. She went to Kevin's side of the bed and thrust the cover off him. Kevin never stirred. She parted his legs and climbed on top of him, inserting the erection inside Kevin, forcing it in with a push that shuddered, inch by inch, inside his rectum. When his eyes shot open with a whining scream bellowing from his throat, Sharon clasped her hand across his mouth and started pounding.

"Momma's good boy, aren't you?" Sharon said in his ear. "Love it when momma gives it to you. Be a good boy, Kevin." And she started thrashing, using her weight to push harder, further, deeper. "Be a good boy for momma."

Good thing about the strap-on, it came with an extra vibrator specifically for Sharon. She ceased pounding Kevin long enough to push it in. Her body shuddered with a pulsating, tantalizing flutter of pleasure. Her head lifted, her throat stretched as she pounded again. She paused, reaching beneath the strap-on to flick the switch on the vibrator that buzzed with a flurry of pleasure.

Sharon couldn't believe how horny she was. She couldn't get enough. And she enjoyed the pain that came with it. She slapped Kevin's head, then took both hands and pushed his face to the side, clawed her nails across his skin, drawing immediate trickles of blood.

"Bleed for momma," she said. "That's it, bleed for momma." Sharon leaned closer to Kevin's head, licked and drank from his wounds. She orgasmed while savoring his thick, salty blood on her tongue, licking her lips with wide-open eyes when the room wavered with a metal crunching yelp. The air around the bed fluttering as the orgasm reached its peak and shot like a tidal wave down the strap-on and across Kevin's back. Sharon watching, staring. Not at the wall behind the bed-the wall was no longer there-but into the depths of what she could only refer to as hell. Darkness reached towards infinity, fires raged across the landscape and blood-curdling screams filled with torture filled the air. Her pelvis gyrated, releasing that last bit of orgasm, when the darkness wavered like a flicker across a movie screen, and the wall behind the bed returned. Sharon snarled and bit Kevin's ear, but not enough to draw blood. Although she wanted to, but Kevin would look better on screen with both ears attached. Sharon removed the erection from Kevin's rectum and stood by the side of the bed, sweat glistening off her skin. Heavy breaths. Whining from Kevin, his hand on his backside. She craned her head to see if he was crying. He was.

Sharon shook her head. "Pitiful vermin. You want to cry? I'll make you cry." Sharon stomped over to the armoire, took out a whip from the top drawer, and snapped the whip across the room, her heart beating like a hateful, angry maniac. Kevin jumped when he heard the sound, staring at Sharon, his eyes wide and fearful.

"Cuff yourself," she demanded. Kevin hesitated. Sharon cracked the whip. "I said cuff yourself, vermin. NOW!"

Kevin nodded. "Ok," he said, moving to the beds center.

"Ok what?"

"Ok momma." Kevin cuffed his right wrist, reached his left hand over, fumbling with the second set of cuffs attached to the headboard.

Sharon noticed how weak he seemed, how emaciated and thin, and how nervous. He couldn't get the left wrist to lock, the cuffs kept fumbling. Sharon cracked the whip across his stomach and Kevin cried out in pain, his left hand going to the wound immediately.

"I'll do it," she said. Kevin's eyes went wide, but he said nothing. After Sharon cuffed his left wrist, she climbed over Kevin, forcing the erection into Kevin's mouth and demanded he perform. Sharon pushed the erection further down his throat as she performed quick successive gyrations with her hips. Another orgasm erupted from her toes to her brain. Sharon laughed, her eyes wide, laughing to herself. She got off Kevin and noticed his erection.

"Oh, what's this?" she said. "Too small for this pussy." And she whipped him. Once. Twice. Three times. Four. Blood down his torso and Sharon leaned in and suckled on his bare chest, lapping her tongue across his bloodied stomach. Held his erection in her hand and with a bloodied mouth, she went down on Kevin.

This newfound power was indeed godly.

4

3:00 PM
Los Angeles, CA
Lilly

She dropped off Sam at her mother's house. Sam was staying for the night and although Lilly cried the entire time she was with Sam, she knew it was best for Christopher. Sam still wasn't sure what was happening, other than the fact that his father was never coming home. The child was confused, trying to make heads or tails from a scenario he couldn't put his finger on.

The nightmares had gotten worse over the last week. Lilly consulted the psychologist who informed her Sam's nightmares might take a long time to resolve. A sign of repressed emotion, with the aliens being a symbol that the child was confused, and the torture a reflection of his pain over his father's suicide. Subconsciously, Sam knew what happened and was attempting to communicate with his conscious mind. The thought that her boys would grow up without a father created a hole in her soul she could never fill. And the thought that one day she would be alone carried an emotion filled with fear. She refused to go there, refused to allow her mind to wander to that inevitability.

And she knew people were talking about her. Blaming Lilly for what had happened, for the way she'd been-too judgmental-and Tad couldn't take it. The result was a lifetime of self-blame, shame, and guilt. She wanted nothing more than to run. To take up a new residence somewhere far away where no one knew who she was or what had happened. Perhaps some place quiet, a small town where she could drift into the unknown recesses of her mind and pretend that everything was going to be all right. A place where she could disappear.

Nonetheless, she had Christopher to contend with and a mountain of financial concerns she wasn't sure how to deal with. Tad had taken out a life insurance policy that, according to the insurance adjuster, would pay off big time. But will there be enough to wrestle her out of the debt Tad had left in his wake of suicide? Possible and likely, although she was concerned that once word of the policy pay-off took hold, people would come out of the woodwork to get a piece. Death by a thousand cuts type of scenario. Lawyers didn't care what they were suing for as long as they knew there was money to be made. Lawyers were heartless vermin, and anyone can file a lawsuit in today's society, even if the lawsuit had zero validity to the claim. It was ridiculous.

Point being, lawsuits went on for years, with the victor being the one who possessed the larger wallet. Lilly understood the only people who make out in lawsuits are the attorneys, because no matter what, she would have to defend herself against the lawsuit, and that took a good wallop of cash off the top.

Maybe a different country is a better place to move? Or a new planet, Lilly thought on her way up the stairs. She heard Christopher in his room, shuffling around and singing and Lilly paused once she reached the second floor, listening.

He'd become her rock. Her constant and her everything. Where he garnered the strength to move forward, she wasn't sure, but he did have it, taking care of the house, Sam, and yes, Lilly had to admit, she herself as well. He sang to Sam every night and was in Sam's room at the first sign of a nightmare, even before Lilly herself had gotten up. Lilly was certain he wasn't sleeping, judging by how his eyes sagged and swelled. Could be crying too, although Lilly hadn't seen him cry, and she was sure he was holding everything in, stuffed down into the abyss that is the human heart. All Lilly did was sleep and cry. Every bone, muscle, and organ hurt with a depression unlike any she'd ever experienced. Hopeless, worthless, and helpless, she hadn't the strength to do even the simplest chore. Food had become an unnecessary commodity, but the bottle helped. The wine and vodka numbed the sensations, although they fueled the sadness and widened the hole in her heart.

She hadn't been out of the house since the funeral. Dropping off Sam took every ounce of strength she could garner and that first step outside the home was like walking into a black hole. Lilly wasn't sure if she took Sam's hand because he asked for it or if she took his hand to help her move from the door. Her feet refused to follow her thoughts, standing in the open door with the sun beating against her forehead until Sam took the first step forward and Lilly's feet followed his lead. It wasn't like she had to go outside over the last week. Delivery brought the wine and vodka; family, friends, and neighbors brought food. So much food and way too much for three people, and Lilly knew she wasn't eating, although she couldn't say the same about Christopher. She hadn't seen him eat, but that didn't mean he wasn't eating.

I should know, Lilly thought when she noticed how tight her jaw was, teeth grinding with a constant quiver in the corner of her mouth. She could feel her nerves splintering and cracking. Signs of a nervous breakdown.

I should go to him. see how he's doing.

Her feet refused to move. Lilly noticed her right hand was shaking. She clenched her fist, attempting to ward off the tremble, angry that she had no control over her body. Eyes roamed left, then right. Her head felt dizzy, but her feet felt like concrete, as if her lower body was battling with the upper half.

Christopher's door opened. She snapped her head towards the quick creak of the door; saw Christopher in the doorway, watching her.

"You okay, mom?" he said. "You've been standing there a while." His voice soft, empathetic.

"I..." She tried to get the words out, but they drifted from her mind, and refused to come out. She noticed how good he looked. Showered with his hair parted down the side. He looked good, and she was proud he was her son. She forced a smile, said, "You look very handsome, Christopher."

"Ma," he said. "It's okay to cry."

Her eyes filled with tears. "I know," she muttered. "I think I'll take a bath if that's all right. Ready to go in about an hour?" They were scheduled to meet Kathy and Jenny for dinner before heading to the carnival. Lilly understood this was a first date, a supervised first date, but a first date, nonetheless. She hoped she wouldn't ruin it for him and wanted to look her best.

Now Christopher forced a smile. "Yeah, that's perfect."

"Okay," she said, as if his agreement allowed Lilly to not have to get all emotional. "Okay," she repeated, willing herself to move. One foot in front of the other, she told herself.

Christopher interjected, "How was Sam when you dropped him off?"

Lilly stared at her son, processing his question. "Fine. Grandma was ready for him. Had all the games set up and said she was going to take him for ice cream sundaes, watch movies, and order pizza." She turned away, eyes downtrodden. "He's going to be okay, right?"

"He will. We're in for a long haul, but we'll be okay."

Lilly smiled, looked at Christopher, then quickly looked away. "I hope so."

"We will," he repeated. "Go take your bath. I'll be ready when you are."

Lilly nodded, then drifted down the hall, those concrete blocks no more. Now she felt like she was floating. All the while, she felt Christopher's eyes on her and wished she had the strength to pull this night off without a hitch.

5

4:00 PM
Somewhere Shiny
SAC John Mills

John could sense his brainwaves moving like a stagnant floating image on a television screen that reminded him of those old televisions that blared static and rolling white noise. His eyes fluttered, and he felt sick, sick to his stomach.

He could feel the gurney beneath him as his sensations returned. Eyes fluttered open to a striking white light. His eyes hurt; tension behind his eyes and a throbbing in his right eye. He could see something at the end of the gurney, small and smeared across his vision. *Smiling?* John stretched his eyelids, attempting to see clearer. A painted, familiar smile. John's head drifted left, then right, as his eyes closed.

Felt a hand on his head, followed by a hoarse voice that said, "Come detective, you're almost there. Just have to open those eyes and see. See me, your Jiggly."

With a heavy head, John moved his head to the right. Eyes barely open, he saw Jigglyspot, the miniature clown he questioned in Westchester, standing over him. Saw two Jigglyspots and shook his head. Focused his eyes and the two became one. He tried to speak, but the words wouldn't come. John Mills pursed his lips and felt how dry they were, his throat too.

"Some water," he heard Jiggly say.

Mills felt Jiggly's small hand on the back of his head lift his mouth to a cup of water. John drank furiously; the water evaporating on his dry tongue and lips before the liquid reached his stomach. He choked on the water and dropped his head back to the gurney.

Heavy breaths, he forced a breath down his throat with a sigh.

"All is well, detective."

Mills felt his brain shed the cobwebs of whatever he'd been through for however long he'd been on this spaceship. That part he remembered, the UFO in the woods in Westchester. He remembered the grey aliens too. Then the thought of that maggot returned with a vengeance and Mills shot up. His chest jumped, not aware they strapped him to the gurney.

"Calm now, detective. Stay calm."

John felt that tiny hand on his chest and Mills calmed himself down. It was obvious he wasn't going anywhere. And why was this clown aboard the UFO? Mills pursed his lips.

"My w-wife?" Mills said.

"Lorraine?" said Jiggly, and John's eyes opened wide.

Mills noticed Jiggly had the golden round top of a red cane in his right hand, his left hand on John's head.

"How do you know her name?" John's voice a dry whisper.

Jiggly laughed and smiled. "Detective Mills, do you not remember me? You should remember, at least now. All those nights we spent together. And our talks?" Jiggly shook his head. "I'm disappointed. Perhaps they gave you a little too much this time. Perhaps your brain has been turned into stew."

Perplexed, John couldn't catch a thought or a memory. Said the only thing that came to mind, "I said, where is my wife?"

Jiggly shrugged. "No worries about good Lorraine, John. She's well taken care of. Your daughter too." And Jiggly leaned in closer to John's eyes, his breath a wretched stank of sewage. "She gives great extraction." Jiggly smiled from ear to ear.

Mills saw an image of his wife and daughter, strapped to chairs with tubes inserted in their skulls. He jumped and flailed. The straps were too tight. And Jiggly laughed.

"My my, John. How angry you've become."

John gave up struggling and turned his head away from Jiggly. He couldn't help the tears. Felt those tears stream across the side of his face.

"John?" Jiggly said. No response. Mills felt lost, frightened, angry. Kept crying. "John?"

He felt Jiggly's left hand leave his head, heard the cane tap the floor when Jiggly's small right hand appeared above John's eyes, fingers glued together, thumb out. His fingers were stained yellow and callused, with what looked like dirt stains or perhaps old, dried blood. Mills followed when Jiggly arched his hand towards him. John's eyes and head moved with it as if some connection existed between Jiggly's hand and Mills' eyes. And John felt calm, staring at Jiggly, whose makeup was cracked and faded, especially over his nose. Mills saw the gin blossoms, faded pockmarks across his nostrils. A small smile graced Jiggly's lips. John's eyes drifted.

"John? Look at me."

John saw Jiggly's eyes then, those glimmering blues captivated Mills.

"Good, John. Good," said Jiggly. "Your help will be required tomorrow, detective." Jiggly breathed deeply, a cross between a sigh and catching his breath. "You understand, solstice is tomorrow, yes?"

Mills breathed, "Yes," and gave a subtle nod.

"And you understand what this means? They will arrive tomorrow. We must be prepared. We require your presence to keep the peace. To maintain ORDER!" Jiggly stomped his cane with a loud smack. Jiggly breathed deeply and although his eyes were steadfast, they seemed paranoid, as if he was concerned with being heard. Turned his voice low when he said, "You've been informed of our most recent predicament, detective. If you don't remember now, know this: the knowledge will come with the arrival of the Dark Lord. Because of the unfortunate circumstances with Mr. E, we have lost a substantial amount of product and have had to make alternative plans. This is where your solidarity will be needed. Because we require new recruits for our celebration and new pods to produce future consumption." Jiggly raised his eyebrows. "You understand, don't you John?"

"Yes," Mills replied, his voice a soft hush.

Jiggly raised his head. "Tomorrow we coronate a new queen."

He stomped his cane twice. "And a new phase towards subjugation." Mills could see the hairs in Jiggly's nostrils flutter with his breathing. "It is up to us to continue reconditioning. Are you with us, detective? Can I count on your abilities to ease us through this transition?"

Mills felt something squirm inside his head. Felt his nose and mouth constrict, facial muscles tense. He had zero conscious understanding with Jiggly's communication and request, his mind devoid of thought. Nonetheless, he understood there was something buried in his subconscious that clicked with an understanding that he will comply.

"Yes," Mills said.

And Jiggly smiled, his eyes turned to his left, and he gave a slight nod then returned to stare at John.

"Good John. I knew I could count on you."

Mills felt Jiggly's hand on his forehead. His eyelids heavy.

"Sleep now, detective."

John's eyelids closed.

"Rest easy."

Felt himself drifting into sleep.

"You will need all your strength for tomorrow."

And then, darkness.

6

4:05 PM
San Luis Obispo, CA
Production Warehouse Four Hours Outside of Los Angeles
Jigglyspot

Jigglyspot craned his head, staring at SAC John Mills. When he was certain the detective had fallen asleep, he turned to CIA Agent Helmsley standing behind a thick glass pane in an observation room six feet from where John Mills slept. Helmsley's grey alien mask sat on the table in front of him and seemed to glare into Jiggly's soul. Helmsley wore the rest of his alien costume.

"That uniform is so close to the real thing you almost fooled me."

Helmsley said, "It's the best yet, right? I love technology. Remember those god-awful rubber costumes? They were so hard to breathe in. But these new ones have a ventilation system. It's cooler inside the costume."

"Kudos to the designer then. We've come a long way in a short while."

"Is he sleeping?" asked Helmsley.

Jiggly nodded while staring at Mills. "That he is." Jiggly smoothed his fingers across John's forehead, brushing the detective's hair from his eyes. "Hopefully, he stays asleep until tomorrow." Jiggly raised his head and looked at Helmsley. "Wouldn't want the good detective to wake up prematurely. We've got enough to deal with without having to coax detective Mills with a longer charade."

"Shouldn't be a problem, I gave him enough thorazine to put a bull down."

Jiggly watched the sleeping Mills. He seemed peaceful.

"What's next on the to do list?"

Jiggly turned to Helmsley. "So much to do. Thankfully, we managed to sneak a few products off the island. They should be here soon."

Helmsley nodded. "Nice. Our guests will be more than happy. Nothing better than young meat."

"Indeed detective. The chef will be ecstatic too. He's been waiting to get his hands on a young lamb."

"So, how will this work, Jigs? What's your plan?"

"Simple," said Jiggly. "Assessment is required. We have multiple roles to fill. Once the product arrives from the island, we'll have a better understanding of our needs for tomorrow's celebration and can plan tonight's event accordingly. Teenagers are always best. For obvious reasons, they can satisfy multiple concerns. Long term being the goal but there's always fun with the matured. For gaming and chance festivities during celebration."

Helmsley was not only nodding, his shoulders and chest were bobbing. To Jiggly, he seemed over excited. "This is great, it really is," said Helmsley. "When was the last replenishing? Was it back in the nineties or..."

"1984. That's when I first met MysterE. All has been running smoothly since then. Recent events not included. But it happens. Eventually, we all must readjust."

"Yeah, it's a shame about MysterE." Helmsley shrugged. "I guess that's what happens when the power goes to your head."

"Don't be fooled by the hype Theo, MysterE has served us well. Unfortunate these circumstances are, but they are what they are."

"Have they chosen a new headmaster?"

"Not that I've been informed, Theo."

Helmsley shrugged, looking at the floor. "I hope it's me," he said, nodding and bobbing. "I really do."

"Highly possible, Theo. You've served the masters well. Come, let us walk. I'm required outside for assessment."

Jiggly walked, cane in hand, tapping the floor to the opposite side of the room where the wall slid open to a concrete hallway.

Helmsley stepped into the same hall from the observation room, grey alien mask on.

Jiggly shook his head. "Take that ridiculous thing off, Theo. We don't need unwanted attention."

"But my face," he said. "I can't be seen."

Jiggly leaned on his cane. "No need to worry about that now, Theo. All who are here are our people. Plus, if you are seen, no one will know who you are. Better for them to see a human face than a grey. The greys are a sorted species and will not be kind if they see you mocking them with that costume."

"Yeah, right. Ok." Helmsley squeezed the mask off his head and placed it on the floor. Shook the hair from his eyes and pulled his arms from the sleeves, then dropped the costume to the floor and stepped away from the costume, which he gathered up with the mask and tossed inside the observation room. He then tucked his polo shirt into his shorts. "Good to go?" he asked, his arms stretched.

"Perfect, my man. Perfect," Jiggly said with a smile.

"You're a good man, Jiggly. I'm honored to be here with you."

Jiggly's eyes narrowed. "My Theo," he said. "Don't go getting all sentimental on me."

"Well, I'm excited is all."

Jiggly leaned into him. "I can tell." Jiggly started walking. "But don't be too excited. The masters don't like it." Helmsley followed Jiggly down the long hall. Double doors at the end, Jiggly pushed through them, stepping into a large, dark warehouse. Jiggly turned to Helmsley, put his finger to his lips. "Be as still and quiet as possible. Our new pod may hear." Jiggly stepped to the wall on his left where a stack of shelves housed a sound system including large speakers, a turntable, and a radio that was bought in the seventies. Still worked, though. Jiggly pushed the power button and hit play. Raised the volume and the room filled with the sound of wood hitting metal and loud huffs and ahh's.

Helmsley laughed and Jiggly did too. It was difficult to contain their humor.

"How has our little pod been?" Jiggly said in a whisper. "Has she been drinking the water?"

Helmsley nodded. "Definitely. I had to replenish it twice now."

Jiggly's eyes lit up. "Wonderful. She will be quite fruitful by tomorrow then. Perfectly planned. I love it when the plan comes together."

"Fact," said Helmsley. "And it's amazing how you smuggled all those egg sacks from Xibalba. Plus, Emmanuelle's blood and the Dark Lord's larva. Especially with all that's going on. Pure genius Jiggs and very impressive."

They continued walking, Jiggly watching the back of the warehouse, hoping to see or hear his new little pod. Although it was dark, Jiggly's eyes adjusted quickly, his extraction from the teenager in Westchester, although waning, continued to aid in the enhancement of Jiggly's senses. He saw a stain in the dark, what he assumed was the blonde hair of his new pod. Heard her shudder and stifle a scream when he came to another door and pushed through it into another hallway. The light was dim in this hall. Jiggly pinched the bridge of his nose. "Close it quietly," he ordered, and Helmsley caught the door before it snapped shut, easing the door closed.

Jiggly led Theo down the hall to a door. Fumbled in his pocket for the key, then unlocked the door. He looked right, then left, scanning and observing.

"No one," Theo said.

Jiggly rolled his eyes. He opened the door. Inside was a chair with a high back and thick arms and legs made from oak. Faded, ripped, and torn red leather on the arms and back. Leather straps on the arms, legs, and back.

"Sit," Jiggly ordered. "Strap yourself in."

"This again?"

"Of course, Theo. It's been two weeks since my last extraction and I'll need as much as possible to aid in my endeavors over the next few days. You're the perfect candidate. None have extracted from you in a day's age. I'm more than sure you are quite potent. I can smell it."

Helmsley hesitated as Jiggly walked to the back of the chair. Jiggly leaned his cane against the chair, staring at Theo with a clenched jaw and narrow eyes.

"I said sit."

Helmsley stared at Jiggly. "This will help me get the position, right? The headmaster position?"

"Of course. As I told you, I've already provided my recommendation to Mr. West. I'm more than sure he will indoctrinate you soon."

Helmsley nodded, smiling from ear to ear. He took his seat, said, "I'm grateful to you Jiggly. Truly grateful."

Jiggly rolled his eyes, easing the strap around Helmsley's forehead, then tightened the straps on his ankles and wrists.

Helmsley tensed. "Ouch," he said. "It's tight."

Jiggly smiled, put his hand on Theo's shoulder. "For your own good. Wouldn't want you to flinch and wind up destroying brain cells you'll need later in life. I'm only looking out for your best interest."

"That's right." Theo leaned his head back, closed his eyes. "Thank you Jiggly. I can always count on you."

Jiggly smiled as he walked behind Theo. A small refrigerator occupied the corner. On the wall were three shelves, all containing equipment for extraction: syringes, scalpels, tubes, and of course, the drill. Inside the refrigerator were samples of numbing solutions. Jiggly pinched a syringe he took from the refrigerator between his fingers, hesitated, looked at Theo from the corners of his eyes, then put the syringe back and closed the refrigerator. Took the drill instead and went to the chair. Jiggly plugged the drill into the socket on the floor. He could tell Helmsley was nervous, his body trembling, his legs and feet shaking.

Theo had been with Jiggly and his faction for quite some time, but his existence was no longer required. Said existence was expendable in the eyes of Jiggly and his people. He was a tool, literarily a tool. Kind of like a vampire's slave, but where the vampire's slave offered blood on the go, Theo provided extraction when required. Plus, he'd been inserted into the CIA for a reason, to keep a watchful eye on Mills and provide reports and research when required, and now that the Dark Lord has chosen Mills, Theo was no longer necessary. Theo's desire to be the next headmaster was ridiculous. The man had zero intellect. People like Theo never understood that you're either born evil or you're not, and if you're born evil, you always know what to do: kill at will and let the dark side rule the world. No one can train you to be evil, and those who pretend to be evil for evil's sake are the easiest to manipulate. Should Theo die, the masters wouldn't blink an eye. The masters trusted Jiggly. He always produced and came through in a pinch. Probably the only reason Jiggly remained untouchable.

Jiggly thought about his little pod, listening to the musical sounds of drumming, oohs and ahhs. He wanted to give her something more to be frightened about. Blood curdling painful screams always sent shock waves of fear through the body. And fear was needed for his little pod. Fear sped up the incubation process and developed strong and quick-witted tadpoles. The more fear, the better.

"I will not be giving you a local," Jiggly said, and Theo's jaw dropped. Fear slithered across his eyes.

"Why not?"

Jiggly shrugged. "We need fear, Theo. Fear for our pod. We need you to scream, and this type of pain will do the trick. Do it for the pod, Theo." Jiggly paused, then said, "Perhaps we will allow you to take her as your own once our tasks are complete. You like her, don't you? She's so sweet, that one. Soft too."

Helmsley smiled from ear to ear. Started laughing. "She is. She is."

"I know. And I also know you've been creeping around her cell in the dark. Touching her hair. And when she sleeps, I know you've been touching her." Jiggly raised his head as Helmsley's stare turned fearful, like a child about to be scolded by an abusive parent. "It's ok, Theo. No need to be erratic. We would have done the same."

Helmsley seemed to relax. His eyes drifted, looking around, thinking, then he looked at Jiggly. "You think they'll allow me to keep her?"

Jiggly craned his head. "I'll recommend it, Theo. You deserve a prize for your loyalty, but..." He shifted his head, maintaining his gaze on Theo. "You have to hold still."

Helmsley shifted in the chair. "Ok. Ok." He straightened his shoulders, sitting stiff and still. "I'm ready." He closed his eyes.

Jiggly smiled, shuffling behind Theo. He toed a step stool from the side of the chair and brought it close to his feet. Jiggly stepped on the stool, his head above Theo.

"Jiggly," Theo said. "What do you think will happen tomorrow?"

"My man," said Jiggly with a smile, a laugh in the back of his throat. "It's going to be a bloodbath."

And Jiggly flicked the switch. The room buzzed with the sound of the moving drill and Theo's wretched cries of fear and anguish.

7

4:30 PM
Hollywood, CA
Tyler

Sitting in the café where he was meeting Pam, all the chatter and goings on were dulled to his ears as Tyler contemplated his latest event with Reilly. Tyler wondered where the power came from; the simple thought that tossed the dead James Reilly across the hall.

Was it supernatural? Otherworldly? Or was he turning into a superhero? His power being the ability to use his mind for protection, or offense should he need it. Tyler felt a hum in the tips of his fingers like a radiating electricity that obeyed his command. His eyes roamed across the café, watching the patrons eat, drink, and converse. No one paid him any attention. He felt invisible, like a ghost. Perhaps he'd been spending too much time with the dead?

He focused on his cappuccino, the thick froth with cinnamon sprinkles sitting comfortable and unmoving. Tyler put his fingertips over the mug, felt the electricity, focused on the power, and moved his fingers in a circular motion, watching as the froth swirled. He could feel it, as if the humming electrical current in his fingers projected to the mug. Quickened his pace and watched as coffee consumed the froth like a spiraling vortex had opened inside the mug and swallowed the milky, thick foam. He then raised his hand and the liquid followed, rising above the mug. A waterspout turning and churning with his fingertips.

He heard a spoon drop and his eyes snapped to the sound when he noticed everyone in the café had paused and was watching him with crooked, narrow eyes. His coffee tornado collapsed into the mug with a splash. Tyler scanned across the café. All eyes were on him.

He raised his hands. "I'm a practicing magician," he said, sensing the tension dissipate. "Not bad, right?" And he smiled when the bell over the front door jingled behind him. Heard footsteps, clunking thick heels, and when he looked up Pam was standing over him. She wore dark sunglasses, those short blonde curls draped across the sides. And in that moment, all the chatter returned, as if the patrons had hit the play button, continuing conversations where they left off.

"About time," said Tyler as he gestured to the empty seat across from him. "Got you a cap too."

Pam cleared her throat as she took her seat, kept those sunglasses on but Tyler could see through them. Her eyes, stiff and wide, revealed a lost and frightened mentality. She said thank you as she took her cappuccino and put the cup to her lips. Tyler craned his head, staring, observing, attempting to get a feel for Pam's current emotional and mental state.

"Not sleeping?" he asked, shifting in his chair and sitting upright and tall.

Pam blew on the cappuccino she held close to her lips, said, "Nightmares," in a soft whisper.

Tyler pursed his lips, gave a slight nod, wanting nothing more than to rip those sunglasses off her face. "I'm sure the cocaine doesn't help." His voice was abrupt; he felt anger rise in his throat. She looked pitiful, and he wanted her to know it.

Pam dropped the cup on the table. Tyler watched as her bottom lip quivered.

"Well, you're turning into a pompous asshole." Her mouth agape, she sat back, hands on her lap.

"Pompous?" He shrugged. "Look at the big brain on Pam, using such big words."

"There you go," she said, shaking her head while turning away.

Tyler watched her; she was beautiful, even if she looked like she hadn't slept in days. He felt empathy surge in his chest.

"Look, I'm sorry. And you're right, I have been acting like a jackass. This is all new to me, too. My head's spinning with so many thoughts I don't know what to think." Pam eyeballed him from the corner of her eyes. "I am," he said. "I'm very sorry. When you do that stuff, I lose my mind. It bothers me. Makes me think I can't trust you. Like you're going off the deep end and taking me with you."

He could see her jaw tense. Pam shifted in her chair, pushed her sunglasses over her head, and Tyler moved back. Pam's eyes were bloodshot and a pale yellow. Thick dark purple skin beneath the eyes gave way to skin that seemed coarse, like sandpaper.

"Are you okay?" he asked, staring through narrow eyes.

"Sure," she said. "I haven't slept in almost a week, Tyler. If that's okay, then I'm doing just absolutely capital." She crossed her arms over her stomach.

She's falling apart, Tyler thought.

"Okay, okay." He raised his hands, then leaned forward, took his mug in hand. "I'm just concerned." She craned her head, staring. "Is it guilt?" Her body seemed to tense from the question. "Because if it is, I understand. We talked about this..." He caught himself, looked around the café and noticed none were watching him. He scanned the patrons, wondering if any of them were a cop, perhaps on a stakeout to gather intel.

Pam shook her head, staring at Tyler. "No, Tyler. No guilt at all. Just nightmares and I could swear there's a ghost in my bedroom."

Tyler's eyes shot up. His whole body shot up. Is it possible she can see Reilly, too? "What do you mean?" He felt his heart racing in his chest.

"What do I mean?" she repeated, moved up in her chair, and leaned in closer. "I woke up last week and my underwear was scattered across the room." She looked away, head shaking. "The whole point was to get rid of him. We were better off keeping him alive. Now I've got some sadistic ghost hanging out in my room. What do I have to look forward to? Ghost sex wasn't on my list of to dos." Her voice raised, Tyler put his finger to his lips, hand gesturing to keep the volume to a minimum. Pam leaned back in her chair, and crossed her arms again. "And I know something strange is happening to you, too. I can feel it. You're not being honest with me. I need reassurance. Answers too. It's like you left me behind and forgot about me." Tyler was sure she would burst into tears right now if she weren't so paranoid.

"I'll give you whatever answers or information you want. All you have to do is ask. I mean…" He paused, looking over the café, making a mental note to keep his voice down. "It was best for us not to talk in case people were watching. I thought it was for the best. That's all."

No response, but Tyler could sense he was getting through to her. Felt the tension ease.

"All that's over now, though. I believe we are in the clear, considering what I've read and heard." Then, after a moment, "I'm sorry. I really am. It's been difficult for me, too."

Pam was quiet. Tension filled the café. He wanted to take her in his arms, conflicted with wanting to provide comfort or squeeze the life from her bones. He hoped for the former. After a long silence, Tyler said, "What are the nightmares about?"

Pam shot him an icy cold stare.

Tyler reached for a napkin, eyes drifted towards Pam. "I guess that's a stupid question."

Her stare turned lost, sad. Tyler saw how her eyes filled with tears, although her body seemed to relax.

"Not really," she said.

Tyler perked up. Her voice inflection changed, now soft and vulnerable. "What do you mean?"

"It's not a stupid question because the answer isn't what you think it is." There was a frog in her voice, and Tyler noticed how she swallowed that frog down her gullet.

Tyler craned his head, eyes narrow. "Understood. What are they about, then?" He waited but received no answer. She turned to the window as if afraid to answer. "Pam?" His voice was soft, caring. He could see her body tense up again; thought he felt her heart race too. "What are they about?"

"Aliens," she shouted, "Human eating fucking aliens."

8

5:00 PM
San Luis Obispo
Production Warehouse
Jigglyspot

Jiggly felt his eyes light up, and it wasn't from the sun that spiked its rays into his eyeballs when he walked outside the warehouse. It was from the extraction. He kept Helmsley strapped in the chair. Theo had passed out from the pain, and Jiggly thought it best to allow him to sleep. He'll need it, Jiggly thought. Gonna be a long weekend. Jiggly left his cane in the room with Helmsley, knowing he wouldn't use it for a while.

As he strolled across the parking lot where a string of warehouses sat vacant under the guise of Hollywood production, Jiggly thought about the carnival a few hours away, the one that will nab him his volunteers in what Jiggly thought was a stoke of pure genius. More than likely patrons-those early go-getters with the little ones-were beginning to arrive. The carnival was set up within a few days. No problem, Jiggly thought. He called his people, and they were ready to go on a moment's notice and they did well; came through in a pinch for their brother, Jigglyspot.

Continuing to walk across the lot, on his way to the truck parked by its lonesome, Jiggly went over his list of to dos. He had to prepare himself before arriving at the carnival and he had to be there within a few hours. Although the carnival was close to four hours away-Emmanuelle's choice, not Jiggly's-that was no problem for Jiggly. He'll use the cane to transport himself to the carnival so there was no problem with his studious arrival, nope, not at all. But what Jiggly was mulling over at this particular moment was what type of clown face he should sport for tonight's festivities. A big smiley face was necessary because Jiggly wanted to keep his potential volunteers at ease. But Jiggly was in a scowl type of mood and he didn't know what to do. Decisions, decisions. He turned his attention to the truck.

The box truck was twenty-two feet long and looked like it was falling apart. Jiggly could imagine the driver coming up from Mexico, the wheels and suspension rickety and rackety along the highway. Carnival of Souls written in large, faded, and thick black letters on both sides. A Ferris wheel beneath the letters. Jiggly admired the painting as he approached. Chipped and faded, the truck had seen better days. Jiggly changed Carnival of Chaos to Carnival of Souls. With so many carnivals across the country, a quick change in one word would help deter any good doers or inquiring police who weren't already under his thumb.

Jiggly smacked the truck with an open palm. Gary, the truck driver, was sleeping in the cab. Jiggly could see him through the side mirror. Gary's stubble had grown thick since Jiggly had last seen him, and he was sweating. His skin appeared moist. Gary is a tall and lanky man, with a narrow face and large nose, beady blue eyes, and thinning gray hair. Jiggly smacked the truck again, three times in a row, and Gary shot up, staring at Jiggly in the mirror.

Jiggly couldn't be mad at Gary for sleeping. The man had pulled off what everyone thought was impossible. All except Jiggly, of course. Jiggly designed Gary's travel itinerary when he was in Westchester-the day after he killed those beaming teens-using what Jiggly knew about the carnivals across the country as a tool for travel. Gary's travel path was pure genius. By using the carnivals, if the police pulled Gary over, he could say he was delivering to the local carnival. Sure, the trip would take longer, but safety was his first concern and Gary had delivered, literally delivered. Imagine, Jiggly thought, if anyone had looked in the back of the truck. Holy shit would that make national news. International news too. Hell, if they caught Gary with all the babies in the back of the truck, it would make interstellar news.

Gary rubbed his eyes and just about fell out of the cab when he opened the door. His hair was wet and greasy; his tired eyes cracked and yellow and he yawned while walking towards Jiggly.

"Tired?" Jiggly said.

"You have no idea."

Jiggly shook hands with Gary who stood six feet tall, hovering above Jiggly. "You will be rewarded for your effort, Gary. I knew I could count on you."

Gary was nodding and yawning when he said, "I hope so. That was one hell of a mission. Got pulled over in Albuquerque. I think the officer took pity on me. I looked so tired. Told me to pull over at the next truck stop and get some sleep. But I couldn't..." And he laughed out loud, said, "Too much extraction. I'm wired to the eyeballs Jiggs. Haven't slept in three days."

Jiggly rolled his eyes. "I'm sure. You'll sleep tonight though. I'll need you tomorrow."

"Of course. Whatever you need." Gary craned his head, studying Jiggly. "Did you just extract? All your gin blossoms are gone. Or is it because you stopped drinking?"

Jiggly smiled at the notion. He hated his gin blossoms. "Gin blossoms don't go away because you stop drinking. I've got Helmsley in the warehouse. That man gives great extraction."

"Fuckin Helmsley," said Gary, laughing. "Haven't seen him in a day's age."

Jiggly shrugged. "You can indulge after you've slept."

Gary's eyes lit up. "Excellent. Although I don't think he'll live up to the hype after the purity I felt a few days ago."

"Did you keep it to one baby as I told you?"

"Sure did Jiggs. Just like you said. Only one."

Jiggly eyeballed Gary with suspicion. He seemed a bit too wired to Jiggly. Multiple extractions from different hosts did that to a human. "Let's see what we've got."

"Sure thing." Gary pulled a set of keys from his pocket as they walked to the back of the truck. He looked right then left before unlocking the thick dead bolt on the door, dropped the lock and key on the bumper, then gripped the ramp and extended it to the ground. Jiggly watched in apt anticipation, scrutinizing every subtle move. Gary walked up the ramp. "You sure you want to do this in the open?"

"It's no matter. Everyone here is one of our own and there isn't another soul for miles."

"Okay," said Gary, then opened the door. Immediately, high-pitched, bloodcurdling screams, cries, and wails erupted from the back. It was maddening.

Jiggly jumped into the van. "Didn't you feed them?"

There was a row of bassinets on both sides of the truck, leaving enough room in the center to walk. The crying and screaming irritated Jiggly. These babies were supposed to be fed and sedated. It was obvious to Jiggly that Gary had not performed as well as Jiggs had hoped. The babies ranged in age from a few weeks to six months old. Twenty-four babies in all. Jiggly walked through the van, assessing each screaming child. All but one. Jiggly tensed his jaw, grinding his teeth.

"This one is dead, Gary. What the fuck did you do? When did you last feed them?"

Gary carried a stare that told Jiggly all he needed to know. Gary had gotten so high on extraction–that part was obvious considering the tube in the dead baby's skull–he forgot to feed them. Stupid Human Scum, Jiggly thought. There was no need for Gary to answer. Besides, anything he would say would be more stupidity, and Jiggly had no time for dumb comments. If he wasn't in a time crunch, he'd slice Gary's throat right this very minute. Mr. Scalpel hasn't tasted blood since the waitress and Jiggly was sure his trusted weapon was hungry. Jiggly noticed his hands were clenched into fists.

"I'm sorry, Jigs," was all Gary could say.

Jiggly looked around, assessing, head shaking. Other than the crying and screaming, the product was in good standing. Plump and soft. The feast will be exceptional with these specimens. Jiggly's chef will be honored to work with such a prime ingredient. Nothing tastes better than fresh young human. His guests will be impressed.

"What do you want me to do, Jiggs?" Gary's voice was soft and defeated.

Jiggly ignored him. Instead, he reached his arm out, his hand hovering over the baby in front of him, palm down. He was looking for the prize, the baby that would satisfy Emmanuelle's itch. He required concentration and closed his eyes, moving from bassinet to bassinet. His fingers started twitching and he could feel warm pumps of electricity in his fingers. There it is, Jiggly thought, and opened his eyes. The baby had blue eyes and a thicket of meat around the bones. Jiggly smiled from ear to ear as he scooped the baby in his hands and lifted the screaming thing over his head.

"Our prize has arrived," he said. "For all things holy and venerable, our prize is here." He nestled the child against his shoulder when he turned to Gary. "Feed this one first and tag his ankle so chef Politiere knows which one to savor."

"Yes, sir. Consider it done."

Jiggly was so happy he found the right one. Happy that Gary hadn't indulged in the child. Happy the baby had made it to solstice. And happy the day was moving smoothly. Not only had he reconnected with Mills and extracted from Helmsley, he has now identified the prize child. All that remained before tomorrow night's celebration was securing new recruits, the volunteers, as Jiggly referred to them. He has vacant positions to fill and queens to hatch. Not to mention some sacrificial ceremonies to conduct, which will require, of course, more volunteers. Jiggly was thinking this year's solstice will be absolutely epic.

Even without MysterE.

9

5:30 PM
Estelle's Diner
Lilly

She felt unsteady, as if a giant weight had barreled down from the sky and dropped on her shoulders. Some cosmic dark energy that infected every cell in her body, polluting her insides like poison. Lilly barely ate her salad, her appetite gone as her stomach boiled with acid. She thought she was going to throw up. Felt the nerves in her jaw constrict and twist with an unsteady quiver. And her hand was shaking, a slight tremble in the fingers, holding her fork over the salad as if she could claim a tomato or boiled egg, bring it to her lips and nibble.

Christopher and Jenny were like two peas in a pod, laughing and talking, sending text messages to each other, emojis and gifs. Lilly ignored Kathy as much as possible. She had no idea what to say to Kathy, all they had in common were kids and books, and it wasn't as if they shared the same point of view on what good literature was, that much had been made apparent during their weekly book club meetings, the two arguing over the writer's use of a metaphor or whether they used past and passed correctly. Lilly thought it was bad grammar and the writer should be tarred and feathered for the inappropriate usage. Kathy was forgiving and considered content and emotional impact over proper grammar. Two mothers with the same, although different concerns. And then there was the proverbial elephant in the room. Tad's suicide. A conversation Lilly chose not to indulge in. After all, it was her husband's suicide and she could choose to talk about it with whomever she chose. One thing was certain; she chose not to talk about it with Kathy.

Nevertheless, what else was there to talk about? She saw Kathy, sitting across the table, attempting to keep up with the children, to get them to join the living and the real by giving up their phones and being present at the table. Lilly was sure what Kathy was attempting to do was to split the air and tension hovering above them. Maybe Kathy had no clue what to say, either. This had to be a strange situation for any person to go through. Kind of like walking on eggshells, although with this scenario, if one of those shells would crack, it would mean that Lilly had cracked, not the opposite. Now that the shoe was on the other foot, her foot, Lilly was out of her comfort zone. She did not know how to act. And as the tension continued to mount, Lilly concluded she needed to start the conversation, for Christopher's sake, at least.

A fly landed on her thumb and Lilly's hand stopped trembling. Felt those little legs on her skin as the fly made neither move nor sound. Seemed to be staring at her. Before she knew it, Lilly had the fly's wings pinched between the fingers of her left hand.

"Nice catch, mom."

Lilly gestured to her son with a head nod and a smug smile. The fly twitching between her fingers. "See, your mom is quick to the punch." She raised the fly. "That's what you can do when you're focused on being present..." She let the fly go and it buzzed and flew away. "And not mesmerized by your phones." Lilly looked at Kathy, who sat across from her wearing a smug smile. Lilly wondered if Kathy approved of what she'd just done.

"So true," Kathy responded, as if she'd heard Lilly's thought. "Those phones will be the death of society. Everything we know about the world has changed because of those phones."

"Or perhaps the evolution of humanity," Christopher said. "They say in the future we will merge with technology. That our brains can be hard wired to the internet." Lilly watched as her son seemed to cower over his declaration. "At least that's what I read." Perhaps it was Kathy's stare that made him curl into a ball and want to be invisible.

It was Jenny who chimed in. "A.I.," she said. "It's not that robots will take over humanity, but that we will evolve into that intelligence. It's really fascinating. I know I'm in." She raised her hand.

"Same here," said Christopher, raising his hand.

Lilly noticed Kathy was smiling. She looked at Lilly. "I love science fiction books."

"Not fiction, mom..." said Jenny. "Just science."

Lilly noticed how Jenny seemed embarrassed by Kathy, whose face turned flushed and pink. She noticed a bead of sweat on Kathy's forehead. Lilly concluded in that moment that she despised Kathy, she saw her as inferior.

"Those who refuse to evolve are destined for extinction," said Lilly, shifting in the booth and sitting tall. "But until then..." She looked at Kathy. "It's all science fiction."

Kathy's shoulders seemed to ease as the tension dissipated. "That it is," Kathy agreed, holding her coffee mug in both hands. Casual conversation then ensued, and Lilly felt more at ease. More sane than off the wall bonkers. Christopher was right when he said it would be good to get out of the house. Maybe it was time, Lilly thought. Time to leave the past behind and evolve.

Into what, she did not know.

10

7:30 PM
Carnival of Souls
Jigglyspot

He was looking for volunteers, searching the crowd for unsuspecting humans. Leaned on his cane with both hands, in full costume. He decided on a frown to help mask his excitement. So many volunteers have arrived. The carnival was a success. Leave it to Jiggly, Jigglyspot thought. He always comes through in a pinch.

Laughter, screams, cheers, and jeers. Games being won, prizes handed out and the food, cotton candy, burgers, dogs, and deep fried breads filled the air with a pleasant nostalgic aroma. But Jiggly kept eyeballing the children, his stomach growling, knowing he should wait until tomorrow's feast. Such food always sat better on an empty stomach. It was better to fast for three days prior to the celebration. Helped to bolster dimensional travel once the fear soaked meat was digested.

Now he heard crying, small tears from small eyes. Jiggly locked in on it, he scanned the crowd, finding the child who cowered behind the basketball game. Couldn't be over four, Jiggly thought when his eyes lit up, started walking with a fast pace towards the child. The sun, setting behind the carnival, cascaded colors of pink and red. Perfect timing, Jiggly thought. Perfect timing indeed. He moved like a phantom, weaving in between customers, whole families who always arrive early. The girl saw him coming, her eyes wide and fearful.

"Young lady," Jiggly said, now that he was close to the child. "Are you lost?"

She looked at him with wide, fearful eyes. Mouth agape, but said nothing.

Jiggly forced a smile through his frown. "It's okay. I'm one of the clowns who work here." Still no answer. "I can help you find your mother. All we have to do is go over…" He looked over the carnival, pointed to the ticket booth with his cane. "There." He turned to the girl; she was staring at the ticket booth. "They can use an intercom to find your parents. Here, take my hand. I'll bring you over." And Jiggly offered his hand to the girl. Her eyes moved from the ticket booth to Jiggly then back to the ticket booth. She seemed to consider his offer, but Jiggly was becoming impatient. He could feel it rise into his throat and tense his bones. "Come now. I've got other things to do."

The girl took his hand and Jiggly led her to the ticket booth, providing information to the employee inside. "You'll be safe here until your mother comes," he assured the girl before leaving.

Not yet, Jiggly thought. That's all I need right now is a mother going bonkers because she can't find her daughter. The cops will crawl all over the carnival looking for her. Not yet, he repeated, his eyes scanning, roaming, and searching, leaning on his trusted cane, watching the entrance. Looking for volunteers when a group of five teenagers entered the carnival. Three males, two females. Jiggly could see a dark energy surrounding them as a smile curled in the corners of his mouth. He closed his eyes, drawing a deep breath in through his nose.

"Beautiful," Jiggly whispered, and he pinched his nose. Started laughing. Another gut busting laugh. He was so happy there were tears in his eyes. And he felt those tears fall from his eyes with a blink. Little tears that dried halfway down his cheeks. Jiggly wiped them away, saw white paint on his fingertips, which he brushed across his red with blue and white polka dot clown outfit. The best part was teenagers stayed late, well into the night, and often past closing time.

The two girls were soft but with an edge in their energetic fields that attracted chaos; usually meant they had an attitude, an edge to their personality, or something to hide. The boys carried an energy all too different from one another. The first, the one buying the tickets, had a confidence coupled with uncertainty, as if he understood everything about his actions were wrong, but why give it up if it's working? The fifth wheel standing behind all of them was an obvious user, kept scratching his arms, a telltale sign of heroin use. Looked like his skin was crawling, he seemed so uncomfortable. Easy prey and an easy play, Jiggly thought. And the last of them, the one whose eyes were searching, steady and calculating, across the carnival, once Jiggly locked in on him, he felt a click in his stomach. The boy's energy was magnificent. He carried a peculiar, unsteady confidence, like a caterpillar that just entered a cocoon. Fearful, unsteady, and unknowing what will happen once the cocoon shreds and tears or how he will fly after emerging, although his internal confidence allowed the mind to rest, accept, and let go.

The boy's energy was screaming for direction, building on his renewed internal confidence. "Freedom…" Jiggly whispered, watching as the one who bought tickets shared them with his friends. "Is never having to say you're sorry." The boy locked eyes with Jiggly. Briefly, the stare lasted. The essence from the teen's stare moved through Jiggly, who welcomed the energy. This boy is rare, Jiggly thought as the group moved into the crowd, one after the other, ticket-boy leading the way. But all Jiggly could see was that stare, watching as the boy weaved inside the crowd, begging for another lock of the eyes.

"What to do?" Jiggly nipped at his bottom lip, staring at the teen, perplexed, and lost in thought. "What to do indeed?"

Amazed when the boy locked eyes with him again, and Jiggly froze. Something in the energy, Jiggly thought. An energy Jiggly hadn't felt in a long while. It felt like home. Reminded Jigglyspot of a younger, and taller… "Me!" he said with a furrowed brow and narrow eyes.

11

8:00 PM
Carnival of Souls
Tyler

"Did you see that clown?" said Tyler as he took Pam's hand, weaving through the crowd, following Jake and Amber. Seemed like they were making a beeline towards the Swooper ride.

No one answered, not even Pam. Tyler noticed her palm was sweating, her hand limp inside his. He wasn't surprised that she was nervous. Nervous wasn't the right word to describe Pam's state of mind. Petrified was more like it. Those nightmares she talked about remained with Tyler. She described them so vividly he felt like he was a part of them and experienced the dreams for himself. But Tyler rationalized the dreams, chalked them up to shame and guilt. Murderous remorse. A deep seed of guilt dropped into the subconscious that was growing roots in Pam's dreams. He wondered if that seed would manifest into strength and hope or become the tree of death where Pam would hang herself later in life. What he understood was that Pam did not want to go to jail, nor did she want anyone to know the truth about the untimely demise of one James Reilly. Considering how petrified she was about her nightmares, the thought, as Pam had explained, of spending a lifetime behind bars with those nightmares was something Pam wanted to avoid at all costs. She understood she would receive no sort of full immunity. Even if she testifies against Tyler for murder, she'll still have to do some time, and that fear was enough to keep Pam from talking.

"Where are we going?" Tyler raised his voice so Jake could hear him.

"The Swooper," shouted Jake.

Amber turned to Tyler. "He loves the Swooper," she said,

following Jake's lead when Tyler stopped in his tracks, scanning the ride as Amber and Jake disappeared within the crowd.

The line was long and snaked around the ride.

"Over here," Jake said before rushing towards the end of the line.

Tyler turned to Pam and Tatty. Pam avoided his eyes, turning away, but he could see she was on the brink of tears. Ned looked like he was about to fall down. "Grab his hand," Tyler said to Pam. No response. Her stare seemed lost. "Pam!" he shouted, and Pam jumped, startled, and looked at Tyler. "He's about to nod out. Grab his hand." Tyler looked around, saw a bench by the Swooper ride, then turned back to Pam. "Let's get him on that bench."

Pam nodded, turned to Ned and took his hand in hers when Ned jumped. "Follow me," she said after clearing her throat.

Tyler led them to the bench when paranoia reached into his thoughts as if he'd been knocked over the head with a wallop of dark energy, a clairvoyance of sorts predicting something sinister was on the horizon. He refused to allow anyone out of his sight as he searched for Jake and Amber. Found them behind the ride at the end of the line, Jake calling for him to join them. Tyler shook his head, pointing to Ned when Jake rolled his eyes. Tyler searched the crowd, looking for the clown.

The energy he felt when he locked eyes with the clown was thick with paranoia, like a stab to his heart or a punch to his gut. He couldn't shake the sensation that danger loomed around every corner. He felt eyes on him too, searching, roaming over him, watching every move. Clowns were everywhere; although none were the clown he'd seen when they first arrived. His clown was small, where all the others were tall. And there were a ton of them. More clowns at this carnival than Tyler remembered at previous carnivals. They were everywhere, as if a horde of clowns had infected the carnival. Tyler counted fifteen clowns, and those were in his immediate proximity. How many more were scattered across the carnival? His roaming eyes found the camera fixed to the side of the ticket booth. He stared straight into it. *Is someone watching on the other side?* He continued his search, finding cameras everywhere, tucked into small spaces and hidden from view, but they were there, watching.

He felt an uncanny sensation that they should all leave. But he knew Jake wouldn't have it and he was their ride home. All the way out here, it would be a hike to get back home and a large fee for a cab ride. A large fee he didn't have, and he was sure Pam didn't either, and, of course Ned Tatty would never spring for a cab ride. He'll come up with every excuse in the book to not spend a dollar on anything other than heroin. Tyler was stuck, felt stuck, too. Like a ball of electricity had barreled down on him and there was nowhere to go, no place to hide. He was in this for the long run and had to see it through.

"Why are you so paranoid right now?" Pam asked, staring at Tyler from the bench. "You look like you're about to jump out of your skin."

Tyler blurted, "Did you see that clown?"

Pam shook her head. "What clown?"

Tyler scanned the carnival. Felt his skin burn and sweat bead on his forehead. He couldn't find his clown.

"Get it together, Tyler."

Tyler shot his stare to Pam as Ned slid against her shoulder. "Get off, Ned." Pam pushed him off and he slid to the opposite side, dropping on the bench.

Tyler shook his head. *What the fuck is going on here?*

His eyes darted from friend to friend. Pam. Ned. Jake. Amber. Amber. Jake. Ned. Pam. Jake and Amber moving ahead in line. Pam staring at him, shaking her head. Ned sleeping passed out. Pam. Ned. Jake. Amber. Pam. Ned. Jake. Amber. Felt his head spinning. Amber. Jake. Ned. Pam. Ned pissing himself.

"That's fucking gross, Ned." Pam jumped off the bench.

Ned's pants were saturated. Urine dropped from his jeans to the bench and in between the wooden slats, dripping to the ground. Pam behind Tyler. He could feel her breath on the nape of his neck.

Calm down, Tyler told himself when the thought hit him.

Where the hell is Reilly?

12

8:30 PM
Carnival of Souls
Jigglyspot

Jiggly watched the teenager on the closed-circuit monitor. The ticket booth camera had a clear shot of him, although he wished the camera had sound. Jiggly would love to listen to their conversation. Jiggly chewed on his bottom lip; sitting in the trailer behind the Swooper ride, he understood this teenager was yards away from him. Something about the boy kept nipping at Jiggly and he was growing frustrated.

Who is this boy? Jiggly thought, eyes narrow, watching, wondering, thinking. Jiggly had spent a lifetime searching for kinship, always keeping a watchful eye for another like himself. Was this teenager a warlock like Jiggly? If so, that could mean a host of possibilities. He could be a transplant, summoned to Earth by the masters. Should this be the case, it meant Jiggly was in trouble, although he didn't believe this was accurate. It would mean the teenager was a few thousand years old and if that was so he wouldn't be acting so erratic, and from what Jiggly was watching on the monitor, the teenager seemed anxious and disturbed, which was not a telltale sign of someone who had lived for so long. Time always manifests in a confident character because for those who relished time knew that the person who understood the relativity of time wins every time. Exception to the rule being the conflict that exists among those with the same understanding, because when this happens, time becomes a simple shifting of energy back and forth and all who are involved win at some point in time. Confused, Jiggly slammed his fists on the table and the monitor shook.

A few additional possibilities existed. Much like Jiggly, he was born on this earth with lineage rooted in the cosmos from long ago. A seed maintained in the DNA and waiting for the appropriate mix of genetics to signal the seed to sparkle with life. Jiggly presumed this was more than likely the case, although he could not be certain. Then again, there is the possibility that Jiggly was wrong on all fronts, and the teenager represented nothing more than today's classic youth.

No matter what the boy was or is, Jiggly maintained a watchful eye on the teenager. Helmsley could prove useful with a profile and family tree on the teen. Although Jiggly will have to wait until tomorrow for the information, Helmsley will need to recover after such an extraction. On second thought, tomorrow was the wrong day. There was too much to do. Jiggly's head was spinning. Thoughts and possibilities and frustrations circled his head as he nipped at his thumbnail, watching the teen, the girl behind him, and his friend pissing on the bench, turn to the camera. Jiggly leaned towards the monitor, took the mouse in his hand and zoomed closer. The teenager's eyes were dark and steady, seeing the camera, possibly seeing through the camera.

"Those eyes," Jiggly whispered. "What do you see?"

Jiggly jumped off his seat, went to the window, and peeked through the blinds. The sun was gone, night had arrived and with it, the ability to see inside the crowd with clarity was minimal, but he could see the teen, his head turned from the window, staring into the camera.

"Me," Jiggly said. "See me."

Jiggly felt a pull; a tug on his face as if someone stood behind him and reached with both palms to his cheeks, then pulled his skin back. His eyes were wide when the teenager turned, staring directly at Jiggly.

Jiggly stepped back and dropped his hand from the blinds.

His eyes staring, head shaking. Jiggly said, "Who are you indeed?"

13

9:00 PM
Carnival of Souls
Lilly

She felt strong and in charge. Where this strength and resilience came from she wasn't sure but it was there, conjured from an abyss of emotions, a cauldron that held the universe inside its walls and Lilly tapped into it and drank with a surge of power filling her gullet with every gulp down her throat. Even when Ms. Finicky joined their group, Lilly never flinched nor retreated.

She was the wife whose husband shot himself. She was the mother whose children's father was a loser. These were the thoughts that had gone through her mind with reckless abandon over the last two weeks. But no more. Lilly imagined herself stepping away from the past like stepping up and out of a bubble into new light and fresh air. She could be anything she wanted to be. A goddess. A criminal. A kingpin or a pawn. The choice was hers, but in the interim, she would be strong and proud and project this newfound pride with a fierce and unforgiving iron fist.

Finicky, Lilly thought. Checking up on my Christopher? Making sure I haven't cracked and placed my boys in harm's way. What was it that Christopher told her? Oh yes, take that stick out of your ass. Lilly laughed out loud, said with a sigh, "That's funny."

"What's that?" Kathy, breaking from her conversation with Finicky.

"Come again?" Lilly said.

Kathy stared at Lilly, perplexed. "What's funny?"

"Oh." Lilly waved her hand. "Nothing. Just a passing thought." And she looked at Finicky. "How are you Ms. Finicky?"

"Carol. The only time I'm called Ms. Finicky is in the classroom. Carol is fine." She seemed tense, at least to Lilly. Nervous was more like it. Then the question came. Lilly was getting used to the question. Although it wasn't necessarily the question, but the manner in which the question was asked, with a nervous vibration, as if the person was bracing themselves for any multitude of answers but knowing and expecting the worst. Because then they'd have to listen when all they wanted to do was run. "How are you doing, Delilah?"

"Lilly, no one calls me Delilah but my mother." And she smiled, couldn't help herself. "But I'm fine. I feel good tonight, like something changed." Lilly surprised herself by being so up front. The stares she received from Kathy and Carol were skeptical and disgusted as if they both screamed inside their heads, *she's gone mad.* Kathy and Carol, Lilly thought. Sounds like a morning radio show.

"Good," said Carol and Lilly could feel her tension ease as her shoulders slacked and her jaw fell loose.

Lilly broke the shared stare with Kathy and Carol and searched the crowd for Christopher. He was in line waiting for the Swooper with Jenny by his side. He was talking, looked like he was giving a speech, and Jenny was his only attendant. She felt herself smiling.

"No matter what happens, you have to keep moving." Lilly heard her voice as if someone else was speaking. "Got to put the past behind you and keep... moving... forward. Step up, put your head down and drive on." She turned to Kathy and Carol. "For my boys. I'm all they have now, and I refuse to falter."

They looked at her like she was mad. Mad or a sadist. Perhaps her mode of grieving wasn't politically correct in their eyes. But what was she supposed to do? Lay down and die? Sink into the abyss and drown at the bottom of a cauldron of emotion and give up and give in? No, Lilly thought. Not a chance. I'm through with that bullshit. Hold your head up, put your shoulders back and tell the world to fuck off because I'm coming and there's not a damn thing you can do about it except get the hell out of my way.

Lilly jumped when she saw the clown beside her. Purple fuzzy hair and sporting one of those red noses, although his facial features seemed strangely off as if he were wearing a mask. His jaw seemed rather large along with his snout, as if he were a wolf or dog or something in between hiding behind a clown mask. Lilly noticed that Kathy and Carol jumped too. And Carol jumped into Kathy's arms.

"I hate clowns," Carol said, staring at Lilly as if she needed to provide an explanation. "Scared to death of them."

But the clown said nothing, standing quietly as he handed Lilly an advertisement. The clown then waved both hands and bowed before moving on.

"What is it?" Kathy said, intrigued. Lilly noticed how Kathy stepped away from Finicky.

Lilly scanned the advertisement. "It's for a new ride. The Shibalba X-Press." She read the paper verbatim. "Wanna go for a ride? Be the first to experience the awe. The fascination. The pulse pounding edge of your seat, death-defying Shibalba X-Press. Present this paper to the attendee upon entrance for a chance to win a lifelong ticket to the Carnival of Souls and a pot of lucky gold valued at two thousand dollars. Drawing will happen at midnight. But don't despair, tear off the lucky number here." Lilly looked at Kathy and Carol, then continued. "There's a serial number on the top and the bottom. The Shibalba X-Press," she repeated. "Chris will love it."

Lilly turned to the Swooper, saw Christopher and Jenny climb into the pod and she smiled. Chris loves spinning twisting rides. He'll sure love this one, she thought. And her eyes kept roaming, scanning the carnival, seeing all the clowns she hadn't noticed before. Handing out tickets to all the lucky people. She turned to Kathy and Carol.

"You all want to go, right?"

14

9:30 PM
Hollywood, CA
Sharon

What a day, what a day, Sharon thought. And tomorrow will be the day of all days. The last day of being meek. The last with this old skin. Tomorrow, she becomes a goddess. Kevin's invitation was for her, not him. The invitation may have Kevin's name on it, but it was meant for her. This she now knew to be true. Tomorrow was her time to shine. And with all the Hollywood elite clambering and mingling, trying to find the next big star, Sharon was confident, as if she knew, her star will rise.

Even as she was pounding Kevin for the last time tonight, her declaration seemed even more real, as if she was creating it through Kevin's pain. He'd become nothing more than a toy, no greater nor lesser than the strap on around her waist. A plaything, a means to an end. A tool she used at will. It was as if he'd disappeared. Disappeared and meant nothing. Invisible even, unless she called on him, then his physical presence would manifest.

She was choking him. Had her hands wrapped around his throat. Sharon required Kevin to experience more pain, more fear. Had him bent over the bed, his ass high, his throat pulled back in her palms. Sharon was standing. She'd discovered that standing was the best position to truly and effortlessly force the dildo as far up Kevin's ass as possible. There was a point inside Kevin, like a button, that when pressed, the room fluttered as if a portal was about to open. She could see it opening when Kevin's fear reached a fever pitch. Fire and brimstone, darkness like dark should be. Black as pitch. Black as night, reached into a millennium of darkness where light could never find a home. She also noticed that when Kevin screamed, flailed, or became stuck in fear, on the brink of death perhaps, that the portal would ripple like waves in the ocean. She wanted to see what was on the other side.

Power and control are what she felt. Like a drug, an addiction to the darkness she welcomed into her embrace. What existed on the other side was what she craved and what she wanted to become. She wasted most of her life thinking she was worthless and hopeless, always second guessing herself, and always giving in. But not anymore. Those years might as well have belonged to someone else. Here she was power. She was strength. Like the iron grip that held Kevin's throat. She felt his windpipe, heard his gagging, and could picture his eyes bulging from his skull, so she squeezed even more and dug her nails into his neck as she pushed her hips as far as possible and held her hips tight against him as she squeezed even stronger.

Ripples pounded across the room like a thunderous rattling boom. Sharon felt her eyes widen.

"Bring me there," she seethed, beginning again the pounding of Kevin. More waves, more ripples, more thunder. "Bring.... me.... therrrre." She could feel heat beneath the ripples. Felt her skin turn hot, burning. The room boomed with a cosmic thunder. The candles she'd lit wavered and then died. Furniture shook, rattled, and dropped to the floor. Bed sheets flailed, and the bed rocked back and forth, up and down.

"Bring me to him, Satan. Come for me," she screamed to the ceiling. In the shadows, she could see creatures watching as if they were the darkness with outlines only perceived with a subtle move. Sharon felt saliva drip off her tongue and lips as she raised Kevin higher, arching his back as she continued to pound and tear at him. Heard chanting that came not from Kevin or Sharon, but from those devils watching. Huffing breaths in unison with a drum or stick slammed against the floor. This was power personified, and Sharon knew she was on the brink, consuming raw power and pure dark energy.

And she wanted more. Wanted to enter and be one with the darkness. To allow this power to consume every cell in her body. She tore her teeth into Kevin's neck, ravenous like an animal. Tasted his blood on her lips and tongue as she heard Kevin scream in horror. He was like a scared little boy, pathetic and weak. She bit down harder, tearing his flesh off in her mouth as she snapped her head back and swallowed that flesh down her gullet as Kevin dropped limp to the bed, although she could still hear his whimpers and cries. A pool of his blood in her mouth and she allowed the blood to seep from the corners of her mouth, drip down her chin to her breasts and she smeared the blood over her body, her torso and around her neck.

When she scanned the room, she was there in that darkness. Those entities receiving the madness she projected like food for the starving, and they ate it whole. She could still feel Kevin but not see him. She'd come into the vortex. Arrived in the darkness and she was a goddess now. Power surging from within, maddening, exhilarating, an enormous monster of energy that tore into her heart as Sharon hollered, still pounding, arms outstretched, and she could feel them then. Those demons and malicious ghosts jumped into her soul.

15

10:00 PM
Carnival of Souls
Tyler

"This is the last ride," said Jake. Tyler had been begging to leave over the past hour, but Jake wouldn't have it and Tyler was growing frustrated. Jake hollered to the crowd standing behind them in line, "This is the ride to end all rides." And he smiled; still holding the advertisement he received from a clown.

Tyler had no reply. He was eager to leave and return home. Home, he thought, never thought I'd say that. And then he thought of Reilly. *Where is he?* Tyler felt abandoned by his ghost. Felt abandoned by his friends too, and they were standing with him. Even Ned Tatty had become coherent. Well, at least as coherent as a heroin addict could be. Tatty had that sunken look to him and Tyler was sure he wanted out of this carnival as bad as he did, considering the stank from the dried piss on his pants had to be nauseating. The lifting Shibalba X-Press caught his attention when the screams from within the ride turned blood curdling.

The Shibalba X-Press is an enclosed spinning vortex able to hold twenty people. And this was the fourth ride for the Shibalba X-Press this evening. A limited run is what they were told, which is why the carnival was giving away prizes for entering. Tyler didn't like the screams. They sent a cringe up his spine. Equally disturbing was the sudden cease of those screams, as if someone had flicked a switch and turned off the volume. Tyler watched as the spinning calmed and the Shibalba X-Press hissed while returning to its settled position.

"Stand back," the operator said. "Once the Shibalba X-Press is empty, the front doors will open. Please allow the passengers to exit through the back prior to entering."

Tyler looked around, searching for the exit, when the front door popped open.

"Here we go," Jake said from the front of the line. He took Amber's hand and led her inside.

Ned was next, followed by Pam, who took Tyler's hand. He noticed her palms were still sweating, her hand trembling. Jake led them to the opposite side, where they all took their designated spots, standing and leaning against the wall. Small gates separated each passenger. Tyler took the chain dangling from the cage and locked it in place on the opposite side.

Jake howled like a wolf, all too excited. Tyler watched as more passengers crammed into the ride. He noted each passenger, finding one he recognized. The boy from the graveyard, the one whose father committed suicide, holding the hand of a girl Tyler assumed was the boy's age. They were followed by three women, one of whom was Ms. Finicky. Tyler swallowed the lump in his throat, his eyes searching the ride, the passengers, looking, hoping to see the ghost, Mr. James Reilly, but to no avail. Tyler was truly alone.

A clown walked around the aisle that separated the passengers from the center of the ride, tugging on each passenger's chain. Tyler noticed his nasty stank as he walked by. Like feces stained on his clothes. The scent boiled acid into the back of his throat as he turned his head away. Startled to see Pam staring at him. The look of fear in her eyes struck his heart. She seemed paralyzed, as if some invisible force was pinning her down. She opened her mouth, but no words came. As if she couldn't talk.

"You, okay?" Tyler said, his voice quiet, mouthing the words. He saw beads of sweat on her brow cascade across her skin. Noticed her trembling lips. And her eyes, her eyes revealed what she wanted to say, *We need to get off this ride.*

He felt a rush of thick hot air across his face, and he gasped for breath. Felt his skin flush with perspiration, looking over the other passengers. Everyone with the same stare, heavy eyelids, and floating heads. He felt sick to his stomach. He reached for the chain, but his hand drifted and dropped to his side. Head flopped back, felt his eyelids grow heavy as he gazed through wet slits. Across the ride, he watched the doors close, eyes drifting to the center of the ride where a fence circled around the center. Inside the circle was darkness, like a pit to the underworld.

He hadn't realized until then that the ride had begun. Slowly spinning, Tyler kept his eyes fixed on the center as he heard a speaker crackle.

"Good evening, ladies and gents," the voice was thick, a husky groveling. "Welcome to the Shibalba X-Press, your last ride of the night. I thank you all for your bravery, your impunity, and your voluntary admission."

The spinning quickened, and all Tyler could see were blurs and smears.

The voice continued, "When you awaken, all you see, and feel will be no more. Slaves you have become for our well doing and our pleasure. Enjoy the ride ladies and gentlemen. Your last forever."

The spinning was in full swing. Tyler's head pinned to the wall, he forced his eyes to remain open, fighting to stay awake. Sudden screams erupted. Tyler's head drifted to the side where he saw Pam, her eyes staring straight ahead, and the look on her face was one of terror and fright, her eyes wide. She was screaming, Tyler knew, although it was difficult to hear. The spinning whirling consumed his ears. Watched as Pam attempted to back up as if something or someone was coming at her, wicked and devious like.

The thought that he was watching Pam relive her rape erupted in Tyler's mind. He could see tears stream from her eyes. Heard her cries, and he could feel her pain like a stab to his heart. A kick to the balls and a punch to the gut. Watched as Pam's lips mouthed the words *please stop, please* as her head flopped to the side away from Tyler. Saw Ned Tatty, looked like he had needles in his arms, four on each side. Tyler felt his head shake and tremble. The ride was moving so fast he thought his brain moved inside his skull. His eyes drifted across his friends, smeared across his vision as he tried to move his head, his pupils pinned in the corners of his eyes as if he could turn his head by moving his eyes. And when his eyes moved, he saw a white vapor, like a billion ghosts, erupt across his vision and his head flopped forward.

In the center of the ride, he could see fire rage. He smelled sulfur and in front of him stood a clown. The clown, the one he'd seen when they first arrived, staring at him, in his hand a scalpel, a smile strewn across his lips. Watched as the clown jabbed that scalpel into Tyler's stomach. No pain. Tyler shook his head.

Nothing but a dream. Tyler didn't know where those words came from, nor if they were his or from someone else.

"No fear in this one."

"Truly special. We have much to show him."

Tyler felt himself being lifted off the ride. Felt heat on his skin as he was draped across a shoulder. Felt walking, movement like footsteps walking down a set of stairs.

"He's not out yet," another voice said. Then, after a long pause, "This'll do it."

Tyler felt a pinch in his neck.

And darkness greeted him.

16

10:15 PM
Beneath the Shibalba X-Press
Jigglyspot

Jiggly was excited. Not only was his Shibalba X-Press ruse successful-the ride ushered in a healthy quantity of volunteers-he was brimming with enthusiasm that he nabbed the teenager he'd been puzzling over since he first locked eyes with him. Jiggly had commanded his clowns to invite the teen and his friends to the Shibalba X-Press. He had to see him, had to look at him and study him.

Jiggly waddled down the steps to the underground. Skipped the last two steps with a jump, then continued down a long dark hallway. A light ahead and he could see his people, his fellow clowns, loading bodies onto the back of a pickup truck they were driving to the warehouse.

"Where is he?" said Jiggly as he approached the truck. "Where is that teenager?"

One of his clowns pointed to the back of the truck. The clown was tall and dwarfed Jiggly who kept walking, following the clown's finger. And the clown followed him to the back of the truck. The teenager looked peaceful, his eyes clamped shut, sleeping, strewn across the truck bed on top of another passenger. Jiggly studied the teen, his eyes roaming across his body from head to toe. Looking, studying, observing, trying to find some mark that would tell Jiggly who this teen was and why he summoned sensations inside Jiggly he hadn't felt in a long while.

"Why are you so special?" Jiggly whispered, his right hand on the teen's forehead, his left hand hovered over the navel. Jiggly closed his eyes, wanting to see inside the boy; his energy and thoughts. "A monster of energy," Jiggly whispered. "But where do you come from?" Jiggly curled his fingers, tightened his hands, felt his lips curl into a grin when he found it. "Conflict," Jiggly said in a hushed growl. "But confidence is growing." Jiggly kept searching, kept feeling. "What is the next move? Where to go from here?" Jiggly's eyes fluttered beneath his eyelids. "Oh," he exclaimed, "We've already crossed the line. How unique this creature is. How strong." Jiggly opened his eyes, turned to the clown hovering over him. "Direction, Apoch. All he needs is a simple push in the right direction. A glimpse into what's on the other side of the realm he's been locked in all his life."

Apoch stretched his arm, pointing to the teen's head. Jiggly followed the finger, craned his head to see the teen's skull. The hair was short, a crew cut tapered across his skull. Jiggly looked up at Apoch and shrugged. Apoch bared his teeth, rows of sharp fangs lined his mouth, and he turned the teen's head to the side when Jiggly felt his eyes grow wide.

The white spot existed on the teen's head. On the opposite side of Jiggly's own white spot. The truck's engine groveled when one of Jiggly's clowns started the truck.

He's one of us, Jiggly thought as the truck moved. His revelation was unexpected. Jiggly watched as the truck kept moving. His clowns around him continued to work, prepping the sleeping volunteers for the next truck prior to loading them. Apoch put his hand on Jiggly's shoulder. Jiggly turned to see the slight shake of Apoch's head.

"I know Apoch," said Jiggly, turning to the truck that was growing smaller with every passing second. "I know." Now Jiggly closed his eyes, shaking his head. "Unfortunate," he whispered,

"This is not the right time."

17

11:00 PM
Somewhere in the dark
Cassandra

She kept feeling sensations bubbling in her gut. Pain wrenched from her navel to her throat as she lay on the floor. Her hand gripped an iron bar to help prepare for the next wave of pain. Cassandra wasn't certain, but she calculated that the pain arrived every hour, and lasted for a few minutes, the excruciating part of the pain that is, although the after effect lasted the length of the hour. She knew it was coming again. Started huffing and breathing heavy, prepping for the pain. Felt sweat run across her skin, saturating her clothes. Cassandra gripped the iron bar even tighter as the pain erupted in her stomach and her body reacted, her knees to her stomach, curled in a ball of agony.

She started to cry, tears filled with fear and the unknown. Heard a click in the distance and the drumming beat erupted. Huffs in unison with the drumming so loud it pierced her ears. And the pain came, writhing up her stomach to her esophagus with a burning sensation that boiled acid to the back of her throat. Felt her eyes close, wet with tears and sweat. She would have screamed if she could. Instead, darkness arrived and escorted Cassandra into oblivion.

Part IV
The Red Carpet Ceremony

1

4:00 PM
Friday June 21, 2019
Carnival of Souls
Jigglyspot

He stood in the middle of a barren parking lot. His clowns had done well, dismantling all signs of the carnival prior to dawn. All that remained was the scent of carnival food and customer fear. Jiggly relished the fact that a hundred people had disappeared last night. Let the police try to explain that situation. And he was certain the story would never hit the news. The major networks had bigger fish to fry, and a mass disappearance had conspiracy written all over it. Why would they cover it? Plus, Jiggly knew, their mandate is to create political upheaval and social divide, and such a story would take too much time and focus away from their agendas. Jiggly shook his head, pacing across the lot, his cane tapping the concrete in unison with every other step.

Jiggly was mulling over tonight's gala in fifteen-minute increments. There was so much to do and so much to accomplish with so many working parts, Jiggly's head spun in a billion directions. And that teen still weighed heavily on him. Tyler was his name, Jiggly had learned. Lived with his father, a drunkard who didn't give more than two shits what his son did as long as he was not an inconvenience to his father. Tyler's mother was a mystery; Helmsley was working on finding out more. Tyler, Jiggly thought, Get out of my head.

Jiggly sat down on a bench. Although it was four in the afternoon, the sky was overcast with gray and black clouds that blocked the sun's rays from shedding light on the vacant lot. So dark the light next to the bench clicked on with a pale-yellow glow. Jiggly's feet dangled above the ground. Cane in his right hand, he twisted the cane in his palm.

This was Jiggly's time to prepare. His own personal tradition prior to the solstice celebration. A time to rehash his accomplishments, and a time to put together what was to come and how he will pull off another festival. Unfortunately, MysterE will not be in attendance this year, and they had torched most of the recruits from his private island at the behest of Mr. West. His reasoning was simple: if those recruits were located, everything concerning what had been going on in plain sight for so long would see the light of day and tear a hole in the fabric of space and time. Well, not really, but it would seem so, at least to Mr. West. But if those recruits were discovered, it would be difficult to suppress the story despite having all the news networks taking direction at their behest. Eventually, they would have to report the story. And how the hell would they spin it? If they weren't careful then people would learn the truth, and truth was what no one wanted. Not even those who slept silently, providing permission on the unconscious level to continue with the master's terrible parade of subliminal tyranny. Nonetheless, Jiggly always knew the truth would arrive one day and all would change in that moment. He simply wished it was not today.

Today, Jiggly thought as he ceased spinning his cane. *What to do about today?* He placed his cane across his arms, cradling the cane like a baby.

He wanted to go over the list of to-dos one more time, but his thoughts looped back to Tyler. Jiggly shook his head, grinding his teeth and jaw, then took a deep breath and touched his white spot, which started to burn and itch after he saw Tyler on the truck bed. As if the white spot understood and required Jiggly to extend the proverbial olive branch. But Tyler was different, Jiggly knew. Hidden away for so long it would take time to show the teen all he'd missed and all he was. If Tyler were raised as he should have been, he would have been under Jiggly's thumb and tutelage at an early age. Would have been shown so many wonderful revelations. But now things were compromised, and Tyler was included in tonight's festivities. Jiggly shook his head. But that can't happen. One less volunteer will not be missed. Instead of the needed one hundred, ninety-nine will have to do. And Jiggly had already handed down the fate of most of those ninety-nine volunteers, designating a purpose for each one of them. Except for Tyler, Jiggly wanted him far away from the others, at least for tonight, to give Jiggly time to pull off the solstice gala without a hitch. Tomorrow will be for him and Tyler alone. For training and programming of the Jiggly kind.

Jiggly's only concern: breaking the connection Tyler has with his fellow humans.

2

5:00 PM
Hollywood, CA
Sharon

Kevin was picking her up at seven. This was her day to shine, to bowl everyone over. And she had the power to do it. Felt it in her bones with a confident state of knowing. A newfound type of confidence, she even did things she normally wouldn't do, like walking around the apartment naked after she stepped out of the shower. Windows wide open. Let them look, Sharon thought. Especially that perv across the street. Mr. Perv is how Cassandra and Sharon referred to him. They caught him staring into their apartment on more than a few occasions. Sharon had always been skittish over the revelation, but today she welcomed his prying eyes.

Let him jack off and sit in his own mojo, hoping to get it up again before I leave. Peasants in this world need to worship what they can't have. It keeps them under the thumb, begging for more.

She studied herself in the mirror, wondering where the change had come from as a snippet of her former self slithered into her thoughts. She felt what she believed was shame. Shame over who she had been or what she had become? Had to be who she was, because she's enjoying who she is. No longer afraid or submissive, as Kevin knew all too well. Sharon craned her head to the right, following her reflection, arms stretched from her hips out, palms towards the mirror. Her hair, wet and matted, cascaded to her shoulders in thick clumps. Those thick hips, at once a point of contention, now looked sassy and sexy. Voluptuous breasts firm and perfect. And she smiled, a thin devious grin, and held her chin up. A combination of perspiration and beads of water glistened across her skin.

"Do you like what you see?" Sharon asked her reflection. She pursed her lips, nodding. "Of course, you do. You are perfect and beautiful." And she paused, turning to the left then right, studying her figure as her hands drifted to her hips, straightened her shoulders, standing tall. Grinned when she accepted the beauty that is Sharon Mable as she studied herself in the mirror. "A goddess, that's what you are." Took a deep breath. "And don't you ever forget it."

She walked to her bed and scooped her phone off the mattress. She sent a text message to Cassandra about an hour ago, demanding an answer. An answer to Sharon's inquiry. **When are you coming back? We need to talk, and you will not like it.**

No response from Cassandra. No response at all to any of the multiple messages Sharon had sent over the last week. Didn't matter though, things had changed since Cassandra left for Atlanta. And she will need to accept the new Sharon. Accept or be gone, either way didn't matter, not to Sharon, at least.

She was chewing on her bottom lip, staring at her phone, when Sharon felt eyes on her. She looked through the window. Yes, the perv was there, across the street, watching, looking, savoring Sharon's body. She could see him sitting by his window; his blinds open a smidge, but more than enough to see. He was an older perv, more than likely in his sixties. Sharon breathed shallow with a smirk across her lips, picturing the perv jacking the jack.

"Be warned, little perv, such action causes the blood to pump to that tiny little peenie. And neglect the heart."

She could feel it, sense it, and see it. The perv's ejaculation, his heart stiff, constricting as he jizzed all over his hand.

"Down you go now, little perv. Out with the old, in with the new." She gritted her teeth and clenched her fist, sensing how his heart stopped and his blood turned cold. "Die little perv, your time has come." Sharon closed her eyes and saw the perv, his eyes wide with fear. No more breath to breathe, and he slumped forward, and this slumping, this vision she indulged in, was confirmed when the perv's window blinds were disturbed. Sharon smiled and shook her head. "Little perv, little perv, you are no more." She could see how the blinds were pushed against the window, could see the perv's head was the catalyst that crinkled the blinds when his head flopped forward.

She turned on her heels, satisfied.

"One down," she said, "So many more to go."

3

5:30 PM
The Warehouse
Tyler

He woke up with a gasp and a jolt, grasping his chest, huffing and wheezing. The room was dark, pitch black, and for the first few moments Tyler thought he was in his bedroom. Started hacking. The air seemed to carry dust, and he was choking on it. Felt those tiny particles in his lungs, his head weary. Hacking and gasping for clean air, hunched over now with his hands on the floor, cold cement beneath his palms, Tyler coughed a wallop of phlegm from his throat to the ground.

His eyes wet with tears from hacking, Tyler felt beads of sweat on his forehead when he noticed how thick and hot the air was, suffocating. Felt a sting on his neck and his hand went to it, the skin sore and tight as he flopped back and smacked the back of his head on iron bars. Felt his face wince with pain as he bounced forward, his hand on the back of his head, when he noticed the surrounding darkness.

The room was so dark, Tyler couldn't see more than a few inches in front of his face. He drew in a deep breath to calm his heart, and with the exhale, the memories arrived. The carnival, those strange clowns, the Shibalba X-Press, and for a moment he felt himself spinning as if he were still on the ride. Tyler shook his head, stretching his eyelids to ward off the spinning sensation. He tried to remember what happened after the Shibalba X-Press, kept seeing that little clown instead. He could hear people talking, speaking in whispers behind the dark fold of his memory. *No fear in this one. He's not out yet. Truly special.*

Tyler moved his head left, then right, attempting to understand where he was. This all seemed surreal. *Where the fuck am I?* None of it made any sense. *What happened?* And where are his friends, Jake, Amber, Ned, and Pam?

Stay calm, he told himself. Just stay calm.

His eyes adjusting, he saw the outline of vertical bars close to where he sat, felt those same iron bars against his back.

Well, he thought, this isn't good.

He looked over his surroundings, hoping to see something or someone. An outline, skin maybe, clothes or anything. Tyler gripped an iron bar and pulled himself up, his back aching as he did so. Started feeling the bars, reached up high but couldn't reach the top, if there was a top, then kept moving, feeling, surveying with heavy breaths and a whining cry in the back of his throat. From what he could surmise, the enclosure was an eight-by-eight cell with bars so close together he couldn't fit his arm through. He searched for a door, a handle, or a segment in the enclosure that would tell him where a door might be. Nothing. *Perhaps they lowered me down. Maybe there's no ceiling and I can climb out.*

Tyler gripped the bars and pushed his knees against those bars to help pull himself up, staring towards the top that receded into darkness. He pulled up a few feet, the bars smooth and his palms tight. Heavy breaths and grunts, his arms shaking. Stretched his neck, his eyes adjusting to the dark and he could see there was a top. About eight or nine feet high, Tyler guessed. He dropped to his feet and leaned against the bars, shaking his head.

"What the fuck?"

He's not out yet.

No fear in this one.

Truly special.

"If I'm so special, why am I locked in a cage? Think Tyler, fucking think."

And he was thinking, trying to think at least, when his thoughts hit a brick wall and his mind went numb. Shallow breaths were all he could hear, *his* shallow breath, eyes wide and staring. He couldn't latch on to a single thought. Couldn't remember what he was thinking when his heart jumped to the sound of feet tapping against concrete.

Red light then beamed into the room and Tyler clamped his eyes shut. Squinting now as the red blaze washed into his eyes. Tyler blinking, eyes adjusting. Heard shuffling outside the cage, coming towards him. Stretched his eyes wide as the tapping, shuffling feet approached. Tyler saw the tiny figure bathed in a red glow approaching, his eyes scanning the girl or woman dressed in tight black leather approaching his cage. Eyes roaming from her feet to her stomach, and up to the eyes. His jaw dropped when he saw those eyes and the tentacles on top of her head.

4

5:35 PM
Cannibal Café
Jigglyspot

At the same time Tyler was discovering his visitor, Jiggly was dealing with Chef Politiere and getting an earful from the world-renowned master chef over the conditions he was forced to work in. Chef Politiere was complaining about the cleanliness of the kitchen. Not that the kitchen was dirty by any means, and Jiggly concluded Politiere required complaining as a part of his act and would have found something to bitch about even if he had to make it up out of thin air. Jiggly could care less about his complaints and would have used Mr. Scalpel to end the life of the master chef if Jiggly had time to usher in a new award-winning chef in the little time there was to prepare for solstice.

And a chef who understood the delicate nature of preparing human meat for a prominent guest list whose palates were as delicate as the baby's Politiere was about to roast over hot coals. Nope, those types of chefs are as rare as Jiggly himself, so Jiggly paid the complaints no real mind, and tuned out the French speaking, nagging, and complaining Politiere to mull over his to-do list for the night. There was so much to do, and time was ticking. Tick Tock. Tick Tock. The guest list that was more than likely at home at this very moment, sucking back cocktails and squeezing their hemmed-up bodies into today's finest fashions, will arrive between eight and nine. No red carpet for this party, although Jiggly was sure they'd parade up and down from the curb to the front door and choose to shine and glitter once the front door opened as if they were royalty or some God among men. Considering the guest list, Gods among Gods was more likely the thought than God among men.

"And what's with the clowns?"

Jiggly heard chef Politiere, although the question faded quickly. Jiggly was staring at the chef, who seemed to size Jiggly up, waiting for an answer. Gary and Helmsley behind the chef, watching the argument unfold.

"Come again?" said Jiggly.

Chef Politiere dropped his shoulders, obviously frustrated. "The clowns," he said. "What's with the clowns?"

Jiggly couldn't help but smile, looking to the right then the left, his fellow clowns were moving swiftly in the kitchen, preparing.

"I do not work in such horrible conditions," again the chef, his thick French accent rolling those r's in horrible.

Jiggly eyeballed Politiere through a scowl. Stepped closer and Politiere put his hands on his hips as if to show he had no fear. And Jiggly smiled and paused before speaking.

"Considering the circumstances," said Jiggly, his husky voice groveling. "They are the best we can get in such a short time."

"They are foul and disgusting creatures. Do they even understand washing and cleaning? Have they any experience at all? Did you smell them?" Politiere was staring at Jiggly's clowns, right hand on his hip, left hand and arm in front of his stomach, palm up, and his nose crinkled as if he'd sniffed a foul odor.

Jiggly was growing frustrated, but there was a simple solution to the good chef's concerns. "Chef Politiere, follow me, please. Need to show you something."

Politiere rolled his eyes as Jiggly walked through the kitchen to the walk-in freezer. Saw his reflection in the metal door with Politiere on his heels. Jiggly pulled the lock pin from the door handle and let it dangle on the chain attached to the wall as he propped the door open. Jiggly opened the door, stepping to the side of Politiere, whose attention remained with the clowns. His nose crinkled when he turned to the freezer and Jiggly could feel the chef's energy darken and sink. Inside was a man strapped to a chair, out cold, sleeping.

"Your husband, yes?" said Jiggly.

Politiere looked at Jiggly as Jiggly held Mr. Scalpel over the chef's groin.

"I figured you'd have complaints," Jiggly said with a slight shake of his head. "You must forgive me for the intrusion on your personal life, but what is done is done. Of course, it is. And I don't have time to stand here and listen to you bitch about fucking clowns, not with who's coming and all I have to do tonight. All you have to do is cook." Jiggly snarled at the chef. Craned his head to the right. "And if you continue bitching, I'll cut that mother fucker's throat and force you to fuck his dead corpse." Politiere swallowed his breath with a gasp, turned to his husband as Jiggly continued. "And should you not cook your finest tonight... I'll cut off your balls and shove em down his fucking throat." He pressed Mr. Scalpel against the chef's groin. "Are we clear?" Jiggly asked, shifting his head to the left. Politiere had his eyes on Jiggly's scalpel. "I said, *are we clear?*"

Politiere paused before nodding.

"Good. Now we understand each other." Jiggly reached for Politiere's shoulder and turned him around. "Then go cook, master chef." He pushed the chef forward. "And be warned," he continued as Politiere walked away. "My clowns are watching you." Jiggly slammed the freezer door shut, slid the pin in to keep it locked, and dropped Mr. Scalpel into his pocket. Leaning against the freezer door, Jiggly pinched the bridge of his nose, eyes closed.

Fucking chefs.

"Jigs?" said Helmsley. "Are you ready?"

Jiggly shook his head, then looked at Helmsley. Gary, the truck driver behind him.

"Of course," said Jiggly, "Follow me."

"Perfect," said Helmsley, "I can't wait to see the designations you've given."

5

5:40 PM
The Warehouse
Tyler

"Who are you?" asked Tyler, staring at the tiny being outside his cage.

"My name is Kera, and I am here to help you."

Tyler eyeballed Kera, who was searching the wall.

"Why?" said Tyler.

"Oh, I have my reasons."

Tyler shrugged. Why argue? he thought. Considering his current predicament, what other options did he have?

"Found it," she said over her shoulder. "Knew it had to be here somewhere. Jiggly always keeps it hidden." And she turned to Tyler. "He's so proficient." And she smiled and cocked her brow, said, "Step away."

Tyler did as instructed, looking over the cage and wondering where the door was when he heard Kera flick a switch followed by a metal clang and the cell shifted with a loud metallic bang. A moment later, the cell lifted with a mechanical hum. He watched it rise high above his head.

"Well, are you just going to stand there or are you coming with me?"

Tyler shook his head, skeptical, thinking the cage would drop the moment he attempted to cross the threshold, and crack and bludgeon his skull with irreparable damage. He looked at Kera, who had her back to him, her head moving from left to right, assessing. Tyler then turned to the cage dangling over his head. Took a deep breath and stepped out. Kera looked at him from over her shoulder.

"Good," she said. "Glad you decided to join me." She returned to searching the room.

"Where are we?" asked Tyler.

"Shh." Kera turned to him. "Follow me and be as quiet as possible."

She took off to the left and Tyler followed close behind. She halted, and Tyler stopped short. She looked left and right, then continued walking.

"Where are you taking me?" said Tyler in as soft a voice as he could manage.

"Out," she said.

"Out where?"

"Out of here," she told him. "To give you more time."

Tyler shook his head. "Time for what? I don't have time. I have friends who are here. At least... I think they're here."

"They are." Kera was moving swiftly, stopping every so often to listen and observe.

"Ok, where are they?"

"Somewhere. I really don't know exactly where, but they are here."

"Understood. I assume we're looking for them next?"

Kera shook her head. "No, Mr. Tyler. Only you."

"What?" Tyler raised his voice and stopped moving. Kera turned to him. "I can't leave without them."

Kera craned her head, staring at him. Confusion turned to pride in her eyes. "I knew you were better," she said. "You'll be good for him."

Tyler shook his head. "Good for who?"

And Kera smiled. "No matter. You will know in time."

Tyler cocked his eyebrows. Shook his head, attempting to find a rational explanation for what was happening. *Am I dreaming?*

"No, you're not dreaming," said Kera.

What the fuck?

Kera smiled, then straightened her shoulders. "If you choose to find your friends, I'm not sure of the outcome. What I do know is I can get you out right now. And with the celebration happening soon, no one will be sent to find you. You'll have at least a day's lead before they do."

"A day's lead?"

"Of course. You don't really think they'll just let you leave and not come after you, do you?"

Tyler craned his head. "I'll just call the police."

To which Kera started laughing. "That was a good joke."

"Joke, that's not a joke. They kidnapped my friends and I, not to mention everyone else on that damn ride. I'm sure the police are already following up on missing persons calls..."

She started laughing again.

"Why are you laughing?"

She stifled her laugh, put her hand over her mouth as her tentacles nestled against her cheek as if to calm her thoughts. Her eyes were wide, as if she was afraid to speak or fearful of divulging too much information. "You don't know, but you should know. You're not afraid to call the police because you believe the police will help..." She moved her head left than right. "But they will not. You must believe me. The police are compromised and limited in what they can do. The masters make it so. Because the masters have always been here. They've got their hands in everything."

He was trying to make sense of her words and beliefs. "I don't understand. You didn't expect me to go to the police?"

She shook her head. "People who shoot their friends dead don't call the police."

Tyler's eyes widened, mouth agape. Took him a few seconds to ask, "How do you know about James?"

Kera had a stare in her eyes and a look on her face likened to confusion. "Well," she said. "James told me about you. I needed more information, and he was the closest one to you."

"James? James told you about me?"

She nodded, a smile across her lips.

"Why?"

"Because..." Kera said. "It was a mutual cause and effect. I needed information and he required suggestions... he's so picky that one."

Tyler cocked his head back. *What?*

Kera turned and started walking. Tyler followed a second later.

"Do you know where my friends are?"

Kera shook her head and stopped walking. "No, but they *are* in here. For what purpose only Jigglyspot knows."

"Jigglyspot?" Tyler asked. "The poka..."

"No, the clown. Common misconception." And she giggled. "Jigglyspot was tasked with summer solstice celebration this year. Your friends are more than likely in one of two situations."

She turned down a long hallway, hurrying down the hall. She had a confidence about her, the way she walked and talked. Tyler found it rather sexy despite those strange tentacles on her head. He wondered how she got them.

"What?" Tyler asked. "What are the two situations?"

She picked up her pace and Tyler noticed her feet were bare. Webbed toes, too. Noticed those tentacles were turned in his direction and staring directly at him as if she had eyes on the back of her head. Are they staring at me? Tyler thought when he looked over his shoulder and saw nothing. Turned back and confirmed those tentacles were indeed watching him.

No response from Kera. She stopped at the end of the hall, scanning both directions.

"Kera? What two situations?"

She was studying the two halls; one went left the other right.

"Kera?"

She seemed to grow frustrated. "Either they have been selected to be hosts..."

"Hosts?" said Tyler. "Hosts for what?"

"Not for what, for whom? And the whom would be the masters."

"Okay," Tyler muttered, confused. "What's the second?"

Kera answered as she started down the hall to the right. "Food," she said. "In honor of solstice. It's a tradition to feast on human flesh and with Mr. E's current predicament, rations are in short supply, so Jiggly had to act fast. There's so many coming for solstice this year, he required additional provisions. Might not taste as good. Baby flesh always tastes better than the older counterpart. Which makes sense if you think about it. Would you rather eat a fresh spring lamb or an old cow?" Tyler wasn't sure if she was asking an actual question or if she was being facetious. Didn't matter, she kept talking without skipping a beat. "If I ate meat, I'm sure I'd prefer the soft succulent flesh of the young over the wrinkled and worn skin of the old. That baby meat probably falls right off the bone. The younger the better is what I'm told. Although, I wouldn't know. I don't eat meat." She paused, and Tyler halted behind her.

"Are you telling me they're eating us?"

"Yes, but I forgot, there is a third option." She started walking again.

"Great, this should be rich. What is it?"

"Breeders. The island needs new breeders."

And Tyler thought, What... the... fuck?

6

5:45 PM
The Warehouse
Jigglyspot

"We have a few marinating already," said Jiggly, leading Helmsley and Gary through a long, dark corridor. He could already hear the whimpers, muffled grunts, and cries as they approached the double doors. "They'll satisfy the feast. And thanks to Gary and some very fine covert driving, the main course was salvaged."

Gary said, "Jigs, does that mean we have more for the island?"

Jiggly threw his hands in the air. "That it does. Our island factory will be replenished soon, and all will go back to normal."

Helmsley said, "What happens to the hosts once the masters leave?"

Jiggly stopped in front of the double door, Helmsley and Gary too. He searched his pockets for the key. "They'll go back to everyday life, agent Helmsley. Much like..." He found the key in his back pocket and made a mental note not to keep it there. One never knows what's lurking behind you in the warehouse. Inserted the key into the lock. "Much like our good friend, Detective Mills."

"How do they not remember?" Helmsley, he appeared genuinely concerned and Jiggly had a fleeting thought that the man was not operating on all cylinders. He should know this information already.

Jiggly eyeballed Helmsley, scanning him from head to toe, and noticed his increased heart rate and pupil dilation. Could be that after last night's extraction, he lost more than a few brain cells. But did he lose more than he could spare was the question on Jiggly's mind. The baseball cap on Helmsley's head had dried blood stained across the rim, which meant the bleeding had stopped, which was always a good sign. His skin was flushed, pale, and moist with dark circles under his eyes and cracked and bloodied lips from when he'd bit down too hard. Another mental note, check on Helmsley after tonight. Jiggly turned the key and the dead bolt snapped open. "They never truly forget," Jiggly said, opening the door as a fresh wallop of stale heat rushed across them. "The memory exists in the subconscious. Most don't want to remember what happened. They choose to keep the memory stuffed down in the subconscious." Jiggly looked at Helmsley and Gary, pausing in front of the open door. A hush, scuffling, scuttling, and gasps could be heard from within the room. "Such is the way of the human mind. Forget your nightly sins and live under the blindness of the sun."

Helmsley shrugged and Gary smiled, his yellow teeth prominent in the dark.

"Who will serve as hosts for Emmanuelle and the Dark Lord?"

"Why, my dear agent Helmsley, that is what our good friend Mills is for. The Dark Lord has selected him as his new host. And Emmanuelle has already chosen hers." Jiggly looked up as if he could see the stars from the hallway. "The induction ceremony will be spectacular." He turned to Helmsley and Gary. "A true and rare sight to see, gentlemen." Jiggly watched as Gary laughed, and Helmsley nodded.

"Cool," said Helmsley, bobbing his head and shoulders continuously as if he were an over excited kindergartener who couldn't wait for show and tell to start. A reaction that irritated Jiggly to his core.

Stupid Human Scum, Jiggly thought, referring to Helmsley. *He's gone zero intellect.* He shook his head, biting his bottom lip. *I'll have to run a diagnostic on him later tonight, after the celebration.* Jiggly raised his chin. "Be ready, gentlemen. Time is wasting and we have much to do. The masters will be here once the sun passes the baton to night."

Jiggly led them into the warehouse, a large open area lined with cages. A separate cage on each of the three walls. The room glowed with red light. Women, adult women, were in the cages on the left and the right, divided by age between under thirty and over thirty.

In between, on the back wall, was the third cage that housed the adult men. Jiggly started counting.

"Why don't they speak?" asked Helmsley.

Jiggly rolled his eyes, shaking his head. "Agent Helmsley," he said, and Helmsley turned to him. "Please be quiet." He raised his hand to show his fingers. "I'm counting."

"Oh, sorry Jigs. I just wanted to know why they aren't speaking?"

"It's the medicine," said Gary. "Paralyzes the vocal cords. Won't last long, though. I'm sure the effects will wear off soon."

Jiggly eyeballed Gary with a scowl and Gary's eyes went wide when he saw that scowl. Gary put his hands up; surrendering and apologizing to Jiggly in the same gesture as he mouthed the words, *I'm sorry.*

Jiggly shook his head, then started counting. Once he ticked off the final number—sixty-eight to be precise—Jiggly started searching. He could use two more in the yard; women, of course. They always need women for the island. As for the men, Jiggly could get away with using just one if necessary, as long as he was a potent son of a bitch. But since the masters preferred feasting from a plethora of human genetics, having an eclectic mix of men was always in good form and helped boost appropriate nutrition. Although in these trying times, we all do what we must, and Jiggly's top concern was not securing male volunteers for the island, but with gathering as many females as possible. Women can only carry one seed at a time and were required in greater numbers than their male counterparts. Sometimes they got lucky and sprouted a litter of two or three, and once they received seven. On that day, MysterE popped a bottle of champagne. Jiggly remembered the day fondly.

His concentration—remembering MysterE and all the fun they had over the last few decades—was broken by his prisoners, whose muffled grunts and rattling on the cell bars rose to a high level as more and more prisoners did the same.

"What are we looking for?" asked Helmsley, shouting over the rising commotion.

"Two more for the yard," Jiggly said. "Sixty-six is the magic number for the hosts and we have sixty-eight. So, two lucky volunteers will do us well to help boost productivity on the island." He scanned the volunteers, his eyes roaming, ignoring the clanking and rattling cages that reached a fever pitch.

"Oh my," said Jiggly, and he turned to Helmsley and Gary. "They are quite the rowdy bunch." And he laughed; Helmsley and Gary did too. Jiggly bunched up his clown outfit and strode over to the under thirty female cage as the inhabitants gasped and moved to the far back, some huddling close together.

Jiggly surveyed his choices, looking for what he hoped would be fresh, unused wombs. Kids were always getting pregnant at an early age these days, most often ending in aborting the poor thing. Don't they know, Jiggly once said, we can use those babies for the masters? Which had given Jiggly the idea to pay off the necessary doctors and agencies for the dead fetuses. An idea that helped raise Jiggly's stock with Mr. West. He scanned across every female when he discovered a skinny blonde with blue eyes and curly hair, sitting with her arms wrapped around her knees. A blank and lost stare in her eyes, Jiggly wondered if she'd come to the awareness that she was a prisoner and wouldn't be making it home anytime soon. Late twenties, Jiggly surmised. Fresh too. He could sense there was never a baby in that womb. He felt his smile brighten and his eyes gleam. She never so much as gave Jiggly a look, kept her head down, staring at the floor. She'll give us at least a good ten years, Jiggly thought. Maybe more if she stays healthy. Looks like a breeder and a cradler. She'll be good at keeping the young ones from going off the deep end. Plus, it'll be humorous to witness one of those little boys satisfying his loins with an older woman. Always is, Jiggly thought and laughed out loud when he felt a tremble erupt in his gut that was immediately followed by tension in his lower spine. Jiggly craned his head, scanning the female with wide eyes, sensing what existed beneath the folds. And Jiggly smiled with the revelation that this woman could mean more to the cause than just a breeder. Jiggly has an uncanny knack for discovering raw talent and this one just needed a little convincing, and she'll be on board with whatever Jiggly required. Satisfied, he turned his attention to the rest of the pack, all huddled together in the cage.

His eyes roamed again, seeking, searching, feeling, and finding. Jiggly grinned while looking her over. She couldn't be more than twenty-two. Dark hair and green eyes. Always a good combination. She was standing with her back to the cage, standing tall too, staring at Jiggly. She must be six feet tall, Jiggly thought. Although it was difficult to see the girl's stomach with all the other ladies huddled together in front of her, but Jiggly knew. Knew she would produce. He had that knack Jiggly did. The knack for spotting a breeder when he saw one.

Jiggly stuck his finger between the bars, pointing at the green-eyed gem. "You," he said, then shifted his gaze and his finger to the young blonde lass sitting on the floor with her knees squeezed against her chest beneath her jaw. "And you. Time to go, ladies." Jiggly backed away from the cage. His green-eyed gem stood paralyzed, her eyes staring at Jiggly. The blonde lass never moved. In shock, Jiggly thought. And that was good because she won't give them too much trouble. "Approach the door, ladies. The rest of you *stand back*," Jiggly shouted. "You'll all have your place and time soon."

Muffled whimpers and panic spread through the cage as the women not selected moved to the back. Neither the green-eyed babe nor the blonde lass moved. Jiggly craned his head. "Let's go ladies. I haven't got all day." He shook his head, then said to Helmsley, "Get the cattle prod."

"Cattle prod?" repeated Helmsley.

"Yeah." Jiggly stared at Helmsley. "Get the cattle prod." He pointed to the cattle prod attached to the wall beside the door they came through.

"Ok. The cattle prod."

Jiggly watched as Helmsley stood in the same spot, shifting his head left, then right. Jiggly shook his head and looked at Gary, who couldn't help but laugh.

"I think you dug too deep with that drill, Jiggs. The guy's brain is like pea soup."

"Well, can you help me out then, Gary, and get the cattle prod?"

Gary's eyes flickered with delight. "Of course," he replied. "I love the cattle prod."

Jiggly felt like he was in charge of a romper room of kids who rode into town on the short bus. Said kids being Helmsley and Gary. Gary, he could understand, the man had to be exhausted after such a long trip. Helmsley, on the other hand, well, silently Jiggly cursed himself for drilling too hard. He definitely did some damage to Helmsley's cerebral cortex. Something he will need to remedy, somehow and someway. Shit happens every so often, Jiggly told himself. Sometimes I go a little too deep. He smiled when Gary offered him the cattle prod.

"Nope, all you Gary. I'll open the door." He turned to Helmsley. "Detective?" he called.

"Me?" said Helmsley.

"Make sure no one runs out of the cage, please."

Helmsley looked over the cage, nodding. "Right," he said and shrugged. "Not a problem. My training with the CIA puts me as the perfect prospect to…"

"Helmsley," Jiggly hollered. "Enough."

"Well, okay."

Jiggly shook his head, then took the key from his pocket and unlocked the cage. "Back away," he ordered, then pointed to the blonde lass as he walked into the cage with Gary on his heels. "Stick that one first."

Gary tested the cattle prod, his eyes delighted with the electrical current, then pressed it to the young blonde lass who jolted back against the ground, fishtailing with quick jerks of her head, legs and feet. Jiggly looked at Helmsley. "Pull her out, detective." Jiggly turned his attention to the green-eyed babe wearing a scowl that Jiggly found rather erotic. "Next," he said, staring at the babe, returning her scowl with a grin. He could hear Helmsley drag the blonde lass from the cage.

"I'll get her Jiggs," said Gary as he approached the green-eyed babe cautiously.

But before he could get too close, she jumped on him, caught the cattle prod in her left hand and gripped Gary's throat with her free hand, attempting to push and trip him up. This is when the rest of the sixty-six started wailing on their cages.

"They're like animals," Helmsley hollered. "Fascinating."

Jiggly looked at him briefly, his mouth agape. He definitely drilled too hard; Helmsley seemed like a different person. He wasn't too bright to begin with. I mean, the man is working for the CIA, but this latest dense intellect is a bit unbecoming of an officer. Jiggly returned his gaze to Gary, who was struggling with the green-eyed babe wrestling for control of the cattle prod. Jiggly thought about helping him, but did he really have to do everything?

"Come on Gary. I know you're tired, but jeez, can we get moving here?"

"I'll get her," said Helmsley, stepping past Jiggly. When he reached for the babe, the raging cattle prod met his hand and Helmsley fell back with a thud, landing unconscious in the cage.

Gary noticed him, and the young babe punched Gary in the gut then jumped on top of him and they dropped to the floor with a thud.

Jiggly shook his head. Fuckers can't do a damn thing right. He grabbed Mr. Scalpel from his pocket, stepped behind the green-eyed babe, and slit her throat from ear to ear with an immediate gush of blood that rained over Gary. He didn't want to do it-she would have brought in a good amount of product-but felt he had to. To show her who really was in charge, and the others, too. Her body slumped to the floor, blood pooling beneath her body. And Gary sat up, covered in blood with the cattle prod now in hand as he looked at the other prisoners, and clumsily stood up.

"Great job, Gary." Jiggly shook his head. "Anything else I can help you with?"

"Sorry Jiggs." Gary breathed deeply, wiping the blood from his face and stretching his eyelids.

"Drag Helmsley out. I'll need your help with the young lass."

"What should we do with him?"

"Helmsley? Leave him here for now."

Gary dragged Helmsley from the cage as Jiggly watched the other prisoners, Mr. Scalpel still in hand, dripping with blood.

"What about her?" Gary pointed to the dead green-eyed babe.

Jiggly backed out of the cage, slamming the door shut.

"Leave her where she is." He locked the door. "A message to anyone who wants to cause trouble." Took long strides backward. He looked over the cages, addressing his prisoners. "Ladies and gentlemen do yourselves a favor and be good. There's no reason for any more bloodshed. Take comfort in knowing that once the sun disappears from the horizon, none of this carnage will matter to any of you. And tomorrow, you'll all wake up at home, comfy in your own beds."

More whimpers and grunts erupted from his announcement, slamming, and rocking on their cages. Jiggly turned his gaze to the young blonde lass that Gary was hoisting over his shoulder.

"I got her Jiggs."

Jiggly bowed. "Thank you, Gary," he said, noticing the perplexed look on Gary's face.

"What is it, my man?" Jiggly hand gestured for Gary to lead the way. "What troubles you?"

Gary started walking, the young blonde lass over his shoulder. "Ya know, Jiggs, what I don't understand is how we account for all these people missing from their homes and families? Seems like a lot of people to make disappear all at once."

"That's the easy part," said Jiggly, following Gary. "People will believe anything nowadays. And when they all arrive home tomorrow, all will be as normal, but with a slight difference. They'll seem strange is all, not to themselves but to those who know them. Always as if something's different or something's missing. But they'll be home and that's all that really matters to people, that their loved ones are home even if they're not present. The trick is in the programming. As time goes by, all the seeds planted decades ago manifest for today. Zero Intellect is what I call it. The morons will believe just about anything you want them to. Like cattle and they don't even know it. And it's not like they can't do their own research to find the truth, they just choose not to. Why spend the time when time is money and time is busy and you can get the story from your favorite news station? Mental baby food is what those news stations pump out time and time again, every one of them. Doesn't matter what side they preach to, they all have the same puppeteer pulling the strings. And it's addictive too, considering the subliminal musical composition behind each story. Our research showed that a subliminal symphonic undertone opens the third eye, and we can slip the messages in easy. Those phones too. Little notifications and a pulse with an accurate wavelength sent right through the phone during sleeping hours strengthens the message." Jiggly laughed when he said it. "That's why I never use a phone. Damn things are the devil."

"Sounds like a plan, but I'm still unsure how we do it. Guess I should just trust the process, right? It's not like we haven't done it before. Well, not like you haven't done it before. I'm just here for the ride."

"True Gary. Very true." Jiggly stepped in front of Gary to the double doors. "Let me get that for you."

"Thank you, Jiggs. She's not that heavy, but she is tall, so it's an awkward carry."

"You're doing fine, my man."

"I wonder who she is in real life. Don't you wonder too?" Gary stepped through the doors. Jiggly followed close behind.

"Don't have to wonder," Jiggly said. "We went through everyone's license and Helmsley did background checks. A few we had to let go for... well, different reasons, really. Mostly conflicts with the masters." Jiggly followed Gary down the hall. "This one, though, this blonde lass, is a schoolteacher. Ms. Finicky I believe."

"Finicky," Gary repeated. "That's a funny name. She doesn't seem finicky."

"Not at all, Gary," said Jiggly, "Not at all."

7

6:00 PM
The Warehouse
Lilly

She couldn't take her eyes off the dead girl lying on the floor with her throat cut. Lilly had tried to keep her eyes closed after it happened, hoping she'd wake up in her bed when she opened them, grateful the nightmare was over, but the panic forced her eyes open. And this isn't a nightmare, is it? Lilly thought. It's all real, just like the girl lying dead in a pool of her own blood. Maybe she thought she was in a nightmare, too. Now look at her? Dead. Life over. Into the ether like Tad.

Lilly woke up in the cell she was in now. Woke up to a blinding red light, muffled grunts, and rattling steel. Woke up to see Kathy sitting in the corner beside her, holding her knees and rocking back and forth. Took a few minutes for Lilly to notice she lost the ability to speak. With so many thoughts and questions rifling through her mind, she first thought she was speaking, but Kathy just looked at her with a crooked stare and gestured to her own throat while mouthing silent words. Nonetheless, all Lilly heard from Kathy were grunts and whines. This is when Lilly saw the cage, her eyes drifting, already annoyed with Mrs. Crawford. Saw all the people locked in with her, walking, pacing, sitting or rocking in silent servitude. They looked like cattle waiting for the slaughter. Spring lambs on the verge of annihilation, and her thoughts went to Christopher when Lilly jumped up, searching for him.

The room was large. A warehouse, Lilly was sure. Cages lined the walls, one on each side except the entrance. She counted sixty-eight adults—now sixty-six—with the majority in the men's cage. Why are the women separated? Lilly assumed the separation had something to do with age since the women in the cage opposite Lilly's held women who appeared much younger than Lilly. No kids, though. No children anywhere. No Jenny Crawford, no Christopher. Her Christopher. She turned to Kathy, still sitting with tears in her eyes.

Lilly waved her hands, caught Kathy's attention and mouthed the words, *Kids? Where are the kids?*

Her inquiry received the painful, worried stare of Kathy Crawford, shaking her head, and mouthing the words *I don't know*.

Lilly started shaking the cage. The thick steel bars barely moved, so she banged on the bars. Her act followed by more adults doing the same. This is when the short little clown came in, followed by two other men. Lilly would swear she saw the clown before and the three of them seemed more like a comedy act than captors. And that debacle with the cattle prod was just dumb, according to Lilly. These guys have no clue what they're doing. At least that's what Lilly thought until the little one cut the girl's throat. And they took Finicky with them, leaving the really dense guy lying on the floor, out cold from the cattle prod.

And Lilly remained standing, watching the blood from the cut throat spread like lava towards the other women in the opposite cage. Cries and whimpers filled the warehouse and Lilly put her hand to her throat, massaging, probing, wondering why she couldn't talk when she remembered what that guy Gary had said.

It's the medicine. Paralyzes the vocal cords. Won't last long, though.

She massaged her throat, hoping the result would be the ability to speak. Even coughed and hacked, then hummed, pursing her lips and piecing together the events that resulted in becoming locked in this damn cage.

What's the last memory? The last thing I remember?

Dropping off Sam. Christopher. The diner. Jenny and Kathy Crawford. The fly she caught. Then the carnival. This is where the memories fizzled like super fuzz with a smear across the back of the eyes. She remembered clowns. Clowns everywhere. And a clown who offered a free ride. What was the ride called? Lilly massaged her throat again. Shibalba X-Press, she thought, attempting to speak the words. Moving her lips phonetically. Hummed. Coughed. Hummed. Hacked. Hummed. Sh-i-bal-ba. Sh-shi-bal-ba-ex-press. Frustration. Hummmmmmmmmmmed, her lips fluttering, feeling the hum in the back of her throat.

"SHIBALBA." The word hollered over her lips. She paused. "Shibalba X-Press," she said, although this time the tone reflected a question as she looked at each person in her cage. All eyes on Lilly. "Shibalba X-Press?" she asked again, receiving head nods and wide eyes registering the word, the ride, with confirmation they were all on the ride.

She continued. "Is that the last you all remember?" Her eyes darting from one prisoner to the next. More head nods.

That's how they got us, she thought. Her eyes downtrodden, trying to think and remember the carnival. Instinctively, she reached for her phone in her back pocket. Nothing was there. Of course not. Of course, they'd take the phones. Probably everything and anything we had, too. Which means they know everything about us. About all of us. Lilly scanned across the warehouse. Looked at the cages and the eyes that stared back, lost and confused, as if she were some savior because she figured out how to speak before the rest of them. They all had the same stare, restless with fear of the unknown.

The unknown, Lilly thought when she closed her eyes. Thinking of Sam and her mother, waiting for Lilly to arrive and the disappointment on Sam's face when she doesn't. How long will it be before Lilly's mother calls the police? But will it matter? Look at all the people here. And where are the children? Where is Christopher? Jenny Crawford? How many people did these sadistic monsters actually take off the Shibalba X-Press? Lilly guessed the number must be close to a hundred, considering all the adults right here in this room with her. Maybe more. How? How is it possible that all these people can go missing all in the same place and they get away with it?

Think, Lilly. Think!

The setup. The carnival. All these cages. This was a planned event. But planned for how long and for what or who? Why do they need all of us? And where the hell is Christopher? Where are the kids? What are they doing to them? They took Finicky for a reason. What did the little guy say? Lilly tried to remember; the words floating across her brain, cloudy and moving like waves of water flooding her mind. He said they only need sixty-six. Sixty-six, Lilly repeated. Why that number?

Lilly gritted her teeth, attempting to piece together this dire debacle when the man on the floor twitched. Others saw it too. Lilly saw their eyes move to see him. Helmsley, she thought. Something like that. *Didn't he say he was CIA?* Lilly wasn't one hundred percent certain, but it was a possibility. There was so much going on, so much blood pumping with worry and fear in the moments before the cattle prod debacle and the cut throat, but he did say something along those lines and was hushed by the little guy.

CIA?

Why?

The man twitched again.

The cattle prod effect must be wearing thin.

He jolted up; his arms limp by his sides. She watched as he fumbled to his feet. Lilly heard gasps and constricted huffs from within the cages. He leaned forward, seemed like he was going to fall over, and Lilly thought his movement was odd, as if some invisible force had picked him up and was moving his limbs with minimal support from the host.

And his eyes snapped open, staring straight at Lilly. His arms shook by his side, followed by his head, trembling and shuddering, as his eyes rolled to the back of his skull. His lips tight, his jaw clenched, his head wriggling so violently Lilly thought his brain was going to explode. Phlegm spit from his mouth and whipped across the open room. Lilly had a passing thought that something was inching its way up into his brain. Some phantom or demon Lilly couldn't see. His mouth opened wide with a loud gasp and all the shaking stopped. He took several gasps, deep heavy breaths as if he needed to catch his breath. Lilly craned her head, watching, mesmerized, when his eyes changed. She watched it happen, looked like black smoke crept into his eyeballs from some unknown source, slithering across the whites of his eyes. Lilly watched through narrow eyes when her hand went to her mouth, watching as his eyes turned to black.

8

6:15 PM
The Warehouse
Tyler

Kera held the door open. Outside and waiting was Tyler's freedom.

"What is this?" asked Tyler.

"This is your chance. Perhaps your one and only. To get out of here. To start a new life. Hide under cover because they will search for you. That's a guarantee."

"What about my friends? All the other people? We need to help them not run away."

Kera seemed to grow tense. Tyler could see how her arms constricted when she clenched her fists. Saw her jaw move, grinding her teeth.

Tyler shook his head. "What is it? I don't get it."

He watched Kera turn to the outside. The setting sun was just over the horizon. A warm breeze rushed through the door. And Tyler thought, Why am I not moving? He saw Pam followed by Jake and Amber, then Ned Tatty. Where are they? Where are his friends? When he looked up, Kera's tentacles were looking at him with a stare Tyler assumed was empathy, although Kera's eyes were downtrodden, as if she were involved in the thought process of regret.

"Kera?" Tyler's voice a whisper carried on the heels of sympathy. "You okay?"

"I guess I expected something different," she said.

"What do you mean, different?"

Kera looked at him. "People who kill their friends don't risk their eternal soul for them. I came here to get you out, so you could help Jigglyspot. To give you time to see him in a different light, like I do. And then maybe you could help him. But this is unexpected, your desire to help your friends after you hunted down and watched one of them die by your hand. It's baffling, to be honest. I don't understand."

Tyler retorted with, "James Reilly was a drug dealing, woman raping, sadistic pig who bullied me my entire life. Me and a slew of others." He was shaking his head. "The damage he would have caused to so many people across his lifetime would have been catastrophic. I couldn't allow him to live."

"Oh," was all she said.

"And I'd do it again if I thought it was necessary."

Kera pursed her lips, nodding. "That would make you judge, jury, *and* executioner." She cleared her throat. "What gives you the right?"

Tyler was quick with his answer. "God," he said. "The crime is standing by and doing nothing when you know injustice continues. Even if Reilly was arrested, he would have received a slap on the wrist because that's what money can buy. If it were me, I'd be going to jail with a public pretender in my corner for the better part of my life. But Reilly..." He shook his head. "His high-priced uptown lawyer would have him home within an hour and the story buried within a week. I refuse to live by that standard. The rich get away with everything while the poor suffer around every corner. I'm tired of the rich game, they're not the end all be all of human existence."

She turned to the outside, and the golden sunset draped with purple effervescence. Seemed to be contemplating, gnawing on her bottom lip as if a new universe had been discovered, although she had to shut the door on the discovery. Now wasn't the right time.

"Jiggly used to hold those beliefs, too." Kera reached for the door handle. "But the path of murder leads to a darkened heart and soul. Corruption of the mind." She pulled the door closed and Tyler glimpsed the setting sun just before that new universe was shut out and the hall became bathed in darkness. Kera's eyes a beam of white light in that darkness. "I was hoping to put you on a different path, so that Jiggly could see there's still time." She wiped her eyes, although Tyler could see no tears as her tentacles rubbed against her neck and face as if to comfort her. "Still time to change his ways, no matter how far he's gone."

"You love this Jigglyspot, don't you?"

Kera looked up at Tyler. "Yes," she said.

"Well, I love my friends too, and I can't leave them here. They don't have the balls to do what's necessary to survive. They'll need my help." He swallowed his breath with a thick wallop down his throat.

"Ok, Mr. Tyler," said Kera. "Let's go find your friends."

9

7:05 PM
Hollywood, CA
Sharon

A stretch limo. Kevin rented a stretch limo for the occasion. At first Sharon was irritated when he was late, but then the limo turned onto her street, and all was forgiven.

Besides, it's good to be fashionably late. All high society elites arrive late because only the meek nobodies arrive early. And this was her night. Sharon's party and all were waiting for her. Let them wait, she thought. It's good for them to learn patience and pay homage to the queen.

These were the thoughts running through Sharon's mind as Kevin escorted her to the limo. On cue, the driver opened the door with a slight nod of acknowledgement. People on the sidewalk watching as Sharon took Kevin's hand and sat in the limo. Perfect, Sharon thought, Let them see my rising star. One day they'll wish for a picture and an autograph. They'll get neither.

Sharon was so lost in her thoughts she never noticed the ambulance across the street. Kevin mentioned the scene after he took his seat.

"Poor soul," Kevin said.

Sharon followed his stare, looking through the window, and saw the EMTs pushing a gurney to the ambulance. A sheet covered the body lying on top of the gurney. And Sharon smiled.

"Ahh," said Sharon. "The perv is no more. Serves him right." And she turned to Kevin. "A perfect start to a fantastic evening."

10

7:30 PM
The Warehouse Somewhere Shiny Room
Jigglyspot

This was Jiggly's time to prepare, applying his makeup and mulling over the evening's events. Greeting his new guests was first on his list, followed by the ceremony and the incarnation of the sixty-six. Then the Goddess' sacrifice followed by Emmanuelle's new form. From there, things get spicy with the offering of blood.

Jiggly spread white paint across his face and head. His hair had grown to a thin carpeted fuzz. He observed the white spot on his head, now covered in paint. Jiggly took a sponge from the counter and blotched the paint off his white spot.

Jiggly recanted previous blood offerings and how they erupted into a sexual frenzy; human blood being an aphrodisiac otherworldly beings could never control even if they wanted to. Sacrifices will then be made to the masters, presenting a lust of power and control. Sometimes-and Jiggly laughed at this-those sacrifices get turned on the offerer, especially if someone has not been holding their weight. Then the presentation of the new brood, followed by their indoctrination through fear and sadism, to prove their loyalty. Finally, one lucky member will be chosen to provide extraction for the group. Jiggly thought about who this lucky person will be.

Hopefully, one of those fresh babes, Jiggly thought, applying black paint beneath his eyes with a thin brush. Just a thin smear, Jiggly thought. His eyes sparkled in the mirror. Perfect touch. He then drew three inverted five-pointed stars beginning below his right eye with the last above his mouth and off to the right. One star larger than the other, although not by much. Stars made to look like tears. Jiggly smiled at his reflection. Took up the red face paint.

"Then the feast will begin," said Jiggly with a tight lip, drawing his voice from his diaphragm. He stretched his face close to the mirror, observing his thin lips before spreading red paint over them, thinking, those little lambs and some tasty surprises. He couldn't help but laugh, pausing his application of red paint. Don't want to mess it up and start all over, Jiggly thought. "Nope. *Times a wasting*," Jiggly sang.

Jiggly pursed his lips, now bright red. Frown or smile? Jiggly knew where he was going; today required a smile for the clown. He pulled it off, this Luciferian nightmare, and he has every right to be proud. He dabbed his index fingers into the red paint, then spread his lips into a tooth filled grin, tightening his jaw. With those painted fingertips, Jiggly spread thin red lines from the corners of his mouth and out across his cheeks about halfway to the bottom of his ears. Saw his eyes in the mirror, sparkling mad as he tensed his facial muscles and pulled those thin red lines up to just below his eyes. He then outlined those red lines with black paint that provided the appearance that the red lines narrowed towards the eyes into a fine, pointed tip.

Crinkled his nose with a snarl. Started posing, pursed lips then a frown, small lips then a kiss as he laughed and chuckled, enjoying the product he'd put together. "Oh, then the Dark Lord will come." Jiggly pinched a dark purple make up case in his right hand. "Thank you, detective Mills." Jiggly popped the top off the makeup case, then took a clean sponge, and dipped the sponge into the paint. "And that's when..." Jiggly applied the dark purple to his eyebrows, right then left, then drew thin lines that stretched from the end of each eyebrow and up towards the hairline. He then used a thin comb to skewer those eyebrows to an up position and the same black brush to outline the purple lines. "The good stuff happens," said Jiggly as he observed his artistic expression. Jiggly washed his hands, then dried them off. Took up his clown hat, the little one, and stretched the string under his chin. The hat sat perfectly crooked. Jiggly loved the job he did. He took up his cane. "Can't forget about you, my dear." He tapped the cane on the tile floor, then posed in the mirror. His transformation now complete.

"Brilliant," he said to his reflection. "The Dark Lord will be pleased."

11

7:45 PM
The Warehouse
Lilly

At the same time Jiggly was turning himself into a work of art, Lilly
was watching the CIA agent. He'd gotten up—this is when he's eyes
turned an inky black—and stumbled backward, falling onto his back
where he remained until he jolted back up a moment ago with a
heavy gasp that echoed across the room then faded with a struggled,
constricted breath. His hand over his chest as he sat on the floor as
if waiting for the cattle prod effect to wane. Then the eruption of
grunts and rattling cages shook the foundation, although with
limited influence on the CIA agent still sitting with his head in his
hands and elbows on his knees.

He looked like he was going to vomit. Lilly noticed how pale his
complexion had turned, his face flushed with red blotches scattered
across his skin. His hat crooked on his head; Lilly was surprised the
baseball cap hadn't jettisoned from his skull when he fell. Now he
was holding his stomach. Lilly looked over the cages and the other
people locked in those cages, grunting and shaking the bars like
monkeys in a lab. Petrified and angry stares plastered across each
visage. The agent's eyes fluttered behind lazy eyelids as his hand
drifted to his forehead. Lilly noticed his expression when his fingers
brushed across his cap—as if he wasn't aware the cap was there—and
a moment later that same hand brushed across his scalp beneath the
hat that dropped backward off his skull.

Sudden gasps and hushed breaths from the monkeys and Lilly's
eyes went wide, her hand to her mouth.

He had no skull, the top of his brain revealed beneath the hat.
Lilly heard vomiting and hacking around the room. Looked to her

left and the woman whose stomach bile splattered beside her feet. Lilly stepped away. Vomit she could deal with, have a couple of kids, you'll get used to tossed up cookies. Lilly turned back to the agent. His skull, from what she could see, was cracked just below the cut line as if someone had drilled into his skull before removing it. Dried blood crusted around his skull from what must have been streams of blood when the removal occurred. Hence the hat, Lilly thought, to cover up the exposed brain. Now he turned over, elbows on the floor as he pushed himself up slowly, carefully, to his feet. He swayed but caught himself, his back now to Lilly and she could see a tube had been inserted into the top of his brain that looped to the back of his skull where she could see the tube was clamped to the agent's ear. He patted his head, his hand jostled when he touched his own brain. Touched his brain again with quick and short pats, then felt the tube, followed it over to the ear.

Lilly saw the dead girl again, amazed by the amount of blood that pooled around the body. So much blood the pool had stretched into a circle large enough to cover the cage floor. Turned back to the agent, who seemed to gather some semblance of stability. Lilly pursed her lips, swallowed hard. This was her chance, maybe her one and only.

"Mister, can you help us?" Her voice was low, barely above a whisper. She felt eyes on her. Eyes from the other cages. Eyes from her cage. She cleared her throat. "Sir? Can you please let us out?"

The agent turned around. His eyes were no longer black, instead they revealed an emerald twinkle as he bent his head, staring at Lilly, confused.

"This is the body," he said. Lilly wasn't sure if that was a question or a statement. His head lolled back, stretching his neck as his eyelids fluttered under the light above. He closed his eyes and shook his head, then snapped his eyes open. Turned back to Lilly. "This brain is mush makes it hard to think."

"Someone hurt you," Lilly said. "I think it was the little guy who did it. He hurt you like he did to that girl in the cage." Lilly pointed through the bars and the agent followed her finger.

"That's a shame," said the agent.

"He'll do the same to you, I'm sure. If given the chance or if he had to. Look what he's already done to you." She shook her head. "You poor thing. You shouldn't have to live like that."

"I think I chose the wrong body," he said, then turned to face Lilly. "This one's so difficult to take hold of. It's like... struggling to think." He touched his skull just below the cut line. His face cringed. "Competing thoughts... so hard to... put... words together."

Lilly saw her chance. "I can help you," she said. "You need help. Let me help you."

His lips moved, but his voice wasn't in sync with his lips. "That's not what Jiggly wants. He'd have my head if I let you out."

Lilly felt her eyes grow wide. She shook her head. "Looks like he already took your head."

The agent started laughing. "That he did. Sometimes he just goes too far. Not his fault really, he just can't help himself." Then his eyes clamped shut, his head shaking, quivering. Eyes open again, looking over the room. "This is so hard." Lilly noticed the agent said this as if he were talking to himself. "This may take time." He shook his head. "I don't have time." He closed his eyes again. "I have to be precise. Have to be in the right place at exactly the right time." Opened his eyes. "Why's everything got to be such a test?" He was shaking his head. "I'm tired of fucking tests." His voice a whining plea.

He seemed distraught, as if some internal conflict were weighing heavy on that mashed up brain. He leaned over and picked up his hat, fit the cap over his skull, carefully. Lilly watched as his eyes reflected some sudden awareness, looking over the cages and the people in them, all staring with wide, fearful eyes. He shook his head, turned on his heels and started walking towards the door.

Panicked grunts, rattling cages erupted. Lilly shouted, "Please help us. Mister, please don't leave without helping us."

The agent stopped, turned his bent head to Lilly, his eyes roaming over her body, her face, her eyes. "I know you," he said, then corrected himself, "I mean, I don't know you, but I know about you. Your husband died, right?" Lilly froze, felt her heart tense and skip a few beats, as the agent's eyes were downcast. "Shot himself.

Closed casket." Shook his head. "Not right. Not right at all. I feel for your kids."

Lilly felt paralyzed. In shock. Her jaw quivered seeing this man, this CIA agent, staring through her as if he were squeezing her heart and soul. His expression changed then, as if he understood the pain he'd caused. He went to speak, but no words came. Instead, he went for the door.

"Mister please," Lilly hollered. "My son, my Christopher, is here. I have to get him. Please." The agent's hand on the door. Lilly walked the length of the cage; hand over hand across the bars, and the other women moved away. "I can't let him go through this. I can't. It's my job. It's my job to protect him." She stopped at the corner. Put her head against the cage. "I'll do anything. Just please let me help my son. I'll come back and you can do anything you want to me. I just want him to go. *Please.*"

"I can't do that," he said. "Can't let you out. Or any of you." He locked eyes with Lilly. "I'm sorry, but this won't end well. It's a damn shame that they always get away with it. Nobody cares." Broke eye contact, looked away, hand still on the door.

Lilly looked around, saw everyone looking, staring, waiting with bated breath.

"You'll be okay though," he said, then turned to Lilly. "Can't say the same for your kids, but I will say this. By tomorrow morning, none of you will care."

His voice was cold, his words cut straight through Lilly's heart. The agent opened the door and walked through as the rumbling grunts and shaking cages erupted. Lilly watched as the door closed with a suctioned thud and with it her last hope.

12

7:50 PM
Somewhere in the dark
Cassandra

Her stomach wrenched with agonizing pain. Felt sick to her stomach, ready to spew chunks, lying on the floor, her knees curled to her chest. Felt her stomach bubble and move. Sweat on her forehead. The room was scorching hot. Her head weary. She tried to stand a few hours ago but couldn't stay on her feet. All she did was sway, and she was scared she would fall over if she remained standing. Holding the bars for support didn't matter anymore; her stomach hurt so much she knew she'd tumble over. Best to lie down, lie down and die. Cassandra welcomed death. Didn't matter anymore, she might as well be dead.

Her legs were restless. Every time her stomach nipped at what Cassandra assumed were her intestines, her legs twitched and jumped. Seemed like there was a house party inside her stomach. And then there was the pain. Pain like she'd never felt before. And it kept coming. Coming in waves and recently those waves seemed to arrive on top of each other. So, Cassandra started counting the seconds in between each wave, wondering how long, how long until the pain was forever. Another reason to welcome death. Now those pains arrived every three hundred seconds. She could feel it coming at the two hundred and forty count. Time to prepare herself, clenched teeth and fists so tight she lost feeling in her hands. And it was heading her way again.

Two thirty-two... Two thirty-three.

She took a deep breath.

Two thirty-four... Two thirty-five.

Thirty-six. Thirty-seven. Thirty-eight. Thirty-nine.

And here we go!

Pain. Unimaginable pain gripped Cassandra with relentless, unwavering abandon. She screamed and wailed, fists tighter than humanly possible. Her legs shuddering and twitching, stomach twisted as her hand went to her stomach and she yelped and hollered. Her stomach was moving, flutters beneath the skin, rapid successive lumps from within as her hand retracted, and she draped her arm across her head and screamed, crying, writhing, and wriggling.

She felt her stomach bubbling with what seemed like a thousand bees swarming in her stomach, stinging her innards. And she screamed even more. Screamed when she felt little legs scurry into her vagina. Her pelvis lifted off the floor then thumped back down, her chest heaved and shuddered as she gnashed her teeth.

And she felt like she should push. Force out whatever was inside.

13

7:55 PM
The Warehouse
Tyler

Kera found a private room with a computer. She punched up an earthly map and used the warehouse address to lock in their location.

"See, this is where we are," she said. Kera sat by the computer, Tyler looking over her shoulder. "But there's so many warehouses. More than a few blocks of warehouses."

"But that's not our concern," said Tyler. "I'm only concerned with…"

Kera shook her head. "That is where you're wrong."

Tyler paused. "What do you mean?"

"It's not just this warehouse, Tyler, it's all of them. There are underground tunnels connecting all these warehouses. Makes it easier to work unnoticed. Your friends can be anywhere and are more than likely in different places, possibly even different warehouses. It could take us all night to find them."

"Then it takes all night," he shouted. Kera shot him a stare of disappointment. "I'm sorry," he said, shaking his head. "I just want my friends."

Kera returned to the monitor. Her tentacles continued to stare at Tyler. She zoomed in on one warehouse, craned her neck, zoomed in closer then pointed. "See this?"

Tyler surveyed the area where her finger was pointing. "Looks like a shop or store or something."

Kera shook her head. "Looks like it, but it's not. You see, this is the solstice celebration and what the solstice requires is an entrance point for all the... human guests."

Tyler shook his head. "What does that mean?"

"It means, Tyler, that I'm sure this store is serving that purpose for this year's Cannibal Café."

"Cannibal Café?"

"Correct."

"You mean..." Kera nodded. Tyler took a deep breath.

Kera continued, "Also, see how the shop is attached to the warehouse?"

"I do."

"Ok, so, since people are arriving at the shop, more than likely this attached warehouse is where Jiggly will hold the celebration. Knowing Jiggly, it will be easier to escort everyone here than transport them across warehouses." She turned to Tyler. "Jiggly likes it when things go smoothly."

Tyler shook his head. "So, you're saying you think my friends are there?"

"I'm saying that it's highly possible and more than probable that they are there or in one of the adjacent warehouses very close to the shop. Jiggly will want everyone in close proximity in case he has to make on-the-fly changes or additions... depends on when the masters arrive. Sometimes they like to go all out if you know what I mean?"

Tyler cocked his eyebrows. "I don't."

Kera pursed her lips, said, "Hmm. Let's keep it that way."

"You're telling me. So, what's the plan? Where exactly are we?"

Kera turned to the monitor, then gripped the mouse and clicked the zoom controls on the screen. A second later the screen changed, the store they were looking at growing smaller and smaller as the blocks of warehouses became prominent. She pointed. "Here."

Tyler looked at the monitor. His heart sank with the revelation that his warehouse was two blocks away from where they needed to go. He shook his head. "Why are we so far away from everyone else?"

Kera paused. Tyler craned his head to see her. Looked like she was thinking. Thinking or hiding something. She took a deep breath.

"Kera?"

She said, "Because Jiggly doesn't want the masters to know you exist. He's hiding you from them."

"Why?"

"Because you are very much like Jiggly. He has a kinship to you and despite himself, it appears he's abiding by the law of his people, and not the masters." Kera sat up, her chair screeching against the floor, as Tyler stood tall and stepped back. Kera looked at him dead in the eyes. "He will be punished if the masters find out. That's why I wanted you to leave. If the masters find out who you are and what we're doing..." She turned away, and Tyler could see she was grinding her teeth. "They may torture Jiggly or banish him into dark matter."

"I don't give a damn about that little shit. I want my friends and to get the fuck out of here with them... and as many others as possible. If we all go to the police with the same story, they'll have to believe us. I'm sorry, Kera, but I don't care about Jigglyspot and his horde of death and darkness. The way I see it, he's made his bed, and it's time he lies in it."

Kera shook her head. Those tentacles wrapped around her skull like a tiara, resting within her hair, staring at Tyler.

"So," Tyler said. "Are you coming with me or not?"

Kera turned to him with a scowl and those tentacles propped up. "Excuse me, Mr. Tyler, but I started this, and I always see things through."

"Perfect," said Tyler, "And here we go."

14

8:00 PM
Cannibal Café
Jigglyspot

Jiggly enjoyed the kind remarks, praise, and, well, let's be honest, ass kissing brown nosing he received when he presented himself for solstice. Kitchen was filled with Jiggly's people–the clowns–scrambling and mixing, stirring, preparing. He rolled his eyes when Politiere complimented him on his use of dark purple and red. "Lights up your eyes," said Politiere.

Jiggly had a fleeting thought where he saw himself drinking extraction from Politiere's husband, with the grand chef a passive observer strapped to the chair Jiggly tied him to. And Jiggly laughed out loud.

"What is it?" said Politiere, his left arm cradling a mixing bowl as he took a quick taste off his spatula and his eyes lit up.

Jiggly grinned as he shook his head. "Nada," was his response. "Are we on schedule?"

"Of course," said Politiere in that French accent. "Guests are arriving on time, as expected."

"Beautiful," said Jiggly. He snapped his arms one at a time, elbow cracks rifled through the kitchen. Stretched his neck that cracked and popped and Jiggly let out an oomph and sigh. Cocked those dark purple eyebrows. "That felt good."

He noticed a few of his clowns looking at him. Jiggly smiled a smug little smile. Apoch, the tall clown–hovering just under seven feet, he often received the nickname Stretch–stood tall, raising his chin as he closed his eyes and gave a respectful nod. Apoch had always been the type with little words. When you're that big, you don't have to say too much or move fast. The world moved around you when you're that big. Jiggly understood the gesture; it was time for Jiggly to greet his guests. Jiggly could hear them in the dining room where a constant stream of chatter and occasional out loud laughter was prominent.

Jiggly gripped Politiere's arm, said, "Is everything prepped and ready to go the minute after celebration?"

Politiere eyeballed Jiggly's hand on his arm. Apparently, Jiggly thought, he doesn't appreciate the gesture. Jiggly bent his head with a slight indignation likened to *I really don't give a fuck about your personal space,* to which the good chef cringed at Jiggly's gesture, as if he understood Jiggly's thought. Politiere responded, "Yes. The longer those marinating the better. Won't take long to cut a throat and skin the meat off the bone. They'll stay alive until that moment. Might hear some screaming and such, but... we aren't really concerned about that now, are we?"

"Not at all," said Jiggly. "Use Apoch. He's a filleting master." He regarded Apoch, who shrugged and Jiggly smiled. "And cutting throats. Plus, his size will stop them from trying anything stupid." Jiggly looked at Politiere, still with his hand on Politiere's arm. "And the infants?"

"The infant product is prepped and ready—except for the live sacrifice for the Goddess, of course. But that is taken raw from what I recall, yes?"

"Always," said Jiggly, his voice rose as he stretched his arms, hands to the sky.

Laughter from his clowns, Politiere too. And then a drop in energy. Laughter cut off, replaced by mixing and cutting and prepping in quiet solitude. Jiggly staring, thinking. This is it, he thought. He pulled it off. The task he'd been given, an impossible task to pull off solstice this year after all that has been happening in their ever-growing circle of depravity, especially with MysterE and all the prep and cover up they've been dealing with. Still dealing with and will be dealing with for some time. But the fallout will be dealt with, tossed under the rug and made invisible. That was the easy part, distraction being the key. Always distraction; give them something else to fear and all those little insipid conspiracies fall by the wayside.

Every solstice for the past few decades was pulled off by Jiggly and MysterE, and Jiggly missed him exponentially at this moment. Jiggly wondered what fate will befall MysterE because it wasn't as though the current circumstance was entirely on his shoulders. There were so many involved. But he was in charge, so someone has to take the fall. Question on Jiggly's mind was if more than forty years of service—service wasn't the right word to use, MysterE single handedly brought the cause to new heights, more than anyone before him—would manifest in praise or darkness? Jiggly hoped for the former.

"Time to go now, Mr. Jiggly." Politiere, still mixing, his voice soft, almost caring.

Jiggly looked at Politiere then turned to his clowns. He stood tall, shoulders back, and stretched his arms and fingers with a crackle, snap, and pop. "Yes, it is," declared Jiggly, and stomped his cane twice on the floor. "Ladies and gentlemen, it is time." He walked to the door as applause erupted in the kitchen. A proud moment indeed for Jiggly. He bowed. "Thank you all," he said, then tapped his cane twice. "Now get back to work," said Jiggly—applause turned to laughter—then turned on his heels and hurried through the door to the Cannibal Café.

15

8:05 PM
Outside the Cannibal Café
Sharon

She took Kevin's hand as she stepped out of the limo. The driver held the door open. She had to admit she was disappointed. Sharon had expected a line of unknowing fans to be outside the café cheering and applauding, snapping pictures and videos. And, as she stood in the roundabout in front of the café, twilight over her shoulder, and the last remnants of sunlight fighting off the dark of night, she couldn't help but laugh at herself. Expectations, she thought, reminding herself that she wasn't attending an awards show; at the most basic level, this was a fancy dinner. At least the private jet that brought them from LA to San Luis Obispo was fantastic. She hoped the café would rival the private jet.

Kevin seemed shaky. His hand revealed the slightest bit of a tremble. He appeared worn and thin, with thick bags beneath his eyes and his neck was swollen where Sharon bit him. Even with his turtleneck choking his jawline, she could see the top of the bandage around his neck. Her mouth watered at the thought of his salty flesh between her teeth, on her tongue, bursting across her palate. She could taste the blood now, sliding down her throat, gushing over her lips, between her teeth, and she smiled at Kevin.

Driving up, Sharon had thought they were in the wrong place. They drove through a neighborhood where warehouses were abundant. So many warehouses and for a brief second, she felt a tremble of fear rush through her veins. A trepidation sensation she dismissed as the last remnant of the old Sharon, the one who second-guessed every natural impulse in her body and mind. She'd taken a deep breath, allowing the fear to subside. This was Sharon's night, her turn in the spotlight and no one, no way, no how, was going to put a stop to the limelight that rightfully belonged to her. By the time the limo rolled through the parking lot to the entrance of the Cannibal Café, that fearful sensation had gone, transformed into confidence.

The front of the café seemed out-of-place out here among the warehouses. Out of place because of the façade. Four tall stone pillars-two on each side-stood prominently attached to the ceiling overhang, which Sharon surmised must be a hundred feet high. She could see, in the twilights last gleaming, the stone masonry of the front of the café that stretched a hundred yards to Sharon's left, the café's entrance on the end of said building closest to where Sharon now stood. In between the stone pillars were steps, at first wide—about thirty feet wide—the steps narrowed like a pyramid to the red front doors. Sharon wasn't sure about the steps construct. The wide red carpet made it difficult to determine the exact make of the stairs; marble is what Sharon surmised. On top of those stairs were what seemed like ten-foot-high double doors that appeared to be made of wood and carried an ancient relic façade with their pointed tops.

Sharon said, "What, no welcoming committee?"

Kevin smiled with a chuckle in his throat. "Not yet, my lady. Not yet."

Sharon stretched her thighs right then left—her dress had bunched up just a bit.

"Are we ready?" said Kevin, holding his arm out.

"Naturally," said Sharon in a silky-smooth voice while looping her arm through Kevins.

"Thank you, Chuck." Kevin slipped the driver a tip.

Sharon's heart fluttered as they took the stairs, her free hand on her chest, the air growing hotter with every step up. Sharon's eyes were on the door. This is it, she thought. Sharon noticed how calm she was, how confident. Even when the doors opened as if on cue to her step—opened by no one, perhaps they are on a sensor—she welcomed the prestige without even a flutter of excitement or star struck panic. Completely calm and cool. Inside the open doors, Sharon saw a small foyer with a table and a mirror above it. And as she stepped into the Cannibal Café, Sharon completed her thought: Tonight... the world is mine.

285

16

8:08 PM
Cannibal Café
Jigglyspot

The Goddess has arrived. Jiggly felt the wind erupt and then die in the same breath. Wind that rushed across the café with a fierce strength, as if to alert all in attendance of the Goddess' arrival, then cut off at the neck as if to tell all to stand. And they did stand. The guests–who had been chatting in murmurs and muttered banter-the maître d', Jiggly's wait staff–three waiters and one bus boy–a cello player, and of course Jiggly was standing, his cane held loosely in his right palm. The dining room reflected the high prestige of royalty–covered tables with white cloth, high back red leather chairs, and a fantastical art collection comprising ancient relics that featured a plethora of pastels depicting the Dark Lord in classic dark robes–and from the inside no one would dare to question if they were sitting in a warehouse.

They waited with bated breath. Quiet. Silence. Heavy anticipation. Jiggly noticed the time, 8:08 PM, as he breathed deeply the galloping glow of night. He scanned his guests, their eyes on the foyer that led to the entrance. The host standing at attention, waiting.

They saw the lackey first, the one who found the Goddess, who offered himself so that the Goddess would manifest. His praise will be forever. Every bone, muscle, and limb tensed within Jiggly. His eyes roaming across the lackey to his arm and the hand that held the Goddess' hand, who, at this very moment, was just out of sight. The split second it took for the Goddess to appear in the doorway seemed to last a century. A collectively held breath choked the restaurant and then she stepped into view and Jiggly would swear there were tears in his eyes, gleaming with bulbs of stars and magical dust, once the Goddess was in full view. He was so happy his eyes couldn't contain the joyful emotion. Jiggly wiped the tears from his eyes and it seemed as if every patron in the restaurant exhaled all at once. A collective sigh–relief followed by admiration with a buzz of excitement–once the Goddess presented herself, stepping up into the foyer.

Magnificent, thought Jiggly. Truly remarkable.

She wore a dark black dress–Jiggly remarked how appropriate her choice of color was–hair cascaded in thick brunette curls to her shoulders, and her skin glowed under the light. Jiggly watched as the lackey presented his card to the host.

And the host said in a silky smooth voice, "Does your guest accept the offering?"

As if on cue, the Goddess replied, "I do."

And Jiggly breathed deeply, savoring the moment.

"Follow me," said the host as he escorted the Goddess and her lackey to their table in the center of the room.

Jiggly watched the Goddess; she seemed to float across the room.

Before taking her seat–which the host moved away from the table–she looked around the room with a smile that revealed satisfaction, accepting the praise from all who were standing. She took her seat and immediately the waiter poured a thick, dark red fluid from a glass decanter to the crystal goblet on the table. The blood from the infant Jiggly had chosen. The waiter waited at the table. The Goddess offered him a nod, accepting the offering.

"Why are they standing?" she asked the lackey.

His reply–voice shaking–came after he forced a swallow down his throat. "My lady, it is customary for the guest of honor to toast those in attendance."

She looked over the room, scanning the eyes and visage of every one of her guests. She eyeballed Jiggly, and he felt a frog in his throat, choked by emotion. Jiggly bowed to the Goddess. As if she knew, as if she'd been here for a lifetime and knew exactly what to do, she raised her goblet.

"I fully accept this offering of blood and wine. In the name of Baphomet, I praise all who bow to him. May your hearts remain dark for all time."

Jiggly smiled when the Goddess revealed a perplexed stare. Jiggly understood why, the Goddess, the skin of the Goddess, the host, wondered where those words had come from.

And she drank, her head tilted back, goblet to her lips, and Jiggly watched as the blood passed those dark red lips, saw the blood cross over her tongue, watched as her throat took the offering. She raised the goblet over her head to thunderous applause. Cello player returned to a rendition of *The Jewel Song*, wait staff returned to their stations, and the guests took their seats.

And Jiggly thought, Everyone is in. Ceremonies can now begin.

17

8:15 PM
The Warehouse
Tyler

Kera had stopped abruptly; a trembling stare gripped her eyes. Those tentacles had stood erect and a moment after rested across Kera's face to her shoulders as if they had bowed.

"What is it?" Tyler asked, craning his head to see Kera.

She started moving again. "We should act fast. Ceremony will begin soon."

"Ceremony?"

No answer. She kept walking.

"What ceremony?" said Tyler, following close behind.

"Your friends, that's who you want out, right?"

"Yes." Tyler picked up his pace to stay as close to Kera as possible. She was moving so fast it was difficult to keep up.

"And then you'll leave? Get them out with you and go."

"That's the plan, yes, but the others too. We can't..."

Kera was shaking her head. "No time."

"What?"

She looked back briefly, her tentacles raised, watching Tyler, but she kept moving.

"We're getting closer," she said.

Tyler shook his head. "Okay?"

Kera came to a doorway and leaned against the wall next to it, craning her head to look down the hall. Tyler noticed how dark the hall was, seemed the red glow dissipated down the hall. Noticed how Kera was trembling. Saw beads of sweat on her forehead. She looked at Tyler when he felt a cool breeze above their heads. He looked up at the large air vent not far above. A grate covered the vent's opening. He looked at Kera.

"Look?" he said, receiving a perplexed stare from Kera. Tyler gestured to the air vent and Kera followed his gaze. "Air vents. I've seen the vents everywhere. We can get around in them without being seen." He scanned the course of the air vent. "If these warehouses are all connected, there's a good chance the vents are too." He paused, staring into Kera's eyes. "We can slip through unnoticed. Might be cramped in some places, but at least we're not in the open. Plus, these types of vents are usually quite large. My dad works in warehouses. He says the vents are made large for easier access should repairs need to be made."

Tyler looked around the hall lined with crates which he stacked beneath the vent. Two crates on the floor and two more on top of those.

"Here, take my hand. I'll lift you up."

She seemed to back away; perhaps it was the tentacles that recoiled, giving off the illusion that Kera backed up.

Tyler shook his head. "What is it?" he said, agitated. "You look like you saw a ghost."

Kera swallowed her breath. "You ever hear the term, point of no return?"

"I have."

"Well," Kera said, staring at the vent. "This is that point for me."

"And you're not sure if you want to cross it?"

"Correct."

Tyler looked over his shoulder to the vent, then back to Kera, whose eyes moved from the vent to him, her tentacles following.

Tyler narrowed his eyes. "Didn't you pass that point when you got me out?"

She shook her head. "No. If you had walked out the door, I would have been gone and no one would be any wiser. Now this, though, it's only a matter of time."

"Time? We don't have time. That's what you said."

"The Goddess is here," Kera said. "She will not be pleased."

Tyler widened his eyes. "If you don't want to go, I understand. But I'm finding my friends and getting us out of here." He turned around, went to the crates, tested them for stability, then looked up. He could see how easy the grate was to remove; small thumbnail sized pieces of metal easily pushed aside will remove the grate. He looked at Kera and those tentacles wrapped around her throat, as if to console their host.

"Follow it through, right?" said Tyler.

Kera stared straight into his eyes. "You don't understand what this night means, do you?" She was shaking her head. "What's waiting for us, for everyone? This may not end well for either of us."

"You said that already." Kera shook her head disapprovingly. Tyler huffed. "Listen, I'm scared half to death myself, but I can't let my friends die without at least trying to help them."

"Connection," Kera said. "A uniquely human trait."

"Something like that, yeah." He went to the crate and lifted himself up with a grunt. He stood, steadying his feet when the crate wobbled beneath him. Tyler waited a moment before unlatching those thumbnail metal clips. The grate fell loosely into his hands, and he guided it down to the floor. He looked over his shoulder at Kera. "You coming?" Then lifted himself into the vent. Darkness bathed the vent, but he could walk, glad he was just under six feet tall, any taller, and he'd be hunched over. Two ways to go, left or right. He looked back at Kera, who was mounting the crates. Tyler helped her into the vent. "Glad you came," he said.

Kera shook her head. "The things we do for that insipid sensation."

"You mean love."

"Whatever," was her response.

Tyler looked both ways. "Any ideas?"

Kera turned in both directions, and Tyler could see those cogs in her brain moving. "We were headed this way." She pointed to the right. "Hopefully, the vents follow the same path." She turned back to Tyler. "Wouldn't want you to see something you shouldn't."

Tyler craned his head to the right. "I think I can handle it."

Tyler thought she hid a smile. "Humans," she said.

"You got that right."

Tyler moved down the vent to the right. Kera following. The two of them disappearing, swallowed by darkness.

18

8:30 PM
Cannibal Café
Jigglyspot

He grabbed Gary the truck driver then strolled towards the warehouse with Gary following close behind.

"Grab Helmsley," Jiggly said. "Get him out. He has to prepare. Ceremony will begin soon."

"What about all those people? Won't they be talking by now?"

"Ahh," said Jiggly. "That's a quick fix."

Jiggly led them to a door, where he paused.

Gary said, "You did good, Jigs. Things are all going as planned. You did real good."

"Once ceremony is complete, then I'll be able to relax. We still have a few hurtles to jump." He shook his head, then took a deep breath.

Gary put his hand on Jiggly's shoulder. "It'll be all right."

Jiggly eyeballed Gary's hand with a scowl and Gary froze before sliding his hand away.

"Keep your wits in check, Gary," said Jiggly. "There'll be plenty of time for celebration once the night is over."

Gary nodded, said, "So, get Helmsley ready for ceremony, then check on the marinades to be sure they're ready to go once the Goddess takes the sacrifice, correct?"

"Exactly. Then bring Helmsley and Mills to ceremony. Dark Lord has selected Helmsley for sacrifice. He found it... ironic. Wants to give Mills a present for his service."

Gary blurted a laugh that Jiggly scowled at.

"Sorry," said Gary, and cleared his throat.

Jiggly shook his head and tapped his cane twice, said, "Let's go!"

He flicked off a light switch beside the door before pushing through the door to the warehouse, where he was greeted by a host of shouting and pleas.

19

8:35 PM
The Warehouse
Lilly

The lights went out and all Lilly could see were the whites of human eyeballs. Stuttered gasps like waves in the ocean rippled through the warehouse. Lilly, standing beside the bars, her fingers gripped those bars in her palms, then gripped tighter.

Something's coming, she thought when the voices rose in the room, echoing off the concrete walls as if the shouting and pleas shouted back. And a door opened. Not from the front of the room where that detective had gone through, but from the back of the room. Lilly's eyes went to that door. She could see a soft light like a far away candle beyond the door, then two silhouettes rippled through that light. Cages rattling, pleas to be let go commingled with threats and anger rifled into the room in a constant stream.

Lilly felt sick, her throat scratchy and swollen. She'd attempted to talk with Kathy Crawford not too long ago, although it had become apparent to Lilly that Kathy did not want to talk. Some people fold under pressure. Kathy was one of those people, but Lilly knew she had to think and keep thinking, because it was the intelligent person, the one who kept their wits in check, who survives such circumstances. Of course, the thought of Christopher being held captive somewhere in this warehouse kept those wits in check. And the fact that her mother, caring for and tending to Sam's needs and desires, should have contacted law enforcement by now was a comforting thought. At least, Lilly surmised, she wanted the comfort, knowing all too well such a call was futile. Large groups of people don't disappear without there being some connection or pay off to law enforcement. In other words, Lilly knew, they were all fucked and Lilly had to act on her own wit to rescue Christopher. And, judging by Kathy's nervous rocking and recent display of debilitating madness, that damnable Jenny Crawford, too.

Lilly cursed herself for thinking of a child in that way. The thought that little Jenny Crawford may be experiencing some of the worst in human depravity, perhaps at this very moment, turned Lilly's gut with shame.

Those two silhouettes were drifting to the center of the warehouse. In step with the walking, Lilly heard what she thought was the tap, tap, tapping of a cane against the floor. The pleas, threats, and rattling reached a fever pitch as the lights suddenly bathed the warehouse in light. A brief pause as Lilly, along with every other prisoner, closed and adjusted their eyes.

Standing center stage was that little guy, now dressed in full clown uniform, his face painted in some damn awful way. The red cane in his right hand looked more like a walking stick for the short stature clown. And the guy over the clown's shoulder, the one who had so much trouble with the cattle prod, a lackey for the clown, stood with a sick grin plastered across his lips.

The clown looked over the warehouse, perplexed. Lilly watched him like a hawk. His mannerisms and body language proved stiff and angry. The guy over his shoulder shrugged.

They're looking for the other guy. The one they left when he got hit with the cattle prod. The one who slipped out of here an hour ago. Had he not returned to heed the service of the clown?

Lilly felt dissension among the clown's faction. The clown was not pleased. Not pleased at all.

He tapped his cane twice to the thunderous pleas of his prisoners.

"Let us the fuck out," "You'll be hearing from my attorney," and "Where are our children?" pleas raged through the warehouse.

"Settle down now," said the clown in that raspy voice that carried a hint of laughter behind it.

"Settle down?" someone said from the middle cage. "Fuck you."

To which the clown seemed to stiffen, eyeballing the man who blurted the proverbial fuck you.

"Well," said the clown. "I guess you all don't want to know what is coming." He turned to the guy hovering over his shoulder. "Like little children they are."

"Where are our kids?" "What are you doing to them?"

"Ahh, the children are safe. Safer with us than any place on earth. Perhaps if you were all better parents, they wouldn't be in their current predicament."

Lilly shook her head. Gaslighting, she thought. Yeah, like it's our fault you drugged all of us and locked us up.

The warehouse erupted then; more pleas, rattling cages, and fuck yous. The clown shook his head. His partner did too, muttered something to the clown, but Lilly couldn't hear what he said.

"Silence!" the clown hollered. "Do you not want your precious answers?"

He waited until the thunderous rattle softened.

"That's more like it." And the clown grinned, holding that cane by his side, spinning the top in his palm. He looked into the eyes of every prisoner—sixty-six Lilly remembered—one by one, locking eyes with all of them, even Lilly and she saw a glimmer wave through his eyes as he ran his tongue inside his mouth. He said, "Your children have been selected to serve the interests of the masters. Unfortunately, we've had to take applications to fill some very necessary positions. Your children will fill that void. Quite precious they all are, as I'm sure you're all aware." He paused, head down, thinking. When he looked up, Lilly felt his anger rifle off his small frame.

"As for all of you," he said. "The masters will be here soon and we require not one of you to interrupt or disturb ceremony." He twisted his cane in his palm. "Considering how loud you've all been, we do not believe you can accomplish this very simple task, even though I've previously explained that you will all return to your homes in the morning, refreshed and anew. I've said this to all of you and still you continue to act like rabid animals." He looked from one cage to the other, and slammed his cane on the ground when he said, "Disgraceful!"

And the guy behind him laughed, although the clown never flinched nor did he acknowledge his subordinate as more fuck you's rang through the room. He stepped forward. "Because of this, because of your failure to abide by my wishes, praise, and help, we've come to an abrupt conclusion." And he smiled, smiled that raggedy devious smirk. He lifted his cane, holding the top end towards the cages, pointing to his prisoners. "We must deliver a clean product for the masters." He looked over his shoulder, gave a quick nod to his subordinate, who nodded back then went to the wall behind them. "We are going to gas you," he said. "But fear not, this is not World War Two, this is not the gas that brings death but gas it is. So you're all less agitated. Less verbal. And more content with current circumstances."

On the far wall were valves with levers and tubes that came out from the wall. The subordinate twisted one valve. Lilly heard hissing. Hissing behind her and she turned on a dime. From the floor, she saw vapor spewing into the cell. Kathy Crawford was the first to swallow a wallop. More hissing, Lilly followed the sound and watched vapor spew into each cell. Suddenly, coughing and hacking filled the warehouse as Lilly immediately stretched her shirt over her mouth and nose. Hurried panics, scrambling to get away or at least to not breathe in the vapor. Huddled masses in every cage, whines, whimpers and cries as people held their hands over their mouths. Lilly drew in a deep breath. A long thick wallop of clean air filled her lungs, and it was there that she held it, closing off her mouth and nose.

Remain calm, she thought, talking to herself, her own cheerleader, her own teacher. She closed her eyes just as the vapor turned thick, too thick to see anything beyond the vapor. She heard the clown and his subordinate laugh. Heard the tapping of his cane as they were leaving the room.

Heard the clown say just before the warehouse door closed, "Find Helmsley immediately."

"One hundred percent. I can't believe he got up so quickly. Usually people are out for at least a few hours, if not more."

"No excuses," said the clown. "I want him here immediately.

The Dark Lord will not be pleased if Helmsley is not here when he arrives."

Lilly heard the door close with a thud. She heard choking and gagging and hacking. Opened her eyes and saw the room was filled with vapor. There was no escape. That white mist was everywhere.

And Lilly started counting, ticking off the seconds in her head, hoping and praying she could outlast the vapor.

20

8:45 PM
Somewhere Shiny
SAC John Mills

He was waiting, waiting for the clown to come and get him. SAC John Mills sat on a metal table connected to the wall. His right ear kept itching. Scratch. Scratch. His pointer finger in his ear moving quickly back and forth, attempting to satisfy his itch. Saw blood on his fingertip and his head shuddered, twisted to the right. Wiped the blood on his pants. Scratch. Scratch. The itch constant, unrelenting, and dissatisfied by his incessant scratching.

His dangling feet moving back and forth feverishly. The aliens are here, he thought. That's all he thought about. That and the itch, his finger a constant player in his ear, digging as far into his ear as he could manage. He had to get in there, as far into the eardrum as possible. Something's tickling his eardrum, something he can't get to. It's constant. Maddening. *Where's the clown? Where did those aliens go? We've got to tell people the aliens are here. Got to let people know.* Felt a squirm in his brain and his neck tensed, back of his head too. Felt the bones in his jaw clench, grinding his teeth with a sour expression as his stomach turned.

They must know. Everyone must know. We can't keep it from them anymore. The world needs to know the aliens are here. The aliens are fucking here and there's nothing we can do about it.

He felt his heart racing, and he jumped off the table.

They've got to know. Got to know.

Finger in his ear. Scratch. Scratch.

Pacing across the shiny room. Something squirming in his ear. Little hairs tickling his eardrum.

Aliens. Fucking aliens are here.

Always have been. The Aliens. The aliens are here.

Pinky finger in his ear now. A smaller digit capable of getting further down the drum.

His head jutting to the left, that pinky finger tapping that itch. Mills' eyes rolled to the back of his skull.

"Something's in there," he whined like a child at the mercy of his emotions. Wanted to rip his head off his shoulders and toss it away. Anything to stop the itching. Pulled his pinky away. Blood dripped off the fingernail, covering his pinky, pooling across his palm, cascading over his wrist. His hand covered in blood.

"So much blood."

His head shook violently. Mills felt saliva and spit spew from his lips. Held his head stiff, took deep hyperventilating breaths. Spit foamed across his bottom lip. Mills could feel the spittle in the corners of his mouth.

Got to tell them. Got to tell everyone.

Pain in the center of his brain, John's eyes closed, his head jutted to the left. Something squirming. Eating, gnawing away at his brain. His hands, clenched into fists, went to his temples. A feeble attempt to ward off the pain. He felt warmth above his lip, his eyes felt wet with tears. Mills looked left, then right. The room seemed to spin away from his ability to see and he raced to catch it, spinning like a dog chasing its own tail, when his hands reached for the wall. The shiny wall that looked back at him revealing how his eyes bled, his nose too. Thick streams of blood cascaded from his eyes and nose. And his breath; his breath fogged the shiny wall, rank like a rotting corpse, hot and dry like desert heat.

SAC John Mills stood staring at his reflection, unwavering, jaw hung loosely, eyes sagging, nose bleeding. Again, the squirm inside his brain, his head shuddered, neck stretched in stutters. Put his finger in his ear, started pacing again, wiggling his pinky as far into the eardrum as possible.

Got to tell them. Got to tell everyone. Aliens are here. Always been here. Always will. Got to tell them. Got to tell. Got to. How to do it? How to tell them? How to know? Where is the fucking clown?

21

8:50 PM
Cannibal Café
Sharon

"Why are they all staring?" asked Sharon, her eyes roaming from one table to the next. She counted thirty-one guests, not including herself and Kevin. The room was quiet other than brief whispers, occasional laughter, and clinking glasses.

Kevin looked over both shoulders, then sat forward. "Maybe you have them all mesmerized." Sharon saw a glimmer race through Kevin's eyes. "In awe of the true Goddess."

Sharon took her glass, the crystal goblet, by the stem. She sipped the warm fluid, thick and salty, over her lips. Closed her eyes. "Exquisite," she pronounced as she opened her eyes, staring at Kevin. After a pause, she looked over the room, trying to put a finger on who was in attendance. Sharon expected big name actors, producers, and directors, but none of the guests were anyone she recognized.

As if he could read her thoughts, Kevin said, "From what I was told, this year's solstice celebration had to be changed last minute and they took some guests off the list for tonight's festivities."

Sharon shrugged, disappointed. *Who are these people who stare so intensely, as if licking their chops in the presence of fresh blood?*

"I assure you though," said Kevin. "As I was..." He moved closer to the table, as if revealing a dire secret. Elbows on the table, his hands folded beside his right cheek. "That all who are here are the people behind the scenes. The ones that really make things happen. Puppeteers," he said and cocked his eyebrows. "Pulling the strings on their little play puppets. Keeping that dark veil forever draped across the eyes of the common people." And he grinned, his head bobbed right then left.

Sharon shifted closer to the table. "Do you know who they are?" she asked. "Like, who are they for real?"

Kevin bit into his thumbnail, nipping at it, stealing glances as he scanned the other guests. "CIA," he said. "Operatives and classified intelligence." He shook his head. "Don't worry about them. They're all here for you, anyway."

Sharon thought Kevin was being sweet. *There's no way they're all here for me?*

Kevin's eyes lit up. "Ira," he said, looking over Sharon's shoulder.

Ira was dressed to the nines; dark red Armani suit brightened his sparkling blue eyes. That bald head polished to a fine shine, his eyebrows ruffled in the corners. Kevin stood up to greet him as Sharon looked over her shoulder. "Always a pleasure." Kevin offered his hand, which Ira accepted.

"Good to see you, Kevin. You've done well. Done well for both of us." And he laughed when he said, "Nothing better than jumping on an opportunity. Can you introduce me?"

"Of course," said Kevin, and he turned to Sharon. "Ira Monteforte, meet Sharon Mable. Promising actress, producer and director, and the spotlight of tonight's ceremony."

Ira turned wholly to Sharon as she offered her hand. "My lady," said Ira, folding her hand within his. "It is an honor." And he kissed her hand. Sharon noticed the stares from the other guests, as if they all stopped, paused and went silent, watching the exchange.

"Pleasure is mine, Mr. Monteforte," offered Sharon when Ira stood erect, releasing her hand. "You know my roommate. Cassandra has worked for you for a long time. Unfortunately, she keeps you all to herself. She's not one to share her possessions." Sharon cocked her eyebrows.

Ira laughed out loud. "No, Cassandra doesn't like to share at all, especially since she's been keeping you from us for such a long time." Ira looked over Sharon with a long silent pause. Sharon could see the hunger in his eyes, as if he was undressing her with those hungry eyes, devouring her flesh.

Sharon eased back in her seat, eyeballing Ira with a similar gaze. "Be sure to send her back to me. She's been in Atlanta for way too long."

Ira seemed to tense up. He straightened his shoulders and glanced back at Kevin. "Of course," he said. "I have a feeling she may make an appearance tonight. After all, with all the work she's been doing, it's only right to give her something to live for. You know what they say, all work and no play make..."

"Cassandra a dull girl," Sharon completed, receiving laughter from Kevin and Ira.

"Exactly." Ira glanced over at Kevin and Sharon. "It was wonderful to meet you, Sharon." He took Sharon's hand again. "I will see you during ceremony."

"Looking forward to it," said Sharon. Ira provided a thank you before retreating to his table. Sharon watched him, wondering who the woman was, dressed in all black and hiding her face beneath a veil, sitting across from Ira.

Looks like? No, can't be, Sharon thought.

She turned to Kevin, who stared at Sharon with stiff and beady eyes.

Sharon said, "So, what is this ceremony?"

22

9:00 PM
Inside the vents
Tyler

Tyler was waiting for Kera to catch up to him. Something was up with her, something was wrong. She seemed to grow more fearful as time went on. Whatever this ceremony, goddess, and Dark Lord are, it was obvious Kera wanted to be far away from the warehouse when they arrive. He understood the risk involved. Understood what Kera had done for him and he understood there will be repercussions if they are caught. So don't get caught, he told himself. Get your friends and get the hell out.

She didn't have to stay with him. He told her so. Told her to leave him be and go back to... wherever. Tyler had yet to wrap his head around the fact that Kera was not of this earth. Although she never explicitly told him so, considering those tentacles on top of her head, obviously she came from somewhere out in the cosmos. And with his recently acquired ghost, Tyler could believe anything. He had questions for Kera, but those questions took a back seat to his mission to find his friends.

Tyler searched the ventilation system that forked to the straight and narrow or to his left. Down the path of the straight and narrow he could see a faint light accompanied by a pungent stench he couldn't put his finger on. On his left, the vent snaked into darkness.

Kera's footsteps behind him. He turned to her, said, "Which way?"

Kera's tentacles stood erect as Kera surveyed both directions. Her nose crinkled. "They're using the gas," she said, her head tilted to the right, staring down the vent towards the light.

"What does that mean?"

Kera bobbed her head left, then right as she pursed her lips. "Jiggly's preparing the hosts for the masters. Getting them to be… complacent. Distracted so the masters can slip in easily." She turned to Tyler, staring at him with those dark brown eyes. "That way, there's no fighting them off. Zero intellect," she said, and Tyler furrowed his brow.

"Zero intellect?"

"That's what Jiggly always says. It's how he refers to human beings. They've got zero intellect."

Tyler shook his head. "I don't like this Jiggly guy."

Kera shrugged. "That's a shame because he has his eye on you. Give him a chance. He may grow on you."

"Aren't you here to help me escape from *him*?"

"Yes, but that's only temporary. To give you time to allow everything to sink in. To teach you knowledge before you're found again. And they will find you. Lucky for you, Jiggly won't allow anyone to hurt you. He'll just wait it out. The man who understands time always wins."

"Still don't know why I'm so important to this guy, but I don't like him. Which way? Straight or left."

Kera stepped forward, head craned to the right, and those tentacles followed, stretching from her head towards the light. She turned to the left, then turned back to the light. "I'm fairly certain your friends are not in the light. Knowing Jiggly, that's where all the adults are. Your friends do not have the same fate."

"So, left then." Tyler started walking. Kera followed. The darkness creeping along the walls seemed to come for them, wanting them, devouring every part of them.

"Somewhere inside Jiggly there's a heart of gold. A light like youthful innocence. You don't know what he's been through."

Tyler was growing frustrated with Kera's defense of the one known as Jigglyspot. "Kera, I don't know if you've noticed, but the guy has kidnapped about a hundred people for some sadistic satanic alien ceremony. Whatever light he had inside of him is gone. You make it sound like he's just misdirected and traumatized. That's ridiculous. I'm sorry, but the guy's a sadistic murdering pig who couldn't give a shit about anyone but himself and getting off on other people's pain and suffering. Not cool Kera. Not cool at all."

"Sadistic murdering pig?" Kera repeated. "This coming from the person who plotted, planned, and implemented the murder of his friend. You're a murdering son of a bitch, Tyler. Never forget that. Denying our nature is like living in a bubble with your head in the sand. Don't fall for it."

"There's a difference. I told you that." Tyler watched as darkness reached for them. Like passing through the event horizon of a black hole, he felt a pull towards the darkness, unknowing but intrigued with what was beyond.

"But in its most basic form, it is still the same. It's called murder, Tyler. Both you and Jiggly are murdering pigs."

Tyler stopped abruptly, turned to Kera, who just about slammed into him. She held his gaze, her eyes burning with fury and those tentacles coiled around her head like a snake. If they had teeth, Tyler was certain they would bite. She crossed her arms.

"What?" she said, her voice harsh and scolding. "You kill for justifiable revenge. He does for sport and game. How long, Tyler? How long until your incessant desire for blood leads to the same? You're like a dog that tasted blood for the first time. It's only a matter of time before you snap those jaws again." And she did just that, snapped her jaw twice, the sound of her teeth snapping echoed in the vent. "You murdering pigs are all the same. *It's justified. They deserved it. Zero intellect. Devolved cockroaches. It's all just game and sport, Kera.* I've been listening to it for centuries. No Tyler, it's a damn choice. Part of the universe balancing itself. Where there's one murdering pig, there's another enlightened soul. Bad energy that murder is. I choose not to indulge."

Tyler knew she was right. He hadn't thought about it much, but he felt a kinship to murder even before Mr. James Reilly. Not to mention the fact that a week ago he'd thought about killing Pam.

"Cat got your tongue?" Kera's sassy and confident poise seemed to bathe the tiny little woman in a veil of protection.

"Hopefully you're wrong," he said. "Because that's not what I want."

"Said Jiggly half a century ago."

His eyes bulged from his skull. Started shaking his head. "If he's so corrupt, what makes you believe he can change or be redeemed?" Tyler wondered if he was asking about Jiggly or asking for himself.

"Because it's never too late, Tyler. Time is infinite and death does not exist, it's just a simple matter of transforming and shifting energy. There's always time for redemption. To help shift the balance back into the fold. Problem is when one side of the scales of balance holds the most weight." She shook her head. "That's when the chaos happens. The universe spinning that scale into a monster of energy and BOOOM!" She slapped her hands together, and those tentacles jumped, seemed to scold him with their eyes. "Destruction. And then all this..." She looked around as if seeing the universe. "Gone. Redistributed into another planet, system, galaxy, or universe. And us with it. And all for what? So some stubborn, pompous people can keep their power." She shook her head. "Control is just an illusion. It's the laws of the universe, Tyler. When energy shifts too much to one side, an equal and opposite reaction must occur on the other or the universe will force the proper balance through chaos and destruction."

Tyler felt like his head was spinning. Kera's words, declarations, and explanations rifling through his mind like a tornado. Couldn't wrap his head around it. Felt awestruck, or dumbstruck, he wasn't sure. Kera stared wild-eyed at him, waiting for a response when a stifling, maddening scream erupted down the vent, coming from the darkness as if the darkness pleaded for mercy.

Tyler looked at Kera. "Maybe we should finish this conversation later."

Another scream; louder and more painful than the one before.

"Agreed Mr. Tyler." She started down the vent, said, "Follow me."

And Tyler followed. Couldn't see his hand in front of his eyes it was so dark. Nonetheless, he knew she was in front of him; those tentacles were watching him. Their sea-blue eyes like the ocean at midnight.

And Kera said, "I have a feeling I know what that scream is."

23

9:05 PM
Somewhere in the dark
Cassandra

Her stomach burned with the force of a thousand stings. Cassandra felt her eyes bulge every time the pain arrived, felt heat like fire rifle across her flesh, turning her brain into a hotbed of activity. The pain spells were lasting longer, and the pause in between each spell growing less and less. Cassandra wondered if there would come a time when all she felt was pain; a constant even flow always existing.

Lying on the floor, knees curled against her chest. She felt her stomach move as if swarming with a million bees, stinging, fluttering, and crawling. She felt acid bubble into the back of her throat as beads of sweat as thick as bullets dripped across her forehead. Breath like fire wafted off her tongue, putrid and vile, the stench turned her stomach and stirred acid across her tongue. The ground was cool beneath her, she knew, but her body was so hot, on fire, raging, she turned that cool ground into a bonfire.

Cassandra never noticed how loud she was screaming. Those screams erupted into a frenzied echo across the room, screaming like a problem child refusing to be controlled. Her eyes dripped thick tears as her lips trembled. And beneath the consuming haze of fire and pain a loud crash, metal scraping followed by a bumbling clang as if something had fallen from high above.

Then scuttling, shifting weight and words, voices. Human throats mumbling. Cassandra's eyes clamped shut, an attempt to remain in the dark, to disappear and spiral into the perils of death. Better dead than a slave. Cassandra thought about the monster in the dark. The one who had been watching her, touching her hair. Always watching. Was this monster in the room now? Has the monster come to carry her into the netherworld where the pain will be forever and terror communal?

Red light now bathed the room in a red glow. Her eyes adjusting to the light and all she could see was a red smear across her eyes like a river of blood. A silhouette by the cage, watching her, outlined in red light. Muffled words and a moment passed before a mechanical clambering erupted. Cassandra stared straight ahead, watching her cage, her bodily shackle, rise off the ground. A flash of darkness, that silhouette ducked under the rising cage, approaching. So close she screamed holy hell.

They've come for her. She knew they would. That inevitability was always a constant. Whatever wicked thing had done this to her would one day come. Cassandra didn't realize she had moved until she slammed her head and back against a wall. Didn't realize she was still screaming. Screaming, not from the pain but from the fear, the fear of knowing and of the unknown.

Eyes adjusting and now she saw the boy crouched in front of her, his hands up as if in surrender.

Pale prince?

Cassandra felt her heart slowing and those hyperventilating breaths seemed to arrive in calming huffs as she tried to make sense of the person in front of her. Young, yes, but not a boy, a teenager caught in-between childhood and manhood. His hands remained poised in front of him. She saw his lips moving, his voice becoming clear as her breathing calmed. Cassandra pursed her lips, swallowing her breath and screams.

"We're here to help," said this boy, this teenager.

Cassandra clenched her jaw, grinding her teeth, seething through her lips. Her chest rising and falling in thick stuttered heaves. And then there was a woman standing over the teen's shoulder, short and thin. A tiny little woman.

"Hide away," she ordered, although Cassandra wasn't sure if the command was for her or someone else, but she saw this woman's hair shift as if something crawled beneath the hairline.

She took a deep, thick breath into her lungs.

"Good," said the teen. "Try to calm down."

He breathed deeply too, as if coaching Cassandra. Three breaths in unison.

"It's okay," said the teen. "My name is Tyler. We're here to help."

Cassandra shot her eyes to the little woman.

"That's Kera," said Tyler and he looked over his shoulder at the little woman, who wore a puzzled although intuitive stare as if she were looking through Cassandra. Her eyes on Cassandra's stomach before she turned away.

"What's your name?" asked Tyler.

Cassandra's eyes darted to him, stiff and wide. She pursed her lips, forcing her name through a dry throat that hasn't talked in weeks. "C-C-Cas-Cassandra."

"Cassandra," Tyler repeated. "How long have you been here?"

She had no answer. All she could do was shake her head.

"It's okay. Don't worry about that now." Tyler's voice was calm, sympathetic, nurturing. "I was abducted too. Kera is helping us out of here." He looked at her, really looked at her as he nodded. "Do you want to come with us? Would you like to leave?"

Is that possible? Cassandra thought. Was this an illusion? Is she hallucinating? Do these people even exist? Cassandra noticed how Kera was surveying the cage, looking up then over then to the ground then to the trough where Cassandra had drunk. Drank because when the thirst is so strong, it drives the mind into madness. The only fix is to drink. Drink or die. Kera walked to the trough, crouched down, looking.

"Cassandra?" said Tyler. Cassandra snapped her head to him. "Do you want to leave with us?" He offered his hand.

Cassandra looked at his hand, then his eyes, then his hand.

"Come with us," he said. "It's okay. We're not here to hurt you. We want out of here just as much as you do."

Cassandra heard a soft splash, and she turned to see Kera with her hand in the trough. Cassandra's skin fluttered, her head shaking, watching as Kera surveyed her hand, or what was in her hand. She breathed, breathed and sighed or grunted. Cassandra wasn't sure. Wiped her hands on her pants and stood.

"Tyler," Kera said, turning to him. For a brief moment, Kera looked at Cassandra with a stare likened to pity with a hint of fear behind that stare. "May I speak with you for a moment?" And she head gestured for them to move away from Cassandra, out of earshot. Walked away from beneath the cage as if this was a command and not a question.

"Of course," said Tyler, then he looked at Cassandra. "Just breathe," he said. "Try to get your wits about you." He was nodding. "We can leave whenever you're ready, but we're not leaving you here. Okay?"

Cassandra never moved as she watched Tyler turn and join Kera. Waiting for the pain she knew was inevitable. And her stomach squirmed.

24

9:15 PM
The Warehouse
Jigglyspot

The time has come, Jiggly thought as he watched SAC Mills through the glass separating himself from Mills. The detective was changing, his brain turning, and judging by the amount of blood dripping from his ears, nose, mouth, and eyes, the change was coming on fast. It was only a matter of time before the Dark Lord appeared and Jiggly could finally enjoy himself. Drink some blood, swallow extraction, and indulge in the flesh.

Mills was pacing back and forth across the room, and Jiggly was sure he was about to start running, slamming his head against the walls in some maddening pursuit of insanity. Jiggly laughed, although beneath the surface, Jiggly felt pity and, simultaneously, jealousy. Like watching an old friend achieve success that wasn't meant for you, although it would have been nice. Would have been humbling had the success landed on his doorstep, because then he would have power, or some form of power at least. Considering his warlock powers never fully manifested-the only warlock powers Jiggly has are the ability to feel and manipulate energy, read thoughts, and see through his choices-it would be nice to have a stronger power, like the well-known elder blast.

Jiggly pinched the bridge of his nose, eyes closed, and took a deep breath allowing the jealous thought to vanish from his mind before he sat down by the desk where the camera monitors were. "Let's see how our volunteers are doing?" Jiggly said, talking to himself. Lulled his tongue inside his cheeks as he punched the enter key on the keyboard. A moment later, the monitor lit up. The warehouse where the adults were kept revealed on the monitor. The room was bathed in white vapor, but he could see the adults. Some crawling across their cages, others hunched over on the floor, some bobbing up and down, while others stood in awe. Jiggly used his mouse to zoom in on the males. To get as close to the eyes as possible. "There you are just don't move," Jiggly said as if the full-grown beer bellied male could hear him. The monitor zoomed in on his eyes with dilated pupils staring wide with wonder. And Jiggly laughed. "Perfect," he said when a loud bang shook the room. Jiggly's eyes darted to the glass where Mills was standing. His mouth gaped open as if some bellowing scream was silenced, refusing to leave the throat. John's face was covered in blood, his eyes rolling, wet with tears and gore. His head shaking, trembling, shuddering. Started slamming his head into the three-inch-thick glass.

"Oh, Detective Mills," said Jiggly. "Seems like the Dark Lord is manifesting." Another crash from Mills, his hands balled into tight fists jabbing at his ears. "I know my man, I know." Jiggly's voice was sympathetic. "Rebirth is so painful. So cold and frightening." Mills then darted, his feet shuffling, running, scuttling, and he slammed into the far wall. Backed up, then ran into the wall again. Two, three, four times, then spun around and went at the wall to Jiggly's left. Jiggly craned his head to watch. "Ahh, resistance is futile, detective." Jiggly sat forward, clucked his tongue, and said, "Stop fighting, detective. Just let it..."

Gary burst through the door, panicked and huffing. "Jig's," he said, after he caught his breath. "We've got a problem." He was still covered head to toe in dried blood and Jiggly wondered if showering was as foreign to Gary as the grey aliens Mills kept talking about.

Jiggly rolled his eyes and sat back in his chair. "What is it Gary?"

Gary was out of breath. He huffed and said, "I can't find Helmsley. I think he's hiding."

"Hiding?" Jiggly repeated.

"Yeah. I looked everywhere. He's gone. It's like he disappeared or something."

Jiggly shook his head. "Gary, you're incompetent at best. He's in here somewhere."

Another loud bang from Mills and Gary jumped. "Holy shit," he said. "Is that Mills?" He stepped closer to the glass. "I've never seen this before... fascinating."

Jiggly looked at Mills again, his hands clawing at his ears. Soon, Jiggly thought. Very soon indeed. He turned to Gary and stood up.

"Gary," he ordered and waited as Gary peeled his eyes away from Mills.

Another slam into the mirror and Gary shook, startled.

"Gary?" Now he was growing frustrated. Shouted, "GARY!" when Gary's eyes snapped to him. "You're annoying me, Gary."

Gary shook his head. "I'm sorry Jiggly. I can't find him anywhere. I looked. He's nowhere in here." Gary looked back at Mills, a look of fear plastered across his face. "The Dark Lord will be so very angry with me."

Jiggly was certain Gary was about to have a full-blown panic attack. Some people just can't take the pressure. Stupid Human Scum, Jiggly thought. Zero intellect useless humans.

"It's okay Gary," Jiggly said, his voice harsh although empathetic.

Gary was shaking his head. "No, it's not. I failed. Dark Lord will be angry. I don't want that wrath." His voice was high pitched and whining.

Now Jiggly shook his head. "No Gary. I'll find Helmsley. He's in here somewhere. He'll come to me like a lost puppy, don't worry."

Relief filled Gary's eyes. "Oh, my lord." His breath huffed, his chest heaved up and down. "Thank you Jiggly. I can always count on you."

Jiggly eyeballed him, his lips curled in a devious smirk. "But I need for you to escort our hostess to the warehouse." Jiggly looked at Gary with a stern and hypnotizing stare. "Do you understand Gary? Ceremony will begin soon and the masters must take their place before the Goddess is presented. Do you understand?"

Gary nodded. "I do. Get the hostess to the ball and you'll find Helmsley, right? But what if you can't find him? What if it takes too long?" He shook his head. His panic returning with a vengeance.

Jiggly raised his voice, "No worries, Gary. If I'm not back by the time the masters arrive, Ira is more than capable of welcoming the Goddess. Just go to the café and inform him, although inconspicuously. Ira will welcome the opportunity, believe me."

Another slam from Mills. Gary's eyes went to him, said, "What if you can't find Helmsley? I'm afraid of what the Dark Lord will do."

"I'll take care of it, Gary. Just bring the hostess in, then get Ira. If you have any trouble with the hostess, grab Apoch. His size always puts fear into anyone he's close to."

Gary nodded. "Okay Jigs. I got it."

Another slam from Mills. This time, the glass cracked, and Gary jumped back. "What about him?"

Jiggly was watching Mills as Mills ran his tongue across his teeth, lapping those incisors, his jaw stretched into an unnatural gape.

"No need to be concerned with this one," said Jiggly. "When the time is right, he will know what to do. Always has." Jiggly turned to Gary, seeing the Glock 9mm now shaking in Gary's hand. Jiggly rolled his eyes. "Put the gun away, Gary. Before you shoot yourself… or better yet, before you shoot me or Mills."

Gary looked at Jiggly, then Mills, then back to Jiggly.

"Now Gary."

Gary nervously holstered his weapon. Jiggly stepped to him and reached for his shoulders as Gary locked eyes with him.

"Deep breaths Gary. Deep breaths. I'll get Helmsley. No need to fret. I need you thinking clear, okay?" Gary nodded nervously. "Go to the hostess. That's easy Gary. She's weak and has been in that cage for two weeks, alone and in the dark. She hasn't the strength to give us a fight. Go Gary. Go now."

Gary looked at Mills, then back to Jiggly, who cocked those dark purple eyebrows. "Okay," Gary said, took a deep breath then repeated, "Get the hostess."

Jiggly pushed Gary's shoulders towards the door and Gary moved to it, repeating, "Get the hostess," as he walked from the room, and the door closed behind him.

Jiggly took a deep breath, his eyes on Mills, who was in the center of the room talking to himself in quick stuttered mumbles. "Got to tell everyone. Aliens are here. Always have been."

And Jiggly said as if Mills could hear him, "That's right, detective. Always have been. But there's no one you can tell. No one who will listen. Not anymore detective. That opportunity was never yours to reveal. But worry not, detective. All your pain will end soon enough."

25

9:18 PM
The Warehouse
Lilly

She felt like she was floating. As if everything was just right in the universe. Lilly snapped her eyes shut, attempting to think, to remember where she was and most of all to remember Christopher was in here too. She had to survive whatever was coming and must keep her wits in check to do so. She held her breath again, uncertain if her plan was working or not. The vapor was everywhere, plumes of vapor so thick even Kathy Crawford, on the floor beside her feet, had disappeared. No chance to avoid the vapor, no chance of getting away. Lilly felt herself drifting as she searched her memory for a thought, a celebration, a time and place where Christopher and Sam and Tad were with her. Anything to jog the thoughts with a clear sign she was locked up against her will.

She could feel the vapor, cool and moist, on her skin. Her nose wet and dripping, she wiped it off, felt beads of moisture trickle off her nose. Her lungs burned for air she'd been holding her breath for so long. Her head on fire. Or was it the vapor that burned? Dizzy now, Lilly grabbed the cage, held on tight as if she were on a ride. A ride, she thought. The Shibalba X-Press. Spinning. Whirling. The world smeared across her vision in a blur. Christopher on her right. She's watching him, terror plastered across his face, wide eyes unable to close.

Close your eyes, Christopher, she thought. Don't look my baby. Don't see the terror they have waiting.

Coughs and hacks beneath the surface, existing inside the memory, although she knew where they came from, reaching from reality into her thoughts. Her legs weak, unsteady, she gripped the cage tight. Hold on, she thought. Does this ride ever end?

The vapor was lasting so long, Lilly could still hear it hissing from the floor. She tried to recant how long it's been. Two minutes, ten or more? Had she been holding her breath this whole time? Impossible, she thought.

She was on the floor, sitting and holding her legs close to her chest. When did she get here? There was no memory of sitting. Felt something move on her left and her heart shuddered. What is it? Her jaw slack as she watched the vapor, mesmerized when Kathy Crawford crawled out of the thick plume. Lilly could see how Kathy's hair was saturated, her eyes wet, eyelids sagged across pupils as large and dark as eight balls. Moist beads of vapor across her skin. Kathy fell into Lilly's arms, her body trembling and shuddering. Lilly held her tight, started rocking back and forth.

Kathy's body felt tantalizing, rippling pure effervescent flutters across Lilly's skin. Lilly's head drifted up and to the left, felt her eyes race behind her skull. Her jaw agape, wide and...

Lilly's eyes shot open wide. She saw Christopher standing over her, quickly growing small as if he floated away, far away, until he was nothing more than a distant star. A blip in the night sky that burned quickly and was gone. Now she's drifting in the darkness. Existing outside of the known universe. Where are we going? she thought. Lilly felt her chest rise and fall, heard her own breathing.

Hold the thought, she told herself. Keep the memory. Remember...

Something. Someone. What is this feeling?

26

9:20 PM
The Warehouse
Tyler

"What do you mean, pregnant?" asked Tyler, looking over his shoulder at Cassandra lying on the ground, curled into a ball. "She doesn't look pregnant." He turned to Kera, her eyes still fixed on Cassandra.

"She's a part of the show," Kera explained. "The hostess, the host for the masters." She turned to Tyler. Those tentacles wrapped around her head, weaved through her hair, staring at him.

"What does that mean, Kera? That she's about to give birth to some demonic entity from the netherworld?"

"The correct term is Xibalba."

"Whatever that is."

"And not just one, Mr. Tyler, sixty-six."

"What?" Tyler shook his head, eyes narrowed. He turned to Cassandra. "How? Her stomach would be the size of a hot-air balloon."

"They're not human size babies. More like spiders. And they're pushing through. That's why her pain is so strong. They're clawing their way out."

Cassandra's body started to stretch and wretch, a low murmuring whine in the back of her throat.

"Here it comes," said Kera.

Tyler watched the clawing murmuring pain soaked Cassandra. "Clawing?" Tyler whispered. "Your telling me she's about to have sixty-six spiders tearing out of her body any minute now?"

"Yes, Mr. Tyler," said Kera as she walked towards Cassandra.

"That's exactly what I'm saying."

Tyler followed as Cassandra bellowed a blood-curdling scream. Kera kneeled beside Cassandra, took her hand in her right palm and touched her forehead, wiping sweat off her brow, then smoothed Cassandra's hair away from her eyes. Cassandra's eyes were on Kera, a profound stare of pain and suffering, fear and confusion, as her head dropped to the ground and Cassandra forced a breath down her throat.

Kera said, "I'm here, my lady. It's okay. It's all going to be okay. Lay back now, close your eyes. I'm going to see if I can help you, okay?" Kera nodded and Cassandra returned the nod. Tyler wasn't sure if Cassandra was giving the okay or if she was mesmerized by Kera's eyes. Nonetheless, Cassandra closed her eyes and Kera released her hand, started feeling Cassandra's stomach, then lifted her shirt. Tyler's eyes went wide when that shirt was lifted. He could see the claws gaping through Cassandra's skin, so many moving parts—sixty-six remember—it seemed like Cassandra's innards carried a wave of spiders, like a river of pulp pooled inside a drain with no place to go other than to wretch and claw out. Kera's hand on Cassandra's stomach, pushing down.

"What are you doing?" Tyler, a slight panic in his voice.

"Guiding them," said Kera. She pointed to the wood trough.

"Guiding them where?"

Kera said, "See if there's any eggs in there."

"Eggs?"

"Yes, eggs."

Tyler looked at the trough: old splintered wood, dark and weathered.

Cassandra started moaning, her breathing shallow.

"Go Tyler," Kera ordered, her hands over Cassandra's stomach. "I need to see if she took all the eggs."

Tyler went to the trough, standing over it, looking in. Red liquid no more than a half inch high, buzzing with flees on top of the still surface. "I don't see any eggs." He turned to Kera.

"Put your hands in," she said. "Feel for anything small, the size of your pinky nail."

Tyler turned to the water.

"Now Tyler." Kera's eyes were locked in on Cassandra's stomach; head close as if she were whispering to those spiders. Her hands moving, fingers stretched, in quick movements circling right, then left.

Tyler shook his head, dipped his hands into the trough, searching, feeling. Felt a thick shell against his fingers. "Found one," he said, holding it above his head. The egg was tiny, like Kera said, the size of his pinky nail, and black.

"Perfect, put it on the floor. Keep looking."

"Why is this so important?" Tyler placed the egg on the floor, dipped his hands back in.

"To make sure they all come out. That we didn't miss any of them. Wouldn't want to leave one in there. It'll crawl out of her stomach and kill her."

"What?" Cassandra hollered.

Kera put her hand on Cassandra's forehead. "No, no, my dear. I'm not going to allow that to happen. That's why I need to be sure how many you swallowed."

Tyler felt for more eggs, swished his hands through every corner. "No more," he said.

"Are you sure?"

"Yes." Tyler noticed how calm Cassandra seemed, as if Kera's touch had a calming effect.

"Crush that egg under your foot," instructed Kera.

Tyler slammed his foot down, heard a quick crack, then said, "What I don't get is if she's about to give birth, isn't that a part of this..." He paused. "Whatever fucking ceremony is happening here."

Kera's eyes were staring at Cassandra's stomach. "I'm not following you."

Tyler shook his head. "What I mean is, is she supposed to give birth here? Seems like that doesn't make sense. If any of this makes sense."

Kera froze, and looked up at Tyler, a perplexed look on her face.

"What?" Tyler huffed.

Kera's eyes blinking, those tentacles raised high, staring in the opposite direction.

"Hide," she said.

"What? Why?"

Kera looked at Cassandra, moved her hands off her stomach and Cassandra tensed and shuddered, a painful groan in the back of her throat. Kera turned to Tyler. "You're right. She's not supposed to give birth here." Tyler noticed Cassandra's wide eyes, staring, unbelieving, unknowing. "Which only means one thing."

"What?" Tyler's voice cracked. Across the room, a door opened.

"They're coming to get her."

27

9:25 PM
Somewhere Shiny
SAC John Mills

"Strength. Power. Control."

Mills wiped his forehead, sitting on the floor, his head leaning against the wall. His hand covered in blood. The pain in his brain, and the itch in his ear, gone. In their place came the voice, low and gruff, as if it came from another world, another dimension. An undiscovered realm outside of the known universe existing in his mind. Mills sniffled and snarled, wiped the snot and blood from his nose.

"Think of all we will have. Together, we can do all things."

Mills closed his eyes, leaned against the wall, exhausted.

"No regrets. Fulfilled desires around every corner, behind every door. Never say sorry. No apologies, no shame nor guilt."

Opened his mouth wide, his right foot trembling, shaking and shuddering, his head drifting wearily.

"Lorraine will be pleased." And the voice laughed, a strong, thick, and sinister laugh that seemed to echo inside the room. "So pleased indeed."

John's head spinning, or is that his mind, thoughts and scenes, an ocean of bones and skulls. The Dark Lord standing on the shore of this demonic ocean of death. His skin the color of burnt ash, and so tall he seemed colossal. Hooves as feet, thick muscular legs like a horse. An erection the size of John's leg. Torso thin, voluptuous breasts, and toned, like his arms, arms that reached into talons. His head reflected a bull with horns tinted gold and red. His teeth were ivory fangs stained with blood and that thick nose exhaled the putrid stench of rotting death.

Eyes like a cat, glittering an emerald red. The Dark Lord grinned.

John slammed the back of his head against the wall. Once. Twice. Three times. Four.

"I'm already in, detective. You can't get me out."

John forced his eyes open, his eyelids weighing like heavy anvils, his vision smeared with blood and sweat. He saw the shiny room around him. Labored breath, his chest struggling to bring in air.

The Dark Lord laughed. "Somewhere shiny, detective. How sweet. Come John. Come to me."

He could see himself stepping into the body of the Dark Lord. He snapped his eyes open, sensing a pull like gravity spiraling him towards the Dark Lord. Mills struggled to break the connection.

Stay awake, he told himself. Don't give in.

And the Dark Lord laughed. "Good John. Good. I want you to fight. I want you to carry that last ounce of strength into my dark heart."

John pushed himself to his wobbling feet. Stood up and had to catch himself from falling back.

The Dark Lord's head craned, watching, observing.

John shuffled to the door, shiny metal, his hand on the doorknob. Locked. Heard his heavy breathing between his ears, felt spit web off his lips. John saw his reflection. His face covered in blood. So much blood. *Is that really me?* Black holes where his eyes should be. Ivory fangs covered with blood tore out of his gums and John jumped into a panic, pulling on the doorknob when his body was thrown backward across the room.

The back of his head smacked against the wall before his body flopped forward. Vision blurred between darkness and shiny metal.

"Stay here a while, John."

Metal. Darkness. Heavy breathing.

"Give me a moment if you please."

Metal. Heavy breath.

"It's going to be so, so beautiful."

Darkness. Heavy breath.

"Sleep now John. Let me complete our union."

Metal. Fading breath.

"All is well, Detective Mills. I am in."

Darkness.

28

9:30 PM
The Warehouse
Tyler

He hid behind a stack of wooden crates, watching. The guy, the man who walked into the warehouse, was startled when he saw Kera. She rushed into the moment. Referred to him as Gary and ushered in urgency when she said, "We need to get her into position. She's about to give birth," amid Cassandra's wails and cries.

Tyler watched-Gary's back to him-while Kera continued to plead. Gary looked over the warehouse and Tyler saw Gary's gun holstered on his right side.

"How did you get here?" Gary asked. "Does Jigs know you're here? He didn't say anything. Hasn't mentioned you at all."

Kera's hands over Cassandra's stomach. Cassandra squirming on the floor, writhing in pain, breathing shallow. Kera said, "Of course Jiggly knows I'm here. You think I'd miss solstice?"

Gary continued looking over the warehouse and Tyler ducked down when his gaze roamed across the crates where Tyler hid. Now crouched down, Tyler watched through the crate's cracks.

"Gary!" Kera shouted. "Help me get her up. They're coming."

A moment later Gary said, "All right missy, let's go."

Tyler watched while Gary leaned forward and helped Kera bring Cassandra to her feet.

"How long?" Gary asked, draping Cassandra's arm across his neck.

Cassandra screamed, hunched over, the scream erupting into painful cries.

"Any second," said Kera. "Pick her up. It's the only chance we have."

Gary scooped Cassandra into his arms. "Let's go, missy, we got devils to birth."

Kera followed close behind and looked over her shoulder at the crates. Tyler watched as she mouthed the word "Go," before turning to catch up with Gary.

They disappeared down a long, dark hallway. Cassandra's wails fading. Tyler heard a door open, then close with a thud. Heard Gary say before the thud, "Turn off the drug."

Tyler stepped away from the crates. Looked over the warehouse. Silence now. Still and calm and quiet. His skin hot, beads of sweat cascaded across his forehead and down across his temples.

He's got a gun, Tyler thought. A gun I can use. If I can get to it.

Tyler looked around the warehouse. Mostly empty except for the crates and prison where Cassandra was held against her will. He pushed the top crate off the stack. Dropped his foot down, snapping the wood.

The wood was worn and weathered, but it would do. A rusty nail poked out of the wood. Tyler swung the wood, assessing how it felt in his hands. Took another look over the warehouse. Alone. Nothing stirred in the open space. Tyler pursed his lips.

Got to get that gun, he thought.

Tyler followed the path where Gary, Kera, and Cassandra went. Down the long dark hallway, ahead a door and beyond the door, another room, another part of the warehouse. Tyler saw smoke or vapor dissipate in that room. Saw Gary standing close to the door. Not too far at all.

29

9:40 PM
The Warehouse
Lilly

They burst through the door. Lilly saw three people enter the room with a hurried anticipation. She heard the hissing vapor abruptly stop, dissipating quickly. She felt perspiration across her face, dripping off her chin and nose. Kathy was still in her arms, her body jerked and twitched every so often. Lilly felt her eyelids open wide, felt her eyeballs bulge and swell. Her breathing shallow. Her shoulders bobbed in unison with her breath.

"Put her down," said a voice from one of the three. Lilly noticed how tiny the woman was, how thin and small.

Watched as Gary—I think that's his name—placed the girl in his arms on the floor as she hollered in pain. Gary addressed the crowd as the tiny woman knelt beside the woman on the floor. "Get ready people," Gary hollered. "The masters are coming."

Lilly looked around the room. Saw how everyone was lying down or sitting with their backs against the bars. None stirred. Complacent. In her own cage, Lilly noticed the same. She shook Kathy. "Get up," she whispered. "Something's happening." She shook again. No response. Kathy's head was buried in Lilly's lap. Lilly opened her arms, and Kathy flopped to her side. Her eyes all black and Lilly cringed, shuddered back. Looked around the cage. All their eyes were black.

And the woman on the floor screamed bloody hell.

30

9:45 PM
No longer in the dark
Cassandra

The pain arrived as if a freight train had crashed into a semi-truck at full speed. She could feel her intestines being nipped at. So much movement she could hardly breathe. Kera's hands over her stomach, guiding out whatever was in. Cassandra wasn't sure if it was the pain that disturbed her the most or the squirming. She could feel tiny legs scurry in her stomach, as if they expected the birth, frenzied and hungry.

Gary made an announcement that Cassandra couldn't hear with any formal articulation; her focus was on the pain and squirming. He held out a switchblade for Kera.

"Here you go," he said as Cassandra felt her eyes grow wide.

"I don't need that?" said Kera.

"What'd you mean? Cut her open. How else are they gonna get out?"

"Primitive humans." Kera shook her head, her hands massaging Cassandra's stomach. She lifted Cassandra's legs by the knee. Cassandra was huffing now as Kera put her hand on Cassandra's forehead. "You have to push now," she said.

Gary put the knife in his pocket as a striking pain erupted in Cassandra's gut and she felt tiny little legs crawling inside her pelvis.

"Here they come," said Kera, and those tentacles raised high, her hands pushing down on Cassandra's stomach.

She felt more legs scurry over her inner thigh. Felt warm liquid across her thigh, jutting from her vagina.

Kera looked at her. "It's just blood," she said so matter of fact.

"Keep pushing."

Cassandra gripped Kera's hand, squeezing tight, her stomach wrenching, feeling, sensing, knowing those little devils were crawling out of her. Cassandra lifted her shoulders and chest, squeezing Kera's hand. Moans, groans, and whimpers escaped from her throat. Felt her face flush, her temples constrict, as she pushed, bellowing a scream from her lungs. Saw how a spider crawled on her stomach, so tiny the little one was. Cassandra's eyes wide.

"Keep pushing," Kera called.

Cassandra shot Kera a cold stare, saw those tentacles staring and pushed with all her might. Felt like a brain aneurysm was on the brink. Felt more legs crawling over her skin. Her thighs and legs. Heard yipping screeches from the spiders as if they were calling to each other. Talking. Cassandra's little children were already talking.

"One more push," Kera hollered. Their eyes met. "You can do this." Kera lifted Cassandra up. "Push!" she hollered.

And Cassandra did push. A screaming, blood curdling, pain-wrenching push that followed with an exodus of spiders jutting from her vagina into the room. Felt a rush of warm blood pool beneath her. Watched as the spiders rushed across the floor, a horde of spiders with blood-soaked feet crawled in a hurried panic towards the cages.

"There they are," Gary said.

Cassandra watched as those spiders ran across the room in all directions.

"Go get em." Gary again, bobbing his head as he watched the spiders crawl across the ground.

Cassandra dropped on her back, breathing heavy, still holding Kera's hand. Her head turned to the right and she could see how the spiders crawled over unsuspecting prisoners. They never moved, the prisoners, some lying down, some curled into a ball on the floor, some staring, sitting with their backs against the cage. Her eyes drifted to the dead body, blood beneath the dead girl with her throat cut. Watched the spider crawl on top of the body. It seemed to be sniffing the dead rot, then ran to the nearest female, who sat with her knees to her chest. The spider crawled up her arm. Cassandra watched as it entered the woman's ear.

"Perfect," said Gary. "We can open the cages now. Let the masters out."

Cassandra's breathing was hurried, her chest rising and falling in quick huffs. Her eyes darting across the room, watching as the spiders crawled into their ears.

Kera turned to her, said, "Can you get up?"

Cassandra thought for a moment, then nodded.

"Gary, help me with her." Kera switched Cassandra's hand to Kera's left. Put her right hand behind Cassandra's back.

"Fuck her," said Gary. "Let her lie there and rot. Shoulda cut the bitch open."

Cassandra heard a mechanical snap, then saw how the cages lifted off the ground. For such a tiny woman, Kera had immense strength; she helped Cassandra to her feet, her legs wobbly. Saw the blood on the floor. My blood, Cassandra thought, as her stomach churned and boiled acid into the back of her throat. She felt sick, weak, her arm draped across Kera's shoulders when screams erupted, wailing voices drenched in pain and fear. Saw Kera's tentacles blink, seeming to retreat as if those pupils sought to run.

"Where are you going?" Gary, he was in front of them, his back to the door.

"Taking her back," said Kera.

Gary shook his head. "I don't think so. I'll take her back, Kera. Why don't you wait here for Jigs? I'm sure he'd like to have a word with you. Besides..." He craned his head, his eyes roaming from Cassandra's legs to her eyes. "I think I'll have a run with this one." And he licked his lips and grinned with a sparkle in his eye. "Can't let a good opportunity vanish into thin air. Plus... I love blondes."

Cassandra cringed, turning away from Gary.

Kera said, shaking her head, "No Gary. I'll take care of her." She stepped to the right and Gary blocked her way.

"What's with you?" he said. "I smell a rat, Kera."

More screams, moans, and groans, and Cassandra could feel how Kera's shoulders tensed.

"You have no idea what you're talking about. Lead the masters to ceremony, that's what you need to do." She stepped again and again Gary blocked her way.

"I don't think so." He was shaking his head, pulled out that switchblade, and pointed it at them when Cassandra saw the door open over Gary's shoulder, slowly and cautiously. "She's coming with me, Kera. I couldn't give a fuck what you say." And he laughed. Laughed with his eyes on Cassandra. "It's gonna be so much fun."

Laughed out loud Gary did. His wide open ear to ear grin was interrupted by a plank of wood and a nail that tore into the side of his head. Cassandra jumped from the sound of wood cracked against Gary's skull. That laugh cut off at the seams as the body went slack. His jaw hung loose. Blood squeezed from his eyes, nose, and dripped off his lips. He dropped to his knees, fell face first on the floor with that nail still buried in his skull. His knife still in hand.

Tyler stood where Gary had been. He went to the body as the screams and bellows from the prisoners erupted into a maddening frenzy. Tyler took the gun and holster from Gary's hip, checked the clip-fully loaded-then replaced it.

Clipped the holster to his hip and said, "Time to go."

31

9:55 PM
The Warehouse
Lilly

The scene was muted. All Lilly could hear was a loud, chronic buzzing in her eardrums. Spiders everywhere. Crawling, whining spiders. Lilly looked down at Kathy, saw a spider crawling across her shoulder towards her ear. Lilly craned her head, staring, saw the spider stare back as if assessing Lilly's intention. Its mouth gaped open with a whine. Lilly shook her head, widened her eyes, head moved back.

The little thing, she thought. And it has teeth, how unique.

The spider gaped again, stood erect as if to be threatening then scurried up her arm as Lilly shuddered back and slapped the poor thing, hard and fast. When she removed her hand the spider was a splat of guts across her skin. Her attention snapped by a loud crack and pop. That guy, Gary or Larry or Barry, whatever his name is, slumped to the ground, some wooden board stuck to the side of his face.

Is he... dead?

Such strange occurrences happening in this room. Lilly craned her head, watching blood pool beneath Gary or Barry or Larry's head. Bulbs of light walloped across Lilly's vision, trying to follow what was happening outside the cage. The cage, she thought. What cage? She looked for it. Nope, no cage anywhere. Looked up. Oh, there it is. They're letting us out, she thought, eyes drifting to the three people standing over the dead body. Lilly adjusted her eyes; blinked hard, then stretched her eyelids.

A gun, she thought. The kid, he looked like a kid, took the gun from Larry or Barry. No, it's Gary, I'm sure of it. That loud buzz in her ear growing louder. Beneath the buzz, commotion, something happening, something big. Felt her heart jump with thick walloping beats as the three people walked out of the room.

Cool, she thought. We can leave!

We can leave.

She shook Kathy. "We can leave," she whispered, or maybe her voice was loud, hard to tell with the buzzing in her eardrums. "Kathy..." Lilly looked at Kathy, her eyes wide and black, mouth open, body limp in Lilly's arms, hair dropped from her skull to the floor. Another spider half in, half out of Kathy's right ear, burrowing into her brain. Kathy squirming in Lilly's arms.

"Kathy?"

Kathy's chest jumped, arms flailing. Her head shuddering, fingers arched, curled into talons. Mouth wide and screaming. Yes, Kathy is screaming. Lilly's knees bobbing, shaking, when the buzzing stopped and all she could hear were screams, hollers, and painful groans. Looked around the room. Bodies lying on the floor, shuddering, convulsing. Some were standing, arms stretched, heads back as if they were inhaling their first breath, and Kathy clawed at her skull, her ears, raking her ears with her fists. Her head shaking, screams erupting from her throat.

A floating film, like an electrical current, hovered around Kathy as her teeth, those incisors, sharpened and grew to a pointed tip, short and sharp as the black across her eyes receded, flowing like a gentle wave into her pupils where the black swirled like a funnel into the brain. Kathy's eyes now beaming a dull dark red.

"Kathy?" Lilly shook Kathy and looked around the room. One parent—a big burly man with an unkempt beard and cheap clothes—was kneeling over Gary. He pulled the board from his skull, then tossed it across the room. Growls and rumbles erupted, growing louder with each passing second. Lilly felt Kathy's body move, unable to take her eyes off the large man hovering over Larry–Barry-Gary as he flipped the body over and touched the forehead. His head bowed as if in a moment of silence for the dead. Lilly's heart jumped into a panic when the burly man snapped his eyes towards her, his eyes the same glint of red as Kathy's were a moment ago.

Kathy. Where is Kathy?

Lilly felt the pull before the pain, her hair grasped in an iron grip. Brought to her feet in one quick thrust and her skull burned from the thick wallop of hair that was pulled from her head. Kathy in front of her; she seemed to move like a snake. Her skin ghostly pale. Veins, red and blue, swelled like spider webs across her skin.

Those sharpened incisors were prominent when Kathy said, "Oh, don't worry, my lovely. We promise to be gentle."

Lilly's head was thrust to the side, exposing her neck as Kathy tore into Lilly's throat, clamped down, and gulped Lilly's blood.

All the while, Lilly heard screams. Heard them before she was aware they were coming from her throat. Eyes wide, blood-curdling screams, constant and forever. Her eyes floating, drifting across the room, and to the line of devils surrounding her, waiting in line for a taste of fresh blood.

32

10:00 PM
Cannibal Café
Sharon

She could hear screams. Sharon noticed how everyone in the room paused when the screams turned cold and curdling. Some closed their eyes as if savoring the moment. Kevin's eyes-wide and withdrawn-carried a guilty stare. Sharon noticed he hadn't touched his food. He looked pale, fearful, and sick. Nervous and unsteady, she saw his hands trembling as his bottom lip quivered.

"Are you okay?" she asked, her eyes narrow. "Looks like someone just walked all over your grave." Sharon sat back, arms crossed, glaring at Kevin.

Kevin said, "I'm just not sure if I can go through with it." He lifted those nervous eyes to Sharon. "Don't know if I'll be able to participate at the level I want to."

Sharon narrowed her eyes even more, staring at Kevin through slits. "Go through with what?"

Took him a moment to answer, as if he was afraid to answer, or ashamed. "You know Sharon." He closed his eyes while shaking his fist in front of him. Opened his eyes and turned to the ceiling, shaking his head before returning his gaze to Sharon. "You've always known. That's why they picked you." And he laughed, more like a chuckle, a nervous laugh. He sat back, folded his napkin over his lap, then smoothed it over with his hand.

"Kevin..." She craned her head, searching for his attention. "What are you talking about?"

Another pause before he answered. "You've always welcomed the devil, Sharon. Welcomed anything that would turn your career into the real." His eyes looking down, away from her stare, although

Sharon willed him to look at her. Look her in the eye and he did, looked right at her with that pitiful stare. "I wish I had your resolve, Sharon. You never were the unsuspecting debutante. You've always had that fire, that dark energy about you. An influence over others with a gentle and commanding tone. I envy you... I do." And he breathed hoarsely. His breath stuttered over shuddering lips. "Don't forget about me, okay? Whatever happens, just don't forget about me."

Touching, she thought when a familiar gong rang through the café. Sharon noticed how the guests all stood up. Five gongs in intermittent successions raged through the room and by the fifth reverberating vibration, the guests all stood around Sharon's table. Sharon looked at them, one by one, faces content, solemn, humble, staring at her. Kevin was the last to stand. He offered his hand.

"Come my lady," said Kevin. "The Dark Lord, Balaam, will welcome you once you've proved your worth. A Goddess you are now. Emmanuelle has proclaimed your transformation. Now you will rise, seated at the head of the table, a Goddess for all to worship."

Sharon knew he was right. Knew this was her moment. The world is yours, Sharon Mable. Yours to conquer.

Sharon raised her eyes to Kevin, a thin grin across her lips as she studied his hand. Sharon raised her chin high.

"You're right Kevin," she said. "The time *has* come." She took his hand, pushing up from her chair.

Ira was the first to holler, his hands raised above his head, palms to the sky. "Hail Satan," he proclaimed. And one by one, they all proclaimed the same.

33

10:05 PM
The Warehouse
Tyler

"You shouldn't have done that," hollered Kera, Cassandra's arms draped around Kera and Tyler's neck as they ushered her into the warehouse, back into the room where they found her. "I would have gotten her out. Now, all is compromised. Jiggly will know what's going on. So will the masters." She shook her head. "Not good, Tyler. Not good at all."

Tyler saw those tentacles glaring at him. "He wouldn't let you leave, Kera. I had to." Cassandra's heavy breath in his ear.

"No, you didn't. You think you had to. That's the difference, Tyler, and it's just another excuse to satisfy that murdering itch."

Cassandra's head rolled sideways to Tyler's shoulder. Her body went limp into Tyler's arms, catching her before she collapsed.

"She's weak," Kera said. "Lost a lot of blood."

"I can see that." Tyler guided Cassandra to the ground. Those big blue eyes staring at him, her pale, flushed skin moist with perspiration, staring at Tyler as if he were the conduit to peace and safety. Her lips dried and cracked. Nappy hair turned dark with sweat and soot. She appeared so sick, so weak and tired. He wondered if she had the strength to continue. Tyler turned to the hallway they came from; screams and hollers rattled the walls. Cassandra heard the same; her eyes darted from the hall to Tyler. "We can't stay here," he told her.

Cassandra mouthed, *I know,* then closed her eyes.

"Time to go, isn't it?" said Kera over Tyler's shoulder.

Tyler smoothed his hand over Cassandra's forehead. "I'm not

going anywhere. Not until I find my friends."

"That's a horrible idea. Look at her Tyler. She can't even walk. If you don't leave now, she's as good as dead."

"Agreed. That's what you're here for. You can lead her out so she can call the police."

"No," she ordered. "I told you already no police. Most of them are aware of what's happening tonight and those who don't know choose to keep their heads in the sand. You need to take her out of here and find a place to hide."

Tyler's lips curled in a sneer. This is not what he wanted to hear. The thought of his friends forever a slave burned inside his blood.

"You can't save your friends, Tyler."

Tyler spun around to his feet, confronting Kera. Those tentacles stood erect, as if in protection mode, as Kera stood unwavering with her arms crossed. He stepped closer, hand on his gun.

"There it is, that fire and rage. You mean to kill me too, Tyler? The one who got you out?"

She seemed to see straight through him, this alien, this woman, with a stare that burrowed through his soul.

"Go ahead," she said. "Pull that gun from your holster. See what happens. How many bullets do you have, Tyler?" She craned her head, looking at the holstered weapon. "Hmm," she said, pursing her lips. "A nine-millimeter. Fifteen bullets Tyler." She locked eyes with him. "And you've got all those masters, Jiggly on the prowl and let's not forget whomever else he has here. Hope you're a good shot, Tyler, because you'll have to kill a slew of masters with every bullet. So go ahead, waste one on little ol' me."

Tyler's breath caught in his throat. She's right, he thought. I'm not even sure what I'm dealing with, and Cassandra won't make it if we continue. He breathed deeply. The sound of his breath echoed in his ears.

"You're not all pure either, Kera," he said, shaking his head. "You've been with Jiggly for years and he's a murdering, raping, putrid fucker. What does that say about you?"

Her tentacles curled around her head, one across the back of her neck, the other around her throat, as if to embrace their host.

"And I got you out too, so what does that say about me?" The sneer across her lips proved he'd struck a nerve.

"It says you seek redemption," he said. "Maybe that's what this is all about. Redemption."

Kera's eyes turned from him, looking away. Shuffling behind him, Tyler turned to see Cassandra pushing herself to her feet.

"What're you doing?" Tyler stepped to her, took Cassandra's elbow, helping her up.

Cassandra shook her head. "Trying to get a grip on what the hell you two are talking about." She arched and stretched her back.

"Take her out of here, Tyler," said Kera. "She will not make it if you don't."

Tyler turned to Kera, then the hall, then back to Cassandra.

"No," Cassandra said. "I'm not going anywhere." She rolled her eyes. "Can't believe I'm saying this, but Tyler is right. I won't let people go through what... whatever it is, I just went through."

Kera said, "You're weak, Cassandra. Haven't eaten in weeks, and you just gave birth to spider devils that have been feasting on your insides for days, if not longer. You lost a ton of blood. This is futile."

Cassandra laughed. Maybe it was a nervous laugh, but a laugh all the same. "I'm aware of what just happened, thank you. They did crawl out of me, didn't they?" She rolled her eyes with a slight shake of the head. "No police, and we're out here in the middle of nowheresville. Even if we walk out the door, where will we go? Hide the rest of our lives? No, I'm tired of running. Tired of waiting. And most of all..." She eyeballed both Tyler and Kera. "I'm tired of these elite bastards getting away with bloody fucking murder."

Tyler was nodding, enjoying where Cassandra was going.

"I say we stick it to the fuckers. Burn this place to hell."

"We lost the element of surprise. They'll be coming after us. A lot of them too. Once ceremony is over, the Dark Lord will order them to find you... us." Tyler looked at Kera, her head moving back and forth. "That is something no one wants, believe me. These are insurmountable odds."

"Maybe you didn't hear me," said Cassandra. "I said stick it to the fuckers. I never mentioned surviving or walking out of here into the sunlight like we're characters in some movie." She shook her head. "I always hated fairy tales."

"She seeks revenge," said Kera.

"You're damn right," Cassandra shot back. "And I can't wait to see the fear in Ira's eyes before I claw them out with my bare fucking hands."

"Holy shit," Tyler blurted. "Damsel in distress just turned into Harley Q."

"You're both insane," Kera said.

Tyler ignored the comment and turned to Kera. "So," he said. "Where are my friends?"

34

10:10 PM
The Warehouse
Lilly

She dropped on her ass to the floor. Fell back, collapsing to the ground. The world spiraled around her, and she could hear her blood trickling in her veins like a stream gone close to dry.

Kathy had torn into her neck, clasping Lilly's head and shoulder as she drank. Lilly could feel the blood leaving, felt her face turn white and ghostly. And then, before the blood had gone forever, before death knocked on her door, Kathy released those incisors. And Lilly's legs buckled, like standing on scarecrow legs.

Somewhere, maybe it was all in her thoughts, or maybe it did exist, in this room or outside, but the gong pulsed through Lilly's body with a shudder tensing her bones. Her eyes wanted to shut out the world, clamp those lids forever and welcome darkness like some old comforting friend, but Lilly refused. Hang on, she told herself, seeing Christopher and Sam, a picture of her sons at their father's funeral. Kathy turned and Lilly could see they all turned as if mesmerized by the gong raging through Lilly's bones. Even the burly bearded one; Lilly could see him through Kathy's legs. Through his legs was that sassy woman, the one whose throat was cut. Her dead, black eyes seemed to stare into Lilly's soul.

"Come." Lilly heard someone holler. The burly man crept into her thoughts, thinking he was the one addressing the others. "All is in," he proclaimed. "Ceremony will soon begin."

And they all moved, shuffling feet moving towards the door on the opposite side. Lilly watched as they left. Some addressed each other. A hand on another's shoulder, a grin or laugh. They didn't look like devils or demons or vampires or zombies. They look like you, she thought. Like everyone else.

The burly bearded man waited by the door, holding it open for the others. And Kathy was the last in line. She stopped and the burly man craned his head, staring at her. His eyes then drifted towards Lilly as Kathy turned around. Both demons staring, earning Lilly's attention as the burly man stepped behind Kathy, his hand on her shoulders, a thin grin on his lips.

She heard Kathy—or the devil inside her—speak inside her mind. Lilly mesmerized by Kathy's glaring red and burning eyes.

My host savors your taste, this devil-demon-vampire said. *Wants more. Unfortunately, only the invited may attend celebration, but know that I'll be back. It's my duty to give my host a gift.* She craned her head. *Looks like that gift is you.*

Big burly man ran his tongue across Kathy's face, his arms around her shoulders.

Until then, the voice said. *Enjoy your brush with death before it claims you forever.*

And she smiled as the burly man laughed out loud, the two of them turning on their heels and through the door that closed with a heavy thud. Eyes drifting, Lilly felt hollow, depleted. That sassy girl still looking, staring. Lilly's eyes drifted to Gary. Saw the blood beneath his rotting corpse.

And the knife wedged beneath his back and the floor.

35

10:15 PM
The Small Observation Room
Jigglyspot

Helmsley was nowhere. Jiggly couldn't find him anywhere. Seemed like he disappeared into thin air. The Dark Lord will not be pleased, Jiggly thought as he scuttled back to the little observation room.

He also heard the gong and knew celebration was beginning. He'll have to miss it to keep searching for Helmsley. There was still time before the Dark Lord manifested completely. Midnight was close, but far enough for him to locate Helmsley. He's probably hiding in the rafters, scared and frightened. Maybe he knows what's coming? His intuition getting the better of him.

Jiggly heard the slams and head knocks from Mills before he entered the room. Apparently Dark Lord was having some fun with his new host before taking center stage in that pea brain of SAC John Mills.

The scene through the glass confirmed his suspicions. Mills had clawed his face from his ears to his lips. Nail marks dripping with blood across his skin as his mouth gaped open and Jiggly could see the Dark Lord's fangs in that mouth. Mills slammed his head against the wall and Jiggly shook his head as he took his seat.

"Go easy, Dark Lord," said Jiggly, clawing the mouse in his palm. "You don't want to cause too much damage. Might take too long to repair that brain." He clicked one of the camera feeds. He needed to check on Gary and make sure the hostess was delivered on time for the masters to manifest. Eyes narrowed when he saw Gary's dead body on the floor. "Shit." The masters must not have liked Gary. Jiggly shook his head. "No one ever likes Gary, fucking moron. I told him to keep his trap shut. Probably said something dumb."

At least he got the job done. The masters were gone, on cue with the gong a few minutes ago. His eyes fell on the woman lying on the floor. Not the one whose throat he cut, another. He could see her chest rising as Jiggly pursed his lips, shaking his head.

One master didn't make it. How unfortunate. One of Ira's people will need to take his place.

He opened another camera feed, checking on the marinades, large adult sized plexiglass coffin shaped boxes, ten of them, although only four were occupied. He could see the bodies in them, suspended in a dark liquid marinade, and the tubes that snaked out of the covers connected to oxygen tanks outside the boxes.

Good, Politiere is on point.

Clicked a third feed. His beloved children in cages. The masters should come for them soon, once the Goddess has taken center stage. He enjoyed watching as they huddled together. Some were crying, some bellowing insane pleas, and still more were quiet, not knowing what to do. And then, of course, there are the older ones who are more than likely attempting to find a way out. Jiggly laughed at the thought. *Stupid Human Scum.* He sighed. "All in a day's work." Started whistling, head bobbing. Despite Helmsley's disappearance-Gary too, although his death was inconsequential–all was right in Jiggly's world. Ceremony was beginning. The Goddess was arriving and the Dark Lord–Jiggly sat up to see Mills, still sitting and gaping and clawing–is on his way. Jiggly sat down. Eyes on the screen and the teenager who seemed to stare at him. Jiggly craned his head. "That little one," he said. "You see the camera, don't you? That's okay, my man. See all you want. You'll see more than you want soon enough." A laugh in his throat, Jiggly ran his tongue inside his mouth. "That's for sure."

Jiggly swiveled in his chair and jumped off as if he were on a spring.

"Fuckin Helmsley," he said, grabbing the doorknob. Started singing, "Where O where, has my Helmsley gone? Oh where, oh where, can you be?" as he opened the door. Kept singing on his way down the hall. And Mills' incessant need to batter his own brain rifled in the hall.

"Where, oh where, can you be?"

36

10:20 PM
Somewhere Shiny
SAC John Mills

He was caught between two worlds. Existing within two dimensions. The first, the shiny room where Mills pounded his skull against the wall, eyes bleeding, clawing fingernails across his flesh, ear itching, and incapable of breathing through his nose it was so bloody and swollen. The second, hell. A river of blood and bones and behind him a mountain of death, rotting corpses where the soul was torn from the body through the eyes, and the stench of cooking flesh forever stained like burnt toast in the air.

Dimension one, Mills a lackey, a battered and disgraced detective who allowed his wife and daughter to serve as playthings for the depraved. He could see Lorraine now, in his mind's eye, naked on their bed, the Dark Lord between her legs, and Lorraine writhing in ecstasy beneath him. He remembers then, remembers the times–so many times living beneath the folds of time–how he sat beside the bed as the demons sought pleasure in Lorraine. And his daughter, so young when she first took a demon to bed, now a teen lying beside Lorraine, waiting her turn for the Dark Lord. How Mills sat, unwavering, watching. And then Mills discovered a revelation: all he's been given has been provided by the Dark Lord. Looking back over the years he understood they had always been there, in the shadows, carried on the wind and under the breath with a curse and dark deed. Insignificant! His existence was insignificant, meant for one simple purpose: to serve.

This futile existence stretched to Xibalba, the second dimension where Mills was trapped. Dark crimson light stretched across the river and mountain of rotting corpses. Devils in the shadows, watching, or perhaps waiting. Waiting for the transformation to be complete when above him a door opened in the sky. Through the door, he could see the first dimension. The shiny room wavered back and forth, he saw the floor, then the air, the door like a camera to the first dimension, seeing the room, the metal counter where Mills remembered he'd lied on for so long, and his eye twitched with the sensational remembrance of that needle spinning in his eye. But then the camera moved, sweeping across the room to the glass, cracked from Mills' head, and quickly the camera went to it. Mills heard footsteps clap against the floor, watching as the mirror grew closer. A body in the cracks, his body. Close. Closer, his head reflected in the cracked, splintered glass. Saw his reflection and it wasn't him. Not all of him.

The eyes burning red, teeth like fangs, incisors prominently revealed with a smile. His skin now dark gray, as if burnt and smoldered for centuries. Smooth, black ivory horns sharpened to a razor tip tore from his skull. And he laughed, those red eyes staring, staring at him. The Dark Lord, Mills thought.

"That's right detective," said Mills, the reflection in the glass Mills, the Dark Lord Mills, the Mills who was standing in that first dimension. "All has been received by the unholy ghost."

Mills shuddered as a torturous, blood-curdling scream erupted on the other side of the mountain of death. A whip slashed across skin and bone. More screams, more flogging and blood.

"Enjoy my kingdom, detective. For in it, you are now a God."

37

10:25 PM
In a Hallway Beaming with Light
Sharon

Kevin had taken her hand, leading her down a long stretch of hallway. The others, including Ira and all who were in the café, led the way. She felt her heart stutter, irregular heartbeat, and the air in the hall seemed to turn thick, as if smog snuck into the hall and thickened upon arrival.

Sharon looked over their heads at the double doors at the end of the hall. Tall doors made from thick wood that seemed like an ancient relic. A tall oversized clown by the door, in his arms were robes, dark robes provided to each attendee. Ira was the first to take one as the line slowed to a crawl, then stopped. Ira wrapped the robe around his shoulders, staring at Sharon as he stretched his arms into the sleeves.

"What is this?" she whispered to Kevin.

"Ceremony," he replied, the word caught in his throat as if the very word attempted to choke him.

Sharon looked at him from the corner of her eye. He seemed depleted, nervous, and his palm was sweating. Her eyes drifted to the bandage beneath his turtleneck, stained with fresh blood. Sharon licked her lips, remembering when she'd bitten him, how the flesh tasted salty sweet and the blood thick and satisfying on her tongue. She closed her eyes, reliving the moment. Kevin's holler when she tore into his neck and how she felt the erection, the strap on, as if it was a part of her, as if it were her erection inside Kevin. And then more memories; the past two weeks playing like a movie in her head. Drinks with Cassandra on a Friday afternoon. Sharon convincing Cassandra to slip her name into the casting call for a new role, which must have worked, considering Ira was all over her tonight. She was sure she earned the role, despite Cassandra's exploits. No more Cassandra since that day. Won't she be surprised when she returns home to find this new Sharon on top of the world?

Kevin's sudden invitation to the big show, where they are now, a royal couple waiting for their crown. Hollywood royalty, the best kind. Kevin's gradual depletion. The changing tide between them, where once Sharon was subordinate now the tables had turned, and it was she, Sharon Mable, who owned the night. Who took him as she pleased whenever she pleased. She saw the devil in the mirror. Sharon remembered that night just over a week ago, Kevin behind her, and Sharon bent over the armoire, and in that mirror was the devil, dark red skin, jagged teeth. How she wanted to be that devil, wanted to feel the power, to know what it felt like to unleash holy hell. And then, the tide turned in her favor. Turned after she drank blood. Remembered drinking from that cup. But was it Kevin's blood? It had happened so quickly. She saw herself, the warmth of that cup against her lips and cheeks. Her breath steaming inside the cup, smoldering towards her nose. The blood, once across the lips, burst like supernovas in her mouth, down her throat radiating inside her stomach, where it remained like a seed. A seed she could see now, in her mind's eye, growing thick. The tree of life, roots planted in her womb, reaching to her feet. Those leaves and branches rising through her veins to her brain.

Sharon's eyes drifted open. The hall was empty. Not even the clown remained. A single cloak hung on a nail on the wall beside the doors. Quiet, so still and silent, Sharon could hear her heart beat, felt her blood raging in her veins. Her shallow breathing prominent between her ears. She looked around the hall. Over her shoulder was the door leading back to the café. Sharon swallowed her breath, felt heat rise across her skin, burning.

This is it, she thought, turning to the double ancient wooden doors. A doorway to a new life. The one you were always meant to live. What you were born for. She took the cloak off the wall, pushed her arms through the sleeves, and tied the rope around her waist. Stuttered, constricted breaths. She has to choose to go through that door; somehow she knew this was true. Once you walk through, there is no turning back. We must be confident in our decisions.

She pulled the hood over her head, fixed her hair beneath the hood, raking the bangs from her eyes.

Turned to the door.

This is it, Sharon Mable. The world is yours.

A sudden, although brief, smile crossed her lips. Sharon breathed through her nose, felt her heart race in her chest, a bead of sweat across her temple. Her hands hot, burning as if hovering over hot coals, igniting her skin in a fire of heat. Felt her lips curl into a sneer that melted into a grin.

And Sharon Mable opened the door.

Part V
The Show

1

10:30 PM
The Underground Tunnel
Cassandra

They were in some underground tunnel dimly lit with a yellow glow from the light bulbs scattered across the walls every twenty feet. Cassandra, weak and faltering, leaned against the concrete wall. Hard to breathe, the air so thick in the tunnel her lungs burned. Cassandra closed her eyes, forcing air into her lungs with deep, heavy breaths. Her thoughts on her stomach and those spiders that tore apart her innards. She could feel them now as if they remained inside, crawling, those tiny legs running, taunting, skittering within. And the bites and nibbles, what kind of damage did those little devils do?

"You okay, Cassandra?"

She lifted those heavy eyelids, staring at Tyler as he stood beside her. Kera in the background, watching them, those tentacles raised high on her head. So strange. So strange indeed.

"Cassie?" Tyler again. He slapped his hands in front of her eyes.

"Her name is Cassandra," said Kera, her arms crossed across her chest.

"I like nicknames." Tyler looked at Kera, then back to Cassandra.

Kera rolled her eyes, then stepped further down the tunnel. Cassandra looked at Tyler. Who is this person, she thought. Who is anyone really? Didn't matter too much, he was obviously on her side. Cassandra nodded, pursed her lips, and leaned her head against the wall.

"Yes," she huffed. "I..." Leaned her head forward, hands on her back. Took a deep breath. "Just needed a break."

"I told you," said Kera. She was staring at them. "She needs medical attention." Kera shook her head. "I suggest taking her out of here. She could be dying. More than likely is dying. The masters are not kind. What do you think they've been feeding on since they hatched in her stomach?"

"That's Cassie's decision, not yours." Tyler's voice was loud, desperate. Kera shook her head then looked down the hall. Tyler's face close to Cassandra's. "Can you make it?" he asked.

She stared deep into his eyes, said, "I ain't no damsel in distress." Cassandra stood erect, shoulders back, chin up. Said with as strong and convicted a voice as she could muster, "Let's go." She walked past Tyler. "I've got a debt to repay." Caught up to Kera and kept walking.

What Cassandra kept thinking, the thoughts that played in her mind, was that Kera was right: she was dying. A slow death, albeit a sure death. When those spiders tore from her stomach, they took something important. Little pieces of Cassandra were in the bellies of those beasts. Maybe too much. She felt hollow, as if they'd eaten through and emptied her stomach.

"How much further?" she heard Tyler ask Kera. Cassandra felt their eyes on her.

Kera answered, "Not far at all."

Good, thought Cassandra.

She wasn't sure how much time she had left in this world.

2

10:35 PM
The Warehouse
Lilly

One, two, three, four, move.

Lilly stretched her arms, palms to the floor, pulling herself towards Gary. That knife gleamed under the light as if it were Lilly's salvation, her only hope.

One, two, three, four, move. Another pull of her body across the floor, air so thick and hot she struggled to bring air into her lungs. She felt drained, for lack of a better word. Depleted. Her neck throbbing with a dull pain where that bitch Kathy bit her. A thick, although slow, beat of her heart pounded between her ears. Lilly's thoughts like a shining star buried in the hollow darkness of space, so far away, so distant she had to search to find them. Search for the reason or reasons to move on. Hunt for Christopher's eyes, Sam's smile and Tad's...

Fucking Tad, she thought. Son of a bitch. You got off easy.

Her limbs trembled. Breath stuttered. One, two, three, four, move. Fucking move. Lilly pulled herself across the floor, closer to the knife. Now on her elbows, she pulled closer. One, two, three, four, move. Her breath constricted, caught in her throat, moving again, arm over arm, her legs limp, following behind as if they couldn't move. As if the small amount of blood that remained in her veins had rushed to her head, erupting like a fire across her forehead.

Fucking Tad. Lilly felt tears in her eyes, her throat choked with cries she refused to relent when the rank stench of the dead Gary-Larry-Barry burned her nostrils. Nose crinkled in a sneer, eyes closed as if she could ward off the stank by refusing to acknowledge its existence.

Lilly's stomach churned, boiling acid into the back of her throat. She threw up, eyes wet with tears. Gawking, hacking. A thin stream of phlegm across her lips caught in the back of her throat, and she vomited once again. Temples pounding, constricted, beating her skull into oblivion. Christopher, she thought. Keep your thoughts on Christopher. He's in here. Somewhere. And they're doing horrible things to him. You've got to survive. You have to help him. Have to get him out of here.

Lilly pulled herself again and again. The knife close, so close. She reached for it, her hands and wrists, forearms and elbows reaching through the pool of Gary's blood as she pulled the knife from between his body and the floor. Held onto it as if it were her savior and Lilly turned on her back, holding the knife like a keepsake close to her heart. Her eyes drifting, the light overhead seemed to batter her eyes with strain. Lilly felt her chest rising, her heart pounding as she pursed her lips, swallowing her breath with a gasp.

Okay Christopher. Momma's coming.

3

10:35 PM
The Ballroom
Sharon

Before she stepped into the room, Sharon didn't know what she was walking into. She could have guessed a million times over what was on the other side of the door. Nonetheless, what she received would not have been one in the million.

She felt as if she walked into a mansion, the ballroom of a mansion. The floors a polished white with cream-colored slivers gracefully and artfully cascaded across marble slats. On the far wall, about fifty yards from the front door, was a mural that featured clay people wrapped in each other's arms as if they were dancing and in between them, a background likened to the tree of life with its roots stretched across the wall as if those very roots held those clay people. The tree's plentiful leaves hovering over them as if protecting the clay people from the sun with the trunk split through the center, tiny in the backdrop as if the roots and leaves were three dimensional, the clay people dancing in between.

The tree represents the hold Xibalba has on this world.

A voice in Sharon's head, her voice, although she did not know how the thought dropped into her mind.

The roots are the underworld, the foundation for life on Earth. The trunk, an extension of the underworld reaching into the Earth to give birth to our product, humans.

Sharon observed the tree, her focus wandering across the clay leaves.

Leaves are for protection, a canvas for which no otherworldly beings can enter.

Sharon breathed deeply and raised her head. The ceiling

reached high above, vaulted to a fine tip, stained glass, biblical and ancient.

And Sharon thought, *I don't recall seeing such a high ceiling outside. It must be six stories high.* Eyes drifting now. To the right of the mural was a grand staircase that led and disappeared into darkness. No lights on. Darkness seemed to swallow the stairs as if those stairs reached into the mouth of madness. Stairs that spiraled to the right then snaked to the left, draped in a red carpet. Sharon's eyes wandered, following the stairs down to the marble floor and the large open room where she stood. So many people, Sharon thought. All in cloaks, all standing still in three circles, one larger than the other, heads bowed, quiet. So silent and still, the quiet carried thick tension to the eardrums. Sharon felt herself drifting, as if she were no longer in control of her legs. The circle parted to reveal the second circle, also parting when Sharon approached. And the third circle parted delicately and on cue. A slight hum caught Sharon's ears, starting in low, then growing loud. The hum an Om, one circle at a time, then repeated.

Ira in front of Sharon, in the center, his hand held out as an offering. Sharon's eyes drifted over Ira's shoulder, to the woman he'd been sitting with, the woman who wore the black veil, now dressed in the same cloak, although the veil remained. Sharon saw the woman's eyes, staring at Sharon. *Was that jealousy or sympathy?*

"My lady," said Ira, although Sharon couldn't take her eyes off the lady in the veil and for a moment Sharon thought she was staring at herself. Years from now, so many years from now. A single tear fell from the veil woman's eye.

"My lady." Ira again, more of a question this time as if he required her attention or wanted to remove Sharon's attention from the veil woman. Sharon turned to him and Ira half smiled when behind her, Sharon heard a door close with a thud followed by the creak of ungreased wheels creeping towards her. A whining cry now. Sharon turned, watching as the circles parted and that clown, the one who handed out the cloaks, was walking towards her, pushing a metal cart. A baby on the top shelf, whimpering and fussy.

"We've chosen wisely."

And those Oms grew louder as the cart approached, raising the room's vibration with a thunderous boom. She could feel the flutter of the Om vibration in her bones. Sharon watched the baby, and the cart moving towards her as the baby's whimpers turned to wails. Sharon looked at the clown, her eyes roaming up. He was so tall, his stature like a beanstalk that seemed to keep growing.

And Ira said, "The Dark Lord waits for his Goddess," addressing the crowd as the OM quieted and ceased to be no more. He went to the cart where the baby continued to wail. On the bottom shelf Ira took a cup, a goblet of gold with gems and rubies that cascaded across the lip. The tree of life was engraved on both sides. Ira raised the goblet. "The blood is the life."

"The blood is the life," the crowd repeated.

He placed the cup on the top shelf beside the baby's head. Lifted the baby in his arms, cradling the child.

"My lady," he said, and forced the child into Sharon's arms. Wails and flailing arms twitched inside Sharon's embrace. And she locked eyes with Ira who took a deep breath as he closed his eyes, his lips curled in a smile and when he opened his eyes, he presented Sharon with a knife, a gold-plated knife with a six-inch blade and equally long handle. "The blood is the life. Bring the Goddess home and you will no longer be a servant to this world."

The knife in Sharon's right hand. Squirming, screaming baby in the crook of her left arm. Ira stepped back. "You will see the inner working of the universe and all of its chaos and beauty." Another step back, slowly, watching her. "Stars will be within your command and life will spawn by your hand. All things begin with the Goddess, commanded by the Dark Lord." The circle parted and Ira slipped into the circle, taking his place among the others. "The blood is the life, Ms. Mable." And he moved his head back and forth. "Take the life, drink from the fountain that flows from the heart of this child."

Sharon watched as Ira took up hands with the people beside him, as did all of them, until all three circles held hands, lifting their arms to the heavens.

"The blood is the life. Drink and let the Goddess in."

The baby's cries reached a fever pitch. Sharon looked down at the child, held the blade above her head.

"Do it, Sharon," said Ira. Sharon looked at him. She could see how his eyes had grown dark and wide. "Become the Goddess."

And then Sharon could hear her own breathing, as if her throat and lungs stole the space between her ears. No more whines from the baby. Ira was repeating, *The blood is the life*. Sharon could see his lips mouthing the words, but silently. All had gone silent, except for the breathing. Sharon raised her arm, the blade high above her head. Took one last look at Ira, his jaw fixed in a demonic grin, eyes wide and black. Sharon looked at the knife in her hand, her bones tense, jaw quivering.

Her hand trembling. And her eyes searched further, past the skylight ceiling to the moon overhead. A drift of clouds passed through the moon and Mars and Venus blinked as if they were complicit in this macabre of death and sacrifice.

Her breathing hoarse as she swallowed her breath. The celestial constellation overhead drifted from focus. Sharon's hand now prominent in the moonlight. She felt her lips curl into a grin as she watched like a passive observer as her hand thrust down. Heard a pop and wet gurgle. Felt the tug and pull of her hand. And a rush of blood gushed across her arm.

4

11:00 PM
The Underground
Jigglyspot

He was missing ceremony, searching for Helmsley around every corner, in every room, but these warehouses were so large, with multiple rooms among a horde of warehouses across six streets with underground tunnels racing to all of them. He could be anywhere, and it could take Jiggly all night to find him. Jiggly turned his key in the lock, and heard the dead bolt click. Wedged his cane between his arm and ribs, then gripped the doorknob and turned.

Jiggly hoped that Helmsley was indulging in some youthful game. Perhaps Jiggly drove a little too hard with his drill. Perhaps, Jiggly thought, he killed off one too many brain cells, extracting too much from Helmsley's pineal gland. Such circumstance has been known to happen, especially when the extractee was older. Not that Helmsley was old. Being in your forties doesn't make you an old man, although the extraction was older, and with fewer amounts, especially since the fluoride had become the norm. Jiggly never agreed with the fluoride provision, calcifying the very gland his people indulged in was not in their best interest. Although his superiors thought differently. The point was to numb the humans' senses, dull their intuition, and, more importantly, dumb down their intellect. Zero intellect, remember? Plus, calcification took years, if not decades. Hence the children, those pineal glands were like low hanging ripened fruit, easy to take and delectable. Of course, the younger the better. The less tainted with fluoride, the fresher the extraction. And that damn fluoride was everywhere.

Jiggly heard hushes, choked back squeals, and under the breath whines when he walked through the door to the kids' room. He hoped Helmsley was here. Jiggly rarely entered this room, even when MysterE was in charge of solstice. MysterE always took control of the kids' room, his favorite. He'd spend hours before celebration in this room. He told Jiggly there was something special about it, tormenting the kids prior to celebration, creating fear in all of them by torturing a few. Fear is what the masters need and MysterE always obliged. To which Jiggly would secretly shake his head.

Jiggly may be a murdering bastard, but he had a line he'd drawn a long, long time ago. He never indulged in a young one, but once those hormones took center stage with a more abstract and self-aware thought process the game was on. Typically, this happened between the ages of twelve and fourteen depending on the deviousness of the recipient-some matured faster than others. He could never indulge in youthful game, thought it was driven by ego because Jiggly enjoyed the hunt and the cerebral game of catch me if you can. Taking advantage of someone who was disadvantaged due to size and cognition, did not sit well with Jiggly, and seemed a bit too over the top. But once they came out on the other side of childhood, thinking they knew everything and were ready to change the world, they were fair game. And that's how Jiggly preferred his extraction, young and hormone filled with attitude. That's right, a ripe teenager does the body good. Plus, that pineal gland was still good with very little calcification.

Although these kids, the ones locked in the room, the ones staring with wide eyes, huddled close together in the dark, scared to all bloody hell, were the age Jiggly refused to indulge in. Had to do with his past. Everyone's got a preference, even murdering bastards like Jiggly.

As he scanned their eyes, Jiggly reminded himself not to talk to them. Talking made them real and when they seemed real, they *were* real and that solidified fact would burn inside Jiggly's veins for the rest of his days. Well, a few weeks at best, but those few weeks would spiral the man into a depression and who the fuck wanted to be depressed? Using avoidance as a defense mechanism is a murderer's best friend. People are into what they're into, Jiggly always reminded himself. Judging people because they were different was a human trait.

And Jiggly didn't like to be human.

Did all he could to not reveal the human part of himself.

And Helmsley isn't here either. Shaking his head, Jiggly flipped the keys around his finger. Low whines and cries, and held back tears, streamlined across the room. He locked eyes with an unsuspecting male who immediately turned away; the boy leaning against the cage, eyes downtrodden, his left hand holding the cage. Jiggly craned his head, staring. He could see the boy was trembling. By his feet, hunched over, knees to the chest and shivering, was a female about the same age. Jiggly wondered if they'd come in together. Perhaps this was their first date, he thought. Some date. The wonder of it all was that all of them, every child in these cages, all they want right now is to see their parents. To be reunited with them. Now that the masters have arrived, that wish will come true.

Which was the crux of it all. The fear that emerges when the child is taken by a parent—demon or no demon—is the most influential of all fears that exist in the universe. Like fear on tap, flowing in a never-ending, constant stream. Nothing tasted better or even came close. Jiggly's mouth salivated; he pursed his lips then swallowed with a deep breath. Twirled that key ring around his finger and tightened his grip around his cane. The boy's eyes were watching him now, staring, as if he were expecting an attack, looking for it, on guard and ready to retaliate. Jiggly liked that. It showed leadership. The boy will do well on the island. After reprogramming, he'll do real good. Maybe one day he will be the one to corral the young for the masters.

Jiggly looked at the female next to the boy, her body shuddering. Maybe her too, Jiggly thought. The future MysterE and his Madame. Amazing how things always come together. He scanned the rest of the herd, huddled together, and they all seemed to gape and gawk and shiver all at once. Definitely not any of them, Jiggly thought, twirling those keys. Started whistling, moved to the door to leave.

"Where are our parents?"

Jiggly stopped at the door, then turned slowly around. That same boy, standing tall, hands on the cage, staring. The girl sitting beside him, shivering and panicked. Jiggly scanned the boy's eyes, unblinking and peering into Jiggly.

"I mean," the boy said. "What is this, some boarding school in hell?"

Jiggly smiled, felt his paint crease across his face. He found that line funny.

"You'll see them soon enough," Jiggly said. "You all will. Your parents are preparing for celebration. They'll be along soon." Turned back to the boy whose head was craned to the right.

"That makes zero sense," the boy said. "Why go through all this trouble just to reunite us? Seems counterproductive."

Wow, Jiggly thought, he is something else. Hardly any fear in him. The Goddess will be impressed.

"What's your name, child?" asked Jiggly.

The boy's head shot back, eyes narrow. "Child? There's no child here and my name is Christopher."

Jiggly smiled again, craned his head, looking at the female by Christopher's legs. "She your girlfriend... Christopher?"

"Maybe. Her name is Jenny, and she's scared. Wants to see her mother, Kathy, as soon as possible."

Jiggly scratched the stubble on his chin. "In time."

Christopher shook his head. "Now," he said, his voice raised.

Jiggly smiled again. "I said... *in time.*"

Christopher looked away, head shaking.

"You know," said Christopher. "You can't keep us here. People have to be looking for us by now. It's only a matter of time before they find us." He shrugged his shoulders. "Doesn't seem feasible that all these people go missing from the same place and the cops don't put two and two together."

Now Jiggly really liked this kid. He's got balls of steel.

"Well, Chris, there's a pivotal point that seems to have escaped your little mind. No cops will come, Christopher. They are plenty aware of where you are and what we are doing. Most of them are our people to begin with, planted strategically over the years." Jiggly shook his head. "Think about it, Chris, you are all here and does it seem like I'm in any way concerned over being caught or for the police to come rushing in with a battering ram to magically rescue all of you? That's just a movie with a happy ending. It doesn't exist. Get used to it, Chris. In the real world, no one cares. Humans..." he scoffed. "They'd sell their grandmother to the devil to get a taste of fame and fortune. Nobody cares, Chris. No one cares at all."

He could tell that Christopher didn't agree with his revelation. His eyes narrowed and his body went stiff, his jaw tight. And Jiggly smiled, enjoying himself.

Jiggly's heart stopped when Christopher said, "Is that what happened to you? Sold your grandmother to the devil."

Now Jiggly felt his lips curl into a sneer and shit, he shouldn't have broken his first rule: don't talk to them. Felt like cracking the little shits skull with his cane. Release some frustration on Christopher's face. Instead, he thought about what was to come. Jiggly would rather witness the depravity of this Christopher and his spiral into madness, which, as Jiggly was well aware, would be more satisfying than a brief interlude of brain bashing murder.

Jiggly tapped his cane twice, said, "Quite the opposite, Chris, but I really must be going. I bid you adieux and may the masters tear your soul apart. All of you, one by one. Be ready for your induction. Be ready..." he said, widening his eyes, "... for slavery."

Screams now from the peanut gallery huddled in the corner and from little miss Jenny. No stir from Christopher, though. He stood, shaking his head.

"Until later." Jiggly bowed, then turned on his heels and went through the door. Just before the door slammed shut, he heard Christopher holler, "My name is Christopher, not Chris."

Jiggly leaned against the door and pinched the bridge of his nose. He could hear the whines and cries erupting from behind the door. Took a deep breath. "Kids," he whispered then shook his head and started walking down the hall. "I think I should move to a new planet. These humans are starting to wear on me."

5

11:15 PM
In the Hallway
Tyler

The door opened with a cracked metal pop. A mechanical hum-sounded like a lawnmower-was heard prominently upon the door's opening followed by a wet gurgle as if a water cooler burped something awful.

"Got it," said Tyler, standing and turning to Cassandra and Kera. Cassandra leaning with her head against the wall. Her face flushed with beads of sweat across her forehead. She looked at him and nodded. Kera's eyes downtrodden, those tentacles weaved snug within her hair. She looked lost. Her body wavered, stepped back, then forward. "Kera?" Tyler caught her by the elbow before she dropped to the floor.

She paused, taking a deep breath, when Tyler released her arm. He could see her chest rising in tune with her heavy breathing. Kera stepped away from him, holding her hand out, and shook her head. Hand on her hip, head bent, eyes staring at the floor. She took a deep breath, then paused. Tyler turned to Cassandra, who stepped away from the wall, staring at Kera.

"You, okay?"

After a brief pause, Kera turned to him, those tentacles hunched over as if pleading for sympathy. "The Goddess is in," she whispered and turned her head around, staring down the hall. Tyler followed her gaze. The hall was empty. Nothing stirred. Her voice shaky when she said, "Get your friends Tyler." She turned around, stared deep into Tyler's eyes. "Now."

Tyler tensed, staring at Kera and the urgency in her stare. He saw fear in Kera's eyes. Tyler, nodding, turned around. Cassandra had already entered the room when Tyler stepped through. First thing he saw were what looked like coffins-coffin shaped anyway-made from plexiglass. A row of ten, one after the other. Six were empty, and looked like they hadn't been used in a day's age, covered in dust and a greasy film. Eyes drifted to the four containers filled to the brim with dark liquid, the lids secured with latches. Three coffins contained what looked like thick sewage with floating chunks dispersed inside the fluid. The fourth coffin contained all dark liquid but no floating chunks. Tubes ran into a hole in the lid of the three coffins with floating chunks that disappeared into the liquid, attached on the outside to a machine—the mechanical hum—pumping what Tyler assumed was forced air. *Perhaps to stir the liquid?* He looked around the room. A walk-in freezer on the far end of the room. Next to it was a table, six feet long and three feet wide, the top made of wood, four inches thick. Beside it was a rolling table with a host of cutlery: a meat cleaver, a filleting knife, and four serrated knives. Tyler recognized one knife as a boning knife, used to cut through bone with ease.

Tyler whipped around to face Kera. She was standing in the doorway, wide eyed and staring. "Where are they? You said they were here."

Kera pointed to the coffins. "In there Tyler."

He turned around and scanned the coffins. Went to the first in line. "I don't get it."

Cassandra interrupted. "They're in this liquid?" Tyler followed as Cassandra's gaze turned to Kera.

"Correct."

Tyler pinched the tube in his fingers, felt air pumping through it. He looked at Kera, head shaking. "Why?"

"For the feast," Kera explained. "The liquid is a marinade to soften and flavor the flesh prior to filleting. Humans get so... tough if cut open too soon. Better to keep them alive until the very last minute. Fresh flesh is always better."

Tyler and Cassandra locked eyes when one coffin gurgled. Tyler looked deep inside the coffin in front of him. Difficult to see but there was an outline in there, a head Tyler thought. Looked at the tube, then the machine and the pump. "This is to keep them alive," he said, then looked at Kera. "They're pumping oxygen through these tubes to keep them alive?"

"Like I said, fresh flesh tastes better."

Tyler looked at Kera, then to Cassandra. Shook his head, then felt over the latches. His fingers trembling as he flicked each latch, one by one, circling the coffin. Heard the same from Cassandra.

"Pull the tubes out first," said Tyler. "Then open the lid and pull them out. Quite obvious they're sedated. I'm sure they'd be thrashing inside if they weren't." Then a pause. "Wait," he ordered, scanning the plugged release on the back and bottom of the coffin. Tyler went to it, popped it open, and the marinade poured from the coffin. He turned to the next one and did the same. Cassandra followed him. The sound of rushing liquid pouring onto the concrete and down into the drains that were scattered across the floor filled the room. Tyler looked at Cassandra, her eyes wide, revealing what Tyler took as sympathy. These were his friends, waiting in line to be filleted like a deer under a hunter's knife. Tyler watched as the liquid drained from the coffin. Watched as Jake's features became prominent. That tube wedged in his nose. His mouth sewn shut. Tyler closed his eyes, briefly, put his hand to his mouth, watching as the marinade drained, his friend Jake Ferris, ghostly pale, eyes closed, tube in his nose, mouth sewn shut. He looked dead. Dead.

"Tyler," said Cassandra behind him.

Tyler turned.

"You, okay?"

He said nothing, just shook his head. Looked at Kera, standing by the fourth coffin. Those tentacles stretched overhead, staring at him, and Tyler forced his eyes away. Amber was in the second coffin. Tatty in the third and...

"Wait," Tyler said, then pointed to the fourth coffin. "Is that who I think it is?" His gaze drifted to Kera, her hands on the coffin, assessing the body inside, her head down, tentacles too.

"Yes," she said. "This is the body of one James Reilly."

"What the fuck is he doing here?" Tyler's voice a high-pitched whine. "How... he..." Head shaking, Tyler's jaw hung open.

"He must be an offering to the Dark Lord."

"From who?"

Kera craned her head to the right, studying James Reilly, searching for answers. "Someone," she said. "His parents, more than likely."

"He was buried a week ago. I was there. I watched his body go into the ground. He..."

Kera shook her head. "No, you saw a coffin go into the ground."

Tyler paused, thinking. He cleared his throat. "But you said..." Cleared his throat again. "You said they like fresh flesh? There's nothing fresh about that body." Tyler's eyes drifted to the body and the bullet hole in Reilly's chest. BANG! Tyler heard the punch of his bullet hit Reilly's chest. Saw Reilly gasping for breath, bleeding out, strapped to the chair by the kitchen table, covered in duct tape. That damn duct tape.

Kera answered, "Could be for his heart. A lot of times, a special offering will be made by a parent to keep the soul tethered to Xibalba, for safekeeping. When a demon eats the heart, the soul is doomed to live in hell for eternity, held at the whim of the demon who ate the heart."

"You're saying his parents did this?" Cassandra, Tyler could see that look in her eyes, that disbelieving stare. She had demonic spiders jutting from her vagina an hour ago, but this is unbelievable. Some things we just can't get used to.

"I'm not one hundred percent sure, but it makes the most sense," said Kera. She looked at Cassandra, then Tyler, addressing them both. "Let's just concentrate on the living and get out of here, please. I'll explain later. Considering our situation, I suggest we move a little faster than we have been. I would like to be home before the sun rises."

"Right," said Tyler, his eyes on Reilly's body, perfectly preserved as if he died an hour ago. Tyler forced his stare to Cassandra. He licked his lips, said, "Can you hand me that knife please," pointing to the cutting board in the corner.

Time was running out indeed. And Tyler thought-knowing his night would not end as soon as Kera wished-Where is Pam?

6

11:45 PM
Looking for Helmsley
Jigglyspot

At this point, all Jiggly wanted to do was cut some throats. Relieve the anger and frustration caused by the missing and elusive Helmsley. He was running out of time, and he knew it. Not that he'd looked at a clock, nor did he need to. He could feel it. The Goddess was in and the Dark Lord was on his way. Briefly he thought about Mills, across the universe, being introduced to Xibalba. What wonders is he witnessing at this moment? Jiggly thought. The transformation coming to a close.

What am I going to tell the Dark Lord? he thought. If I can't find Helmsley, what do I do?

This was a new situation for Jiggly. No one had ever gotten away, and he cursed himself for leaving Helmsley after the cattle prod knocked him out. How could he have gotten up so quickly?

Now Gary was dead courtesy of the masters. Helmsley was missing and Jiggly knew he couldn't spare any of his clowns to help him search. There was too much to do and too many milestones to cross before the Dark Lord was presented. He was sure Apoch was on top of everything. Thank the universe for Apoch. He always helped, even if he didn't agree with Jiggly. Apoch was like that little brother Jiggly always wanted. A little brother close to seven feet tall, but a little brother just the same.

Jiggly was walking to the other side of the warehouses. He didn't like being so far away from ceremony. If something goes wrong, he cannot intervene. When he first started his search, he'd thought it would be easy. Who the hell could have predicted that Helmsley would go off like this? Not even a peep from the hiding

Helmsley. *Where the fuck is he?*

Jiggly wasn't singing anymore; wasn't whistling either, as he pounded across the concrete. Felt streams of sweat cascade from his forehead and across his temples, knowing his clown makeup was far from perfect. Felt like he was all dressed up for nothing. Fucking Helmsley. If the Dark Lord didn't want this asshole so much, he'd cut Helmsley's throat himself. This hide and seek game was childish bullshit.

If he doesn't find Helmsley soon, Jiggly will have to bite his lip, swallow his pride, and face the wrath of the Dark Lord, which he found rather ironic considering the years he'd spent with Mills.

This night was feeling more like hell with every passing minute.

7

11:50 PM
Xibalba
The Dark Lord SAC John Mills

When Mills stepped over the hill to investigate where the sound of torturous bellows emanated from, he hadn't expected a welcoming committee.

Gargoyles, he thought. They look like gargoyles, all hunched over, some of them with wings, all with rows of sharp teeth. Some with horns and all had claws. They greeted him as if relieved to see Mills. Grunts and scoffs are how they communicated and there had to be a million of these gargoyle looking things. They scurried over to him as if to cuddle themselves beneath his arms and snuggle close to his torso, lifting his arms so they could hide beneath as they escorted Mills to the sound of torture.

Perhaps, Mills thought with a fleeting inclination, they are looking for reassurance for a job well done.

Mills' eyes scrunched and squinted from the hurricane winds that breathed heavy against his eyes and face, burning hot. Although Mills welcomed the heat, it felt like coming home. Over the horizon, mountains bathed in darkness spit brush fires across the indentured hills as black smoke rushed across the dark sky. His ears filled with the sound of burning, crackling, and raging fire, as the gargoyles led him forward across a cracked path of cobblestone. And when he looked down to his feet, he could see lava seep in between the cobblestone path.

They were all around him now, all those little gargoyles surrounding Mills as if they required approval and wished to provide protection, leading the detective to...

The gargoyles parted as if on cue revealing a waist high rock slab propped up by an overgrown sphere made of the same rock, three of them, and on the slab, strapped to it by hands that Mills thought were made of gold with thin fingers sharp at their tips, holding his wrists and ankles, was Helmsley. His skin covered in sweat, skin that carried the color of fire. Naked, his head lolled to the side, and Mills could see how his chest rose and fell in quick, shallow huffs.

Mills craned his head, staring, waiting, anticipating that this dream, this nightmare would end abruptly, and he'd wake up in his home, in bed next to his wife. "Helmsley?" said Mills and the gargoyles all screeched like monkeys, started jumping, scurrying, and flailing.

Mills approached closer as Helmsley's head rolled to the side facing Mills, his eyes wide and all black, metallic black. His mouth hung open and Mills could see he struggled to breathe. Struggled to speak as a gargoyle leapt onto the slab by Helmsley's head, jumped up and seethed at Mills as his small claw-like hands grabbed Helmsley's hair and flew away, his wings batting across the air with Helmsley's skullcap in his hand. Mills watched as the gargoyle circled across the landscape to the fiery volcano gurgling with lava and tossed the skullcap in.

"I'm sorry John," hollered Helmsley.

Another gargoyle, flying, landed on the slab, crouched down next to Helmsley's head and dipped its head closer to the brain, then lapped its long, dark tongue across it.

"Helmsley, where are we? What is this place?"

"Please don't hurt me, John. I'm so sorry for what I've done."

Mills shook his head. "What're you talking about? Where are we? Is this a dream?"

The gargoyle that lapped its tongue across Helmsley's brain poked its sharp finger into the organ. Brain on its fingertip, the gargoyle swallowed with a shudder.

"Hell, John," screamed Helmsley. "We're in hell."

John looked up, staring at the landscape. "Doesn't feel like hell. It feels like…"

Home, Mills thought, and the volcano growled, the wind howled, and thunder erupted in the far beyond. Those dark clouds pumped with lightning. His gargoyles all snickered, sneered, and bellowed. Mills looked at the gargoyles, felt himself smiling. They were like pets that brought a smile to the owner's lips.

"You're changing, John, and you don't even know it. This is not a dream. *This is really happening!*"

Mills snapped his head to Helmsley when his scream erupted. He saw the gargoyle, that long fingertip splitting Helmsley's torso, burning an incision from his navel to his chest. Mills then saw Helmsley's eyes and his reflection in those black eyes. Like staring into a dark mirror.

He craned his head to the right because he wasn't sure what he was looking at. Was it him, detective Mills, who was staring back or…

"Hello John," said the reflection, and Mills could feel his mouth move. "How do you like my humble abode?"

*****

The Dark Lord stood in front of the shining, glimmering wall, his lips curled in a sneer. Mills' face covered in blood. Blood from his ears now dried and cracked down his neck, the blood from his eyes, nose, and mouth the same.

"I see you found Helmsley," said the Dark Lord Mills. "A gift for you John. Enjoy Xibalba. We shall meet again, my friend. We are one now." The Dark Lord Mills gestured both hands at himself, towards Mills' torso. And then he smiled, a conniving, confident grin. "Eat his heart," said Dark Lord Mills. "Be satisfied and watch as I provide power to this coil." He dipped his chin to his chest, eyes staring, never moving from his reflection. "Now take leave. All is in my hands, John. You have nothing to concern you… ever… again."

The Dark Lord Mills closed his eyes and breathed deeply, then craned his head to the left and up, cracking his neck. He seethed through gritted teeth, his upper lip curled in a sneer.

"The Goddess waits," he breathed. "And I… I am the seed that keeps its hold on this world."

8

11:55 PM
The Room with the Coffins
Cassandra

She cut the sewn mouths before pulling the tube from their noses. Cassandra had taken the shears from Tyler to clip the stitches. He looked nervous, angry too, and she knew there was something more to Tyler's story. Tyler was so put off with the fourth body. Obviously, he knew this person. More than likely he was a friend since Tyler had been at the funeral. But there was something he wasn't saying, as if he expected someone else to be in the fourth coffin.

And Kera, whatever she was with those tentacles that seemed to have a mind of their own. Cassandra wondered when she'll take them off. How they were fastened to her head she wasn't sure, but they were creepy and Cassandra had enough creepy over the last two weeks to last two lifetimes. Kera's attention remained with the dead body, which, once the lid was removed, stunk something awful. Bury the dead, she thought, they stink up the place. Tyler was searching the room, looking through cabinets and assessing possible weaponry; the cutlery was indeed a weapon. Other than the coffins, the cutlery, the walk-in freezer, the door they came in through and the other door tucked in the corner on the opposite side, there wasn't much in the room.

Cassandra believed they'd be going through the opposite door they came in from. Why go back when you could go forward? But what was beyond that door she didn't know, knew Kera and Tyler didn't know either. And all she wanted to do was burn the whole place down. Get out and survive-if possible-but burn the place over the shoulder as they walked into freedom. Where life would go after that didn't matter. What mattered was survival and revenge, although what Cassandra couldn't stomach was leaving other people to the demise she'd experienced firsthand. Not a chance would she allow that to happen. Not a chance at all.

She felt a warm liquid drip down her inner thigh, rolling down her leg to her ankle. She looked down at the bead of blood that dripped to the floor. Yes, she was losing blood. Losing time. What did those spider devils do while inside her? What damage did they cause? She'd lost so much blood and now more was leaving. She felt weak, her head weary, but that was only temporary. Survival was forever. After she'd pulled the tube from the last of Tyler's friends— the girl he called Amber—she addressed Tyler. "Do you want to wake them up?"

Tyler ceased his exploration—he'd been opening cabinets against the far wall-and paused, staring at Cassandra. She watched his eyes turn to Kera, drift to the dead body, then back to Kera. Cassandra turned to Kera, too. She was massaging the body, speaking quietly—too quietly for Cassandra to hear coherently. Those tentacles dipped down to her shoulders. They seemed to carry a stare likened to sympathy. Kera never stirred. She continued whatever ritual she was performing. Cassandra turned to Tyler.

"Can you help me?"

Tyler didn't move, his eyes lost, staring at the dead body.

"Tyler!?"

He blinked rapidly before turning to Cassandra. "Ice water," he said.

Cassandra craned her head. "Come again?"

"Well, we're dealing with an obvious sedation, on what we don't know, but usually if someone is overdosing you douse them with cold water. If we can do the same, I'm sure we can wake them up."

He had a point, Cassandra thought. She'd seen movies where that happened. A slap in the face could help, too. "Where can we get ice?" she asked, focusing on keeping her voice as calm and quiet as possible.

Tyler pointed to the back of the room. "The freezer," he said, looking around the room. "Even if it's just frozen meat or something like that." He went to the counter by the butcher block and the sink directly next to it. Above the sink were metal cabinets. Tyler opened one and took out a large metal pot.

Cassandra turned to Kera, still preoccupied. Okay, she thought, I'll get the ice. Tyler ran the water, put his hand beneath it as Cassandra went to the freezer, popped the pin lock from the door and opened it with a suctioned pop. She was greeted by freezing cold air that billowed like smoke from the walk-in freezer. So much cold smoky air it was difficult to see more than a few inches in front of her face.

She stepped in and was immediately enveloped in cold air that seemed to rush from the freezer as if it wished escape. Cassandra took a few more steps in, and, as the cold air filtered from the freezer, she could see clearly and her heart froze, her hand went to her mouth, stifling the scream erupting in her throat. Cassandra was staring at a row of human bodies hung on meat hooks attached to the ceiling. Her eyes darting from one dead body to the next. Three rows of dead bodies, all hanging on hooks, that disappeared into the white fog. Eyes frozen closed, blue icy skin, and those mouths were sewn. She wondered if they were alive when they were hung on those hooks. Frozen to death, she thought, shaking her head and forcing her eyes away. Felt acid boil in the back of her throat, her gut twisted into a knot. Cassandra held her hand over her mouth as if she could ward off any puke and vomit that decided to reverse gears. Coughed a few times, her bottom lip curled over her teeth.

"You, okay?" Tyler, his voice seemed far away. Cassandra heard water running.

She was staring at the dead body in front of her. He looked no more than twenty.

"Cassandra?" Tyler again.

She cleared her throat. "Yeah," she called, forcing her eyes from the body. "I'm fine." Cassandra looked around the freezer, spotting a wide metal shelf on her right. Three shelves with nothing on them other than a plastic canister. She looked in, saw it was filled with frozen eyeballs, and she immediately turned away. Clamped her eyes shut, attempting to ward off the sickly sensation to puke. When she opened her eyes, she was staring at the dead body hanging beside her. Eyes gently closed. Closed forever, and behind those closed eyelids, she now knew, was nothing. Dark black holes would stare at Cassandra should those eyelids open. She turned away and scanned the freezer. There was no ice in this damn freezer.

Cassandra took the plastic canister and stepped out.

"Ice?" Tyler asked and then a moment later when Cassandra didn't answer. "You, okay?"

Cassandra felt the cold on her back as she looked at Tyler, craning his head to peer inside the freezer. His eyes narrow, drifted from the freezer to Cassandra to the canister in her hands.

"What's in there?" he asked, pointing to the plastic.

"Your daily dose of eyeballs," she said. "Lots of them, too. Closest thing to ice I could find."

"They use them for soup." Kera, her hands gently caressing the dead body, staring at Cassandra. Those tentacles too.

Cassandra thought, How the hell does she know that?

"Here," said Tyler, stepping closer to Cassandra. "I'll take them."

A sound like a latch or dead bolt clicked open snapped their attention to the far door. Four dead bolts on that door. A second sound, second dead bolt unlocked.

"Hide!" said Kera. "Hide now."

Third dead bolt unlocked.

"Where?" said Cassandra with a shrug.

"In the freezer." Tyler, and she noticed he was now holding a meat cleaver. He looked at Kera, whose tentacles were raised high over her head. "Now!" demanded Tyler, and Kera gave up her inquiry with the dead body.

Fourth dead bolt unlocked.

Cassandra looked down, seeing those eyeballs staring at her. Tyler gripped the crook of her arm and she followed him into the freezer at the moment the far door opened and Kera slipped in behind them, closing the freezer door with a gentle hand.

Tyler said, "I'm gonna hack up whoever the fuck that is."

9

Midnight
The Ballroom
Sharon the Goddess

Sharon's eyes fluttered behind closed eyelids, seated within the confines of an oversized throne that dwarfed Sharon, raised high by the masters and royal guests as they continued to chant, cheer, and laugh, parading Sharon and the throne around the ballroom. She could feel the blood inside; it was hypnotic. Sharon licked her chin, ran her tongue across her lips and then her teeth. The taste was exquisite. Her body shuddered with a hypnotic sedation of fluttering ecstasy. Felt a trickle of blood cascade across her windpipe.

She drank, Sharon did, from the chest of that baby. She could see the memory that had been reality a half hour ago. Saw herself raise the baby above her head and offer the blood to her audience, who all dropped to their knees when their turn arrived to kneel at Sharon's feet and beneath the fountain of red that spotted their chins and lips. So many of them; all in attendance to provide worship to the Goddess. Worship to Sharon.

Her thoughts returning to the first moment when the blood touched her lips with a quiver across the tongue and down the throat. But even more was the sensation, the turn, as if some energy forced itself inside her skin. Her mind. Spotting her memory with glimpses of another world, a rare dimension and portal to the underworld. And then power, conscious power where guilt and shame were no longer necessary and the term *I'm sorry* was no longer relevant. Had no reason to exist. Sharon felt that energetic force-field enter the crown of her skull, bloom inside the center of the brain then cascade into her throat where it swelled like a balloon and Sharon would have coughed under normal circumstance, although there was nothing normal about any of the events that have transpired over the last two weeks.

Sharon swallowed the balloon and felt her shoulders weave like waves in the ocean, back and forth, that energy inside her heart. She could sense it in there, closing the organ off to the outside world. Saw a green ball of light with slivers of black, like ink spilled into a green ocean, circling and slithering like snakes around the green globe, as it turned into that inky black until all that was green was now black, and her heart felt as if it turned to stone without a care in the world. Nor a care for the world as the energy walloped further down, bursting within the solar plexus with a burning flutter and she felt her lips curl into a grin, capturing the energetic ball that now drifted down, further down inside her gut where the energy was absorbed and blossomed at the base of her spine. Sharon could see, in her mind's eye, a red rose wither and turn black; that same black ink as the heart had turned.

Sharon's eyes snapped open. She was standing in the center of the ballroom. Those three circles surrounded her. She looked around, those cloaks worn with pointed hoods hiding their eyes within. They stood still and quiet, their hands formed a triangle. Sharon looked at them as if they were beneath her, her chin raised high as a fierce wind tore across the ballroom. The circles parted, one at a time. Two people moved at the top of each circle, their shoulders turned inward, connecting each circle, and creating an opening like a bottleneck. And standing outside the circle was the Dark Lord, head forward, chin to his chest, his skin the color of burnt ash. Two thick and long horns jutted from his forehead, black and smooth. Eyes red, blood red, with green pupils that surrounded a crystal blue iris.

Sharon felt her arm reach out, palm up. Felt her mouth move, heard her voice say, "Come, my darling. I wait for you."

The room remained silent as the Dark Lord walked slowly towards her. Sharon felt her blood turn hot in her veins. Her heart pounding in her chest. Felt her nose curl, heavy breathing as the Dark Lord approached, taking her hand in his.

"My love," she said, staring into his eyes. "You look ravishing."

"As do you, my Goddess. Do you like this body?"

Sharon pulled him closer. "Do I ever." Her hand on his neck pulling his lips to hers. Open kiss, tongues lapping. Sharon unbuttoned his pants, pulled down the zipper in a slow movement. The Dark Lord standing, his head raised high as she stretched his pants to his ankles. Dark Lord stepped out, took Sharon's hand and pulled her close. His hands beneath her cloak, raising the dress beneath, and lifted her from the hips, taking her close to him.

"Give me your seed," said Sharon. "Allow our grip on this world to be... forever."

"As you wish, my lady. As... you... wish."

The Dark Lord reached his arms beneath and around Sharon's legs, pulling her close; going inside and Sharon quivered and groaned when he entered. Sharon's hands on his shoulders, thrusting her body against his. Her skin fluttering wet with ecstasy. Jaw clenched, teeth gnashed, eyes wide with maddening rage. Sensations, pulsing, forcing, thrusting until she felt the blossom in her womb and her toes tingled. The Dark Lord held her, his erection pulsing inside as she closed her eyes, seeing the seed scurry into the womb. When she thrust her eyes open, Sharon felt her body cringe, tighten, restrict, her mouth agape, teeth barred, seething. A growl in her throat erupting across her lips.

"The seed is in," said Ira and Sharon craned her head to see him, eyes narrowed into slits as she stretched her neck, observing the masters, as their shoulders moved like slithering snakes. "Hail the Dark Lord. Hail the Goddess. Hail Satan."

Then the familiar gong, like a crystal bowl, rattled five times to usher in the moment that reverberated inside Sharon's ears. Her mouth close to the Dark Lord's neck, and she could see how the masters disrobed. Music, electrical, thumped with a thick beat as if signaling the coming of an army, and the change in time. Saw how the masters danced, hands on hips, gyrating. Beneath the music and heavy breaths were the cries of babies. An orgy of wails and cries. An orgy of masters, wrapped and knotted together like snakes in the grass. And Ira walked across the room, providing blood to the masters as the babies' cries, one by one, became no more.

10

12:05 AM
In the Freezer
Tyler

When he first stepped into the freezer, Tyler wasn't expecting the rows of dead bodies hanging from the ceiling. The cold cringed his skin, sent goose bumps up his arm and caused the hairs on his arms to rise. His breath plumed like vapor across his lips as he stood with his back against the wall beside the door. Cassandra and Kera were hiding somewhere deep inside the freezer, their presence hidden by a cold fog that lifted off the floor. Looked like the haze that lifts off a pond in the dead of winter. The meat cleaver in his hand seemed to disappear; his grip had gone numb. His breathing heavy, his lungs felt frozen, constricted. Fast talking gibberish outside the freezer door. Someone complaining, he was sure, judging by the tone of voice. Tyler heard the voice but had no intellect to understand the voice. Whoever was in the kitchen was talking in another language; French, Tyler assumed.

Cold, so cold, Tyler thought when he raised the cleaver close to his eyes. His hand cold and turning blue. His plan was simple: let whoever was outside step into the freezer and meet Mr. Meat Cleaver. He was hoping to swipe at the neck and roll the head across the floor. Although he'd settle for the eyes or head.

Now came the sound of banging pots, pans, and utensils as if whoever was out there was relieving frustration. Or looking for something. Tyler regarded Mr. Meat Cleaver. Could be, he thought. How else were they going to hack up dead bodies? Probably kosher style, slit the throat, then start hacking. A leg here, an arm, a... Tyler shook his head, gnashing his teeth, his jaw clenched. Noticed his heartbeat was perfectly calm when out of the fog Kera appeared, wide eyed, with those tentacles raised high. He didn't like the look in her eyes. They were reporting some plan he was sure he wouldn't agree with.

Kera whispered, "He's going to come in here."

Tyler shrugged. "I hope so," he said and regarded the cleaver.

"What comes from that? Then they'll be looking for us, aware we are here. This could compromise your escape."

He didn't like where this was going. "Well, you can't make an omelet without breaking some eggs." He turned away.

"That's not what you want," she said. "You want to escape with your friends. That's what you said. Let me talk to whoever is out there. Get them off the trail to give you time."

Tyler turned to Kera. "That's a horrible plan." He was shaking his head, shoulders slightly hunched. "They'll kill you for sure. NO... we hack this fucker up and we stay together. That's the only way."

"No Tyler," she commanded. Those tentacles raised high, eyes narrow. "We do this my way. If it weren't for me, you'd still be locked up and waiting for Jiggly and all your friends out there would be dead. You owe me that much."

More hollering and complaining from the outside. More cabinet slamming and stomping feet.

Kera's hand on his chin, she moved his head to look at her. "There's no time," she said, and Tyler could see fear in her eyes, although that fear also carried commitment, conviction. "Get them out, Tyler. Your friends, all of them. As many as you can."

Tyler's eyes narrowed, his nose scrunched as he shook his head. "NO!" He moved to the door, gripped the handle.

"Tyler!" Kera called, loud too. Tyler snapped his head around with a fierce ferocity. Noticed how the bitching and moaning outside stopped abruptly when Kera's body tensed. Her fingers formed a triangle, and she pushed those hands towards Tyler.

He felt a push in his stomach and chest, as if some invisible hand thrust him backwards. And backwards Tyler went, as if he'd been pushed by a giant. Hit the freezer wall and pain raced across his neck and head, falling to the floor on his ass and pain wrenched up his spine as Mr. Meat Cleaver was tossed from his grip, and scuttled across the floor.

"I said no Tyler. No more murder. I can't stand it."

Tyler looked on in awe of the tiny little alien woman with those tentacles glaring at him. Her hands circling and Tyler watched as something that looked like fog circled around her hands as if she caught the very atoms in between himself and Kera and commanded them at her will. Looked on, mesmerized, as a slithering fog wrapped around him from his ankles to his neck, then over his head. Fog that quickly turned into ice. A thick wall of ice. Tyler cringed, attempting to back up as if he could move through walls. But there was no place to go, and quickly there was ice all around him, like a personal prison made just for him. He looked around. Mr. Meat Cleaver was out of reach.

Kera knelt in front of the ice. He could see those tentacles. Saw Kera through the ice.

"Let me the fuck out," he bellowed and punched the ice. Pain jutted up his arm, rattling to his elbow, and raced to his shoulder and neck.

"Save your strength," said Kera, her voice low, sympathetic. "You must listen to me now, Tyler. Listen to this instruction please; it is very important and highly significant. You have no reason to be concerned about me, Tyler. But you must make it a priority to maintain your attention on your friends. All of them and the others who are in here. I wasn't able to completely understand what is happening tonight until I saw the dead body of your friend, James Reilly. His presence is significant. His corpse is meant for more than a simple tether to Xibalba. This night... this night, Tyler is meant to capture a stronger hold on your planet and your species. If that is to happen, their presence here will be forever and the streamline of their indulgence will spiral your species into chaos, upheaval, and eventually Tyler, slavery. Cut out the heart of James Reilly, Tyler. Don't allow the Dark Lord to eat the organ. You must burn it, Tyler. It must be consumed by fire and turned to ash. This is the most important task you have tonight. Now I know Tyler. I understand how the constellations exist in this system. There is a door, Tyler. A door that is opened every so often, and when that door is open, it is a window through time and space. Tonight, the stars are in alignment for that opening. The yin and yang of the universe, two beasts that seek to be fed. Which one is fed will determine the fate of your species. Don't let the Dark Lord eat the heart, Tyler."

She stood up, and Tyler watched her, hovering over him. She looked like glass through the ice.

"No matter what happens tonight... burn the heart, Tyler. Burn the heart."

He watched as she moved from the ice. Tyler heard the freezer door open. He turned to the door when a haze of cold air billowed around his ice prison, unable to see.

He heard the conversation. The person who was outside was obviously the chef responsible for pulling off this feast of human flesh. He questioned Kera, unrelenting in his conviction. Said he would not be responsible for spoiled meat, pleading to Kera, who attempted to placate the man and his fears.

"You are coming with me!"

That's the last Tyler heard before the door closed. And when he looked up, the ice around him began to melt.

11

12:15 AM
On his way to the Small Observation Room
Jigglyspot

He missed the orgy and for that his anger burned his brain, turned his skin hot with flame and he could feel how his makeup was running in streams across his face. The Dark Lord had surfaced, and Mills was now in Xibalba. How lucky was Mills? Jiggly thought. He will make an excellent king.

However, this fact did little to curb Jiggly's frustration. He missed ceremony, missed the coming of the Goddess, and the seed union. Hopefully Politiere was hacking up bodies at this very moment. Everything had gone as planned since Emmanuelle contacted him two weeks ago. This toppling of adversity provided a small sense of pride for Jiggly, although he would rather witness these events firsthand and not through his ears and bodily vibrations, instincts that confirmed all was right in the world.

And then his failure curled his blood as he stepped into the small hidden room for what Jiggly hoped was his last time tonight. He gripped his clown hat and tossed it across the room, tired of that damn string nipping at his stubbly beard. He'll have to swallow his pride and inform the Dark Lord of Helmsley's disappearance. He searched every part of the warehouses, and still no Helmsley. Jiggly had a passing thought that Helmsley—in his newfound erratic brain—had left the warehouse unaware of what he was doing. Something Jiggly would have to remedy soon. If he's picked up—CIA agent or not—and told them the story, he'll more than likely be committed or, at the very least, detained. But this is where Jiggly's people would intervene. The CIA was always in the shadows, sweeping the pieces under the rug or into the sea.

He took a seat in front of the monitors while staring into the shiny room where Mills had been. Blood covered the floor and the smell of sulfur burned his nostrils as a light slithering smoke lifted off the ground like fog across a lake in the coldest winter. The Dark Lord had done well, Jiggly thought when he clicked the mouse and the computer screen lit up with life. Jiggly's plan was simple; he was going to check all cameras to see if he could locate Helmsley. One last attempt at saving face before swallowing his pride and admitting defeat. He jinxed himself, Jiggly did, when he paraded around and accepted applause. Felt like a fool for getting all dolled up when he should have been on top of Helmsley and never allowed him out of his sight. All that preparation and here he was, a fucking failure. Jiggly gritted his teeth as he surveyed the monitors, his jaw tight. That kid Christopher was staring at the camera. Staring at him. Fucking kid is eerie, Jiggly thought. Made his skin crawl. He'll make a great master one day. It's like he was born for it.

Jiggly clicked the icon for the camera that was in the holographic room where ceremony was taking place. His first thought upon seeing the masters standing at attention, was that he hadn't missed the union or orgy although that thought process quickly turned skeptical when he saw Chef Politiere standing proud in front of the Goddess and the Dark Lord who had taken their seats on their designated thrones. Politiere's right hand was on the shoulder of a rather short person Jiggly couldn't see from the camera angle. He shook his head because the scene made little sense.

Something's wrong, he thought. Something's very, very wrong. What the fuck is Politiere doing in there? He should be filleting and deboning at this very moment.

Jiggly's heart was racing; he could feel it pounding against his chest.

He watched as one of the masters, a big and bulky bearded man, stepped forward. Jezebel, Jiggly thought. Makes sense she would choose such a body. It fit her internal self-projection. He saw Jezebel's mouth move, a sneer across her lips, and then Politiere turned to Jezebel, his mouth moving. Jiggly's eyes darted around the monitor, remembering that this particular camera did have sound. He clicked the speaker icon on the computer, and sound filled the room. It was Politiere who was speaking.

"I refuse to be held responsible for what this... thing has done."

Jiggly's eyes narrowed. *Thing? What thing?*

Jiggly craned his head as if in doing so he could see clearly the person in between Politiere and Jezebel. Jiggly gripped the mouse, hovering the cursor over the camera's controls on the monitor, moving the camera so he could see. See...

Kera?

Jiggly's mouth agape. *What?*

The scene seemed too surreal. Was this actually happening here and now, at this very moment? Impossible, he thought. *This... this is... WHAT THE FUCK?*

He looked closer, his eyes inches from the screen. Jezebel was speaking, but the sound had become muted in Jiggly's inquiry. All he could see was Kera. Kera standing in between the chef and Jezebel. Kera, her tentacles hiding inside her hair, their eyes watching like a child hiding under the covers, too afraid to shutter their eyes from seeing any monsters who were on the attack. But Kera was prideful, standing tall and erect. Her eyes drifted to the camera, as if she knew Jiggly was watching.

And she smiled.

And Jiggly's heart sank.

12

12:20 AM
The Ballroom
Sharon The Goddess

This putrid vermin had no place standing in front of her. And the chef was irritating. His mannerisms were annoying, and she couldn't stand that fucking accent and the way he carried himself. If she weren't so hungry, she'd tear the fucker's heart out. The intrusion frustrated her. She'd just taken the seed that would manifest in a stronghold on this world, and now this... this insurgency.

And a smile from this vermin, staring off over the Goddess' shoulder. Sharon craned her head to the left, glaring at this Kera. She pointed at her.

"Why do you smile at such a time?" Sharon asked.

Kera looked at Sharon, and her smile disappeared. She said nothing, stood silent and raised her chin, and those tentacles hid further within her hair. Jezebel squeezed Kera's neck.

"Answer her," ordered Jezebel, the voice a gruff and thick baritone.

Kera's face winced, but she said nothing, simply looked at Sharon with indignation.

Sharon stood, pushing off the throne's arms to her feet. Sharon felt her smile curl across her lips. "You're protecting someone." She stepped slowly towards Kera and Jezebel's hand forced Kera forward with a squeeze of her neck. "Who?"

Kera turned to Sharon. "No one. I work alone." And she laughed. A nervous laugh.

"I think not," said Sharon. "You're from the Mintaka System. It's quite obvious to us that you are." Sharon craned her head, peering into Kera, searching for heart flutters and pupil dilation.

"How did you get here? Only those invited to this planet are allowed. Someone had to provide you with entrance. Who?"

Kera was shaking her head. "Not a chance. I'm loyal to those who are my friends. Your wickedness does not scare me, your Highness." She said the word with insult behind her voice. Jezebel's grip tightened.

Sharon observed Kera's heart flutter. Quite obvious Kera was covering for someone. Some person who was here with them, and who knew the location of ceremony. Could be SERN, but their will had been taken long ago. These damn humans, she thought, there's always a rat in the horde.

"Tell me, Goddess…" Kera, her eyes determined and staring at Sharon. "When your hold on this world is broken, what will you do? Go back to burning and torturing your own? Or will those tables turn because of your failure? Will it be you who is then burned and tortured? What, dear good Goddess, would hell be like for you?" And she smiled a wide grin before she continued. "What depths of despair wait for the soul that has inflicted so much pain on others for so long? I'm sure there's millenniums worth of suffering waiting for the dear precious Goddess." Kera lifted her chin, proud, eyes narrow, and that smile continued, never ending.

Sharon returned the smile. She looked at Jezebel, whose mouth opened and closed with a snicker that crinkled Jezebel's nose. She looked back at Kera.

Sharon laughed then, the laugh bellowed from her gut to the ceiling high above. And Kera laughed with her as did Jezebel and the Dark Lord. Politiere stood confounded, nervous, his eyes darting from Sharon to the Dark Lord to Jezebel to Sharon whose laugh reached the heavens—or Xibalba. And Sharon thrust her fist into Kera's chest and gripped her heart. Sharon's eyes wide, locked with Kera's. "I guess you'll know, my dear. Once your heart is in my stomach." Sharon thrust her hand from Kera's chest, the heart in her grip. She took the first bite with a smile, staring deep into Kera's eyes before she dropped to the floor with a thud.

And Sharon ate that heart, her chest bursting with waves of love and empathy. Kera's heart was filled with pure love. Love that

Sharon's blood curdling hate wrapped around and swallowed. She could feel that love dissipate with that last bite, captured within a dark cauldron filled with terror. When she finished, she addressed Jezebel. "Find the traitor. Find them all. Have the children brought immediately for indoctrination. We move fast now. This..." She gestured to Kera, lying dead in a pool of blood, her chest torn open. She noticed how those tentacles scurried within Kera's hair. "Putrid vermin has compromised our plan." She addressed the masters. "All of us, there's a snake in our midst. Weed it out, stomp on it with destruction. We must be focused. We must maintain. Leave the human hearts with me. They will serve the child indoctrination."

"And bring the heart to me," said the Dark Lord.

Sharon turned to him. "Yes. Bring the Dark Lord the heart."

Jezebel stood tall like a soldier accepting orders. "Consider it done," she said, then addressed the masters. Called out three names and ordered them to follow.

Sharon hollered, "And bring me Jigglyspot. He must answer for this intrusion."

"As you wish," said Jezebel who, along with the three masters, were leaving the ballroom.

Sharon sat on her throne when another master approached.

"Goddess," the master said, a female. "We may have a lead. A woman who was not indoctrinated. She remains in the room where the masters manifested. May I receive her?"

Sharon bowed. "You may. And if she refuses..." She turned to the Dark Lord, and he returned her stare with a snicker and a grin before she turned to the master. And she said with a gleam in her eye, "... bring me her heart."

13

12:30 AM
The Room with the Coffins
Cassandra

"How do I take out his heart?" asked Tyler, standing over the body of James Reilly.

Cassandra, holding one of the three pots filled with eyeball ice water and about to toss that cold water across Tyler's friend Jake, stopped in her tracks. Water sloshed back and forth in the pot. Staring at Reilly, she then looked at Tyler, whose lost, unknowing stare seemed to reach out to her for reassurance. The cleaver he'd been holding resting on Reilly's legs.

"You have to crack the chest bone," she said. "Then force it open."

Tyler nodded, then quietly took the cleaver. His free hand on Reilly's forehead.

She saw Tyler raise the cleaver and quickly she glanced at the water and all those eyeballs. Heard the cleaver meet Reilly's chest bone with a thud and a crack. She stepped closer to Jake's coffin. He looked dead, lying in the coffin, sleeping. She heard cracks and pops with a constricted, hard breath. Tyler was prying the chest bone open with his hands when he cried out, winced, and pulled his hands away. Blood dripped from his palms. And the smell, the stench from the now hacked open, dead body of James Reilly, was like none she'd ever experienced. Cassandra gagged and felt acid in the back of her throat. The putrid stank was thick and unrelenting, invading her nostrils and crinkling her nose. Tyler seemed unaffected.

"Fuckin' chest bone's sharp." He clenched and shook his fists, then reached into the open chest and Cassandra felt her jaw slacken, the pot in her hands growing heavier with time, and her arms ached. Saw how Tyler ripped the heart from the chest, heard arteries popping and tearing. Tyler put the heart next to Reilly's throat, with those arteries still attached. They disappeared inside the open chest, and Tyler took the cleaver again and hacked them off. He then turned and looked at Cassandra.

"Go ahead," he said. "Wake them up."

Cassandra was staring, looking at Tyler now holding the heart in his hands. "Where are you going to put it?" she asked, then looked around. "There's no fire in here."

"For now, in my pocket. I don't have many options." Tyler squeezed the heart into his pocket, then looked at his shaking hands, his fingers curled and stiff. Cassandra saw blood drip off his palms. Saw the slits across his palms where the bone had sliced across his flesh.

All too surreal, thought Cassandra. But what wasn't surreal about this night or even the last two weeks? Kera said to burn the heart, but all Cassandra wanted to do was get rid of it by any means necessary. Walking around with a heart in your pocket felt wrong.

Tyler went to the sink, turned on the water, and put his hands beneath the faucet.

"Go ahead," said Tyler, rinsing his hands. "They need to get up. I'd like to be gone before that French guy comes back."

Cassandra looked at the eyeballs again and for a moment, she wondered whose eyeballs they belonged to. Obviously from the bodies hanging in the freezer. But who are those people? Or who *were* those people? Life shouldn't end with your eyeballs plucked out and used for some cannibalistic soup. She shook her head and doused Jake with icy eyeball water, and he immediately jumped up with a gasp. She did the same to Amber and Ned Tatty. All three with the same reaction. All three now hacking and coughing. Tyler had taken a towel from the bottom shelf of the sink, tore it in half, and wrapped each half around his palms.

"Can you tie these off?" Tyler gestured to his hands as his friends continued to hack and cough, obviously disoriented. They hadn't said a word. Not yet at least.

Cassandra forced her stare away from the eyeballs now defrosting inside their respective coffins, and put the pot down, then tied off Tyler's makeshift bandages. Her stare drifted to Tyler's pocket, where the heart was. She pictured it beating inside his pocket. How surreal would that be?

Cassandra turned to Tyler's friends, their eyes glassy, drooping eyelids and shivering. They had yet to say a word. She looked around the room, searching for something for them to wear. They were naked, after all. I guess marinade works better when the immersed body is naked. And of all the things going on right now, that made the most sense, however sick it was.

She went to the metal cabinets on the back wall.

"What're you doing?" asked Tyler.

She opened a cabinet. "Giving them some sense of dignity." And she gestured to her own body, then to Tyler's friends. The first cabinet was empty, so she opened all of them, finding a stack of robes, all black, in the last cabinet. She took out four and joined Tyler.

It was Tyler that addressed his friends first. "You all alright?" Their eyes drifted to him, confused. They said nothing.

Cassandra took one cloak and draped it across Amber's shoulders. She was shivering, and she looked at Cassandra with a disoriented stare.

"It's okay, hun," whispered Cassandra.

Amber went to speak. Her face winced and her hand went to her throat. Forced herself to say in a grumbling, crackling voice, "My throat hurts." She looked at Cassandra with a fearful stare.

"Understood," said Cassandra, her arm across Amber's shoulder.

Tyler said, "Not surprised. You've had a tube stuffed down your throat for at least a day now. It's probably irritated. But that's not the important part. What is important is that you can all walk. Run is more like it, but walking will do for now."

Jake was shaking his head. He coughed and said, "What happened? I can't remember anything."

Ned, his head drifting, said, "Neither can I. My head feels like a thousand pounds."

"Probably the effect of whatever they gave you."

Amber stared into Cassandra's eyes. "I want to go home," she muttered.

"I know, honey, we all do. And we will." She looked at Tyler.

Jake repeated, "What happened?" His eyes on Tyler.

"The Shibalba X-Press," said Tyler. "I think they gassed us or something because I have no recollection that we got off that ride. All I know is we all ended up here."

Jake pursed his lips and swallowed with a wince and a gasp. "Where is here?"

Tyler shook his head. "Not exactly sure, but we're in some warehouse. There's some sick shit happening in here too. Some rich fucker's satanic cult was about to fillet all three of you and serve your flesh up for some cannibalistic ritual." He paused, seemed to check himself. "However hard that is to believe. But that isn't the worst of it. We still have to find Pam and then find a way out of here."

"Pam?" whispered Amber.

Ned Tatty said, "Where is she?" Of all three, he looked the worst.

Cassandra wondered when they'd recognize they were in coffins. And moving on from there, when they'll recognize the dead body with the chest split open and the heart missing. She squeezed the fourth cloak around her head. Looked much nicer than the tattered nasty clothes she had on.

"I don't know, no one does. But I'm not leaving until I find her." He paused, looking over his friends, assessing, giving them a moment for current circumstances to sink in. "So, here's the plan. Once we find the quickest way out of here, I want all four of you to get the police and bring them here while I look for Pam."

Cassandra snapped, "I told you I'm not leaving." Tyler paused.

"Yeah," said Jake. "We can't leave Pam."

Tatty said, "I still don't understand what's happening," through a cough, his voice raspy.

Amber leaned her head on Cassandra's shoulder. She was shivering, her lips turning blue. "Let's get this cloak on you," said Cassandra. "You're freezing." And she did just that, fitting the cloak over Amber's head and shoulders, then squeezed her arms into the sleeves.

"Listen, Tatty, here's the long and short of it. We were abducted. I mean, look around you, you're sitting in a plastic coffin. This girl too, although..." He gestured to Cassandra and his voice trailed off. He shook his head. "But that doesn't matter. She's in the same boat as we are. Pam too, and everyone else on that ride. We need to get out of here, and fast. They're coming and if they find us, they'll kill us. So, the fucking question is, *Can you all walk?*"

It was Amber who replied. Her voice cracked and whining, her eyes brimming with tears. "I don't know if I can. I can't feel my legs."

Ned Tatty said, "Are these eyeballs?"

"Eyeballs?" said Jake.

"Fucking eyeballs." Ned Tatty jerked and twitched, attempting to get out in a hurried frenzy. He tipped over his coffin and slammed into the body of James Reilly that crashed, plexiglass coffin and all, to the floor, as did Ned Tatty.

Amber was whining and crying on Cassandra's shoulder. "I don't want to see eyeballs."

"Okay," said Cassandra. She gestured to Tyler to help her.

Ned Tatty said, "Fucking eyeballs everywhere." After a moment's pause, "What the fuck? Is that Reilly?"

"Yeah," said Tyler, wrapping his arms around Amber's back and under her legs. She buried her head in his shoulder. "Don't look," Tyler whispered, lifting her from the coffin. "Cassandra," he said. "Help her, please." With his hand on her back, Tyler let her feet down. Cassandra held her shoulder, and Amber leaned against her.

"Get me the fuck up!" screamed Tatty. "What the fuck is Reilly doing here?"

Tyler stomped over to Tatty and crouched in front of him. "Keep your fucking voice down."

"James Reilly's dead body is staring at me, and you want me to keep my voice down?"

"Yeah, Ned. Unless you want to be dead too. And all of us."

Amber said, "I think they're just asleep. I've got that prickly feeling from my toes to my thighs."

"C'mon," said Tyler, offering his hand.

Cassandra, "That's good. Keep moving. You'll get the feeling back soon."

Tyler helped Ned Tatty to his feet, who put his hands on the overturned coffin to steady himself.

Cassandra scanned the room as Tyler walked over to Jake.

"You, okay?" asked Tyler.

Jake's head drifted towards Tyler, and he laughed. "Yeah, fucking peachy. You?"

Tyler laughed, too.

Jake shook his head. "I don't care about eyeballs, just help me out."

Tyler gripped Jake and hauled him out of the coffin, standing him up when his right leg jerked and buckled. Tyler caught him before he fell. Cassandra saw how he looked at Reilly's body.

"Why is Reilly's body here?" asked Jake.

Cassandra exchanged stares with Tyler.

"I don't know. There's not much more I do know other than what I already told you," he lied.

Jake nodded, then looked at Amber. "You, okay?"

She was moving her feet and lifting her knees one by one. "No," she whined. "I haven't got a grip on what's happening. Not yet." She looked around the room. "But we're together. I guess that's a good thing, considering." Cassandra saw how she regarded Tyler and paused. Amber looked at Reilly, then back to Tyler. Cassandra thought she was piecing together current circumstances, fitting the puzzle together, so to speak. She could see the cogs turning in Amber's brain, and she wouldn't take her eyes off Tyler. Maybe she *couldn't* take her eyes off him.

Ned Tatty said, "That smell..." His nose crinkled, his chest heaved twice, and he threw up, tossing marinade all over the coffin and floor. Hunched over and threw up again. "How can you stand it?"

"You get used to it," said Tyler, and Cassandra noticed how Amber stared at him, wide-eyed and fearful.

Untrusting? Cassandra thought and felt how Amber tensed with a constricted swallow.

Tatty tossed marinade again, his skin a ghostly pale, red-rimmed eyes, and vomit dripping from his bottom lip. Tatty wiped his chin off and hurled some more.

"Jesus, man," said Jake. "Maybe you should step away from the dead body."

"My fuckin legs won't work, asshole."

Tyler took the cloaks from the coffin where Amber had been and handed Jake his cloak. "Need help with it?"

Jake shook his head and took a limped step forward. "They're getting better," he said regarding his legs, and draped the cloak over his head.

Tatty was holding his nose and Amber buried hers in Cassandra's shoulder, perhaps to ward off tossing her marinade. Tatty moved to Tyler, limping, but doing better. Tyler handed him his cloak, and he draped it over his head with shaking hands.

"Okay, Tyler," said Jake. "What's our next move?"

"We've got two options. Door number one or door number two." He gestured to both doors. Door two was the door they had originally come through with Kera. He cleared his throat and Cassandra wondered if Kera flashed in his mind's eye, because Kera definitely flashed in Cassandra's thoughts, wondering what had befallen their little savior. "Door two, we know where it leads, door one... that's a different story. We have no clue where it goes, but..." His voice trailed off. Cassandra could see he was searching for the right words.

"But what?" asked Jake.

Tyler looked at him. "We..." He looked at Cassandra. "We know what's beyond door two. There's not much we haven't covered and from what we... understand... is that Pam is on the other side of that door." He pointed to the far door. "Somewhere at least. Probably with the rest of the people they took from the Shibalba X-Press."

"So that's the play then," Jake interjected, and he hobbled one step closer to Tyler.

"Yes. Only problem is, we don't know what is beyond that door," Tyler added, then looked at all of them, one by one, assessing. "So, we will need to protect ourselves."

"What do you have in mind?" Tatty, his voice soft and weary.

Tyler craned his head. "Well, all we've got are some filleting knives, things like that. They'll have to do. But there's no way we can know what weapons they will have. Good thing is we have the element of surprise." And he paused, looked at each one of them and said, "If you have to, if it comes down to it, don't hesitate. Hack the fucker up like chop suey."

And Cassandra felt Amber tense with a shiver that raced down her spine.

14

12:40 AM
The Warehouse
Lilly

She passed out. Had been dreaming of Tad, drifting together, young and naïve, before the boys. Before Christopher was even a thought. They were waiting in line for the Shibalba X-Press when Tad turned and said, "Everything changes after this. Everything and anything that was will change." In the dream, Lilly knew Tad was gone. She felt it, the understanding and awareness of current circumstance. "Don't leave," she said. "Just stay here with me. Please!"

But then Tad was gone, and Lilly was standing outside the Shibalba X-Press listening to Christopher's screams. And she rushed in with the sound of a loud bang as the door shut behind her. She winced and shuddered with a jolt, staring into darkness. No light on. No sound. All she could see was blackness, as if she stepped into a void where light was no longer welcome. Heard feet shuffling towards her.

Heard a voice. "There's my lovely, lovely." It was Kathy Crawford's voice. As promised, she'd come back for Lilly.

Lilly's eyes were closed, listening to her own heavy breathing and the steps slapping across the floor, coming closer.

"Lovely, lovely." Kathy again, and Lilly pictured Kathy skipping across the room towards her.

Lilly forced her eyes open. Her head throbbed. She felt weak, depleted, running on empty.

"The Goddess wishes to see you. But I think I'll savor that delectable blood of yours first."

Closer now was Kathy, and all Lilly could see was blood, coagulated, and sticky. She felt it on her skin, across her head and face. And her arms were tingling, numb beneath her body.

"So sweet it is," continued Kathy, her voice close, so close Lilly knew she was standing over her. "I can hear it flooding through your veins."

Lilly moved her prickly numb fingers. Her eyes wavered, slow and tired, to the eyes staring. The dead eyes of Gary-Larry-Barry, black to the core, staring at Lilly like some metaphorical foreshadowing of Lilly's demise.

"I know you live. I can hear your heartbeat and the slow rise of breath in your lungs. Come, my lovely, fight as much as you wish."

Lilly's fingers wrapped tight around the knife in her palm.

"Fear turns the blood even sweeter." Kathy's voice close to her ear, and Lilly could smell the warmth of her breath; it stunk like sulfur. Kathy's hand on Lilly's shoulder. "Come, my lovely, let us eat." She turned Lilly around.

Numb fingers or not, Lilly refused for the opportunity to pass. She buried that knife in Kathy's Crawford's neck and a spout of blood jutted from the puncture. A surprised stare widened Kathy's eyes as she let out a wet gurgle, her hand on her neck as a growl erupted from the back of her throat. Started in low and grew, grew loud, then deafening. Kathy's head snapped back, the scream filled her mouth, filled the room. Her arms leapt from her sides, outstretched as Lilly pushed away from Kathy Crawford, across Garry-Larry-Barry. And Lilly could see beneath Kathy's skin how whatever had taken over Kathy Crawford's body raced beneath the flesh, circling, spiraling around her neck when Kathy belted out a loud thunderous cry and that spider, that thing, jettisoned from her throat, and over her lips.

Like a black cloud swirling in a thick puff of smoke. Lilly saw red eyes gleam inside that black smoke. It looked like a gargoyle. A gargoyle with wings. Small, jagged teeth and a snake-like tongue waggled at Lilly as this gargoyle thing dipped its head closer and Lilly backed up even more when the gargoyle tensed and constricted, belting out another scream as it stretched its wings, its arms and talons, as if pleading to the almighty for mercy. Now a whirlwind of furious wind filled the room like a hurricane with a vengeance that raced towards the gargoyle. And the gargoyle's expression changed to fear as the wind rifled up the gargoyle's chest, exploding from within into a bright white light. Lilly clamped her eyes shut, shielding herself with her hands raised against the light. Her face scrunched and tense. And just as quickly as it came, the wind was gone, the light dissipated, and beneath it Lilly heard gurgling and heavy breath.

She opened her eyes. The gargoyle was gone. The gurgling was coming from Kathy, lying on her back, blood pooled beneath her, holding the knife still stuck in her neck. Lilly searched Kathy's eyes and that stare that captured fear. Her head shuddering. Lilly put her hand on Kathy's cheek. "I'm so sorry." Blood coughed and spit over Kathy's lips, cascading from the corners of her mouth and dripping to the floor.

Kathy was attempting to catch her breath, to speak. Lilly took her hand. "I'll find Jenny." Lilly was hovering over Kathy with one hand holding Kathy's and the other on the back of Kathy's head. Kathy gurgling and struggling to hold on. "I promise," said Lilly, her voice a low whine.

Kathy managed her last words, which arrived in a wet, bloodied gurgle over her lips. Her chest heaving up and down as she spoke. "You... have... to." Kathy's eyes staring at Lilly. "What will... become... of them. What waits... you *have*... to..."

Lilly was nodding when Kathy froze, and she could hear the final breath release from Kathy's lungs. And all was still and quiet. Lilly felt the cry and wail in her chest rise to the back of her throat, but she forced it down, turning that holler into a whining cry. Felt her tears fall across her skin. Heavy breath as she gripped the knife and yanked it from Kathy's neck with a wet tug. Kathy's head lolled to the side. Lilly dropped the knife, her breathing heavy and stuttered. Her chest heaving with thick breaths. Her hands working nervously, shaking, trembling, and disrobed the recently deceased Kathy Crawford.

15

12:45 AM
Inside the Small Observation Room
Jigglyspot

If he could cry, he would, but that right had gone a long time ago. What Jigglyspot felt was hatred and confusion. His thoughts swam as if a floodgate had opened. Quite obvious to Jiggly, there was more happening tonight than he'd been aware of, and it was only a matter of time before he was summoned for questioning by the Goddess and the Dark Lord. This was his show after all, and he'll have to answer for the insurgency. But Jiggly already knew what the most prominent question would be: How did Kera receive entrance to the show?

Widely known in Jiggly's circle was the fact that outside influence on planet Earth was restricted. The only way otherworldly beings could enter Earth's atmosphere was by invitation, and there were very few people on the planet who not only understood this, but who were also capable and knowledgeable enough to offer entrance. It was the cane. The cane Jiggly was gifted by the lord of all lords—referred to as Mr. West. When wielded properly, the cane opened a portal for space travel. Jiggly thought about Mr. West. Should he go to him and request assistance? West might dismantle Jiggly himself if he learned about Jiggly's mishandling of the cane. It was West's brilliance that punctured a hole in the fabric of space and time. West had humanity wrapped around his pinkie and made the Goddess and Dark Lord look like scampering children or out-of-control teenagers with their master minions. But of course, they served Mr. West's narrative, which is why he tolerated their exploits for so long. As long as they continued to follow his declaration—Mr. West had high ambitions to turn Earth into his own Xibalba—they'll remain a welcomed addition to accommodate his plan. A plan Jiggly always marveled over. West was a diabolical genius, probably the best in history.

But Jiggly thought better about going to Mr. West. It was not a good idea, not yet anyway. He mishandled West's most prominent gift—the cane—and West will not be pleased when he discovers that Jiggly was opening portals for otherworldly beings for no reason other than personal gain. Jiggly was a spoke on a wheel and that wheel belonged to West. Not even a spoke, Jiggly was one of those accessories children put on their wheels to make the spinning look cool. He'd been loyal to the cause for decades, even if he'd done so under duress and punishment. Jiggly always believed that when life hands you lemons, you make lemonade, and he's been stirring that lemonade to his benefit for decades. But now Kera had undermined his loyalty, exposed him to the Goddess. The Goddess who ate her heart and Jiggly knew what that meant, but he refused to allow himself to go there. He could commission Mr. West if needed. If he can set everything right tonight, Mr. West will more than likely oblige his request.

His only question was what to do next. He was, for lack of a better word, in trouble. At a crossroad, and if he zigs or zags in the wrong direction, it will be him in Xibalba, that was for sure. He was certain the masters were looking for him now. He felt like a fool, all dolled up and clowned out, and everything about his plan had been turned on its head. Gary was dead, Helmsley was missing, and Kera betrayed him. What she actually did, he wasn't sure. What was she doing here? Knowing Kera, it had something to do with that kid, the teenager Jiggly had become so fond of, the other warlock hiding beneath the folds of time, much like Jiggly had been before his purpose was revealed. Before he understood who he was and where he came from.

Jiggly decided then that he needed to see the boy for himself. Did Kera release him? Is that why she came tonight? But she didn't know about him? How could she? Who could have told her? Jiggly searched for answers, but none came, other than more questions. If Kera released him, where was he now? Had he gotten out? Jiggly knew that if he did get out, that would be an entirely new can of worms to deal with. The boy's demise would be forthcoming and there was one thing about Jiggly most people did not know.

Jiggly would never kill one of his own. His fellow clowns had put up with Jiggly for a long time because of his cosmic debt, but they would not stand behind Jiggly if he were to turn on his own or have any contribution to it whatsoever. This was a pickle of all pickles.

But his clear direction forward starts with a trip to the underground to see if the teenager is still there. If not... well, Jiggly wasn't sure what to do. The masters should be looking for him by now—his absence during ceremony more than likely raised some red flags—and he had to act fast.

Seems like everyone is under the gun tonight.

16

12:50 AM
The Warehouse
Lilly

She was dressed in the cloak, standing by the door where she'd seen the other adults exit after–after those spiders took control of them. Took control of Kathy Crawford, who was lying in a pool of her own blood, dead by Lilly's hand. Dead because she was one of them, a devil or demon or whatever the hell was going on here.

B will they know it's Lilly beneath the cloak? Lilly, who was not one of them.

She touched the knife wedged in her pants pocket beneath the cloak. If I have to and only if I have to, she told herself. She must find the children, Christopher and Jenny specifically, although she was certain there were more children being held against their will. How many she had no way to know. And she didn't want to think about why they were here. Considering the spiders, had a similar fate befallen the children? She hoped not. She hoped she did not have to stare into the demon eyes of her own son.

What will you do then, Lilly?

Better not to think about it. Better to hope for the best. She thought about Ms. Finicky. They took her away for a reason. Maybe Finicky was with the children now?

She turned to the door. No window. No way to know what she was walking into or where she'll be once she goes through. Touched her pocket again as if the knife could grow legs and run away. It had not. She wouldn't be surprised if it had. She had so little information on her current predicament she braced herself for any possibility that may come barreling at her with lightning speed. What she knew was, although those spiders were in control of the adult bodies, they could be expelled by killing the host. She looked at Kathy Crawford and swallowed the lump in her throat.

But there were many of them. Too many for Lilly to shove the blade into every one of them without recourse. And they were strong, stronger than humans. That fact Lilly discovered when Kathy Crawford had yanked her by the hair. She seemed to lift Lilly with gentle ease.

Okay, so they're strong, but they can be killed. It is, after all, a human body they possessed.

Lilly looked back at the door, her jaw tense and tight. Maybe there's a leader, she thought. Of course, there is. There's always someone pulling the strings, like that little guy, the clown. He seemed to call all the shots. Maybe if I drive this knife into his throat, his reign will be over. Maybe the others will leave then? Wishful thinking, she thought. Probable, but unlikely.

Still, it was worth a shot.

Lilly clenched her jaw and gazed at the dead Kathy Crawford and Gary-Larry-Barry. Her last thought–before she walked through the door–was how many more dead bodies would join them tonight?

17

12:55 AM
Xibalba
SAC John Mills

He heard the wind before he felt it. Standing over Helmsley, Mills searched the landscape when the wind rushed against his brow with a fierce howl. And those gargoyles all started jumping and yipping as if they knew something was coming.

Behind the wind, on the other side of the mountain, Mills heard terror filled screams erupt like thunder. He looked at the mountain and he could actually see the wind. It circled in black and red colors, spiraling around the mountain.

Heard Helmsley repeat, "You're changing, and you don't even know it. It's not a dream, John. *This is really happening!*"

Mills forced his eyes away from the wind to look at Helmsley. "Why do you keep saying the same thing?"

"Hell John, we're in hell."

And somewhere in the distance that other voice, his voice, SAC John Mills, although the voice carried a different tone, more sinister and thick. Eat his heart, the voice said. *Eat his heart.*

"Hell John, we're in hell."

The wind kicked into overdrive with a whirling spin like when a drain is unplugged. Lightning pumped and popped within the wind like some sadistic electrical game fought for dominance over the wind. Mills felt it across his skin, hot, burning hot, as those gargoyles yipped and leapt into a frenzy.

"You're changing, John, and you don't even know it," said Helmsley. "It's not a dream, John. *This is really happening!*"

Mills looked at Helmsley. "Stop saying that. You're starting to really *piss me the fuck off.*"

The wind ferocious. Yipping, clambering, hopping, and screeching.

"Hell John…"

Eat his heart.

"We're in hell."

Eat his heart.

"Stop fucking saying that." Mills heard a growl erupt in the back of his throat. He licked his lips, staring at Helmsley, wanting to…

Eat his heart!

And beneath the wind was laughter, a sinister growling laugh. The yipping turned to squawking, squawking turned to high-pitched hollers. Mills looked around. All the gargoyles were now jumping and hollering and yipping.

"You're changing, John, and you don't even know it. It's not a dream, John. *This is really happening!*"

Mills raised his fist and noticed it wasn't his fist. What Mills raised in an effort to plunge his fist into the chest of Helmsley was a talon. Long, sharp fingers and nails, and darkened skin like burnt ash that rippled up his arm.

"Hell, John…"

Mills stood observing his hand and arm, watching it change.

"We're in hell."

Yipping hollers and screeches, the howl of the wind kicked up a few octaves, and Mills' eyes darted to the swirling vortex that captured the wind. Something in the wind, inside the vortex. Something's coming.

"Hell, John…"

Something is definitely coming. Mills could see it, a light in the center of the vortex that beamed in all directions with the wind swirling around it like a frame in some sadistic film.

"We're in hell."

John's arms drifted to his side as he craned his head and the yipping, screeching squawking filled his ears. That light, that beautiful light, dissipating, and behind it Mills saw who was coming.

And Mills said, "Is that a woman?"

18

1:00 PM
The Room with the Coffins
Tyler

He was kneeling with his ear to the door, listening for any movement, a grunt, or a laugh. Anything to tell him what was beyond the door. All Tyler heard was his own breathing.

"Is it clear?" Jake, Tyler turned to him, to all of them, lined up and ready to go, fear plastered across their faces. All except Cassandra. She seemed ready and willing to go the long mile.

"I don't hear a thing," said Tyler. "But that might not be good, either. Silence ain't always golden."

"What choice do we have?" Tatty, he was scratching his arms; Tyler could see red fingernail marks across his forearms. And he seemed shaky too, nervous. But not the fear kind of nervous, the, *I've got something to do and I don't have time for this* nervous.

"Exactly." Tyler lifted himself to his feet. Transferred the meat cleaver to his left hand, then unlocked the first deadbolt, slow and steady. His hand calm, his movement smooth, holding his breath each time he unlocked a deadbolt. Looked over his shoulder after the last lock clicked open. "Be ready for anything." One hand on the doorknob, he squeezed the meat cleaver tight in his other hand.

Opened slowly. Just a crack. Light beamed through the crack from the other room. Listening. A slight creak from the door and he could hear how everyone held their breath. Tyler paused, then craned his head to the right, looking in. He could see a waist high stainless steel table with bowls, cutlery, and cookie sheets scattered across the top. Craned his head some more and saw a line of sinks followed by a stove.

A kitchen, Tyler thought, and he turned to his friends with a quick glance. Made sense it would be a kitchen, considering his friends were soaking in marinade less than an hour ago. But no sounds. No scuffling, no rambling, no shuffling, and no talking. All was quiet.

He turned to Jake, hovering over his shoulder. "Stay here. I'll check it out. Seems quiet." Jake nodded, and Tyler scanned his friends. How nervous they all were, how restless and scared. Looked at Jake and whispered, "Hold the door closed. I'll be right back." And he slipped through the door.

The kitchen was large and filthy. Stunk like rancid meat and Tyler's hand drifted to his nose, his nostrils burning from the stank. And it was cold, so cold Tyler's breath plumed off his lips. Directly ahead was an opening, no door, just an opening to another room, which was bathed in darkness. A walk-in freezer on his left, the door slightly open. Cold air drifted from the open door into the kitchen. On his right, on the other side of the kitchen, was a separate alcove with a wide opening. The room was dark, and Tyler approached cautiously. The room was a good six feet deep and ten feet across and filled with what Tyler assumed were incubators. Plastic coverings with tiny mattresses inside the enclosures, but no babies. Where are the babies? Tyler studied the incubators; saw blood stained on one mattress. He didn't want to go there. Couldn't go there.

Babies! he thought. *Fucking babies.* His hand over his mouth. He clenched the meat cleaver tight.

And then he heard it, a whimper, crying. Someone was crying. He scanned the room. Where was it coming from? Heard it again. The freezer? Yes, it was definitely coming from the freezer. And Tyler knew all too well what these sick fucks kept in their freezers. Could it be someone was still alive, hanging in the freezer? Tyler pictured them on a meat hook, crying their eyes out, waiting for death, and hoping it would arrive soon. Tyler approached with caution, walking between the table and the sink.

Heard whimpering behind the door. Tyler looked around, darted to the opening, and hid next to the door, listening.

"Killed my husband."

Tyler heard the voice, and the tone was familiar.

"What did he do? What did he do?"

The accent was French.

The man was wailing. Tyler, thinking, his head bowed in thought. Has to be the same guy who caught Kera. There's...

His thought trailed off. On the opposite side of the freezer, off to his left and through a short foyer, Tyler saw one of those swing doors, like those in a restaurant that separate the dining room from the kitchen. A light was on in the room beyond the door. He stepped into the foyer, scanning his surroundings. Looked more like a supply closet. Boxes, aprons, cutlery, and napkins were on a table against the wall on his right.

Heard the Frenchman repeat, "What did he do?"

Tyler went to the swinging door and looked through the window. It was a restaurant. An empty restaurant, but a restaurant just the same. Tables scattered across the room, a bar in the corner. He could see plates and glasses on the tables. Looked like whoever had been dining had gone in a hurry. But everyone? Kera had said some ceremony was happening tonight. Made sense that's where these guests were now.

Tyler bowed his head in thought when he put his left hand on the wall to the right of the door and heard a pop. He snapped his head around. A door was open, just a crack. A door made to look like the wall. Tyler went to it, opened it a bit more. Stone steps spiraled into darkness.

The other side, Tyler thought. Highly possible that Pam is down there. Turned back to the swinging door, looking through the window. There's got to be a way out through...

"You!" He heard the Frenchman behind him.

Tyler turned quickly.

"You slit his throat."

Tyler's eyes went wide. The chef was holding one of those filleting knives, his eyes wide and wet with tears.

"You're one of them," said the Frenchman, his face pinched in hatred. "One of the clowns." His voice filled with rage. Tyler watched the knife, and he clenched his meat cleaver tight, holding it by his thigh, out of the Frenchman's sight. "Where's your master, Jigglyspot?"

"Who?"

"Don't berate me. Everyone knows who Jigglyspot is."

"Mister, I have no clue what you're talking about."

The Frenchman didn't seem to register what Tyler said. Or he didn't believe him.

"You didn't have to kill him. He didn't do anything to anyone."

Tyler could see the chef's tears streaming down his face.

"Mister," said Tyler, as calm as he could. "Drop the knife, you're making me a little... nervous." He cleared his throat.

The Frenchman's eyes went wide. "Nervous," he said, scowling at Tyler. "Oh, I'm making you nervous?" His hands were trembling.

"Don't do it, mister," ordered Tyler. "Maybe we can help each other."

"Help you..." he hollered and rushed at Tyler with that filleting knife raised high over his head. "I'll kill you."

Tyler buried his meat cleaver between the Frenchman's eyes, stopping him cold in his tracks. He took two steps back and dropped his knife, which hit the floor with a steel clang. Blood streamed across the man's nose and across his lips, dripping off his chin as he stood there with a dumbfounded stare, as if he wasn't aware there was a meat cleaver wedged in his skull. Tyler noticed how the wall door bumped against the doorframe, then opened again. The Frenchman wobbled on his feet, then dropped like a sack of bricks, and Tyler saw Jake standing in the kitchen.

He said nothing. Just stood there, nodding as if to tell Tyler killing the Frenchman was necessary. Or maybe he had no idea what to think, but Tyler didn't have time to counsel his friend. He stepped on the Frenchman's chest and gripped his cleaver. Pulled and tugged. That sucker was in there good. The Frenchman's body wiggled when Tyler pulled and yanked, the Frenchman's eyes still open, staring at him. Pulled again and the cleaver slid out of the skull with a wet jerk. He scuttled back two steps, then caught himself and looked at Jake.

"Help me with him," said Tyler. "Let's put him in the back room in case someone comes." Tyler wedged his meat cleaver in the back of his pants and stepped over the body. "Jake!" he said. Jake was staring at the Frenchman. "Jake," said Tyler in a loud whisper when Jake looked at him. Tyler cocked his brow. "Grab his legs."

Jake said nothing. Tyler was sure he was in shock. Kept looking from Tyler to the Frenchman, then back to Tyler.

Jake said, "You killed him," while staring at the dead body.

"Yeah, I know."

Jake looked at Tyler.

"Are you gonna..." Tyler gave up, started dragging the Frenchman when Jake walked past him. Tyler paused so Jake could grab the ankles and together they carried the bobbing, swaying dead body into the kitchen when the scream erupted.

Tyler turned and saw Amber with her hand over her mouth. He dropped the body and rushed to her. Cassandra was in the freezer, the door wide open, and yes, there was someone strapped to a chair with his throat slit. But Tyler's focus was on Amber because Tyler was sure she was about to scream again.

"Amber, don't," ordered Tyler. "He was gonna kill me," he pleaded, his hand on Amber's shoulder, her eyes on the dead body. "Amber!"

Slowly, her eyes drifted to Tyler, and he could see how her pupils contracted with fear. She was trembling, shaking uncontrollably. Cassandra stepped out of the freezer. Ned Tatty leaned against the wall. He looked worse for the wear, still scratching. Seemed he didn't give a shit about the dead body.

Amber moved her hand from her mouth. "Jake, no."

And Tyler turned around. Jake was pulling the arms, bringing the body further into the room.

"What?" he said. "We've got to Amber. This is a matter of survival." He kept pulling until the body was in the room, away from the foyer. He stretched his back with a heavy breath. "They get heavy quick."

"I want to go home." Amber, Tyler turned to her. She was staring right at him. Through him. She stepped away. "I... I... I don't trust anyone. I want to go home."

Jake said, "What about Pam? We can't leave without Pam."

Amber never took her eyes off Tyler. Now she was shaking her head. "She's probably dead already."

"What? How can you say that? We don't know that Amber." Jake again, he was stepping closer to her.

Amber's tears were streaming down her cheeks. Her lips trembling. "I want to go home."

Tyler didn't appreciate the way she was looking at him.

"Baby, do you understand where we are? Or where we don't know we are." He shook his head. "We don't even know where here is or how to get out. We..."

"The restaurant," Tyler said, and everyone seemed to tense up.

Jake turned to him. "What?"

"Right through that room. I saw it. There's a restaurant in there. Which means there has to be a door to the outside." He looked at Jake. "Let her go," he said. "The three of you, go." He looked at Tatty, Cassandra, and then back to Jake and Amber. "Go get the police."

Jake was shaking his head. "But we don't even know where we are. They could've taken us anywhere. How do we know where to go?"

"I'm not going anywhere." Cassandra, Tyler regarded her briefly, then turned back to Jake.

"You'll figure it out. It's better than being in here. We'll look for Pam," he said and looked at Amber, still wearing that frantic stare. "Even if we can't find her, you'll bring the police and—"

Ned Tatty stepped forward. Tyler looked at him. His eyes were wide, his hands reaching, reaching for something, pointing, his breath stuttering across his lips, his jaw moving up and down, but no words arrived off his lips.

"Spit it out, Tatty," hollered Jake.

"What the fuck is that?"

Tyler turned. They all turned. At first, Tyler noticed nothing. His eyes adjusting to the dark room. And then he saw it. Wasn't sure what he was looking at. It looked like a tree trunk just outside the doorway. But tree trunks don't wear clothes and Tyler was sure he was staring at a clown outfit, a black and white clown outfit. What he'd first thought were tree limbs were arms draped to the sides of that trunk body. But here was the crux of it all: there was no head. The trunk reached past the top of the doorway. Tyler stepped back, gripped the meat cleaver, and pulled it from his pants.

Are those feet? he thought, staring at what he assumed were big floppy clown shoes. And then one of those clown shoes moved, stepped forward into the doorway as Tyler saw the trunk bend. Now he saw the head duck beneath the doorway and stretch inside the kitchen, where this clown stood over the dead body.

A clown indeed. He must be seven feet tall. Tyler's eyes raised to the clown's face as his head also rose. The clown's head was the shape of a thumb, with painted green hair like an eraser glued to his thick skull. His face seemed to be plastered in a permanent scowl, even with the thick red painted smile across his lips and those gleaming eyes painted the shape of stars—possibly to provide a twinkle to what looked like a stare of death and pain. The man looked pissed. He continued to study the body. Tyler looked at the dead Frenchman, then looked at the cleaver in his hand.

Tyler had two thoughts at that moment. The first, I need a bigger knife, and second, I hope that wasn't his friend.

Not a word from the clown, but his eyes moved. They moved and then blinked before finding Tyler. His head craned to the left as if he was studying Tyler's thoughts. Then he looked back at the body, his nose crinkled twice with what Tyler assumed were quick sniffs.

This is when Tyler noticed that not one peep or squeal nor a gasped breath had come since this giant clown had stepped into the room. Tyler watched with a dropped jaw as the clown bent over the body, gripped the Frenchman's head in one hand, stepped to the side of the dead body and with his other hand gripped the Frenchman's leg and hauled the dead body in one smooth jolt and dropped the dead Frenchman on the table with a loud bang causing all the bowls and cookie sheets to jump and drop off the table with a metal clang. Someone let a whimper escape, but Tyler wasn't sure if it was Amber or Tatty. Tyler looked at his friends. Amber with her hand over her mouth, Jake looked like he'd seen a ghost, his skin ashen, his lips trembling, Cassandra was studying the large clown, sizing him up it seemed, and Tatty was plastered to the wall as if he could disappear through the wall to get away.

The clown let out a breath that buzzed his lips with a flutter, as if he was overworked and now he had to keep working. Tyler looked at the clown standing on the other side of the table, but he was so big he seemed to be right on top of Tyler. The clown stretched his hand out, palm up. Tyler's lips quivered while staring at that baseball glove sized hand. Noticed blood stains on his callused fingers. Fingers that then clenched and shook. Tyler's eyes drifted up, up, up, and locked eyes with the clown who gestured to the meat cleaver Tyler forgot was in his hand.

Unknowingly, Tyler handed him the cleaver, and the clown raised his shoulders, standing tall with the cleaver in his left hand. He pointed to the door with his right hand.

Tyler said, "I think he wants us to leave."

The clown nodded.

"Come on," said Tyler. "Let's go."

Now Tyler could hear stuttered breaths from his friends. And the clown smiled. Tyler could see how yellow and jagged his teeth were, as if he'd chipped more than a few of his teeth. Tyler looked at the dead body. Chipped on bones, he thought, then looked at the clown, who gripped a sharpener from the knife holder attached to the table in front of him. He started sharpening the cleaver.

Tyler's mouth agape.

He's not going to...

The clown dropped the cleaver down and in one fell swoop, the Frenchman's leg was severed. Amber stifled her scream.

"My god, what the fuck is this?" Tatty, still plastered to the wall, and the clown turned to him with a scowl.

Tyler searched for something to say, some word, anything.

"Ned," he whispered. "Come over here." He turned to Jake. "Go." Jake took Amber's hand, leading her out the door. Cassandra followed, and Tatty, although reluctant, peeled himself off the wall and stepped cautiously around the table, the clown watching him the entire time as he moved behind Tyler. Once Tatty moved past him, Tyler said, "We come in peace," and the clown started sharpening again. Tyler guessed hacking off the leg wasn't as smooth as the clown had wanted. Tyler backed up, watching the clown as he walked backward to the swinging door. That scrape, scrape, scrape sharpening the cleaver followed him. When he turned around, his friends had gone through the door to the restaurant. Jake was last, holding the door open, waiting. Cassandra was staring at the popped open wall door.

"Tyler," said Jake. "C'mon."

He looked at Jake, then Cassandra. Jake was trembling, Cassandra the definition of calm. He looked back at the clown as he dropped that cleaver again; saw how he was carving the flesh off the bone from the Frenchman's severed thigh.

"Tyler." Jake again. "Let's go."

Tyler shook his head. "I'm going to find Pam. Take them away. Call the police."

Jake shook his head. "Amber is right. You don't even know if she's alive."

"Doesn't matter. If she is, I need to find her."

"Are you insane? Did you just see what happened or am I living in a fucking asylum?"

"Jake," said Tyler. "It's okay. Just go. Stop wasting time."

Jake shook his head. "This is crazy."

"Maybe so, but I still have to find her."

"Fucking Tyler." He was shaking his head, disbelieving.

Tyler said, "Go Jake. Go now." He went to Cassandra.

"You too?" said Jake, staring at Cassandra.

She nodded. "Damn right I'm staying. These fuckers messed with the wrong woman."

Jake shrugged, shook his head, and rolled his eyes. "You're both fucking insane."

Tyler looked at Jake. "Good luck," he said after a pause.

"Yeah," said Jake. "Good luck all around."

Tyler nodded. Took one last look at Jake through the door window, watching as he joined Amber and Tatty in the restaurant. Heard the cleaver drop against the table and he flinched, then paused. Paused for a brief second before he joined Cassandra.

19

1:20 AM
The Warehouse
Jigglyspot

He was standing beneath the cage where he'd put his fellow warlock. The cage that now hung from the ceiling just out of Jiggly's reach. The room was bathed in red light but there was no warlock, no teenager waiting.

"Fucking Kera," whispered Jiggly. "What did you do? You should have gone home."

Jiggly thought about that night last week in the Cummings' home when Kera was about to go home, and the little girl came knocking. Jiggly had thought Kera went home when he tucked little Lindsey under the covers. Did she slip out before he set the alarm, or did she wait for the Cummings to leave before she made her move? Didn't matter; what did matter was the fact that the deed was done and now all was compromised. Jiggly gritted his teeth, grinding his jaw when his thoughts went to Apoch and his other clowns. More than likely, they were now aware of Jiggly's position. What will they think of their brethren now? Their fallen from grace warlock. Jiggly had pushed the envelope on so many occasions he wondered if they'll stand behind him now. After a while, everyone wears out their welcome. Foolish, he thought. I've been foolish all my life. Why would they stand with me?

Jiggly was feeling like a man without a home. A man without a planet, if truth be told.

"Did you find what you're looking for?"

Jiggly snapped his head around. Standing behind him, about fifty feet away, were four masters. He recognized Jezebel immediately, even in her newfound human form-the big burly bearded man. She was scowling at him, her skin a dull, red glow. And her three minions were standing behind her; all staring at Jiggly as if they'd caught an unknowing suspect. One of those minions had their arms crossed, standing beside Jezebel, his head bent as if he could see inside Jiggly's mind. It was this minion who spoke next.

"What *are* you looking for?"

"One of our volunteers has escaped. I'm wondering if Helmsley had something to do with it?"

"Ahh," said Jezebel. "Old Helmsley." She moved her head around, scanning through the darkness. "Where is he?" Eyes staring at Jiggly now, and her grin revealed teeth bathed in red.

"Who knows," retorted Jiggly, staring at his cane leaning against the wall beside the masters. "Been looking for him for hours." He walked towards them, a slight wobble in his step. Eyes on his cane-he needed to get to it before the masters noticed its presence-within an arm's reach from where they stood. What Jiggly did not want was for the masters to get their bloody paws on his cane. Mr. West would not be happy should that happen, not in the least. Jiggly looked at Jezebel, sensing her mistrust and skeptical nature. She followed Jiggly's stare. Noticed the cane Jezebel did, Jiggly was sure of it-judging by the sudden tension in Jezebel's body language-but Jiggly retrieved his precious gift before Jezebel had a moment's chance. He cradled the cane in his arms like a baby. "What're you all doing down here? I've never seen masters leave ceremony before." And he cocked his eyebrows, feeling his makeup crinkle above his brow.

Jiggly looked from one master to the next, assessing every one of them. They were all staring at his cane. He didn't like the way they were looking at it. Like heroin to a junkie.

It was Jezebel who answered. "You've been called for Jigglyspot. Goddess has requested your presence."

"Is Emmanuelle not happy with the volunteers? The children must have satisfied her itch. How could they not? Most of them are as pure as a first snow?"

Jiggly watched while the masters exchanged glances. Not one

word was spoken.

"What?" said Jiggly. "Have I missed something?"

Jezebel answered, "You'll find out Jigglyspot." She stepped forward, that big frame hovering over Jiggly. "Come with us."

20

1:30 AM
The Ballroom
Lilly

She entered a hallway after stabbing Kathy Crawford. A long hallway with three doors. One down the hall thirty feet away, the other directly across. Both were single doors, but the door down the hall on her left was a double door made of old wood. She could hear voices coming from the other side of the double doors, so Lilly fastened her hood over her head, hiding her eyes, and entered a room she wasn't expecting; out of place and out of sorts was this room. Looked like it belonged somewhere else, in some medieval mansion with its long spiral staircase and glass ceiling.

She had slipped in during some ceremony. All in attendance wore their cloaks with the hoods over their bowed heads, standing in three circles in front of two thrones. Sitting on those thrones were two people, one woman and one man. The Queen and King of hell, Lilly thought.

It was the queen who was speaking when Lilly entered. "Bring the next offering," she'd ordered, and without a moment's pause, a second set of double doors off to Lilly's right creaked open. Lilly looked at the double doors, noticing how all the bowed heads remained bowed, her eyes scanning across those pointed hoods. Behind the door a puff of what Lilly thought was smoke or vapor— maybe the same vapor that Lilly experienced while in the cage, although she wasn't sure—filled the entrance, highlighted by a faded white light beaming from somewhere behind the vapor.

She saw nothing else.

But she heard it, whimpering like tears held back.

"Come, child," said the queen. Lilly's eyes darted to the queen, who stood from her throne. Lilly could see blood across her face and chin. "There is nothing to fear." Her voice cut through the crowd like a jagged knife.

That whimper again as Lilly searched the spaces between attendants.

"Come." The queen's voice a hollered frustration, Lilly's eyes darted to the queen, her arm stretched with her hand offered palm up.

Lilly searched again.

"Good child, come to me. Come to Emmanuelle."

Lilly saw something move, small and blonde. A child walking, no more than six years old, a teddy bear clutched in the crook of her arm close to her chest. Lilly could see she was crying. Those tears were streaming down her blotched face, sniffling back tears. And those eyes, Lilly saw them as she approached the queen, seemed mesmerized, confirming to Lilly the vapor was indeed the same drug from the cage. She was walking across what looked like a wedding aisle. This child, the bride, waiting to be married.

The whimpering child took the queen's hand. Lilly could see the girl was trembling and how the queen grinned at the child, turning her around to face the hooded crowd.

The Queen addressed her subjects. "Who wishes indoctrination for this child?" The Queen's chin raised high. "Who among you accepts this offering?"

One of the hooded subjects stepped forward, and the Queen regarded this person. "Ira," she said. "Always willing to indulge." Her smile ear to ear. "Who do you choose to indoctrinate?"

Lilly saw this Ira, his back to Lilly, raise his hooded head, scanning the room. His arm stretched, pointing. "My dear friend Hilary, her time has come."

From the opposite side of the circle, Hilary stepped forward. The Queen regarded this woman. "Come," said the Queen, offering her hand, which Hilary took. Then to Ira, "Come," and Ira stepped forward. The Queen took their hands, offering the child's tiny paws. "Go now," said the Queen. "Enjoy yourselves and your indoctrination."

The circles huffed as if their breath choked their throats, the exhales forced across their lips. Ahhh. Ahhh. Ahhh. Ahhh. The King slamming his fists against the arms of his throne in unison with the Ahh's.

Lilly watched as the queen took her seat. Watched as Ira, Hilary, and the unsuspecting child took the stairs like some demonic family walking into darkness.

Ahhh. Ahhh. Ahhh. Ahhh.

The girl whimpering all the way up, but she never rattled or attempted to break free. She kept the teddy bear tucked between her arm and ribs. They arrived at the top of the stairs and stopped. Ira turned to Hilary and Lilly watched as he looked down on the little girl who also looked at him. Lilly could see that he was smiling, a soft smile as if to comfort the girl.

Ahhh. Ahhh. Ahhh. Ahhh.

She studied the circles, then looked at the Queen and King. All were watching the Ira three as both Ira and Hilary stepped forward and Lilly could see how the air in front of them swirled like a vortex to another dimension. Lilly's eyes mesmerized by it. She could feel the power that existed inside the vortex. The girl cried, "NO," trying, attempting to not go into the vortex. Her whimpers and pleas rang through the room as Ira and Hilary pulled the girl forward with her feet dragging across the ground.

Ahhh. Ahhh. Ahhh. Ahhh.

Her teddy bear fell down the stairs, tumbling over to the third step where it flopped and stopped.

Ahhh. Ahhh. Ahhh. Ahhh.

The girl was screaming now, that high-pitched blood-curdling scream only children can make. Screaming *NO NO NO* within cries and hollers and more screams as they stepped into the vortex and disappeared and the girl's screams with them.

Ahhh. Ahhh. Ahhh. Ahhh.

The stomping and Ahh's ceased with a long, huffing breath. Lilly bowed to keep from being seen. She stepped into the circle and all who were there parted and stepped over to make room for Lilly when the queen said, "Bring in the next indoctrination."

Those doors creaked open again. And Lilly waited, hoping to see Christopher come through those doors.

21

1:30 AM
Xibalba
SAC John Mills

The wind had turned into its own animal with a hurricane fury. Mills watched as the tiny woman emerged. She was indeed tiny, short and thin, although she moved with a fierce step. Mills could see as she moved closer two lacerations high on her forehead, as if some appendage had been torn from her skull and was now bleeding. Blood dripped from the wounds, cascading across her skin. Her eyes were large and round and opened wide as if concern drove her actions.

One of those gargoyles approached her; Mills witnessed the gargoyle drop to the burning ground and squeal as if it meant to deter her from Mills. She kept walking, approaching Mills and Helmsley.

"Hell, John," hollered Helmsley. "We're in hell."

Mills turned to the weary Helmsley, screams from the other side of the mountain, blood-curdling screams wrought with *No No No Please* raged from that mountain as the wind erupted even more and Mills dug his feet into the ground to keep from being whisked away. His eyes narrowed by the sheer force of the gale.

"Hell, John." Helmsley, John looked at him.

"We're in hell," Mills said in unison with Helmsley. Helmsley's head drifted to the right, and Mills followed his gaze as the tiny little woman stepped closer. That swag and sass, conviction and determination, inside each step.

"Detective John Mills?" she hollered through the wind.

No answer from John as he scanned this tiny woman, toe to head. Her short dark hair was pushed by the wind and those lacerations dripped with beads of blood that were tossed into the void and carried on the heels of the wind to places unknown.

"We're in hell, John."

She stepped forward. "Yes, Helmsley. We know where we are."

Mills said, hollering over the thundering wind, "He's just scared."

"Detective," she hollered, then shook her head, her eyes never leaving John. "Helmsley is not truly here. Not his body, at least." She craned her head, peering into John's eyes as if she could see his soul. "This is a simple projection of Helmsley's consciousness." She turned to Helmsley and Mills noticed a hint of compassion behind her eyes and the movement of her hand towards Helmsley's head. She kept her hand close to his skull, hovering over it. "It's meant to deter you, detective."

Mills watched as her hand cut through Helmsley's body, not disturbing him except for the glimmer that became Helmsley's body, which wavered with the passing of her hand.

"They want you to think it's real."

Mills' mouth agape, he lifted his gaze to the tiny woman. "Why?" His head shaking, confused.

"Let me guess… they want you to eat his heart, right?"

Mills stepped back. *How could she know that?* His eyes narrowed, moving his head to the right, assessing this tiny little woman.

She continued, "If you believe it is real detective and you eat his heart, their hold on you will be forever." She paused then, and Mills could not remove his eyes from her. "The real Helmsley is… alive and breathing back at home, detective. Back where the shiny room held you captive. Do you remember that place, John? Do you remember where you were?"

John's head seemed to take on a life of its own. He noticed his head was twitching back and forth with a paramount *No* answer.

"You will, detective. There's more going on than you're aware of. So much more John and you, the unknowing and unwilling participant. They've deceived you for so long, detective. It's not your

fault. I want and need you to know. No matter what I show you."
She was shaking her head. "You always have to remember, John, it's
not your fault. But I have to show you. I need you to see, detective.
See what they are doing." Her voice changed to desperation. "You're
the only one, John. This all comes down to you and what you do
now." The wind blew fiercely, as if this tiny little woman was a threat
to its dominion. Threatened by her words. Gargoyles now dropped
around her from the sky to their feet, squealing and yipping, baring
their teeth and staring, staring with blood-red eyes at this woman.

"I need you to come with me, detective. I need you to come with
me now."

"Where?" said John, shaking his head with a shrug.

John followed her gaze as she craned her head around, then
pointed. "Over the mountain, John." The burning lava mountain
stood in the background. "To where all the screams are coming
from." She turned back to Mills, staring at him. "Will you come,
John? Will you come with me? Will you help me, detective? Help me
stop the devil from the stranglehold he has on your species." She
offered her hand, tiny little fingers attached to a tiny little palm.
"Will you come, detective?"

John looked at her eyes, his gaze drifting to the mountain
behind her, the gargoyles—now a horde of gargoyles surrounding
this tiny woman—and then to Helmsley, whose mouth kept opening
and closing, repeating the same statement. Then looked at her,
nodding. "Yes," he said. "Yes, I will come with you."

"Excellent, detective. Please, take my hand."

John reached his arm out, clasping her tiny hand in his.

"Thank you, detective."

John said, "Who are you?"

She wrapped her tiny fingers around his hand and lifted her
eyes, staring with compassion and empathy. "My name is Kera. And
we have met many times before."

22

1:40 AM
The Underground
Cassandra

They heard screams, little whimpers, a holler, a sinister conniving laugh, and whining voices pleading for answers before they heard the shocking bolt of electricity. The door from the kitchen led to another underground tunnel. This one had a dirt floor, with concrete blocks for walls, and scattered across the tunnel were old crates. Fluorescent lights shed a dull glow across the tunnel. Cassandra made a mental note on the crates; they would burn quickly. Her plan was simple: burn them all to hell. If it comes down to it, choosing death over this satanic hellhole was no choice at all. She would make that choice for all involved. Even for Tyler, if she had to. Tyler, whose myth and mystery was growing in Cassandra's thoughts.

His friend Amber, Cassandra was sure, was afraid of him. For what reason, Cassandra did not know, but her fear was apparent. The girl cringed every time Tyler talked, but that was expected, considering current circumstance. Nonetheless, something was off, something Cassandra was unaware of. The teenager had a dead heart in his pocket, a gun in the other, and a filleting knife in his back pocket. And what was with that clown? He seemed to know Tyler, or at least know of him. At the very least, the clown had no concern with regards to Tyler.

And then there was Kera. The gentle creature with those tentacles. If Cassandra hadn't had a horde of spiders birthed from her womb, she wouldn't believe any part of what she'd seen so far. But she did, and putting the incident off as a mere nightmare would not only be naïve, it would be downright stupid. Quite obvious,

Cassandra thought, we are dealing with the unknown here. So, keep your wits about you and strike to kill. There's no way she's allowing anyone to get away with what they've put her through and once she finds that mother fucker Ira, she'll return the favor. Return the favor with blood.

What she knew, and what she felt trickling down her leg, was the constant stream of blood. Cassandra was certain those little fuckers had torn apart her insides. How much of them, and exactly what part she didn't know, but it was there, the pain in her gut, and the blood. So much blood. And if it weren't for Kera, Cassandra was certain she would not have survived the birthing process. She knew Kera's hand guided them in the right direction out, because if not, Cassandra knew they would have found a way out, through any means necessary. She kept thinking of that alien movie, the one where the alien rips out of the bowels of its host. Her stomach cramped every time the thought appeared. Turned her blood hot and caused her heart to race.

Another scream. This time Cassandra knew it was from a child, a girl, although boys at that age can often hit that high-pitched squeal too. "Leave me alone," the voice said. "I don't want to go. *Mommy, please.*"

It was this last part that made Cassandra's skin crawl, as if the mother were the predator to her own daughter. Tyler jogged forward, ahead of Cassandra. She saw how that heart bobbed in his pocket. He went to the door, the double grey doors that were typical doors as exits from any building or staircase. Small windows on both doors; she wondered if they were painted because all Cassandra could see was black. Tyler stood to the right of the window, looking in. She watched as his head craned to the left then right.

"Mommy, please." That voice again, whining, confused, and terrified. "I don't want to."

Tyler shook his head and leaned against the door. He looked at Cassandra, his eyes narrow.

"You're bleeding." Tyler pointed to the floor beneath Cassandra's legs. Spotted blood stained the ground.

She watched as blood dripped off her ankle to the floor, a

constant although intermittent drip. Her stomach hurt something awful, like a cesspool stirring in her intestines. Toxic is how Cassandra described the sensation. As if that toxicity was inside her veins, tainting her blood. She turned to Tyler. "I don't have time to bleed." She gestured to the door. "What's in there?"

"Kids," Tyler huffed. "Locked in cages." He craned his head towards the window. "There's another cage on the right, but I can't see who's in it."

Cassandra nipped at her bottom lip, staring at the window. She could see subtle movement, like blurs smeared across her vision. "What was that sound?" She looked at Tyler.

"What sound?"

"Sounded like lightning."

"Oh," said Tyler. "It's a cattle prod."

"Cattle prod," Cassandra whispered. As if on cue, a shock and jolt of electricity raged inside the room. Screams, wails, and cries followed. She went to the window, looked in from the side. She could see the other cage, but not much more. The windows weren't painted black; they were filthy with scum, dirt, and grime. She could see an adult female tugging on the wrist of a child.

"It's your turn, little girl," said the adult. "Let's go! The Goddess waits for you."

"Mommy, no," the girl pleaded.

Cassandra moved away from the window and put her back against the wall on the side of the door. "You still have that…" She looked at Tyler, holding the gun beside his face. "Gun."

"Yeah," said Tyler, staring through the window.

"Put it away, Tyler."

"What? Are you crazy?"

"No," she said. "But once that gun goes off, we lose the element of surprise. Do you see any of them with guns?" She was staring at Tyler, who held that gun as if it were the last weapon on earth. "Stealth, Tyler. Quiet and reserved, that's how we win this." Tyler was shaking his head. "You know I'm right. That gun is a last resort. Use it sparingly. What else do you have?"

"Well, we both know what happened to the cleaver. That would be good to have right now."

Cassandra pulled the boning knife from her cloak. Looked at Tyler, still holding the gun, and she shrugged. Tyler shook his head.

"All right," he said, holstering the gun, albeit reluctantly. "We'll play it your way." He took a filleting knife from his front pocket, licked his thumb, then rubbed the blade clean. Looked through the window. "That lady is dragging that kid somewhere. Hard to see, but it looks like they're gone." A bolt of electricity, Tyler's head craned to the right. Quickly, he moved away, his back to the door. "There's another in there. Looks like he's got the cattle prod."

Cassandra looked down to her cloak. Noticed blood on the cloak between her legs. Just spots, really, nothing large. She tightened her grip on the boning knife. "I'm going in," she said.

"Okay," said Tyler, staring at Cassandra.

She fit the hood over her head, then slipped the knife within the sleeve, holding the handle to conceal the blade. "They'll think I'm one of them. Once I distract him..." She locked eyes with Tyler. "Stab the fucker."

"Sounds like a plan," Tyler whispered.

Cassandra stepped forward, tensed her arms, then went through the door.

First she saw was the man with the cattle prod who caught her attention when he ripped the prod across the bars on the far cage Tyler couldn't see. She saw the kids in the cage jump with fear, huddled together, whimpering and crying. The man's back was to her, and the sound of electricity must have covered the subtle suctioned closing of the door behind her; he never stirred. Directly ahead, hunkered down in a cage, were a host of older kids. At least older than the little ones locked in the opposite cage. Middle school is what Cassandra thought. Separated by age for... some sadistic reason Cassandra refused to allow into her thoughts. Their eyes staring at Cassandra, waiting. She stepped closer to the cage and counted eight children. Cassandra craned her head, attempting to get a glimpse of their faces, their eyes.

Saw in the back of the cage, huddled in a corner, her knees to her chest, shivering, a woman who looked much older than the others. The woman hadn't noticed Cassandra, not yet anyway.

Another electrical bolt from the cattle prod.

"What're you doing here?"

Cassandra turned slowly to the cattle prod man. His beer belly hung over his jeans. Someone's father, husband, or son who brought his family to the carnival not expecting a spider to crawl into his ear and take over his brain and body. More than likely his child was among the jailed children or had been brought to... somewhere else. Cassandra turned around, stepped back towards the cage, staring at the man.

"We got this," he said rather annoyed, as if Cassandra meant to take away his fun.

Cassandra saw Tyler in the window, looking in. The man's back to the door.

"Daddy, please," said a little girl in the cage where the man had raked the cattle prod across. Cassandra put her age at around seven. She had tears in her eyes and thick bags beneath them.

"Daddy," the man said, mocking the little girl while glaring at her. A wide grin across his lips as he turned to Cassandra. "She'll be calling me daddy alright. Very soon, too."

Cassandra's stomach turned, and the man craned his head, staring, sizing her up.

"You're not..." his voice trailed off. "You're one of them," he said. "The humans they're looking for." He tossed the cattle prod in the air, flipping it, and caught it again. "Perfect," he said, moving his head back and forth. "Absolutely perfect." He pressed the cattle prod and a bolt of electrical current crackled at the top. He stepped closer and Cassandra moved back against the cage and squeezed the knife's handle in her palm.

Cassandra saw the door open.

"Not too perfect after all, you putrid excuse for a human being." Cassandra's eyes narrowed, glowering at him as Tyler raised the knife over his head.

"Daddy!"

Tyler drove the blade down into the man's skull with a quick thrust.

"Dadddddddyyyyy!"

Cattle prod hit the floor, and the man stood with an unknowing stare when Cassandra saw blood drip down his skin and the most god awful sound erupted from his throat. A yipping screech as his mouth opened to an inhuman width and from his throat, torn from the man's bowels, a demon with glowering red eyes emerged from the body, screeching and writhing and wriggling. Long, jagged teeth parted wide and yipping. Its wings stretched erect from the throat as the man's body flopped back with a thud and the demon emerged continuing to screech, yip, and shudder as it reached for Cassandra only to dissipate and burst into small particles like burnt ash floating to the ground. And all Cassandra could hear was the little girl screaming at the top of her lungs for her father to come back.

Tyler stood over the body, dumbfounded. He looked at the body, then at Cassandra. And that little girl's screams were relentless. She wouldn't stop screaming. Three other children sat by their lonesome in the cage with the girl, all with their eyes closed.

"Chill the fuck out, kid," snapped Tyler. He had that look in his eye that Cassandra did not like. It was cold and sinister. The girl bellowed even louder. "I said shut the fuck up. You're gonna get us all caught."

"It's okay, don't look sweetheart. Don't look. Close your eyes. Close your eyes and don't look."

The voice came from the cage behind Cassandra. It was the older woman, now standing, her fingers between the diamond shaped steel. The little girl's cries screeched across the room.

Tyler said, "Ms. Finicky?"

The woman, Ms. Finicky, turned slowly to Tyler. She seemed scared, which was obvious, Cassandra thought, considering. But she seemed even more frightened of Tyler.

"Yes, Tyler. It's me. Let me out so I can console her."

Tyler looked at the girl still screaming, although the high-pitched screeches had settled down. "Good," he said. "I can't stand that screaming."

Cassandra searched the cage. The door was on the other side. She went to it.

"You just murdered her father. Of course, she's screaming."

A lock secured the door with the key in it. Cassandra turned the key and popped the lock, thinking, Whoever else was in here, they're obviously coming back.

"Well," Tyler said. "Every great kid's movie begins with a dying parent."

Cassandra looked at Tyler; he was watching the girl.

"I'm sure she'll be a princess soon."

Cassandra's stomach turned as she opened the door.

"Tyler," huffed Finicky. "That's disgusting."

"Doors open," said Cassandra, and Finicky turned to her, staring. Perhaps, Cassandra thought, the fact that freedom was within reach did not immediately register in that Finicky brain just yet. She just stared. "This is a rescue attempt."

"I know." Finicky still waited, as if sizing up Cassandra. Her voice carried a choked back cry when she said, "I'm just... processing what is happening." She locked eyes with Cassandra. "It's a lot to take in."

"Lady," said Cassandra. "You have no idea." Cassandra surveyed the others in the cage. Three boys, four girls, all around middle school age, huddled together. "You're all free, but I suggest we get this train moving. I'm more than sure they'll be back."

She eyeballed Finicky, who suddenly darted out of the cage, stepping cautiously around the dead body. Tyler now kneeling, surveying the skull and the knife wedged inside it. Cassandra watched as Finicky went to the far cage.

"It's okay," she said to the now subtly whining girl, her eyes filled with tears.

Tyler said, "So if we kill them, we're just killing the body. The host. That demon just leaves." He looked up at the ceiling. "Where did it go?" He clucked his tongue several times.

Cassandra turned to Finicky, who already had the second cage door open. She was holding the young one who'd been screaming. Hugged all of them in that cage, Cassandra could hear her consoling them. "We're getting out of here," she told them. Cassandra turned to the kids in the cage where Finicky had just been.

"Hey," she shouted, earning their attention. "We need to go." She gestured outside the cage. "Let's go."

"Jenny," called Finicky. "Please come help me."

One of the girls, a blonde with blue eyes, scuttled out of the cage to join Finicky. The others in tow behind her huddled together.

"Where's Pam?" asked Tyler as Cassandra stepped out of the cage. He was staring at Finicky. "Ms. Finicky," he called and Finicky, holding the child, looked at him from the corner of her eye. "Where's Pam? Was she in here with you?"

Finicky nodded. "Yes, she was. They took her. Took her and the other children."

"Where?" asked Tyler.

Finicky gestured to the far wall bathed in darkness. Cassandra could see it was another tunnel.

"Where does it lead?" Tyler again, he was staring into the tunnel.

No answer. Tyler asked again.

"I don't know. How could I? That dead man was keeping us here and the other one was grabbing children and taking them into the tunnel."

"They took Christopher too," said that Jenny girl, she was holding two children close to her thigh.

"They took a lot of them," said Finicky. "Do you have a way out?"

Cassandra heard footsteps outside the door she and Tyler had come through. She gripped the handle in her palm when the door opened. It was Jake.

"Oh, thank god," muttered Finicky.

"What're you doing here?" asked Cassandra.

Jake looked at her, then at Tyler and the dead body with the knife still planted in the skull. A pool of blood creeping beneath the skull, spreading wide towards Tyler. "I couldn't leave," he said.

"Where's Amber and Tatty?" asked Tyler.

"They went for help. But I don't know how long that will take. We're in the middle of nowhere. Nothing but warehouses everywhere. It'll take some time before they find a phone."

"So, there is a way out," said Finicky. She looked at Jake. "Can you take us?"

"Well, yeah, that's why I came back. To help find Pam." He looked at Tyler. "Where is she?"

"Not here," said Tyler as he yanked the blade from the skull with a sloshed stutter. Wiped the blood and brains on his pants and stood up.

"But where?"

Tyler turned to him. "I don't know. Not yet, but I will find her." He gestured to Ms. Finicky. "Help Finicky get these kids out."

Cassandra saw how Jake's eyes seemed to swirl in his head. "Finicky," he repeated.

"Yes," said Tyler. "Help her."

"Take them to safety."

"Yes, then call the police. Tell them to bring the swat team."

"Swat team?"

"Yeah," called Tyler. "What's wrong with you?"

Jake's head snapped up, staring, confused. "Nothing," he huffed. "I'm okay." He turned to Finicky. "Fancy seeing you here."

Strange, thought Cassandra. She noticed Jake's right eye seemed strange too, as if some dark spot had formed on his eyeball.

Finicky said, "Not fancy at all, Mr. Ferris." She corralled the children and stepped out of the cage with them clinging to her waist. "Let's go," she said. "It's time to leave."

Cassandra turned to the dark tunnel, attempting to see, but her vision wouldn't reach more than a few feet. She heard mostly silence and occasional talking, incoherent words. She put her hand up, could feel electricity in the darkness beneath the folds, a current consuming the tunnel.

This is it, she thought. Point of no return.

"Take her." Finicky, Cassandra turned to see her transfer the girl to Jake. She turned to the rest of them, all staring with wide, tearful, and dark eyes. "Follow close and be quick." She turned to Jake. "How far is the exit?"

"Not far at all."

"Good. You take the lead. I'll be last in case anyone…" She swallowed whatever breath wanted to choke the words from her throat. "Or anything comes."

Cassandra watched as Jake looked at Tyler as if for approval. Tyler nodded. Cassandra could see the girl in Jake's arms was shivering. Her head on his shoulder, thumb in her mouth.

"Let's go, Mr. Ferris," ordered Finicky.

Jake was blinking rapidly, staring at Finicky. "Okay," he said, then addressed the kids. "Follow me."

He led them through the door, kids in tow, single file, as if they were walking to the school cafeteria for lunch.

Finicky was last. She turned to Tyler standing over the dead body. "I know what you did, Tyler. Pam told me. That's why I don't mind leaving you here. What waits for you…" She regarded the tunnel then shook her head. "I don't want to know, but I'm more than sure it's deserving of your evil deeds." Then, a moment after, "Godspeed, Tyler. And may he have mercy on your soul." And she was gone. Out the door that closed with a thud. Cassandra watched her through the window, disappearing down the hall with a hurried step.

Tyler was staring, his blank gaze burning through the door.

"What was that about?" asked Cassandra.

Tyler regarded her, shook his head, and wedged the knife in the back of his pants, kneeling beside the dead body's feet. He grabbed the ankles.

"Tyler?" Cassandra huffed. "What is she talking about?"

Tyler pulled the ankles, dragging the body towards the back cage. He said, as a matter of fact as anything she had ever heard, "Let's just say I've been a very bad boy." And he continued to drag the body.

Cassandra felt her jaw drop; watching him drag the dead body he'd just planted his knife into. Watched as the blood scraped across the ground, leaving a blood trail in its wake.

And he's got a heart in his pocket, she thought, shaking her head. Obviously, there was more going on than Cassandra realized. Doesn't matter, she thought. When you're facing an evil demonic threat, maybe having a badass mofo on your side is a good thing? She took a deep breath when she felt the electrical current at her back, like prickly heat with bumps and jolts across her skin. She turned to the tunnel, saw how it started swirling, and Cassandra stepped back.

Something's coming, she thought, feeling the current as if it were drawing her into it like gravity at an event horizon. Her jaw dropped when she saw eyes in that current.

"What the…"

She felt her body propel backward with a sudden jolt. Felt herself flying across the cage when the back of her head slammed against it, and she dropped to the ground with a sudden twist of pain that raced from the small of her back to her neck. Cassandra saw the adult female step out of the vortex, snarling. Felt blood drip from her nose. Eyes weary. Saw the woman's sneakers step into the cage.

And then, darkness.

23

1:50 AM
The Warehouse
Jigglyspot

There are a few things Jigglyspot wouldn't put up with. He was
thinking about these few things while the masters escorted him
down the long hall leading to the adult cages where they can enter
the holographic travel room where the Goddess was. The first was
idiocy. He loathed stupidity to his core. Idiocy has no place in the
world and if you were born without enough brain cells than you
were better off dead because one day you might become president
and then that stupidity would run the nation—and the world for that
matter. And there's been too many of them already. The second was
being called for. And, more specifically, being called on for
something he had no control over. People were always placing
blame on others as if every situation required a scapegoat so the
powers that be could point their bony little fingers and say, "look,
see what he did," as if they were children arguing over gummy bears
while sitting at recess. Shit happens and shit goes wrong when
you're dealing with the cosmic forces of darkness.

So, what's a Jigglyspot to do in such situations when you've got
four masters watching your every move? You make the call to those
who can get you out, even when said call is of the telepathic kind.
That was one thing about the clowns: they always took care of their
own, which included Jigglyspot since he was raised as one of their
own, providing Jigglyspot with a lifetime of protection, no matter
how sick and tired of his antics they had become. You don't kill a
clown if you know what's good for you, that's for sure.

Perhaps the new Goddess had forgotten such things. Or perhaps
she no longer cared. But then again, Jiggly thought, maybe she's

unaware that Kera had ties to Jiggly, although Jigglyspot was sure Emmanuelle knew everything Jiggly had been doing, which was more of the sure bet. Either way didn't matter, not now at least, because one thing was certain, his friend's heart was in the Goddess's belly, and that fact burned his brain more than Jiggly expected.

He could see the door growing larger the closer they approached. He saw the eyes in the walls before the lights went out, bathing the hall in darkness and Jiggly ducked down, heard the crunching and quick breaths caught in fear. And when the lights went back on a moment later, Jiggly's clowns had done their job, and done their job well. All four masters were dead; three of their human hosts were sprawled across the floor bleeding from their half eaten skulls and brains. That was one thing Jiggly knew, eat the brain and the masters can't escape, they simply perished along with the host. Good thing his clowns could change colors and blend into the environment unseen, like a chameleon changes color. But Apoch continued to eat the skull of Jezebel, the big bearded burly man. His jaw opened around the head. Those razor-sharp teeth cut through the skull like a hot knife through butter. Jezebel's body wriggled within Apoch's embrace as blood gushed from the open skull down Apoch's chin, soaking his clown outfit.

The two other clowns-Jimmy and Fred, as they enjoyed being called when setting foot on planet earth-were standing over the dead, wiping blood off their chins with the back of their hands.

Apoch belted out a belch as Jezebel dropped to the ground with a thud and Apoch's jaw returned to normal form. He looked at Jiggly, shaking his head.

Jiggly stood up. "Don't give me that shit, Apoch." He pointed his cane at Apoch. "If you were me, you'd have done the same. And take off that ridiculous clown mask. The carnival is over."

Apoch crossed his arms over his chest, stood proud and tall, chin up, eyes peering down at Jiggly.

Jiggly rolled his eyes, then shook his head. "Fine, keep it on if you like it so much, but I'm not starting a planetary war because of what happened to Kera. She knows what she did and what the potential consequences would be if they caught her."

"What do you think will happen when the Goddess learns what we've done?" said Fred regarding the dead bodies, his painted frown a reflection of his internal turmoil. "There'll be retribution. And Apoch likes the clown look. We all do. If we were to reveal our true nature on this planet there'd be mass hysteria."

Jiggly said, "And if Kera's people learn the Goddess has eaten her heart, they will start the damn war." He looked at Apoch. "And that's not good for Mr. West. His wrath will be felt across the universe for impinging on his plans, and who do you think he'll blame?" Jiggly shook his head. "I'm not feeling that wrath. I'll tell you that. Not after all I've done."

Now Apoch was shaking his head, waving his finger in front of Jiggly.

"That's not why we're doing this, Jigs, and you know it." This was Jimmy, a large, massive clown with the plastered face of a happy clown.

"I don't have time for the insipid emotion of love, Jimmy. That notion had gone a long time ago."

"Lies," said Fred. "We all appreciate Kera. She's like a sister."

Jiggly breathed deeply, looking away from his clowns.

"So, what's your plan?" asked Jimmy.

Jiggly squeezed the cane in his hand, digging the bottom into the ground. "Simple enough," he said. "Tell all the clowns to take up arms in the ballroom." The clowns exchanged stares. "I'll get to Emmanuelle. On my cue, unleash holy hell."

Apoch bent forward, his hands tucked beneath his arms.

A moment later, Jiggly said, "I can't do anything about that. It's his choice."

"A replacement?" Jimmy, he turned from Apoch to Jiggly. "That means you can finally come home."

To this Apoch snarled, tensed his arms and shoulders and pointed at Jiggly's head, at his white spot.

"I know Apoch. Fuckin warlocks have been used and abused for centuries. Who is he not to take on that wrath? I can't do anything about it. It's cosmic law, remember. I've had to suffer the same and you know it."

Apoch looked away. Jiggly could see how tight his jaw was.

It was Fred who replied. "You always do things for the wrong reasons, Jiggly." He touched Jiggly's shoulder. "That's why they go wrong. Maybe this time you should do the right thing for the right reason and not because of West and what he wants."

"I'm a murdering son of a bitch, Fred. That's who I am."

"No, you're a warlock. Start being proud of it and stop using the past as an excuse to continue your tirade against the universe to get your rocks off, which is all it's about, really. In the end, at least. You punish other people because you hate who you are. Start taking some personal responsibility. We've been waiting for so long Jiggly, soon even we won't be able to stop the crown from deviating from your antics, whether or not you were raised by us. Plus, it's insulting to our heritage. We are a peaceful species who only fight to save our own."

Jiggly said nothing. He had no retort, knowing they were right. A moment later Jimmy said, "What about them?" pointing to the dead bodies.

Jiggly shook his head. "Leave them be. They can't tell the Goddess anything." Jiggly understood the masters were now trapped in the bodies lying on the ground. Eating the brain definitely comes in handy in such situations. There's no means of escape.

"What will you tell the Goddess?"

"Simple," said Jiggly. "They've gone to take up arms against West, as the Goddess desires. That much has been made apparent with recent events. She's challenging his earthly dominion. Trying to take over and earn a seat at the right hand of Baphomet."

"Is West here?" Fred, his eyes wide.

Jiggly was tapping the dead Jezebel with the bottom of his cane.

"Ya know, Fred," said Jiggly as he looked at Fred, raising his chin, then tossed the cane in the air and caught it quickly. "You never can tell."

24

2:00 AM
The Ballroom
Lilly

Where are they going? Lilly thought, watching the next set of three become devoured by the vortex on top of the stairs.

There was no rhyme or reason to the selection process. At least none that Lilly could decipher. They brought a child before them; the Goddess offered the child, then one of them stepped forward to claim the child while another volunteered–the Goddess's words, not Lilly's–to escort them into the vortex. And then the vortex took them. Devoured them like tender little morsels. She had yet to see someone return from the vortex, except for Ira and Hilary-no child with them though-and she wondered if she'd made a mistake. If she should try to leave and search for Christopher through other means?

The door opened to usher in a new child. The bright light emanated from inside the doors and Lilly closed her eyes, scrunched from the bright white light, forcing them open to see the child in the door. And there, standing with his shoulders erect, was Christopher. He was looking, staring, observing the surrounding light, and Lilly could feel her heart thump inside her chest. The moment she'd been waiting for had arrived. She had to talk to him, had to get him alone to talk about a plan for escape. Lilly held her breath, her bottom lip wedged between her teeth. She bent her head, conforming to the surrounding others. Felt her blood curl in her veins and grow heavy. She has to be the first one, she thought. Has to make sure she steps forward when the Goddess calls for volunteers. Her thoughts swimming with endless possibilities. Each child so far had received two volunteers, and all had gone through the vortex on top of the stairs.

She was grateful she had the switchblade. But could she kill someone in front of Christopher? If she has to, she will. But what the plan was after Lilly had no idea. And then the most dire question erupted in her mind: Where would the vortex take them?

Lilly swallowed that bulge that grew in her throat, watching through the corner of her eye as Christopher made his way into the circle. She could see his feet and his legs in her line of sight.

"And what is your name, child?" asked the Goddess.

No answer. Lilly raised her head, just a bit, enough to see. Enough to know that Christopher's eyes were wide and staring. He looked mesmerized, his eyes like eight balls, black and wide and round. And he looked clean and pristine, not like someone who's been held captive. He looked fresh, and all dolled up. Lilly wondered if they had given him the same drugged vapor she'd experienced herself.

"Child," hollered the Goddess. Her raised voice snapped Lilly's head towards her. She tightened her grip on the switchblade.

Looked at Christopher, his head raised, staring, staring at the Goddess.

"What is this?" he asked, his voice loose and soft.

The Goddess craned her head, her eyes devouring Christopher. "Indoctrination, my dear." She kept her eyes on him, and Christopher's head lolled from side to side, observing the ballroom. Goddess screamed, "Tell us your name!" And Christopher jumped the same as Lilly.

"Christopher," he said.

"Christopher," the Goddess repeated. "How nice to make your acquaintance." She eased back on her throne and Lilly could see how that other one beside her, the Dark Lord, snarled at her son. Goddess said, "Who among you will indoctrinate good Christopher?"

Lilly put her foot forward but brought it back quickly when another master stepped towards the center. "I volunteer," said this other master with a thick manly voice. Lilly sized him up quickly. He was skinny, young too, maybe late twenties.

"My Kevin," said the Goddess. "So good of you to join us."

Lilly noticed how Kevin was staring at Christopher as if he were a hot lunch. She did not like that look. Not one bit. Kevin's hands on Christopher's shoulders.

"And a volunteer from the masters?" called the Goddess.

Lilly stepped forward this time, closer to Christopher.

"I do," she said, putting her hands on Christopher's shoulders.

Christopher, watching her, said, "Mom?" in a dreary, confused voice.

Lilly saw how the Goddess grinned. "I love it when it's the parent who indoctrinates." She turned to the Dark Lord. "It amps up the fear and we drink it down like wine."

The Dark Lord laughed. "Indeed," he said, his eyes staring at Christopher.

"Go," said the Goddess. "Enjoy your indoctrination, Kevin. You've earned it."

"Thank you, Goddess," said Kevin with a bow. "I will not disappoint you."

Lilly's body tensed. Say something, she thought. "Come, child," she said, taking Christopher's hand when those Ahhs began.

"Yes, Chris..." said Kevin. "Let's go."

"My name's Christopher."

"Whatever," replied Kevin, holding Christopher's free hand.

Together, the three of them took the stairs. All the while, Lilly's eyes never left the vortex, a swirling ball of silvery circles spiraling like a downward spiral. She could see nothing else. No end in sight to tell her where the vortex led. Her heart was pounding in her chest. She felt her face turn red and flushed as she gripped Christopher's hand tight.

"Where are we going?" asked Christopher as they took the last step, the vortex spinning as if welcoming them to it. Lilly didn't answer. Didn't answer because she didn't know. "Mom?"

Lilly looked at her son with his pie-eyed stare and her heart sank into her gut. It was Kevin who answered.

"Don't worry, kid. Let's just put it this way…" He pointed to the vortex. "That's the tornado, and beyond the tornado is fucking Oz." He looked at Christopher, and Lilly wanted to cut that demonic stare off his face. The way he was looking at her son turned her gut. "And I'm the fucking wizard, and your mom, she's Dorothy. And the wizard and Dorothy are going to have a jolly good time with our little pet, Toto." He started laughing. Belting out high-pitched cackles with apt excitement.

The vortex growled, and Lilly shuddered. Sounded like an elevator about to open.

Kevin looked at her. "Do we go in now?" His eyes narrow, waiting, anticipating, as he licked his lips.

Lilly turned to the vortex and felt heat on her skin as a scorching wind blew her hood off.

"Well?" hollered Kevin.

Lilly turned to Kevin, then to Christopher with his enormous eyes staring, then to the vortex that seemed to call to her. She gripped Christopher's hand as tight as she could and stepped forward.

And all three stepped into the vortex.

25

2:10 AM
Xibalba
SAC John Mills

It seemed like they were walking for an eternity. Howling heated wind against his skin, his eyes scrunched, following Kera up the mountain. Torturous screams bellowing from the other side of the mountain. The air seemed to glow with a dark red film that wafted the metallic taste of blood across John's lips.

Kera was relentless in her endeavor, as if the fate of the world depended on them traversing the mountain. She walked with a furious step, those little legs widening the distance between herself and Mills. He kept hearing Helmsley with his loud and vicious declaration, "We're in hell, John." And Mills was beginning to believe this was true. But how? Did he die when that spaceship took him? Or when those aliens tore into his eyeball? Or, perhaps, it was that little worm that entered his ear. Maybe it ate his brain and brought him to hell.

"John!" Kera called, her voice loud enough to crack John's thoughts. She was standing at the top of the mountain, her tiny frame dwarfed by the expanse of the dark blood red sky above as the wind howled into a hurricane fury. "We are here." She offered her hand. "Come with me, John. You need to see this. You need to see what they're doing."

John studied her hand, so tiny, like a child. Raised his eyes to meet Kera's.

"It's okay, John. It's okay to be afraid. I am too, detective, but we have to stop it. We have to stop it all."

He could see how she steadied her hand against the wind. A loud bang erupted from the other side of the mountain like a butcher barrels a cleaver through bone, its thin blade met by the butcher block. But it wasn't the loud bang that cringed John's spine; it was the blood-curdling scream that immediately followed. A child's scream, John was sure. He rushed to it, urgency in his bones, heart fluttering, eyes wide. He met Kera at the top of the mountain.

Saw the expanse over the mountain that raged on forever. Seemed like there were a million planets in the sky. Ahead of him, he could see mountainous terrain with lakes of fire and flocks of gargoyles flying by the thousands across the skies. No millions. Looks like they're getting ready for an invasion, thought Mills. The air thickened with the sound of crackling fire, screams, and the stank of death and sulfur.

"My God!" John huffed. "It goes on forever. It's like the entire universe exists here." He looked over the expanse of stars millions of miles away, but right on top of them.

"Not quite, detective. But it keeps growing, swallowing system after system. Galaxy after galaxy. Bringing darkness and fear to every corner of the universe, turning light into darkness. It's how it eats, how it survives. It wants to live, the dark energy wants to live, to dominate and control until its evil tirade rules all we see... all we know... bathed in darkness and fear."

Everywhere his eyes roamed, he could see torture. But not just humans, he could see grey aliens strung up to black horses, their limbs torn from their bodies. Humans disemboweled, their intestines drawn from their stomachs by a spinning picket. Gargoyles laughing, providing the torture. Kera, by his side, dropped to her knees with a crunch. Whatever this mountain was made of, it wasn't normal. Wasn't rock or dirt, nor minerals or sediment. John realized then that the mountain was made from the bones and flesh of their victims. Forever entombed in this hellish place. He looked over Kera's pale skin, her quivering lip and wide tearful eyes staring, fixed on the very bottom of the mountain.

John followed Kera's stare. Beneath them were humans and demons with their wide red eyes, burnt skin, and horns, who worked in unison, torturing.... children. Children that John first thought were dolls, all prettied up, their skin seemed to be made from cloth.

But there was no cloth; John could see how their blood and organs were devoured by human and demon alike. He watched as one demon stole intestines from one of those doll looking children, laughed and ate it up as the child lay motionless, her eyes wide, as if she dissociated from the pain and carnage.

John shook his head. "Is it real?" he hollered through the howling wind. He looked down at Kera. "How can it be real?"

Kera looked at him, and John could see the pain in her eyes. "It is John. It is as real as you and I." She sifted her hand into the mountain, gripped remains in her hand and squeezed them out like sand between her fingers. "As real as the battered bones of a millennium of death and torture." A single tear fell across Kera's cheek.

John whispered, "They look like dolls."

"Made to look that way, John," said Kera, and John snapped his head to her. "It's easier for the human host to torture them when they look like a doll. Makes it less real."

"How did they get here?"

Kera pointed to the far right, where a spinning vortex stood as if plastered to a wall. Every few seconds he saw a glimmer race out of the vortex to reveal a ballroom that faded along with the glimmer. "From there, John. It leads back to earth. To where we were before. We have to go back, John. The Dark Lord has taken over your body, and we must confront him. We must kill him, John, him and the Goddess. They can't keep doing this. Look at what it's done to your world." She was shaking her head. "It's just not fair. It's not fair at all."

More screams, more torture, and John could see the sodomy. He turned away and looked at Kera. "If he has my body, how do I defeat him?"

"Simple John, you fight him, he's given you his power, you're just not aware of it because you haven't used it. You're too afraid. Don't be afraid, John. Let go of fear."

He turned back to the torture, to the humans and demons tearing the children apart. Their cries, hollers, pain, and fear rose to John's ears. "What about them?"

He heard Kera rise to her feet, turned to her, and that stare that burned through his soul. "You can stop it, John. When we go down there, you can stop it all, burn them down, and rescue the children. You can save them all."

John stared into the eyes of one of those demons and his heart trembled, watching the demon tear into the flesh and bone of a child's arm. "How can I defeat that?" He pointed to the demon and looked at Kera.

"Simple John. In here, in Xibalba, at this present moment, you SAC John Mills, you *are* the Dark Lord. You can cut through them like parchment paper. Send them into the void so they can do no more harm."

John shook his head. "I'm no Dark Lord. I'm no lord at all. I'm just a scared and frightened man. All my life I've been a coward. I'm no lord Kera, dark or light, I'm no lord."

Kera laughed. "Look at your hands, detective. You are indeed the Dark Lord."

John craned his head, perplexed, then raised his hands over his eyes. Saw how his arms were dark-skinned, how his fingers were like talons, thick and massive. Looked down at his body, saw how his skin was dark, thick with muscle and how his feet were no longer feet but looked like the hoofs from a raging bull. Raised his head and ran his tongue across his teeth, noticing sharp fangs had replaced his pearly whites.

"There's just one thing, detective. A warning you must heed."

John snarled, staring at Kera.

She was shaking her head. "Whatever you do, detective, do not eat anyone's heart. If you do, you'll become consumed by it. By the blood and power. And all we do here will slip into the void and be no more. You're using dark energy, detective. You must tread cautiously."

John breathed deeply, his breath burning across his lips. "Okay," he said,

"Where do we begin?"

26

2:15 AM
The Underground
Tyler

He heard Cassandra crash into the cage before he saw the demon woman. A tall, thick in the hips middle-aged woman with short curly hair. Eyes as red as blood. She'd gone over and checked her cohort; the one Tyler had murdered. Crouched down beside the body, she clucked her tongue. "Not good," she said, looking over the empty cages. She turned to Cassandra, unconscious on the floor. "Where are the children?" she asked as if Cassandra could answer. Tyler hid in the back of the room, waiting for the right moment to leap out. He touched his gun. Not yet, he told himself. Not until he had Pam. He has to get her out of here. He owed her that much. Considering all they've been through, he refused to allow her to go down a path into slavery. He had to get her out, no matter what his consequences were.

"Come, little ferret," said the demon woman. "I've got questions for you."

Tyler watched as she picked up the cattle prod, watched as her thumb turned down the strength of the electrical current, her thumb rolling across the intensity wheel. Walking across the cage, she raked the prod across the steel. Blue sparks and electrical thumps raged across the room.

"Little ferret, so mischievous and coy," goaded the demon woman as she raked the cattle prod across the cage once more, entering the cage where Cassandra was. "I'm gonna pump you up with so much electricity your eyeballs are going to pop." She laughed and stepped forward.

Tyler watched as Cassandra's eyes opened, her eyeballs rolling.

She seemed so weak, pale, and sick.

"I'll ask you once again, just one more time, and then I'll find them myself." The demon woman looked around the room. "I mean, you can't be hiding them in here. I'd smell them, so sweet and delicate that soft flesh is." Her eyes closed as she raised her chin, breathing in the air with a graceful smile. Cassandra's body shuddered as she attempted to sit up, and when she moved, Tyler could see blood on the floor. "You're no master, my dear. I can smell your insides. So familiar to me. I enjoyed nipping on your intestines. Feeding on your womb." She zapped the cage with an electric jolt from the cattle prod as Cassandra rolled over, grunting through a restricted breath. The demon woman grabbed a handful of Cassandra's hair and lifted her off the ground as Cassandra screeched and winced. A scream erupted from her throat. The demon woman raked that prod once again, holding Cassandra in her left hand, the prod in the right as Cassandra wailed, her body flailing, feet kicking.

"Where are the children?"

Cassandra wiggled in the demon's hand. "Fuck you," she hollered. "You get nothing from me."

The demon woman rolled her eyes. "Wrong answer," she said, and shocked Cassandra with the cattle prod. Her screams erupted into a frenzy, her skin burning, her body jolting. Blue electrical sparks raged from the prod as the demon woman's snarl scrunched her eyes. She kept the cattle prod on Cassandra's chest.

She's killing her, thought Tyler. He pulled the gun from the holster and hurried into the room. "Leave her the fuck alone, you sick, twisted bitch."

The demon's eyes widened as she brought Cassandra in front of her like a shield, then tossed her across the cage. Cassandra's head snapped against the steel. She landed with a thud and Tyler felt the gun pull from his hand, as if some invisible force had taken it from him. Felt the push in his gut when he was tossed backward. The demon woman's hands in front of her as if this invisible force came from those hands, and Tyler crashed against the wall, falling forward on his knees. His hands hit the floor, stopping himself before crashing face first into the cement. Pain jolted from his hands to his shoulders. His limbs numb and burning. Heard the electrical current again and when he raised his eyes, the demon woman was zapping Cassandra, her body flailing on the ground. And those eyes, the demon red eyes, glowered at Tyler as the scent of burning skin raged in the room. He clenched his fists, gritting his teeth when the prod ceased. The demon woman craned her head, staring, studying Tyler.

"My, my," she said. "It's you, isn't it?"

Tyler's knees stung something awful, his bones crackled and popped as he raised himself to his feet, all the while never moving his eyes from the demon.

"Funny," she said. "I thought you'd be taller."

Tyler stepped forward, ignoring the demon, his anger pulsing in his veins, feeling energy swirl around him, thickening in front of him. He could feel this energy in his navel, reach to his limbs, his fingertips, and he snarled when he thrust this energy from his hands towards the demon woman whose eyes widened just before the energy collided across her bones and tossed her backwards. Cattle prod dropped from her hand as her body crashed against the cement sliding across the cage. Tyler used the energy force and lifted her up. His anger consumed every bone in his body, every breath in his lungs, and every thought in his head. He wanted to tear the bitch apart, choking her throat, squeezing the windpipe as the demon choked and flailed. He wanted to rip her throat out, wanted to see blood in the air. And-as if this energy, the same energy that had tossed the Reilly ghost from his bathroom, obeyed his thoughts-he watched as her windpipe tore from her neck. Blood speckles raged across the cage. Tyler forced her body back to the cage, tearing her skin open as the demon woman raged with screams and hollers that were not human, yipping and squealing, the noise like an echo through the open throat, whistling and hissing, as blood and bile rushed from the open wounds. He tore her body from the inside out, her innards spilling to the floor as her skin melted off her bones in a raging, fiery plume. Smoke billowed off the body as the demon screamed her last, and her bones dropped to the floor.

And Tyler stood, confounded by what he'd done. Where had this power come from? Cassandra's body jolted, and Tyler could see she was foaming at the mouth. He rushed to her, stepped over the intestines and blood and bones now smoldering on the floor. Kneeled beside Cassandra, and took her in his arms.

"Come on, Cassandra," he pleaded. "Don't go, girl, stay with me." He smoothed his hand over her face, brushing the hair from her eyes. Saw how much blood was between her legs, her robe stained a dark brown, wet and slick with blood. He put his hand over her heart. Still beating, he thought. But the beat was slow and weak. "Come on, Cassandra," he hollered. Her eyes closed, her body soft in his arms. He felt that same energy now, but he could control it. Felt it in his hands like a toy, a plaything he could move at his whim. Felt her heart and used the energy to pump the blood, get the heart beating in regular rhythm. "Come on, Cassandra, wake up, girl."

Her body jerked in his arms, and she gasped for breath.

"There ya go." Another deep, gaping breath. "Perfect. Keep it coming. Breathe deeply."

She started coughing, gagging, her body jumping, jolting, shuddering, her head saturated with sweat. And then her eyes were open, wide and dry, staring.

"Welcome back," he whispered.

Cassandra shook her head, eyes closed as she breathed deeply. "Get me up."

"Okay," said Tyler with a laugh behind his voice. He helped her to her feet when the vortex began spinning with a whir. It called to him. As if he was meant to go through it. As if everything led up to this point. The vortex seemed magical, with silvery circles spiraling.

"What is it?" Cassandra breathed.

Tyler went to it, standing close, watching. All he could see were silvery, spiraling circles.

"I don't know. But I have to go through it." He turned to Cassandra. She was staring at the vortex, her fingers holding the cage to steady her feet. She looked like death, eyes sunken and dark, skin deathly pale, blood dripping from between her legs.

"Cassandra," he called, and her eyes moved in his direction. "Are you coming?"

She looked at the vortex and then at Tyler. She swallowed her breath, and her jaw quivered. "It calls to you," she said, then looked over the room. "I believe, Tyler, this is when we go our separate ways."

Tyler nodded, then turned to the vortex. Put his hand up and felt the electrical current as it reached towards him with tiny sparks across his skin.

Tyler said over his shoulder, "Do what you have to, Cassandra. I hope you make it." He turned to her. "See you on the other side."

He turned to the vortex.

"Wait," called Cassandra. Tyler turned again. "I've got to know why, Tyler. Why does that vortex call you?"

Tyler paused, thinking. "I'm not sure." He looked over his shoulder at the vortex. "But I think it's..." Another pause. He was tired of fooling himself. He knew why; it was just difficult to admit. The thoughts, the voice in his head he'd been listening to since that day in middle school when the thought to murder Reilly first manifested, guiding his actions and devious nature. They've always been with him, manipulating and feeding on his tragedies. Leading him to... He squeezed the heart in his pocket. Leading him to murder. He'd thought the voice was his, but now he knew, he understood this was not true. Had he been a demonic pawn?

"Think it's what?"

Tyler stepped closer and reached his hand into the vortex; a tingling sensation tore up his arm.

"Think it's what, Tyler?"

He raised his free hand and stepped closer. "Because... *I* am the one who killed James Reilly."

And Tyler stepped into the vortex.

Part VI
Take a Bow

1

2:20 AM
The Ballroom
Sharon the Goddess

Everything in the universe in its most basic form is energy, right down to the smallest sub-atomic particle, buzzing and vibrating electrical waves across the universe in frequencies designed by nature and permeated by thought, choice, and belief. Hence control of the subject and control over the dominant frequency consuming the universe. All in the universe is a shifting of these energies and frequency vibrations. A recycling pattern of energy. For those few evolved souls in the universe, knowledge of this cosmic makeup can lead to ultimate power. Problem is when your opponent beats you to the punch, hence Emmanuelle's dilemma. It was West who had all the control. West, who had penetrated the cosmic prison that separated Xibalba from the rest of the universe through manipulation. He was the master of all masters, seated at the right hand of Baphomet. A status once reserved for Emmanuelle. West had a hold on this planet the likes that none had ever accomplished, and he did so by knowing and understanding their minds, desires, and hearts. Humans, at their core, were silly innocents, like children in a candy store the size of the universe, completely in awe and simultaneously afraid and overwhelmed by the vastness of that store. It is this innocence of heart that fuels the energy Xibalba requires to live, breathe, evolve, and expand its reach across the universe, the destruction of innocence, its perversion and desecration through fear. Xibalba ate it up like candy and the one who opened the floodgates between this world and Xibalba sat at the right hand of Baphomet, and there were no points for second best.

West had thwarted Emmanuelle, and this night represented her revenge. Years of planning and manipulation had brought her to this point. It wasn't pretty or perfect, although the result was all that mattered; Emmanuelle will have her hold on this world and will remove West from the right hand of Baphomet.

The plan had been set. A plan that has now come to fruition. The game was chess, not checkers, and she'd played her pawn perfectly across the board. Now, as she sat on her throne, Dark Lord beside her, masters in waiting with heads bowed and cloaks donned, her chosen white knight's arrival was forthcoming, and with him Emmanuelle will slip her queen into position. Her breath caught in her throat when she heard the vortex begin its spiral, locked in on the energetic frequency of the vortex and, more importantly, the frequency captured on the other side of the vortex. The frequency was indeed the white knight; Emmanuelle could feel his vibration in her bones.

And Sharon the Goddess grinned, watching the silvery glistening glasslike spiral swirl as the Xibalba wind raised heat inside the ballroom, arriving on cue as if it knew, knew what Sharon the Goddess, Emmanuelle knew. Sharon's eyes widened with glee and delight, the vortex spiraling inward, capturing the white knight. Only one more hurdle for him to pass, the in-between, and the realization that the past could come to a screeching halt with the power she can provide.

Sharon's voice a whispered snarl, "Check mate West."

"Check... mate."

2

2:21 AM
In the Airshaft
Jigglyspot

Jigglyspot watched from the airshaft, his little portal for voyeurism. Being called for by the Goddess brought a beneath the surface perspective into focus, and things were now making sense to Jiggly.

They had followed him. For how long he wasn't sure, and he didn't have time to reach that far back into his memory to find the divergence, the glitch, and change in time. If he didn't know any better, he would have thought it was Helmsley. His sudden disappearance would be proof of the accusation, but Jiggly knew better, or at least he thought he did, because where was Helmsley after all? Plus, the man's brain was fried last night, there's no way he could pull off a coup without making dire mistakes. Although that could be why he was hiding, having put all the arrangements together prior to his makeshift brain surgery performed by doctor Jigs. Jiggly laughed just thinking about it, laughed because there was nothing else to do.

One thing he knew, above all, was that West will not be happy with Emmanuelle's rebellion nor her undermining underhanded ploy to gain power in the eyes of Baphomet. Power was all about the hold one had over the world, but whether that was an in your face type of power or a behind-the-scenes power was a choice. West preferred the latter, Emmanuelle the former. Jiggly sided with West, it's always better to operate in the shadows. If history has taught Jiggly anything, there is one trait about human beings that always worked in the favor of remaining behind the scenes: they're easily manipulated, although, when confronted, are a force to be reckoned with. Hence the flaw in Emmanuelle's approach.

Jiggly searched the ballroom, finding the hidden gems in the room, his clowns cloaked by walls and doors and stairs. So many of his brothers were in attendance, their loyalty brought a smile to Jiggly's face. He counted one of his clowns to every three masters. A battle was about to erupt that will be worthy of inclusion in the demon archives; if they win that is. History is always written by the victor. The Dark Lord remained in waiting, the Goddess the same. He could see how she waited for her time to come as the vortex began its spiral.

No way, Emmanuelle, thought Jiggly. No way you get away with this, take over and condemn me to absence.

Jiggly's plan was simple; send that bitch back to Xibalba for another century.

Vortex spinning, Jiggly rose to his feet, felt that conniving grin creep across his lips and crinkle his nose.

"Time to go," he whispered. Turned around and started waddling down the airshaft. Tapped his front right pocket where Mr. Scalpel waited while gripping his cane in his other hand. One thing is certain, Jiggly thought,

There will be blood!

3

2:22 AM
The Xibalba Ballroom
Lilly

She never expected to end up in hell. How is that even possible? Lilly never believed in heaven or hell, yet here she was, certain she'd arrived in hell and damnation. Fire, brimstone, screams filled with torture, and darkness greeted Lilly the moment she stepped outside the vortex. As far as the eye could see, the expanse of darkness seemed to drift on forever. And then her eyes adjusted as blips of fiery red and blue bulbs of light scattered across an opaque wall forming boundaries around her. Boundaries in the form of a translucent room, and as Lilly looked around, she recognized that the room's shape reflected a mirror image of the ballroom she'd just come from. Like stepping into an alternate dimension that existed on top of or beneath the surface of earthly reality. Although this ballroom was a shell of the former. It was dark, like those moments before sunset when darkness crept across the walls to usher in the totality of night. Looked decrepit, as if the ballroom had been abandoned a millennium ago. Dust covered the floors, and the walls had cracks like spider webs that reached everywhere the eyes could see.

They came out of the vortex at the same location, at the top of the stairs, and the first noise was a scream, a child's high-pitched squeal that Lilly knew carried fear and pain no child should ever endure. She caught Christopher by the shoulder just before he collapsed. She pulled him closer, kept her hands on his shoulders while concealing the knife in her right palm. Quite obvious to Lilly, they drugged her son, his eyes beaming wide and staring. Another high-pitched squeal followed by a loud bang, laughter, and more cries, wails, and pleas. Lilly was certain it was a girl's voice, a constant terror filled cry rolling through the room so loud if it had been a solid substance, it would have consumed the whole of the ballroom and beyond. That voice, that plea, the eternal cry, curled Lilly's blood, festering in her heart like a knife twisting in her chest.

"Ahh, such a sweet sound, isn't it?" Kevin stepped in front of Lilly and Christopher towards the top step. His hands clenched into fists and raised high over his head. "Can you feel it?" he growled, looking around, his eyes wide. "The energy in this place… just like they said. It's *magnificent*." Lilly could see the grin curling across his lips as Kevin closed his eyes and a shudder ran through him. His teeth grinding, his lips parted. "We can do anything here." Lilly watched as his teeth turned jagged and his eyes turned black.

He stepped to Christopher and Lilly jerked her son closer to her, although Kevin didn't seem to notice. Didn't notice Lilly staring at him, either. He was devouring Christopher with his eyes, as he ran the back of his hand across Christopher's cheek.

"Little pet," said Kevin. "Always the little pet. You're my ticket to the big time." He squeezed Christopher's jaw. "Not bad, is it? A simple sacrifice for the greater evil." He looked over the room. "And your soul here, watching from oblivion." He turned to Christopher. "Perhaps if you're good, I'll bring you with me. Keep you in my employ, so you're always close. We're going to share ourselves… *Christopher*." And he smiled, a big grinning smile.

Lilly's heart jumped when the little girl's scream reached another fever pitch. Her mind swimming with thoughts she refused to entertain. Sweat beaded off her brow and raced down her skin. She felt stuck, confused, as if all her swimming thoughts competed for center stage in her mind. She felt numb, as if her brain was overwhelmed and decided it was best to shut down. Perhaps it was this place, she thought, looking around the room. She looked at Kevin and the stare in his eyes narrowed Lilly's. He bent his head, staring into the dark recesses of her mind as if her pupils were a portal to her thoughts.

He stepped to the side and gestured to the hall. "Shall we?"

Lilly looked into the hall. Saw doors every few feet on both sides, as far as her eyes could see. She gripped Christopher close, squeezing the knife in her palm, and hobbled with him, clutching at her cloak, as the little girl's cries continued, growing stronger and louder as they walked further down the hall.

"Mom, I don't want to," said Christopher, and Lilly recognized he hadn't said a word until then. So unlike her son, typically he was never one to be quiet.

It was Kevin who answered. "Oh, keep quiet Chris. We'll have plenty of time for conversation later. Pillow talk, Christopher. Do you know what that is?" And he laughed out loud, started singing beneath his breath, "*It's gonna be a hot time in hell tonight.*"

Lilly hadn't said a word either. Perhaps she was in shock, or perhaps there was nothing to say about the current situation. She was beginning to believe that it was she and Christopher who died and not Tad. And this was their hell to endure. They walked past door after door as if they were on an escalator.

Remember the knife, Lilly thought. She felt weak, as if her veins were tapped, draining all her strength into a flood of weariness. Felt like floating now, her eyes growing lazy with heat and sweat.

"*Hell toniiiiiiight!*" Kevin's voice a sultry baritone. He sounded like a parlor singer from the fifties.

A door opened on their right, fifty feet away.

"There we go," said Kevin.

Lilly felt drawn to the door as if some mystery existed on the other side she was intrigued to discover.

"I wonder what they've conjured for us to see? What depths of despair await Christopher? I wonder what you fear?" The door seemed to come at them now as if they had stopped and the door moved on its own volition. "Oh Chris, I know this is fear manifested in real time. I'm so excited, Christopher. You and I attached at the hip. Let me be the one, Chris. Let me be the one to escort you to a new dystopia, one made just for you..." Kevin was standing at the open door. "Your own private hell."

They were standing in front of the door, but all Lilly could see was light. Mesmerizing, blinding light. Christopher gripped Lilly's waist in his arms. A subtle growl behind the light and the little girl's shuddering screams twisted Lilly's gut. She looked at Kevin, his skin grown burnt and dark, his teeth jagged and long. His eyes were twisted black balls, and the horns were smooth like raven claws.

Kevin hollered, "Time To Gooooo!" with a wide grin plastered across his lips.

Christopher screamed, "Mooooomm, no!" when Kevin thrust him from Lilly's arms into the room. He glowered at Lilly. "You're next."

She heard Christopher scream, and she stepped inside. At first, the light blinded her. But the light quickly dissipated, and she found herself in Tad's office. Tad sat at his desk, a revolver in his hand. He looked at Lilly, said, "So sorry," and blew his brains out. His head snapped back then flopped forward, and the canoe that had become his skull when that bullet tore through it immediately turned to normal. He looked at Lilly. "So sorry," he said and shot himself again.

"I had my suspicions when you didn't know what to do with the vortex." Kevin's voice, directly behind her, seemed a million miles away as she watched her husband's bloodied skull drip skull fragments across his face.

She looked around the room; saw Christopher in the corner facing the wall.

"I should have known. This is your hell, isn't it?"

Lilly's jaw hung loosely as she turned to Kevin, saw how his head was craned to the right as if he were staring through her when his fist connected with her mouth, and she dropped with a thud to the floor. Her knife tossed from her hand.

"So sorry." Another gunshot and she heard Christopher scream.

Kevin crouched beside her, staring. "Thank you, dear sweet Goddess. My reward is that I get two." And he smiled. Lilly felt the back of her head throb. Pain raced down her neck. "Come, Christopher, I want you to see this." She felt paralyzed, tried moving her hand and fingers with no such luck as panic struck her heart, feeling the warm drip of her own blood across her mouth. "You and your father are now voyeurs to pain and fear. I want you both to

watch. Watch as I sodomize your mother. And then Christopher…”
Kevin laughed then, laughed out loud, and stared into Lilly's eyes.
“Then I'll watch you do the same.”

4

2:23 AM
Xibalba
SAC John Mills

"What is it?" asked Mills. "I don't understand what I'm looking at."

Mills watched Kera roll her eyes for what he thought was the hundredth time. They were standing at the bottom of the mountain, watching as the air glimmered in red and blue blips. One moment there was a ballroom, the next it was gone, as if some magician were playing tricks on John's eyes.

"I know I saw it... saw all of them on our way here. Now that we've arrived... where did it go?" Mills was studying the glimmer. He looked down at Kera, standing beside him as she studied the same area where the glimmer came and went. Noticed her head was bleeding again, fresh blood jutted from the open wounds on Kera's forehead. Instinctively, he ran his finger across the wound, catching blood, then dropped his finger between his lips and cheeks, the taste a perfect combination of sweet and salty. His body shivered as the blood ran down his gullet to his stomach, sucking on his finger like a baby's binky.

"Taste good?" Kera said, her tone sarcastic as she shook her head with a stare of pure disgust.

Mills nodded, finger still in his mouth. Kera rolled her eyes and stepped closer to where the glimmer should pass them once again. It seemed to come every few minutes. Mills raised his chin. Above them, a flock of gargoyles raced across the dark sky. They disappeared when they flew over the glimmer and reappeared a moment later, further away.

"That's interesting." Mills watched the gargoyles fly into the distance.

Kera turned to him. "What is?"

Mills gestured to the gargoyles. "When they flew over, they disappeared." He stepped closer to the glimmer, hands feeling the air as if there was a wall when there was none. He felt energy. Electrical currents moved through his hand as a shock of electricity raced through his arm. Mills jumped back, pulled his arm away.

"What is it?" called Kera.

Mills looked to the right, watching as the glimmer was speeding towards him. He had only one second to react. Mills grabbed Kera by the elbow and leaped into the glimmer as it passed. Electrical currents shocked and tossed him around, losing his grip on Kera. The sudden shock was enough for Mills to clamp his eyes shut, wincing in pain as he felt his body drop with a pounding thud to the ground. He heard himself snarl and growl. Electrical currents painfully wrenched through his bones. Felt like he was floating for a long while before he snapped his eyes open. The empty pit in his stomach burned and consumed his thoughts. And when he opened his eyes, he was in the ballroom he'd seen from before. Dark and dreary was this ballroom, as if life had abandoned the ballroom long ago. Stunk of mildew and dust and charred embers. He saw Kera standing over him.

"Good job, detective. I guess you're more keen than Jiggly thought."

Mills pushed himself off the floor like he was lifting a thousand pound sandbag. Got himself to his knees and stopped, hands on his legs, breathing heavy.

"It's the gravity," said Kera. She was looking over the empty ballroom. "Between worlds, it's much stronger, makes the body heavier."

Mills shook his head. "What is this place?" He looked at Kera as she continued to study the ballroom.

"I'm not entirely certain, but I believe this is the hotel where Mr. West first got his hold on the earth. It was burned down a long time ago. This must be the energetic stain that remained. Somehow, West harnessed its power to open a portal between worlds." She was shaking her head when she turned to Mills. "They're like little children, detective. Little children…"

She was interrupted by a terrifying, blood-curdling scream. The screaming was endless, and Mills felt his blood boil in his veins.

"My god," hollered Kera. "This must all stop."

Mills felt rage build in his chest. And when he arched his shoulders, he noticed how Kera seemed tiny, even smaller than she'd been before. She looked at him, her head rising to meet his eyes.

"Dark Lord is taking his hold on you, detective. In this place, you are whomever your thoughts reveal. You can turn into smoke if you wanted. It is in your power."

Mills stood erect, his line of sight at the top of the steps. His eyes roaming to the dark hallway on top of those stairs. "Tell me something, Kera." His voice thick and guttural. "What happens to them?"

"To who?"

"To the masters you talked about and the people they are bringing here. If I destroy them here, what happens to them on earth?"

Kera thought and thought, Mills waiting patiently, watching her. "It's never happened before, so I'm not sure. I assume the masters will lose their hold on their earthly hosts and the others will disappear from earth and remain here. Why do you ask?"

That scream was endless; it irritated Mills like he'd never been irritated before. "Because, Kera, I'm going to kill them all."

Mills turned to Kera, grinding his teeth and snarling.

"Understood, detective."

"So, how do we get back once the children are safe?"

"I'll have to figure that one out. But I saw three people go down the hall after you threw me in, so I'll look for the vortex. I'll find it. You just focus on the children and not eating anyone's heart."

And he smiled a wide grin as he transformed into smoke and slithered up the staircase.

5

2:24 AM
Inside the Vortex: The In-Between
Tyler

He felt the pull more than the push. The push at his back into the vortex and the pull across the vortex threshold. Felt all his atoms release as if he were boiling water and he'd become the vapor, a conscious awareness more than a physical presence, materializing on the other side into...

My room?

Tyler stepped into his bedroom, although it wasn't really his bedroom, not the way it was now. It was his room, but his room from when he was a child. Posters of superheroes were taped across the walls, the comforter on his bed reflected the same. His toys scattered across the floor when his bedroom door slammed open and in trampled his father, drunk as ever. He looked directly at Tyler, the teenage Tyler, looking through him, before he turned those eyes to the young Tyler, hiding beneath his superhero comforter.

"Hiding again, boy?" his dad grumbled. Tyler could smell the stale stank of beer on his father's breath. An all too familiar stench.

Tyler turned to the bed and saw his child self hiding beneath the covers. Tyler remembered how he used to pad his body with as many layers of clothes as he could find, wedging old magazines in his pants he'd steal from school, friends' houses, and anywhere he could find a magazine. Anything to help with the lashing he was about to receive from the angry, drunken hand of his father. He could hear his younger self beneath the covers, holding his breath, holding back the tears because if he wailed, if he so much as welled up a tear or whimpered a cry, the beating would be tenfold. Boys don't cry, remember?

"Gonna give you something to hide about." His father unbuckled his belt. Tyler watched as he did so, his anger boiling in his throat.

"Leave him alone," teenage Tyler screamed, but his father did not relent, staring at the teenage Tyler as if he knew he was there. Tyler shook his head, stepped in front of his father as he raised his belt and stepped to the bed. But his father stepped right through him. Started belting his younger self.

Tyler looked at his hands; shimmering translucent glimmers ran across his fingers. He looked at his dad, his back now to Tyler as he drove his belt across the young Tyler's back. Tyler saw himself, his younger self, peeking through the covers that he'd wrapped around his head. He was staring at Tyler, but not really looking. His eyes had gone cold and dark. He disassociated. Tyler remembered then how he would disassociate as a child. Whenever the beatings came, he'd put his mind somewhere else to forget the pain and fear. But this was the night when his father took it to the extreme. A beating was one thing, what came next was...

Tyler pursed his lips and swallowed the lump in his throat, listening to the slap of the belt across his back.

Powerless, that's how he felt. Even here, in this separation of time and space, he felt powerless. What was the point? Tyler thought. What is the point?

"To remind you where you come from," said a raspy voice behind Tyler. He snapped his head around to the large and short woman behind him. She was bent over, studying his toys and train set. Her hair a mop of short curls. Looked like a bag lady wearing a moo-moo that was clearly too big.

"Why?" asked Tyler. "I've made peace with the past."

That belt and whipping kept coming, young Tyler whining and desperately attempting to stifle his cries.

"You cryin yet, boy?" his father said, and Tyler knew when it was coming. He wished to be gone by then.

The short woman turned to the young Tyler, then to Tyler

himself. "Apparently not." She craned her head, staring at Tyler.

The belt came down in quick successions. Tyler heard himself, his younger self, stifle that scream, a wedge of blanket between his teeth.

"Take back the power, Tyler," said the woman, offering her hand, palm up.

Tyler looked at her palm and the blue pill resting on her skin. Confusion, eyes narrowed, and he looked at the woman.

"What is that?"

The woman shrugged. "Something that'll ease the pain. Make you less…" She paused, searching. "Help you adjust."

"Adjust to what?"

"Acceptance!" she said as if she were attempting to find a common ground with Tyler, blurting out any word she could find to do so.

Now that belt came furiously and without pause. Tyler remembered how he wished he'd used those magazines across his back. He could still feel the welts that had formed there. He turned away, turned his head away from the young Tyler.

"I can't do anything about this," he hollered, hollered over the sound of the belt and the whimpers from the young Tyler. "What's the use of showing me this?"

"Oh," said the woman. "I see now. I was wondering when you'd show up."

And everything suddenly stopped. The belt lashing, the cries, the whimpers that were about to erupt. Tyler knew where that scream led and what came after. When he looked up, the room was bathed in darkness, as if he and this woman were standing in the middle of the universe. Shooting stars raced overhead.

"You're the warlock," she said, and Tyler snapped his head towards her.

"What?"

She smiled. "The warlock. The one they've been waiting for."

Tyler shook his head. "What does that mean?"

"Decisions Tyler. You have a decision to make." She turned to her left, and Tyler followed her gaze.

In the darkness, the vortex spiraled. First as waves of darkness, then changing to the silvery spiral.

Tyler watched the vortex, mesmerized by the liquid-looking spiral. "What decision?"

"You shall see soon enough, Mr. Tyler."

Tyler forced his eyes from the vortex to the woman staring at him.

"Best to go now, Mr. Tyler. They have been waiting for you."

"Who?"

"In time, Mr. Tyler. All in time. The vortex calls to you. You must answer."

"Who are you?" Tyler's eyes narrowed, staring at this puppet looking woman.

"I am the preparer. I try to help the children as much as I can."

"By drugging them?" He shook his head. "All you do is amplify the fear and you know it."

She looked ashamed and how Tyler knew what he'd just said was true he did not know other than that he could feel it, sense it, and that sensation brought with it a knowing. This puppet looking woman was as evil as all of them. He could feel her wretchedness, like a virus infecting his cells. It felt dirty and congested, like venom in his blood. She turned away, refusing to look at him, and it was then that Tyler saw the birthmark on her neck, between the jawline and her ear. Oddly, the birthmark resembled the head of a goat.

The birthmark teased Tyler. Seemed all too familiar, although he couldn't place it. "Who are you really?"

The woman craned her head around, a snarl in her throat.

Seething, she said, "Time to go, *Mr. Tyler*," and pushed Tyler into the vortex.

6

2:26 AM
The Ballroom
Sharon the Goddess

She stood up from the throne. Her heartbeat caught in her throat as she stifled her breath, the vortex spinning wildly. Felt her eyes widen as she looked over the room. Dark Lord was on her left, a smug smile across his lips, waiting. Emmanuelle's minions, the masters, lined up in the appropriate circular stance as a symbol of the three levels of the universe, their heads bowed in silent reverie. She thought of Jezebel then, more than likely taking her time with Jigglyspot. Emmanuelle knew Jiggly wouldn't go down without a fight. She chuckled, thinking about it. Wished she'd been able to see the look on his face when he discovered he'd been the pawn in Emmanuelle's game.

The thought brought her to turn to the right, where the warlock's friend waited. The girl Pam was close to Emmanuelle. She'd done well, Emmanuelle thought. All of Emmanuelle's preparation had come to this moment in what had taken decades to culminate, waiting for the exact right moment to strike. An orgy of evidence, that's what it took to wrangle in and dismantle the dreaded Mr. E. Officially referred to as MysterE, because of his untarnished ability to slip through the cracks every time the feds got close, and the truth was about to see the light of day. MysterE was West's prized accomplishment. He'd taken him under his wing at a very early age, nurtured him and polished him for what would become one of history's greatest veils.

But like all things in the universe, they transcend and transform. Most of the time they change on a dime, but not now, although it may seem that way to anyone outside Emmanuelle's circle. And she was ready to take the baton and lead the armies of darkness across the globe and beyond. The thought sent a shiver up her spine as she closed her eyes and relished the moment, grinding her teeth and seething. She could feel the change in her bones, and, with an enormous grin, she opened her eyes to the vortex and the warlock who now emerged.

7

2:28 AM
The Underground
Cassandra

She watched Tyler disappear into the vortex. One moment he was there, the next, gone, vanished into the vortex. All that remained after the spinning stopped was a dark hallway. She had assumed something was up with Tyler, considering how Amber cringed every time he said something questionable or took up arms against current troubles. Cassandra was more than aware Amber didn't trust him.

Despite these insurgencies, she felt his absence now that he was gone. Her heavy breathing the only sound in the room, alone, her mind racing with possibilities, processing all she'd been through. And what the next step was. What should she do?

The voice behind her was husky and thick, bellowed from the gut and throat. "In such instances, I'm always of the opinion to burn the whole place down."

Cassandra snapped around. Standing in the door was a clown, a very short clown who looked like he'd seen better days. His makeup cracked and smeared with perspiration, his clown outfit disheveled, and his eyes revealed a man lost in madness. His stare cut through Cassandra and her stomach turned, noticing the scalpel in his right hand and the cane in his left. He followed her gaze, then turned to her.

"Oh, no alarm for you. I was going to sneak up behind you and cut your throat, but you needn't worry about that now."

"That's not at all comforting."

He bobbed his head right, left, right, left. "Be that as it may, I do not care." He took a step closer, and Cassandra jumped back and the clown stopped moving.

"Who are you?"

"I am the one they call Jigglyspot, and I *need* to go into the vortex."

"You're the one Kera is fighting for," said Cassandra. "The one she's trying to help."

"And you are the one she saved. If it weren't for Kera, you'd be dead by now."

"I'm aware."

"Are you aware she is no more?"

"What?"

Jigglyspot paused. "The Goddess ate her heart." He was gnashing his teeth, staring at the floor. "An act I intend to reverse." He raised his eyes. "So, if you would kindly move away from the vortex, I won't have to apprise my earlier plan."

Cassandra turned to the vortex, or where the vortex should be, then looked back at Jigglyspot. She stepped back, towards the cage, and out of his way.

"Thank you." Jiggly walked towards the vortex, stopping when he was passing Cassandra, staring at her, staring through her. "You wish your revenge..." He craned his head, assessing. "And I suggest you take it. That is the only reason I haven't cut your throat." And he smiled, his makeup creased across his cheeks.

"You're not very charming."

"Nor do I intend to be. But the fact of the matter is this, plain and simple, what cannot happen is for Emmanuelle to keep her hold on the planet. The vortex must be closed and destroyed. No matter what, we must blow this place to hell. And since you are here to exact revenge for your predicament, we have a mutual cause and effect. We both want people dead." He rolled his eyes. "Doesn't everybody?"

"What do you want me to do?"

"Ahh, simple really, fill the place with gas then blow it sky high."

"But then everyone will die, the innocent too, and you. There's got to be a better plan than mass destruction."

Jigglyspot smiled from ear to ear. "None are innocent here, my lady."

Cassandra shook her head. "Not true. Children are here, parents too. People who are here against their will."

"All who are here have come of their own accord, with very few exceptions."

"Not true!" she shouted, shaking her head. "Not true."

Jiggly paused and raised his chin, his eyes wide and staring. "I don't have time to discuss the cosmic makeup of the universe and how they relate to the subconscious mind, but I assure you, they are. Seeds planted long ago, the Goddess has been very busy. What we have here tonight is the result of those years. And here I am, thinking this was just another celebration to usher in the new solstice. How wrong I was. Foolish really."

"What're you talking about?"

"Doesn't matter, really. Soon enough, one way or another, this will all be over. So, if you decide to do as I say, be sure to use the gas, starting with the gas valves down the hall, then make your way into the kitchen and the gas stove and oven. There is a door in the dining room that will lead you to a hall and another room on the left. Go through it and into the warehouse and you'll see all the valves. Keep turning on the gas; twist as many valves as you can. Gas is how the place is heated. Turn the valves on one by one but do so quickly. At exactly three a.m. the portal will take a permanent hold on this building and will serve as Emmanuelle's doorway to usher in an army of darkness from Xibalba. It would be best if the hold is no longer here."

"Shwhat?"

"Xibalba."

"What the hell is that?"

"Exactly." Jiggly cocked his eyebrows. "You can do that, can't you? Think about all the good you'll be doing, keeping hell and damnation from casting its dark hand across the globe."

"Seems like that's already happened."

Jiggly smiled. "Clever girl," he whispered. "But look at it this way: in doing so, you'll allow humanity to have a fighting chance."

Cassandra shook her head. "I won't kill innocent children. Not happening on my watch. I'm here for one person and one person alone."

Jiggly thought a while. "Ira?" he asked, and Cassandra nodded. "He has been a dastardly bastard now, hasn't he? Brought you here, did he?"

"Yes, kept me in that cage for a lifetime."

"Then your revenge is owed to you, my dear. How about this, if I toss Ira's head down the vortex, will you then do as I ask?"

Cassandra considered his offer. "I'm not killing children."

"Understood, then we will have it as this. Once the gas has been turned on, I'll personally dispatch the children to you. Whatever you choose to do with them is up to you. I'll leave their fate to your hand."

"Why would I trust you?"

"Simple," Jiggly hollered. "The enemy of my enemy is my friend. I wish to not only dismantle Emmanuelle but also cut off her means of transport, in honor of Mr. West, my mentor." He bowed his head, thinking. "After learning of these events, it will satisfy him to know I did all I could to stop Emmanuelle's rise. I sense his presence. He is here somewhere, watching and listening to all that has transpired." He looked at Cassandra, his stare burning through her soul. "Understand that today is solstice, but not just solstice on this planet, but on Xibalba too. And when the stars are in alignment between the two worlds, a portal can be opened. Granted, in order for the portal to remain open, someone who has an equal hold on this planet and another must offer a heart to the Dark Lord before the witching hour has arrived. At least that is one way to keep its hold, while the other is for total desecration of all who are here and have taken part in this little ritual, and I'm more than sure Emmanuelle won't shed too many tears for her dead minions and masters. Plus, I believe they have secured their new lackey-even if he is unaware of it-but we can divert all their plans by blowing this place sky high. Do this for me and I will release the children to you. Seems like a small price to pay to get what you want."

Cassandra thought about his offer. How else was this going to end? Was it not going to end in a hellish fiery blaze, no matter what she did? At least, she rationalized, she'll be able to save some children... and she'll have comfort in knowing that Ira no longer lived.

"Well, Cassandra? What's it going to be?"

Cassandra eyeballed Jigglyspot, staring, and nodded her agreement.

"Perfect," said Jigglyspot. "Good to know not all you humans are selfish, degenerate fools." And he stepped to the entrance of the dark hall. "Look for the head rolling down the aisle. That's your cue to begin the gas."

Cassandra stepped away from the cage. "And the children?"

Jiggly paused, his hands in front of him swirling. "Listen for the screams," he said.

And Cassandra's heart sank. She pursed her lips and swallowed her breath, staring at Jigglyspot. *Did I just make a deal with the devil?*

"No devil," he said, "Just a Jigglyspot."

8

2:29 AM
The Ballroom
Tyler

He emerged from the vortex into what looked like a ballroom, large and open and brightly lit, with a tall glass ceiling and floors made from marble. In front of him were three circles, one inside the other, lined with people wearing dark cloaks; their hoods covered their bowed heads. A path cut through the circles leading to the opposite side where there were two thrones. A man sat on one of those thrones. Standing in front of the second throne was a woman, her eyes burning through Tyler as she gently removed her hood. Blood on her robe from the neckline to her knees. Blood on her lips and chin and smeared across her cheeks. She smiled at Tyler and took a step down from the throne. She looked to her right.

"Come," she said, holding her hand out. Tyler watched as the person cloaked to the woman's right took the offered hand and stepped into the path. The woman returned her gaze to Tyler. She took the person's shoulders and stepped behind.

Tyler stepped forward and noticed how the man sitting on his throne sat upright, watching Tyler. His features were difficult to see, but Tyler noticed his fangs when his mouth gaped open like some demonic greeting. Everything was so quiet. He wasn't sure what to make of it. Hadn't expected a welcoming committee. He was looking around the room when the woman called his name. "Tyler," she said. "We've been waiting for you."

"What is this?" Tyler felt his heart race in his chest, his voice choked in the back of the throat that he now cleared. Noticed how the fanged king leaned forward on his throne. Tyler saw the dead body on the floor just off to the left of the throne. Dried blood beneath the body. He was sure it was Kera. Tyler's eyes narrowed when he glared at the fanged king.

It was the woman who spoke first. "Your induction Tyler." She stepped forward, away from the cloaked person who turned on their heels, head still bowed, behind this woman.

"Induction for what? Who are you?"

"My name," she said with a slight bow and curtsy. "Is Emmanuelle. Goddess of the watchtowers of the north and you, Tyler, are my prized possession."

Tyler felt his face warm with a blushing heat. "What the fuck are you talking about?"

Emmanuelle continued. "I must admit she had you pegged appropriately from the start, but your friend gave chase too, too much. His parents insisted. For years, they insisted it was he Mr. West was looking for." She paused, and Tyler could see a glint in her eye. "But you put an end to that debate, didn't you?"

"Debate? What debate? Lady, you're driving me insane. I'm here…"

"You still have his heart, correct?"

Tyler stopped cold, felt the blood drain from his veins. Kera's voice in his ear: *Don't let him eat the heart.* He looked at the fanged king.

"What's the point?" he said.

Emmanuelle chuckled beneath her breath. "The point is, Tyler, that the Reillys sought to destroy you. Your friend's parents were next in line to take over the business of one Mr. E., with their son serving as their right hand." She looked around the room as if what she was saying was a secret held for only those in attendance. "But we intervened, did we not, Tyler? Put an end to their plan." She clucked her tongue, moving her head left and right.

"Lady, I don't know what you're talking about."

She paused, then laughed. "You know, Tyler, I would think you'd show more appreciation for what we've given you."

"Given me?" He shook his head. "Are you serious, lady? My life's been nothing close to a gift."

"Not until now, no, but we had to make sure you were the right one, so we had to make it hard, impossible even, and you came through. Shot James Reilly right in the chest and watched him die. I love it. His murder was your initiation. To make sure we had the right man for the job."

"What job?"

She stepped closer to him. "You are one of us, Tyler. All you've endured was necessary to prepare you for this moment. But your suffering ends tonight. All you wish and desire will be yours. Just say the word and you will have it."

"I don't think so. Life doesn't happen like that."

"It does for those who take what is theirs without remorse."

"I just want..."

"Pam?" said Emmanuelle as she stepped backwards, turned around, and reached her hand to the cloaked person standing at attention. "Come," she said as the person took her hand. Emmanuelle pulled the hood off and there stood Pam, her eyes slowly lifting to lock with his. "You want her, don't you Tyler?"

"She's a friend, is all."

Emmanuelle craned her head, a skeptical stare in her eyes. "Come on, Tyler, I've heard your thoughts at night. Here she is. Take her as you will. Toss her to the side when you're done with her. We don't mind. Slit her ear to ear if you wish. The choice is yours, but know this, Tyler." She looked back to the fanged king, then to Tyler. "When you walk with us, you can do whatever you want, when you want."

"Why me?" he asked, staring at Pam. She hadn't said a word, hadn't even moved.

"Because we require a foothold in this dimension. Someone to serve our interests. A commandant, so to speak. And in return, unlimited power is yours to do with as you wish. But you must provide reassurance, Tyler. You must prove loyalty."

"And how does that happen? What do you expect me to do?"

"Simple Tyler. Offer the heart to the Dark Lord."

"What?"

"The Dark Lord," she repeated, turning and pointing to the fanged king. "Offer him the heart of James Reilly and you will take your rightful place by our side."

"Why would I do that?"

Emmanuelle turned on her heels. "No Tyler, the only question is why wouldn't you do it? Think of all you will have. All the power. There's no reason not to."

Tyler looked again at the Dark Lord, to Kera's body, then to Emmanuelle. He laughed and shook his head. "Not that easy, is it? You need me to volunteer, don't you?"

Emmanuelle nodded.

Tyler chuckled. "I hope I'm not your only hope, lady..." He pulled the boning knife from his back pocket.

Emmanuelle laughed back. "No, Tyler, of course not. There is always another." She stepped back, and Tyler could see how frustrated she'd become. She stepped behind Pam. "You want her destroyed. Very well then, let's show Pam what true pain feels like." Emmanuelle stretched her fingers and Tyler watched as electrical sparks raged from her fingertips towards Pam's back. The strain that erupted across her face told Tyler those electrical sparks were wrenching her insides as she dropped to her knees and hunched over as a painful moan escaped her lips.

Emmanuelle said, "See how easy it is Tyler? All it takes is a flick of the wrist and the pain can be forever." Tyler could see how she tensed her arms and shoulders. Electrical currents rushed from her fingertips, turning Pam's skin red and blotchy.

"Bitch," Tyler called and went to swing the boning knife when two arms wrapped around his neck and shoulders. A blade nipped his throat.

"Oh Ira," said Emmanuelle. "I can always count on you."

Tyler felt the heat of Ira's breath across his right ear. "Drop it," he demanded.

Emmanuelle upped her game, tensed those arms, and the power erupting from her fingers brought a holler from Pam's throat.

"He said drop the knife, Tyler." Emmanuelle, her nose

twitching, staring at Tyler.

Pam's nose was bleeding; her body shuddering, groaning painful whimpers, her fists clawing against her head, as blood dripped from her eyes and Tyler heard the Dark Lord laugh above the raging electrical currents.

Ira pushed the blade further into Tyler's neck. He could feel blood trickle down his throat.

"I said drop it." Ira again and he yanked Tyler's head back, digging the blade a nip further into his throat.

Tyler dropped the knife, the steel clanging against the marble floor. Ira thrust Tyler from his grip to the floor, then kicked the knife away. Tyler watched as Pam dropped onto her back, wriggling. The Goddess refused to relent as Pam clawed at her head, hollering and screeching, and Tyler could see blood dripping from her ears.

"Leave her be," Tyler commanded as he snapped his head towards Emmanuelle.

The smile on Emmanuelle's lips was from ear to ear. She craned her head, glowering at Tyler. She ceased the electrical current from her fingertips. "Offer the Dark Lord the heart, Tyler. If not, Pam will die, followed by the rest of your friends and all you hold dear."

Tyler looked at Pam. She was clawing across the floor, crying and screeching, obviously in pain. Tyler stood up, hands out in surrender. "Okay," he said. "Just leave her be." He looked around the room. To the cloaked people standing idly by. Emmanuelle's eyes roamed over him as she licked her lips in anticipation. To Ira standing, a thin smile across his lips, holding the knife in his right hand. And then to the Dark Lord, standing in front of his throne.

"Come, boy," said the Dark Lord. "Kneel before me. Offer the heart and we will take our rightful place and rule the universe in the name of Baphomet."

Tyler rose to his feet, standing, staring at the Dark Lord and the eyes that peered through narrow eyelids. Looked to Pam and Emmanuelle.

Emmanuelle hollered, "Get down. On your knees, all of you." And all the cloaked people kneeled. Emmanuelle smiled, and Ira's head and shoulders were bobbing with anticipation. Ira's tongue across his lips, his eyes wide. Tyler turned to the Dark Lord.

"Come, boy." He lifted his chin. "Kneel before me." Seething, his jaw tight, gritting his teeth. "Take my hand." He reached his hand out. "Swear allegiance and loyalty with the offering." His eyes closed.

"Go now Tyler." Emmanuelle, Tyler snapped his head around to her. "Or the next move I make is twisting this little bitch's neck." She gripped Pam by the nape of the neck and lifted her to her feet. Tears flowed from Pam's eyes, her lips stuttering, her face winced and pinched in pain. Emmanuelle gripped a handful of her hair and yanked her head back. "I said now, Tyler," Emmanuelle hollered as Pam's painful whimper erupted in the ballroom.

Tyler turned to the Dark Lord. He stepped forward, his footsteps slowly tapping the marble floor, staring at the Dark Lord when he saw something twitch in the corner of his eye and saw Kera's body slumped across the floor and those tentacles hiding within her hair, staring at him as if pleading for help. They looked sick, depleted, their blue hue turning pale and frail. Perhaps they can't live without a living host? Perhaps, they were dying a slow, and torturous death. Tyler turned back to the Dark Lord, his hand raised above Tyler's head.

"Kneel before me," he said. "Then take my hand."

Tyler knelt before the Dark Lord and touched the heart in his pocket.

"Good," said the Dark Lord. "Now, take my hand and swear allegiance to Baphomet."

Tyler looked up when he heard a choked back scream. Looked back quickly and saw Ira convulsing and shuddering, his eyeballs attempting to jump out of their sockets when Ira dropped to his knees and a short little clown stood behind him. One hand gripped Ira's hair, the other circled around Ira's neck, across his throat and circled back around as blood rushed from the wound across Ira's throat, soaking his cloak. Tyler heard Emmanuelle gasp when the clown said,

"Sorry I'm so late, Goddess. But as they say, better late than never." And he yanked on Ira's skull, pulling and tearing his skin and tendons, bones splintering as he ripped Ira's head off his shoulders, his spine still attached to the head that the clown tossed behind him into the vortex. The clown kicked the body over and blood spouted across the marble. Tyler saw a blood-soaked scalpel in his right hand. "I couldn't make it on time, so I thought I'd crash this blasphemous ritual back to hell." He pulled a red cane from his clown outfit and slammed the bottom to the floor.

Tyler's eyes snapped to Emmanuelle. She was staring at Ira, but quickly turned to the clown. "Foolish," she uttered with a sneer.

The clown returned her stare, shaking his head. "No, Emmanuelle, the only fool I see here is you."

Tyler heard the muffled scream before he saw the other clowns. They seemed to come out of the walls, out of nowhere. They ate the first few cloaked people outside the circle. Ate their heads and dropped them to the floor. The cloaked people stood quickly, then stepped away from their dead cohorts.

"My masters," Emmanuelle called while staring down at the little clown. "Destroy them all!"

There was a moment, a pause before all the fighting erupted, before the high-pitched battle cry raged across the room and all the bodies collided with angry yelps and growls, when Tyler thought he and Pam would just walk out the front door. But when the Dark Lord yanked him off the ground by his hair, the thought dissipated quickly.

"Now," said the Dark Lord, turning Tyler's head to him. "You will offer me the heart."

Perhaps it was the fear and adrenaline pumping through his veins that released the power from Tyler's fingertips. The same power that tossed James Reilly across the hall, and the same that tore the minion apart in the cage. It felt like magic released from his fingertips that rushed towards the Dark Lord and tossed him, crashing against the far wall.

Tyler looked at his fingers, then to the Dark Lord, sitting on his ass against a mural that beamed and swirled with demon looking people cascading across a large tree. The stare in the Dark Lord's eyes was pure hatred as he rose to his feet, and the roar that erupted from his throat was ear piercing.

And Tyler said, "Let's get this on... Dark Lord."

9

2:35 AM
The Underground
Cassandra

She heard the vortex before she saw it spinning. Watched as a round object came hurling out of the spinning silver and dropped on the ground, rolling towards her. Blood sprayed off the decapitated head, the spine rattled across the floor as it tumbled over and over, then stopped in front of Cassandra's feet. Ira's eyes were open, a stare of pain and disbelief plastered permanently across his face.

Cassandra crouched down and picked it up, staring at the dead eyes of Ira Monteforte. Just a Jigglyspot, she thought, running her tongue inside her mouth. She took the head and propped it up against the back of the cage when she heard screams and fighting coming from inside the vortex and a voice shouting orders that sounded all too familiar.

"Sharon?"

Can't be, she thought. Cassandra shook her head, looked back at Ira's dead skull, then made a beeline for the hall.

Time to burn this place to all bloody hell.

10

2:36 AM
A Private Hell
Lilly

"Come, Christopher," said Kevin, the crook of his arm wrapped around Lilly's throat. He was on top of Lilly, her cloak pushed up high to her chest, her stomach burning against the hot floor. Hard to breathe, she felt sweat drip across her skin. He was still inside her, Lilly's rectum burning; she could feel blood trickle down her inner thigh.

Eyes wet with tears, gagging and struggling to breathe, she saw Christopher sitting beside his father. His eyes circling, lost in fear, his head and shoulders bobbing back and forth.

"So sorry."

Bang! Tad's brains blown across the back wall and Christopher jumped, startled, and panicked, when Kevin released her throat. He gyrated his hips and Lilly coughed and choked, drawing air into her lungs. Felt Kevin push himself to his feet, his nails raking across her flesh as he stood. Lilly curled into a ball, drawing in deep shuddering breaths as she peered through wet, narrowed eyelids at her son standing. Obeying.

"Take your rightful place by our side," demanded Kevin. "Claim your birthright. Even your mother belongs to you."

Lilly's ribs cracked when Kevin kicked her. "Turn over," he hollered. "I want you to look into your son's eyes when he takes you." Pain wrenched from her brain to her toes. Every inch of her body ached. Her thoughts burned inside her mind like little fires erupting in her skull. Another kick, this one to the spine. Another kick. Four. Five. Her body wrenched and stretched with the last kick, turning her over. Her throat burned something awful, but she squeezed words from her throat. "No, Christopher, don't."

Kevin offered his hand to Christopher. Kevin's skin looked burnt, dark and charred, and Lilly could see the fangs jutting over his bottom lip. His red eyes glowered at Christopher, and he smiled. "Come now Christopher. It's so easy and sweet. Your mother is a delectable treat." His long tongue lapped across his lips to his chin.

Lilly looked at her son, standing, staring at her with a look that equaled confusion. Lilly shook her head. "Don't Christopher, please."

Christopher reached his hand out and took Kevin's offering.

"Oh, my man," seethed Kevin and he led Christopher to stand in front of him, the two looking down on Lilly. Kevin's chin just above Christopher's shoulder, his lips close to Christopher's ear when he reached his finger to Christopher's cheek and Lilly could see how Christopher's skin burned where Kevin touched him. Christopher's face scrunched, gritting his teeth, allowing the burn. "Ahh," said Kevin and he glared at Lilly. Said, "He likes it," as a smile crossed his lips. Moved his head slowly back and forth as he gripped the back of Christopher's neck. Kevin pushed him forward two steps and wrapped his hands around Christopher's throat then squeezed. Christopher's eyes bulged from his skull, his skin flushed a burning red and Lilly could see how Kevin's hands burned his skin, smoldering smoke lifted from his fingers. He clawed at Kevin's hands and Kevin yanked his hands away with a sudden jolt, then pulled Christopher's head back by his hair.

"Little bastard."

"So sorry." BANG!

Christopher shuddered, then returned to that sedated state. Kevin was snarling and seething.

"I'll tear your head off, little boy, if you try that again."

Kevin forced Christopher to his knees.

"Don't move Ma," said Kevin. "This is going to be spectacular."

"No." Lilly shook her head, tried flopping over to run, but Kevin snatched her by the hair, his movement lightning fast, and pulled her back, sliding her beneath Christopher. Kevin behind him.

"No worries, mom." Kevin cocked his eyebrows, staring at Lilly with a sickly grin across his lips. "He's gonna get some, too." And he laughed. Laughed and lapped that tongue across his lips again, forcing Christopher forward between Lilly's legs. Lilly pleading, trying to move, to be free. Kevin's grip inhumanly strong, pinning her to the ground. "This is all so beautiful. In honor of Baphomet, I give you the ultimate evil."

Lilly watched as Kevin squeezed his hand around Christopher's throat, and forced him closer, further up between her legs. Christopher's skin turning in front of her eyes, the color likened to burnt coal.

"So sorry."

BANG!

Lilly cried, "My god... please help me."

"God?" Kevin raged, then bellowed a laugh from the back of his throat. "God, my lady... is not allowed in this place."

11

2:38 AM
In the Kitchen
Cassandra

She'd gone back up into the kitchen. Had to shield her eyes from the dismembered corpse rotting on the table. He'd been filleted like a deer under a hunter's knife, the stench putrid and foul, burning acid into the back of her throat, her stomach churning. She told herself repeatedly not to look. The last thing she needed right now was hurling chunks of stomach bile. She had to focus on the mission at hand. What Jigglyspot told her to do. Burn the place to all bloody hell, and do it before three A.M. Cassandra didn't understand the rest of what Jigglyspot had declared would happen after said time should she not accomplish this dire mission, but she knew it was not good. Hell on Earth type of shit.

She thought about Tyler as she twisted the knob on the oven while covering her mouth with her free hand. She opened the oven door, then twisted the stove knobs when the hissing sound of gas whistled from the burners. Was she sealing his demise by her current actions? She saw a box of matches sitting on the top of the stove. She took them and squeezed the box into her cloak pocket. Would he be able to get out with Pam? Or was it poetic justice, his consequence for murder? She couldn't be sure, but what Cassandra did know was that something wasn't adding up with her newfound friend Tyler, a nagging feeling that there was a larger picture, a pawn at play she was unaware of. In a world wrought with manipulation, Cassandra reminded herself to find the heart of the matter, to feel energy instead of listening to words. To trust her intuition. Beneath the surface, Cassandra knew, Tyler's foundation was pure; she witnessed this firsthand with his relentless pursuit in rescuing his friends.

She looked around the kitchen, making sure her eyes passed over and above the dead body. She could hear fighting, howls, and screams, aware that Jigglyspot and Tyler were a part of that fight as she hurried into the dining room. Tables still set up, half eaten food, dirty plates, glasses half full. Eerily quiet, with a thin layer of fighting commotion in the distance. She found a door, went through it, and entered a long hallway. Painted white, all white like the beaming light of midday. A door on her right and another on her left. Double doors at the far end of the hall and beyond those doors, the sound of combat was paramount. She looked at the door on her left and went to it with a hurried step when she heard that familiar voice again and stopped in her tracks, her hand hovering over the doorknob.

Sharon?

Hesitation when the thought erupted. If Ira took Cassandra, perhaps Ira knew Sharon was involved. Perhaps they'd taken her as well. Was it possible Sharon had experienced the same fate as Cassandra? She scanned those double doors at the end of the hall, standing tall as if they were guards themselves and stepped to them. She had to know. If Sharon is in here, she couldn't continue with her current mission. She'd have to get her friend to safety.

Cautiously, Cassandra gripped the door handle and twisted, holding held her breath as she cracked the door open and felt her eyelids stretch wide when she witnessed Sharon, some mystical dark energy jutting from her fingertips. Her skin burnt and dark. Her lips curled up high, revealed jagged fangs, and her eyes were a demon red and blazing with hellfire. And she had Jigglyspot...

She felt the force before she heard the crack. Felt herself thrown backward. Wood shrapnel from the shattered double doors followed her, and she crashed against the ground. The back of her head smacked against the tile. Cassandra saw the master lift off the ground and race into the room where she witnessed a supernatural surreal battle waging in a large and open ballroom, as if the room existed in hell. Felt pain rattle in her skull, tightening behind her eyes. Heavy head, Cassandra's eyes drifted closed.

12

2:39 AM
The Ballroom
Jigglyspot

He saw the wave of magic barreling towards him and Jiggly crouched down behind the red cane, twisting his grip on the cane and enveloping a protective shield around him that held strong when the Goddess's magic rammed into his own. He was completely aware he was no match for the Goddess. Even with the power of the cane, his ability to wield its full power was beyond his understanding. Simple parlor tricks. That's what Jigglyspot could do with the cane compared to what West could produce with its power. Using the cane for protection and distraction is what Jigglyspot was hoping for. But he had to get close to the Goddess, a task that was becoming increasingly more difficult with the passing of time and Emmanuelle's relentless barrage of hellfire.

Around him, his clowns fought valiantly in his defense against the Goddess' masters. And that kid, that Tyler, Jiggly knew, had the heart of James Reilly in his pocket. Knew the Dark Lord required the heart and once the heart is simmering in his stomach, West will be challenged for his hold on this world, having lost his path to total domination where no demon, man, woman, or child could dethrone him. The earth would then belong to the Dark Lord and Emmanuelle. Human beings their pets. Jiggly shook his head, the Goddess's power immense, bearing down on him with the strength of a thousand men.

Apoch tossed a master across the room, crashing into the double antique doors, splintering the wood into shards of wooden shrapnel. Watched as that same master leapt from the hall into the room towards Apoch, whose attention was on the master who crashed her shoulder into his stomach. Apoch must have known the master was flying towards him because he tossed the master's shoulders up into the second master, their bodies crashing into each other, falling with thuds on the marble floor. Apoch grabbed the head of the closest master and bit down, tearing off the skull at the neck. His jaw opened to an inhuman size as he bit down with a struggled crunch then chewed on the skull, gulping it down with a big nasty choked back swallow as blood, brain, skull, and bones jutted across his lips and down his chin, spilling over his throat and clown outfit. Blood gushed from the severed neck and Apoch growled at the second master on the floor, staring with narrow eyes at Apoch.

"Really Jiggly," said the Goddess. "You should have remained the pawn. I would have offered you asylum. But now Jigglyspot..." Jiggly could see how she clenched her hands into claws, the magical power immensely barreling down on him with a powerful fury. "I'll do no less than tear you apart."

Jiggly gripped his cane tight, the magical power beaming from the cane acted as a shield against Emmanuelle's relentless barrage of dark magic. "Seems you've lost your warlock, Emmanuelle. What will you do without your precious warlock?" He watched as Emmanuelle glared out of the corner of her eye at the Dark Lord and Tyler. The kid was good, Jiggly thought, warding off the Dark Lord with his own newfound power. Admittedly, Jiggly was a little jealous at that moment, wondering where this new warlock received the magical power. The elder blast was a power that had never manifested in Jiggly's favor. It was beyond his scope of understanding. Wished he had it now, though, considering the Goddess was unleashing holy magical hell.

Did he possess the strength to continue? Jiggly knew he was running out of time.

13

2:40 AM
The Xibalba Ballroom
The Dark Lord SAC John Mills

He tore them apart. Slithered into their bones, and turned them into dust. The children carried a purity that salivated his tongue. His stomach ached with a hunger he'd never experienced. He wanted to eat them, consume their hearts and savor their blood on his palate, knowing that if he did, he would feel whole. But Kera was his conscience. She followed him into each room, watched as he consumed the masters and indoctrinating humans, and took the children into her arms. He could feel himself growing stronger with every life taken into his soul, although his bloodlust refused to be satisfied. He looked at the children as if they would provide that satisfaction. But Kera was gentle, a trait that Mills now worshipped, finding her gentle nature mysterious and thrilling.

"No," she ordered, her head shaking, the children huddled behind her, tearful, whining, and screaming, fear and pain raised to the forefront of their minds and lips.

Mills felt and heard his own growl erupt in his throat, his nose curled.

"No!" Kera demanded. "You have one more room, Dark Lord. Take it and let's go home."

Mills inhaled deeply through his nose, raising his chin, looking down on the gentle Kera. "It's okay to eat them?"

Kera paused before she confirmed his inquiry with a gentle nod. "All but the children and the hearts. Both are off limits."

Mills closed his eyes as his body shuddered. Seething, he clenched his jaw, gritting his teeth with his hands clenched tight into fists and shaking by his sides.

"Do you feel them?" asked Kera. "Can you smell their fear?"

"Yes," Mills answered with a hush as he opened his eyes. He bent his head, staring at Kera. "I wish to consume their fear, their blood." His eyes lit up wide with delight. "And their hearts."

Kera shook her head. "No, Dark Lord Mills. You will eat no hearts tonight."

His eyes closed again, gnashing his teeth. The thought of hearts like a calling from the unknown. To consume them would mean elation, satisfaction, and bliss. But also, desecration and corruption for the detective, a line he understood he could not cross, for that would mean the end of SAC John Mills. The thought, want, and desire was immense; he could feel it in his veins as if his blood required hearts. He could smell them and hear heartbeats all around him.

"Resist," said Kera. "Resist the urge. Your hunger is almost gone, detective. One more room and we take the children back. One more room and we win this contest." Mills opened his eyes to Kera. "They'll never expect you, John. You're the fly in their ointment."

"One more room," Mills repeated. He closed his eyes, breathed deeply, and transformed into smoke. "Follow meeeeee," he said, slithering out of the room into the hall towards the last door.

14

2:41 AM
The Ballroom
Tyler

The Dark Lord stood tall. His grin forever plastered across his lips. His skin burnt black and charred. Dried blood flaked off his skin.

After Tyler used his newfound power and sent the Dark Lord reeling against the wall, Tyler thought he'd retaliate. Instead, he tore the head off the closest master to him. No cut across the throat like the clown had done to that guy Ira, no, the Dark Lord gripped that head in his talons and Tyler heard tearing, cracking, and popping as the Dark Lord wrenched the masters head off the shoulders, blood flooding from the neck and down across the body that dropped to the floor. Dark Lord's eyes never left Tyler. His lips curled into a small smile. Tyler felt a tingling in his fingers, as if this newfound magic called to him, wanting to be used. Electrical sparks raged off his fingertips as the Dark Lord gulped blood from the decapitated head.

Tyler looked away and saw how the clown and the Goddess were engaged in a supernatural battle. Masters and clowns collided, the clowns taking on a horde of masters. The clowns moved quickly, like blips of light as they projected themselves into different places. One moment they were standing tall, the next they were behind a master, tearing off a head, eating a shoulder, their jaws opened to inhuman sizes like a python swallowing prey.

"Do you wish to drink?" said the Dark Lord, holding the head for Tyler to see. Blood dripped from the torn neck.

Tyler clenched his fists, shaking his head. "No, I wish to tear every inch of flesh off your bones."

The Dark Lord raised his chin, a sinister and foul laugh raged off his lips, staring at Tyler. "Turn your anger on those who deserve it. We have been your guides all your life. It has been us who have given you your power. Nurtured every thought you've ever had. Encouraged every notion and dream. It is we, the Goddess and I, who have been with you all your life. You are our product, a gift from Baphomet to quicken our desire. Even your magic is a gift from the Goddess." The Dark Lord stepped forward and tossed the head across the room, screaming, "You belong to us!"

Tyler opened his fists, his fingers stretched, and projected magic from his fingertips that barreled into the Dark Lord forcing him back, but the Dark Lord drilled his feet into the ground, sliding across the marble, and stopped Tyler's magic from forcing him to his knees. Tyler's magic fizzled from his fingertips and the Dark Lord stepped forward and growled.

"Foolish boy," the Dark Lord raged, his hands in front of him, palms up, conjuring a ball of energy in his palms. "You are no match for me."

And he tossed magical energy towards Tyler. The energy raged in red and black, racing towards Tyler and he lifted his hands, propelled his own magic towards the Dark Lord's energy. Two balls of magic collided with a pulsing explosion that tossed Tyler and the Dark Lord backward. Tyler slammed against the marble floor, sliding on his back. His legs scuttling across the ground as he quickly rolled over and leapt to his feet, spinning around like a spider on a wheel, then stopped and stood tall. The Dark Lord growling. Tyler wasn't sure how, but he hurt the Dark Lord.

"Come on," Tyler screamed, holding his palms up, fingers curled, gathering magic in his fingertips.

The Dark Lord stood, watching him, and Tyler could feel how his magic was more powerful than before. Raging blue and white electrical sparks collided and became one within his hands. Dark Lord stretched his arms and just as Tyler was about to toss his magic into the Dark Lord, Pam stepped in front of him. Her black eyeballs staring at Tyler.

"What're you doing?" Tyler, his head shaking, raging hellfire magic like electrical sparks raged across his fingertips, the magic held at bay by his thoughts. "Move the fuck away," he hollered as the Dark Lord hid behind her, grinning, staring at Tyler.

"She is with me," raged the Dark Lord.

Tyler jerked his head back, confused. "What?" he whispered, "I don't believe it."

15

2:42 AM
A Private Hell
Lilly

"What's wrong with you?" screamed Kevin as he flung Christopher backward by his hair. Lilly saw how Christopher winced when the back of his head hit the wall. Lilly scrambled to her feet. Kevin standing in front of her, his attention on Christopher. "You're supposed to be stronger than this. More sinister."

Christopher's eyes were blank, as if there was no consciousness behind his eyes. Lilly gathered her strength and leapt onto Kevin's back. "You son of a bitch. Leave my son alone." She scratched his eyes, sinking her nails into his flesh.

Kevin hollered, snatching Lilly's hands in his, prying her hands from his eyes as Lilly attempted to wriggle her hands free when Kevin pulled her forward and dropped Lilly face first into the marble floor. She saw black when her head bounced off the marble. Felt and heard her jaw and nose pop with an immediate gush of blood across her face.

"Fuckin bitch."

Kevin pulled Lilly to her feet by her hair.

"Hurt me?" he screamed and punched Lilly dead in the face. Followed by another, then a third punch. His hand on her throat, squeezing with the power of iron. "Fuckin' kill you, bitch."

Now both hands were wrapped around Lilly's throat. Suffocating, she felt her eyes bulge from their sockets, staring at her son standing, his eyes rolling in his head. Kevin raised his right arm; his hand clenched in a fist and barreled his fist down across Lilly's face. She felt her cheekbone crack as his left hand squeezed her throat, choking the air from her lungs. She was dying. Kevin was on the brink of taking her life. Her thoughts were with Christopher. *What will happen to him?*

Another anvil fist from Kevin, this time across the eye, and she heard the bone crack, felt a bone pierce her eyeball. She heard hoarse breathing, struggling, not knowing this was coming from her own throat. An attempt to live and breathe that quickly dissipated when Kevin wrapped his hands around her throat. His smile ear to ear. Beads of blood covered his face. Her blood.

She could feel nothing but pain. Her whole body wrenched in agony, every bone and muscle felt bruised and battered, her left eye swollen shut; she looked into Kevin's eyes with her right eye and saw smoke slithering behind him. Kevin raised his right hand again, high above his head.

His sickly grin revealed his jagged bloodied teeth when he hollered, "Time To Die!"

And then he stopped. Seemed to freeze like a recipient of Medusa's stare. Except his eyes. His eyes wandered as if Kevin had realized some internal catastrophe requiring immediate urgency. His left hand released her throat and Lilly dropped with a thud to her ass, hacking and coughing air into her lungs. She looked up at Kevin, still standing. Saw smoke in his mouth puff out of his nostrils and ears. His eyes captured in fear as his body shivered, then turned into a shudder, his whole body trembling.

She saw it in his eyes first, the blood dripping from his black eyeballs as his skin split and tore as if some mystical force were using a razor to slice his flesh into a million cuts. A low, painful moan erupted from Kevin's throat. Blood seeped from every cut and tear. His throat drowning and gurgling on his own blood, his fingers clenched like talons by his sides, his head thrown back, his throat ballooned to an inhuman swell that immediately ripped open with a flood of blood. One last scream came from Kevin, like a whistled gurgling scream through the torn throat, when Lilly heard his bones all crack, splinter, and pop, and he exploded across the room. Lilly shielded her eyes from the flesh, blood, and guts that rained over her. She scurried further back and when she looked at the place where Kevin had been, her eyes went wide. The devil was standing over her, snarling.

He craned his head, staring at her. Staring through her. Said, "What's that smell?" as his eyes roamed over Lilly as if she were his next meal. His breath was shallow, like a hush over his lips he was attempting to control. His eyes lit up wide, gritting his teeth, he breathed in deeply through his nose, his head turning slowly to Christopher. "Your heart," he said. "It's fascinating." He stepped towards Christopher, who was staring with wild roaming eyes at this devil. Noticed Tad was no longer in attendance. "I neeeeeeed it."

He took another step towards her son when the voice came.

"No, Dark Lord."

Lilly turned to the open door. A tiny woman was in the door. A horde of children clinging to her.

This devil or Dark Lord or whatever she just called him took another step towards Christopher.

"I said NO!" this tiny woman ordered, and she stepped into the room with the children clinging to her.

"But his heart," said the Dark Lord. "It's different from the others. Soooo wonderful."

The tiny woman shook her head. "But you are not the Dark Lord, John. You are detective John Mills and if you eat his heart, you can never leave here. Don't do it."

Lilly stood up. Every bone in her body ached and popped. She looked at the tiny woman who was sizing her up.

"How are you different?" the tiny woman said and now Lilly noticed how her forehead had two bloodied wounds. "Spiders?" she asked, head shaking. "Did they not get you?"

Lilly shook her head. "No. I saw what they did to the others and how they changed. I tried to help, but I couldn't. All I wanted to do was save my son." She gestured to Christopher and this tiny woman looked at him as the Dark Lord turned on his heels towards Lilly.

"No," screamed the tiny woman, and the Dark Lord stopped cold. She looked at Lilly. "We will need you to take the children through the vortex and bring them to safety. Can you do that?"

Lilly nodded as she continued to stare at the Dark Lord.

Dark Lord said, "Why her?" He turned to the tiny woman. "Are you not coming with us?"

The tiny woman shook her head. "I can't, detective. I am dead and my heart eaten by the Goddess. My eternity in this place has begun. There is no way for me to leave." She gestured towards Lilly and Lilly could see tears in the woman's eyes. "Come," she said. "Take your child."

Lilly cautiously stepped around the Dark Lord towards Christopher. "Why is he like this? Like he's not here." She wrapped her arms around him.

Tiny woman answered. "Because they drugged him. Confusion manifests fear in abundance and it is fear that they feed on."

Christopher was complacent, as if still unaware and mesmerized over current circumstance.

Dark Lord said, "If you're dead, does that mean I am too?"

He said this as if he were a child discovering for the first time the ills of the world, and when Lilly looked into his eyes, he seemed more like a frightened child than a demonic entity.

"I'm sorry, John, but yes, it is true. You cannot go back to your old life." This Dark Lord John was shaking his head, contemplating. "But you can help these children, John. You can defeat the Dark Lord and Emmanuelle and send them back here. You can find the light if you choose to but returning to your home, your wife, your daughter, your life..." She moved her head back and forth. "I'm sorry, John, but that hope was never meant to manifest."

Lilly saw blood tears fall from his eyes as madness and rage cemented across his face.

"They killed you, John. Make it right," said the tiny woman. "Save this woman and these children. Fight for your soul, detective. It's the last right you have." She paused before asking him, "Will you do this, John? Will you still fight knowing your cause has passed? We have to know John. The vortex is opening, and we must bring the children through. They will need you on the other side. They will need your strength to survive. Will you help them, John? Will you do this for them?"

Lilly watched as the Dark Lord was staring at the children, wide eyed and battling confusion behind his eyes.

"John?"

He nodded. "Yes," he said. "Yes, I will."

"Good John. Good." She looked at Lilly. "Let's get you all home."

16

2:43 AM
In the Hall Bathed in Light
Cassandra

She felt a hand lift her head before her eyes opened. Pain shot up her neck to her brain.

"Looks like a concussion. I don't know, I'm no doctor. Try to open your eyes."

Cassandra did just that, opened her eyes. Her head pounding in her skull, rattling off the bone and the light that rushed into her eyes caused the pain to strengthen. And as her eyes adjusted, she saw the man holding her in his arms. She'd never seen him before. He wore a baseball cap and she could see a ring of dried, crusted blood across his forehead, below the rim of the hat. And he smiled.

"You'll be okay," he said. "But you have to get up. Everything's about to pop out there and we need your help." Cassandra was trying to understand what he was saying, her head weary. His voice seemed like he was talking underwater, his words swimming to her ears. "I got all the gas turned on just like Jigglyspot said to do. And I got the children out too, most of them at least. And a way to transport them." He shook his head. "Fuckin' Pam, that bitch. All of them." He clenched his jaw, gritting his teeth. "We have to make sure Tyler doesn't turn. If he does, they'll win. And we can't allow that to happen. Do you understand? He doesn't deserve it. They've been manipulating him since the womb. He can't give in."

It hurt to move, but Cassandra gave a quick nod.

"Good," he said. "Make sure of it. And when it's done, be sure to hide because they will come looking for you." He helped her to her feet. Leaned her against the wall and for the first time since her eyes opened, Cassandra heard all the fighting and commotion coming from the room beyond the shattered door. He looked towards the room, then back to Cassandra. Stopped cold, looking down and bent over, grabbing something off the floor. He squeezed the box of matches into her hand. "No matter what, make sure this place blows sky high before three A.M."

Cassandra gripped the matches and nodded.

"Good." He turned towards the open door and walked towards it.

Cassandra was staring at the matchbox when she turned to him, head shaking. "Who are you?"

He turned to Cassandra and smiled, then turned around and stepped through the door, hollering over his shoulder, "I'm the reason this is all happening."

17

2:44 AM
The Ballroom
Jigglyspot

He felt heat across his skin from the Goddess's hellfire magic and thought for a brief second about how his clown makeup had to be fading to nothing. Either that or his makeup was burned permanently into his skin. He felt charred, his skin singed and growing hotter by the second. Goddess's magic erupted now into a hurricane wind; Emmanuelle's attempt to force the cane from Jiggly's hands.

His eyes felt like they were on fire, but he peeked through his narrow eyelids, his pupils burning. He twisted his grip on the cane and his protective shield strengthened under the hellfire magic.

This was a dance Jiggly knew he could not outlast. And he had to get close to Emmanuelle, had to put his hands on her, squeeze that gullet and send the bitch back to Xibalba. He had an idea on what Emmanuelle's logic was, get past three on the clock and take over, or, at the very least, secure a hold on the planet that would allow the Dark Lord and Emmanuelle to walk freely between Xibalba and Earth. Then we would see a war on Earth that stupid human scum couldn't possibly fathom in their puny little minds. Jiggly refused to allow Emmanuelle that privilege. She'd used him as a pawn, and he was not happy. His loyalty had always been to Mr. West, and always would be. Jiggly worshiped West and to honor his loyalty, West provided Jiggly with all the means necessary to carry out his insipid little desires. But that didn't translate into Jiggly getting off with a simple slap on the wrist should Emmanuelle and the Dark Lord have their way. This was a coup of cosmic proportions, and Jiggly could only hope he was on the winning side.

He had to get to Emmanuelle. Everything depended on his ability to strike down and take her out.

Now the magic subsided, eased up on the strength and power and Jiggly could hear the Goddess speak. "There's no way you can win Jigglyspot. You're too weak. Too pathetic. You always have been Jiggly, the little pathetic joke among us higher immortals."

Jiggly felt blood gush from his nose and ears. Tasted blood on his tongue too; the Goddess's magic was tearing him apart from the inside as if that black magic carried nuclear power that disintegrated his organs and skin. He struggled to breathe; continuing to hide within his protective shield he knew was wearing thin.

"Come on Jiggly," said Emmanuelle. "Is that all you have? The cane from West is you're only protection? Are you too afraid to face me without it?" He looked through his shield, saw how the Goddess had her fingers clenched in front of her, ready to unleash holy hell. Jiggly used the pause to twist the cane again, attempting to open a portal to the Goddess for a surprise attack. One twist, two twists, three, four and the Goddess unleashed holy hell. Jiggly gripped his cane tight to steady himself from the sheer force of Emmanuelle's magic. Felt his feet sliding back across the marble floor. His skin burning, melting the flesh off his bone. Turned his head around to shield his eyes from the brunt of the Goddess's impact. He could see how his clowns had their hands full. War was raging inside the ballroom. Apoch battling six masters at once, his other clowns tearing apart masters, most of them at least. He saw a few of his clowns lying dead on the ground and he gritted his teeth in a sorrowful and mourning gesture. His clowns had arrived to fight along with him, a gesture Jiggly took to heart, knowing his only real family still had his back and they've paid the ultimate price. He knew he will have to honor their loyalty. If he survives. And that kid Tyler, Jiggly could see him through the blood, carnage, and fighting across the ballroom. He saw how the Dark Lord used Tyler's friend as a shield, and Jiggly could see they were in a new dimension, understanding the Dark Lords play to separate Tyler from the fighting, to get him alone, a similar ploy Jiggly remembered had been done to him long ago.

Don't fall for it, thought Jiggly. Be done with it and tear them all apart. They want nothing for you and all for themselves.

The Goddess's magic eased and Jiggly used the moment to twist the cane. His hands singed and burning, he saw how his burnt flesh flaked off his hands. It hurt to twist, his skin cracking and tearing, and pain shot through his fingers.

"Oh Jiggly, we have a problem," hollered Emmanuelle. "So stupid Jiggly. You really believe anything you're told. Must be that human side of you. Zero intellect, right? Isn't that what you call them? Stupid Human Scum." And she laughed. Laughed as if Jiggly were nothing and she was in complete control. "And all this time, you were just the same. Stupid little man that you are." She was shaking her head and snarling. "You deserve total obliteration. I think I'll serve your heart to West. Personally shove it down his gullet."

Jiggly saw the magic spiral towards him. His eyes went wide as Jiggly looked over his cane. One last twist and he heard the click in the cane. "Got it," he said and disappeared. The ballroom now bathed in black and white, hurling winds and screeches coming from all directions. This was his path to the Goddess, a dimension existing on top of and beneath the third-dimensional reality. The place where evil travelled unseen in this world, courtesy of the power of the cane. He could walk among them without being seen. Jiggly held the cane in front of him as he pushed through the howling winds towards the Goddess.

Goddess released her magic, sweeping the room with her eyes. Jiggly forcing his way towards her through fierce winds igniting burning fires all around him.

"Jigglyspot," the Goddess raged. "Come out, come out wherever you are."

18

2:45 AM
A Familiar Scene from the Past
Tyler

It was as if the light had gone off. After Pam stepped in front of the
Dark Lord, the room had gone dark, bathed in darkness and silence.
Every sound had fallen silent except for Tyler's breath and the
rhythmic beating of his heart. Then, a light revealed a room as if
he'd been transported to another place. Another time.

Tyler was standing in James Reilly's living room, a gun gripped
in his hand, but not the gun that was flung from his grip by that
demon. No, the gun in his hand he knew all too well. It was the gun
he used to put a bullet in James Reilly. Alone. He heard a door open
with a creak and then close with a thud. His head snapped to the
sound, eyes narrowed. He craned his head towards the kitchen, felt
an eerie sensation tickle the nape of his neck. Shallow breathing, or
struggling to breathe, followed by a loud gasp and gurgling.

"What is this?" he whispered, looking around the room. He
remembered it intimately; Tyler had studied every inch of James
Reilly's house for years. But how he was here now, he wasn't sure.
Confusion. Is it a dream? A nightmare? What the hell is going on? A
sudden gong filled the room. Tyler remembered it, the grandfather
clock in the corner announcing the top of the hour. Tyler saw the
time on the clock. Four AM. Again, more gurgling, Tyler followed
the gurgle, knowing what to expect as he went into the kitchen. Low
and behold, James Reilly was there, at the kitchen table, duct taped
to the max, blood from beneath Reilly's clothes seeped past the duct
tape, dripping to the tile floor. But no Tyler. Or rather, no Tyler from
the past. This Tyler dismissed it; he must be here after the Tyler
from two weeks ago had left the house. James Reilly jumped in his

chair with a loud gurgling gasp of breath, his eyes wide. His face scrunched in a horrible wince of pain. Sucking in air as if through a straw. Still alive? Tyler thought. He had been sure James Reilly was dead before he left the house two weeks ago.

Wind in the house now, raging from the living room, swirling fierce like a tornado and converging in the kitchen across from Tyler. Lights flickered on and off as the Dark Lord manifested from within those howling winds. Tyler stepped back, back, back against the wall. The Dark Lord's eyes glowing red and glaring. Behind the Dark Lord, a door of darkness stood like a portal to another dimension. Tyler raised his gun and squeezed the trigger; unloading into the Dark Lord until *click, click, click* signaled an empty chamber. Dark Lord smiled at Tyler, brushing off his torso where the bullets had entered and disappeared.

"It's that fight we adore Tyler," said the Dark Lord. "So many only fantasize about taking life, but you... you, Tyler, are truly special." His voice quiet and almost gentle. "You take life without remorse. You kill indiscriminately. As do all who hold godly power. It is our right, for we are the pupils of yesteryear and the gods of tomorrow. Our evolution can't be stopped. *We* are the future's inevitability."

Gurgling from James Reilly. Tyler looked at him; saw the fear in his eyes, and the terror of death's finality.

Tyler turned to the Dark Lord. "What is this? Some sadistic, ritualistic indoctrination?" He shook his head. "I'm not into it." He looked around the room, trying to see past the walls and furniture.

I'm not in this place.

Dark Lord continued, "Come," he said, the order catching Tyler's attention. Dark Lord's arm stretched, gesturing towards the hall bathed in darkness. Tyler's eyes narrowed. All he could see was black until the outline of a face pressed against the darkness. Pam. Blonde hair blue eyed Pam. Tyler's Pam, his partner in murder, stepped out of the shadows. "Now we are whole. Our star-crossed lovers are in attendance."

"Lovers?" Tyler looked at Pam, then turned to the Dark Lord. "I don't know who you've been talking to, but we aren't lovers. Not even close. And it's quite obvious that what you've got here is a poor puppy looking for a golden bone to chew on." He gestured to Pam, then to the gurgling, gasping Reilly. "After this bag of shit got what he deserved, all she's looking for is another ticket to stardom." Tyler chewed the inside of his cheek. Shook his head and glared at the Dark Lord. "Is she even real?" He was looking around. "Or is this some sadistic kindergarten romper room type of shit? Share with your friend's bullshit." He breathed deeply. "No, I don't think so. I'm willing to bet this is all an illusion. None of it is real. We're still in that fuckin warehouse and you, ya son of a bitch..." He gestured to the Dark Lord. "Are about to die."

Dark Lord gritted his teeth. "My patience wears thin, Tyler. Even your precious Pam wants you to offer me the heart."

"I will not unleash slavery across humanity. That's fucking insane."

"But you can kill anyone you want because of what they did to you?" raged Pam.

Tyler shrugged with a sigh, staring at Pam. "Reilly was a piece of shit who would have caused more harm to people..."

Dark Lord interrupted, "So right you are Tyler. But you don't know the larger picture. Reilly was the replacement for Mr. West's most prized human. He would have unleashed hell on your people, seated at the right hand of West and in control of his minions. You were right to kill him. All the suffering you saved by taking his life. Which is why we want you with us, Tyler. To set everything right."

"By subjugating the rest of the world? I don't think so."

"You know as well as we do Tyler how small-minded humans are. They require order. They need to be told how to live."

"That's not up to you to decide."

"Enough of this." Pam, she stepped away from the darkness. "You..." She pointed to Tyler. "You owe me most of all. The hell you've put me through. I want what's mine. Give the Dark Lord Reilly's heart so I can find peace. I'm owed that much. You know what Reilly did to me. I want to know he'll spend the rest of eternity in hell. The fact that they set him up to take over the planet turns my stomach. Give him his heart, Tyler."

Tyler shook his head. "Not a chance, Pam. Reilly is dead, and that's a good thing, but a soul is eternal, and I'm not his judge in the afterlife."

"But you can judge him in this life?"

"It is what it is, Pam. Free choice and such. He fucked with me and I got my revenge. It's over. Reilly hurt people and would have hurt a shit ton more if I didn't do what I did. Looks like I made the right decision. I kill for the greater good."

"You kill because you love it," said the Dark Lord. "You kill because it is in your nature to take life. Because of the power murder provides. Do it again, Tyler. Do it for me and for the greater good. Offer me his heart and take your rightful place by our side. West will never be able to stop us. The game is chess, not checkers and this here, Tyler..." He gestured around the room. "You, Tyler, represent check mate. The only reason Reilly was the ravenous bastard he was is because of West. We can destroy him together."

Tyler was shaking his head. "You really need to look back at history, Dark Lord. Cut off one head and two more grow back. Please, I'll find this West myself if he's so bad and put a bullet in his head, but I'll never join you."

Dark Lord closed his eyes, breathing deeply, a growl in the back of his throat, and as he opened his eyes, that growl erupted with a sonic boom.

Tyler felt the Dark Lord's grip across his throat before he was aware the Dark Lord had moved. The back of his head crashed against the wall as pain jutted down his neck and spine. Dark Lord held Tyler off the floor by his throat, his lips so close, Tyler could smell the stank of his breath.

"Let's try this again, Tyler. Give me the heart."

One word squeezed off Tyler's lips. "Never," he said, "Never."

19

2:46 AM
Through the Vortex to the Other Side
SAC John Mills

He could taste hearts on his tongue, the sensation and hunger more powerful than he'd ever experienced. And that child they just saved, the scent of his heart was delectable, beating just for him. He wanted to punch a hole in the boy's chest, tear out his heart and drink blood from it as if that heart was a fountain of thirst-quenching water. He tried to push the thought from his mind as he stepped into the vortex. The others had gone first, the children and the mother, kids clinging to her, afraid of the Dark Lord Mills. He'd looked over his shoulder just before he stepped in. He saw Kera standing, watching. She was a brave little thing, Mills thought. Destined to live in hell forever.

"Remember who you are, John," Kera had said. "You're a good man, detective. No matter what you see or feel, keep that thought always and you will defeat the Dark Lord."

She smiled too. The little woman was destined to hell for eternity, and she was smiling. Her smile was the last image John saw before the vortex swallowed him and he stepped into the ballroom at the top of the stairs, where raging sounds of battle filled the ballroom. The mother and all the children huddled on top of the stairs, watching, looking, unknowing what to do.

The mother hollered over the sounds of carnage and mayhem, "Can you turn again?" John noticed how frightened the woman seemed, unsteady and untrusting. Was it him she didn't trust? John tried to remember what Kera had said. He looked at the boy, the mother's child, his eyes rolling in his head the same as the other children. Mills locked in on the boy's heartbeat. Had to peel his eyes away and try to forget, swallowing the lump in his throat. The mother asked again, "Can you change into smoke and distract them?"

John thought about her inquiry, snapping his focus on the heart.

She said, "Remember what Kera said. We have little time. Help me get them out."

John looked over at the children, then scanned the ballroom. He saw clowns devouring human beings. Masters is how Kera referred to them, demons incarnated inside human hosts. He knew they were dead already. There was no saving them. And the clowns? John was afraid of clowns, always had been. Now he understood why. Scary wasn't the right word. The clowns' mouths opened like pythons, their teeth sharp, tearing off heads with large gulps. He continued to scan, and found Kera's body, her mortal coil, on the ground in a pool of blood. John's heart sank seeing her like that. He gritted his teeth as anger boiled in his veins. He continued to scan the ballroom, finding...

"Me!" He saw himself choking the throat of a young man surrounded by a thick dark cloud that circled around them. Inside the circle he could see hurling winds tearing through what looked like a kitchen. His mouth opened, jaw loose, awestruck.

"John!" the mother hollered as the children screamed something awful. John snapped his head around. One master was climbing the stairs and John could see he meant harm to the children.

"Come now, little ones," said this master. "All the fun we will have."

But John just stood there, confused, when the mother kicked the master dead in the face. He fell backward and tumbled down the stairs as the mother pushed the children behind her. Now more masters found them. The clowns were not enough to stop them. The master down the stairs stood up, snarling.

"Get back," the mother told them. "Get down."

She huddled them against the wall as the master climbed the stairs, cautious this time.

"Careful now," said the master, climbing the stairs. "There's no need for concern. I'm just going to tear your flesh off your bones."

The mother stifled a scream and cry. John looked at her, saw the fear in her eyes as she looked at him, her eyes pleading, her stare anxious and frantic.

"It'll be okay," she lied to the children as the master stepped on the landing. Two more masters right behind him. "Close your eyes, babies. Don't look."

The master grabbed a handful of the mother's hair and yanked her off the floor. Her bloodied, battered, and bruised face looked frantically at John. The master's blade, the knife in his hand, slashing across the air towards her throat. John caught the master's hand just when the tip of the blade touched the mother's skin. His free hand wrapped around the nape of the master's neck, and the master's grip released the mother's hair. John glared at the master, squeezed his neck with such force the master's bones and spine cracked, popped, and splintered in his palm, the neck disintegrating within his scolding hand. His head dropped onto his shoulders then fell back, tumbling down the stairs, leaving a bloodied trail. The body, spouting blood from the open neck, dropped with a thud to its knees, then fell forward gushing blood like a river towards the screaming children. The two masters on the stairs stopped cold.

John turned to the mother with a snarl in the back of his throat. "Follow meeeeeee."

20

2:47 AM
The Ballroom
Lilly

She followed the Dark Lord with the children huddled as close to her as possible. She skidded down the stairs, watching as the Dark Lord tore every master to shreds. Lilly eyed an open doorway where she remembered she'd come through, but now the doors were torn apart. A lone woman stood in the doorway. Lilly remembered seeing her, the one with the spiders crawling from her womb.

And Lilly thought, If she doesn't let us through, she'll have to die. Lilly looked over at the Dark Lord. He was creating a clear path towards the spider crawling woman. She scanned the kids clinging to her, huddled close, whining, crying, screaming with their eyes clamped shut. The horrors they'd been through Lilly didn't want to think about. Couldn't think about. She just needed to get them out. End this nightmare and pick up the pieces after. Survival was the only thought on Lilly's mind.

21

2:48 AM
Standing in the doorway of the Ballroom
Cassandra

She watched as Jigglyspot disappeared. Saw how the guy who awakened her was walking cautiously and stealth towards a dark cloud, dodging masters and clowns, walking among them unseen and unscathed. She could see Tyler inside the dark cloud, and when she scanned the ballroom, she saw a mass of children huddled close to one of those masters. Where was she going with those kids? Cassandra thought.

And all the mayhem and chaos in the ballroom turned muted when Cassandra heard the voice of the Goddess, Sharon's voice. Cassandra scanned the back of the Goddess's head. Looked like Sharon and when the Goddess shifted, scanning the room in search of Jigglyspot, Cassandra confirmed her suspicions. She was indeed Sharon.

Sharon the Goddess.

Sharon, her roommate.

Sharon, who convinced Cassandra to cheat, lie, and steal her way into stardom. How was she here? How is she a goddess? A goddess with power? There was only one way that could be. Sharon had orchestrated Cassandra's capture, working with Ira the entire time. What else could explain the current circumstance? She looked at the box of matches in her hand, then turned to Sharon, gritting her teeth.

"No way," said Cassandra. She stuffed the matches into her cloak pocket. "No way she lives." And she stepped into the ballroom behind Sharon.

22

2:49 AM
The Reilly's Kitchen
Tyler

"Give me the heart, Tyler," seethed the Dark Lord. His grip was like iron. Tyler felt his windpipe crushing within the Dark Lord's grip. Felt his eyes roll to the back of his skull.

He heard Kera's voice, *Don't let the Dark Lord eat the heart.*

"Give him the heart," screamed Pam. "You owe me that much."

"See," said the Dark Lord. "Even your true love wants it done. Give the heart to me." Tyler felt the Dark Lord's hand squeeze the breath from his throat as his feet kicked empty air, his eyes rolling behind his eyelids, struggling to breathe. He stretched his fingers, wanting to use his newfound power, but the magic fizzled across his fingertips and died.

The Dark Lord laughed. "No such luck, Tyler," snickered the Dark Lord. "We giveth and then we taketh away. It is in our power to do so. Only when you stand with us will your power be forever." He tightened his grip around Tyler's throat and thrust the back of his head against the wall when Tyler winced, his face pinched in pain, the Dark Lord forcing his head into the wall and squeezing his throat with all the power in the universe. And Tyler could feel the breath dissipating from his lungs, his head on fire, his eyes bulging from his skull, struggling to breathe. Tyler nodded. "Good," said the Dark Lord, releasing his grip and Tyler collapsed to his knees as the Dark Lord turned zend stepped away. Tyler gasped for air, holding his throat.

"Really Tyler, we have little time. Offer me the heart and all this carnage will be done."

Tyler raised his head, staring at the Dark Lord standing over him. Dark Lord raised his chin. "Offer the heart, Tyler. The time has come."

Tyler touched his pocket. He felt the heart, noticed it was beating inside his pocket. His throat was dry and burning, eyes wet with tears. He took the heart from his pocket and yes, it was beating in his hand.

"Yes, Tyler. Offer me the heart."

Whatever you do, Tyler, don't let him eat the heart.

Tyler cradled the heart close to his chest. He looked at Pam, standing; her stare burrowing into his soul, filled with hate. Scanned the room and saw how the room glimmered around them and within that glimmer Tyler could see the ballroom. Staring at the Dark Lord, he saw that glimmer again and a guy wearing a baseball cap sneaking up behind the Dark Lord. And Tyler smiled. Started laughing, laughing uncontrollably.

Pam said, "What the hell is so funny?"

Tyler said, "Fuck off, assholes. You'll never get this heart from me."

He scanned the room, Pam, the dead Reilly, and the Dark Lord, and felt a click in his stomach. Felt their anger and disbelief. Couldn't help himself. All he could do was laugh.

Dark Lord said, "So be it... Tyler," and rushed towards him.

23

2:50 AM
The Ballroom
Sharon the Goddess

She scanned the ballroom. Jigglyspot was using the cane, the magic that allowed the recipient to walk unseen by the third-dimensional eye. She could not see him; she had to feel her way through to him. Electricity sparked off her fingertips, her magic begging to be used. Tried not to focus on the fact that her masters were being used as food for those insipid clowns, nor how the Dark Lord was about to take the warlock to Xibalba for eternity when she felt wind across her cheek. Close to her now. Sharon reached out-her reflexes like a cat-and took hold of Jigglyspot's throat and watched as the fifth dimension spit the clown into her hand.

"There you are, Jiggly," said the Goddess. "I was thinking you tucked tail and ran."

Jiggly's eyes bulged from his skull. Sharon's grip was like a locked vise around his windpipe.

Jiggly managed to squeeze across his lips, "Mind your back, Goddess."

Sharon stared wild-eyed at Jiggly, confused, when she felt someone wrap their arm around her throat and squeeze, yanking her head back.

A voice in her ear, "Hi Sharon, care for a little girl talk. Just between us friends."

24

2:51 AM
The Ballroom
Lilly

Lilly hurried the children across the ballroom. The Dark Lord John was tearing apart masters, parents who had brought their children for thrills and chills at the carnival, now possessed by creatures from hell. Parents of the children that clung to her waist as if she were the last lifeline in the universe. Lilly led them towards the hallway, towards the busted doors and on the heels of the Dark Lord when he stopped cold and turned, staring across the ballroom, a confused stare plastered across his face. Lilly looked over at what had stalled the Dark Lord, the children clinging to her waist, screaming, hollering, and squeezing her ribcage, their little hands strong with fear. She saw the Dark Lord across the ballroom within a cloud of hurling winds. Two Dark Lords, they looked identical.

Dark Lord beside her whispered, "He's going to give him the heart."

Lilly cringed as a master lunged towards her, but John caught the master by his throat before he could reach her and snapped the man's neck in his hand. The possessing demon rushed from the host as the body dropped to the floor. The demon screeching and yipping above them, the children screaming, hollering, and clawing at Lilly, and with a sudden puff and poof of air, the demon was gone. Lilly's heart jumped in her chest. She clung to the children and rushed them towards the hallway as Dark Lord John continued to stand and stare, unmoving. The spider crawling female was no longer in the hall guarding the entrance. Lilly rushed the children into the hallway, their feet trampling across wooden debris. Brought them through the door at the end of the hall, into a dining room where they rushed past table after table to the entrance, bolting through the front door into the hot dark of early morning.

25

2:52 AM
The Ballroom
SAC John Mills

He froze when he saw himself across the ballroom. His first thought was that he could live again if he reclaimed his mortal coil.

You're dead John, there is no going back.

Kera's words rattled in his skull as if she were talking to him from the far reaches of hell and damnation. *Don't eat any hearts.* But that kid is about to offer the heart to the Dark Lord. To him, SAC John Mills. Or the other Mills. What happens if *he* eats the heart?

Kera's voice erupted in the center of his mind: "You'll be locked in Xibalba for eternity."

And that, John thought, he could not allow.

His attention snapped by a man wearing a baseball cap, stepping cautiously into the gray smoky clouds. Behind the Dark Lord. His heart beating like a rabbit thumping in his chest, scared to all bloody hell. And who is the teenager standing around the one with the heart? Mills could feel her heat, anger, and rage. He could read her vibration and, in doing so, understood her intention. *She is on the side of the Dark Lord.* The boy needed help and before Mills could blink, he was a tornado of smoke barreling towards them.

26

2:53 AM
The Ballroom
Jigglyspot

His throat felt like it was about to pop inside the Goddess' grip.
Jiggly had seen the female walking behind Emmanuelle, her
intention obvious to Jiggly. When she gripped Emmanuelle's throat,
Jiggly used the moment to his benefit. He pulled the hidden blade
from the cane and sliced across Emmanuelle's stomach, swiftly
inserting the blade back into the cane in one fell swoop, then
dropping the cane by his feet. At first, he thought his cut wasn't deep
enough. A thin line of blood seeped across her stomach, soaking
Emmanuelle's cloak. Her face pinched, gritting her teeth, as a
painful groan choked her throat and Jiggly gripped her jaw and
squeezed.

"Excuse me Goddess," said Jigglyspot. "I must retrieve
something for a friend." Jiggly buried his hand in Emmanuelle's
belly as the Goddess's teeth clenched and her jaw tightened. His
little fingers took hold of the Goddess's stomach, pulled it from her
belly and yanked it out, raising the stomach to Emmanuelle's eyes.
"Before you die, Goddess, I need this heart." Emmanuelle's
intestines spilled across the floor as a low whining groan rose from
the bottom of her throat. Jiggly looked over Emmanuelle's shoulder
at the female with her arms wrapped around Emmanuelle's neck.
"You may want to let go now." The girl's eyes went wide. "This won't
be pretty." And Jiggly smiled, stepping away from the Goddess.
More blood dropped from the stomach, pooling beneath her as that
groan erupted over her lips, reaching a fever screech and wail. The
blood was lava hot, hissing as it hit the floor in a flood from
Emmanuelle's stomach, eating away at the marble and burning her
feet that disintegrated and melted into the hot lava blood. The

Goddess wretched and screamed, her head whipping from side to side as the female on her back stepped away from the blood. Emmanuelle's legs disintegrated into the pool of blood and intestines, her scream whistled like the beginning of a sonic boom. She started screaming, "I can't believe it. You killed me, Jigglyspot. OH what a universe. What a universe." Her legs gone, her torso dropped to the floor, melting, the pool beneath her growing, spreading. "I'll be back Jiggly. Oh, you can't do this to me." Her eyes burning with blood dripping down her cheeks. "If it takes an eternity, I'll be back for you." Her voice screeching, yipping, yawping. Down to her neck now, melting into that bloodied pool. "I hate you Jigglyspot. I hate you always."

One final scream erupted from her throat before her mouth disintegrated, her eyes raging with hellfire, staring at Jigglyspot.

"It's okay, Goddess," said Jiggly. "Go to heaven."

Down to her forehead now, and her hair caught fire, burning bright then smoldering quickly, leaving nothing more than a pool of melted skin, bone, blood, and disintegrating organs. The blood now smoldering, a wretched stench lifted in the air as the blood cooled and solidified across the ground into large broken chunks likened to lava rocks. Jiggly looked down to the stomach in his hands and went to town, tearing the organ between his teeth and swallowing large chunks of stomach. His eyes closed when he bit into Kera's heart, then swallowed the heart pieces with a prideful satisfaction. I release you, Kera, he thought. Go to the next life, my lady. He swallowed the last chunk, then bellowed a belch across the ballroom. Jiggly looked at the female when the ballroom rattled; the walls shook with a sonic boom as if something were attempting to get in. Another sonic boom and Jiggly said, "I hope you got the gas on."

27

2:54 AM
The Reilly's Kitchen
Tyler

The Dark Lord rushed at him, took him by the throat once again, and squeezed the air from his gullet.

"Kill him," said Pam.

"Give me the heart, Tyler, this is your last chance," growled the Dark Lord.

Tyler cradled the heart. If it was the last thing he ever did, he refused to offer the heart to the Dark Lord. "Never," muttered Tyler, thrashing against the Dark Lord's grip, his feet kicking air.

Dark Lord said, "Then I'll take your heart and feast upon it for all eternity."

Dark Lord reached his free arm back, ready to drive his fist into Tyler's chest when Pam said, "What is this smoke?"

Dark Lord froze, his eyes scanning around them. Tyler saw smoke slithering around Pam and a man in a baseball cap walking behind the Dark Lord, coming from out of the shadows, stepping into Reilly's house from the ballroom.

When Tyler looked at Pam, her eyes were bleeding. "Someone turned off the lights," she whispered, and Tyler could see how her cloak became soaked with blood.

Dark Lord said, "You die now," and thrust his fist towards Tyler, but the baseball cap wearing man drove a butcher knife into the back of the Dark Lord. Tyler watched as the tip of the blade tore through the Dark Lord's chest. His arm dropped to his side, his hand on Tyler's throat slid off, and Tyler collapsed to the kitchen floor. He looked up, gasping for air, and saw how Pam's skin split and tore into shreds, falling dead in a pool of her own blood. Dark Lord stood frozen, staring at the tip of the blade protruding from his chest. Blood dripped down his stomach, a disbelieving stare in his eyes. He turned around, said, "Who are you?" when Tyler dropped the heart, jumped up, thrust the knife from the Dark Lord's back, then slammed it in again, collapsing to the ground, exhausted. Dark Lord fell to his knees, then dropped on his back, and the knife punched out of his skin, tearing a gaping hole in the Dark Lord's chest.

Tyler saw smoke slither around the body, entering through the nose.

"I'm the one whose heart you've been trying to eat," said the baseball cap man.

Tyler looked at him, said, "Reilly?" in a hushed gasp.

The answer he was looking for interrupted by a loud sonic boom and quickly, the Reilly house dissipated, and Tyler was back in the ballroom.

28

2:55 AM
Outside the Cannibal Cafe
Lilly

There was a bus waiting outside the entrance. Lilly stopped cold on top of the staircase when she saw it. The children stumbled into her, but she regained her balance before tumbling down the steps.

The white bus, old and rusted, stood idling in front of the building. Lilly wasn't sure if the windows were tinted or just covered in muck and dirt, but she was certain there were kids on that bus; little heads were looking through the dirty windows. The bus door opened with a creaking suctioned slap and Ms. Finicky rushed from the bus to Lilly's surprise, remembering how the little clown and his minions had taken her from the cages, an event that seemed like a lifetime ago.

Finicky looked like she'd seen better days, her hair nappy, her skin moist with sweat, makeup smeared across her face. She seemed out of breath. "Come on," she hollered. Finicky looked at Lilly as if Lilly were insane, just standing, not moving. "We've been waiting for you. We have to get out of here, and fast. This whole place is going to blow sky high."

Lilly shook her head. She turned to the children. "Let's go," she ordered and together they all ran down the stairs towards the bus. Finicky helped the children on, Lilly at the back of the line.

"Wear your seatbelts," said Finicky.

"How did you get out?" Lilly was staring at Finicky. Something felt off about her.

Finicky said, "We were standing out here for the longest time not knowing where we were. A few of the older kids went to try to find help and then some guy in a baseball cap drove this bus to us.

He said to take it and drive the children away." Lilly watched as, one by one, the children hurried onto the bus. She could see their heads finding empty seats. "He said there were more children coming and at three o'clock the building will explode but to wait for all of you." She shook her head. "I don't know how he knew, but he said to drive off at five minutes to three if you didn't come. We were about to leave when we saw you."

Lilly noticed Christopher was staring at Finicky. He turned to his mother, his eyes spiraling in their sockets. "It'll be okay," said Lilly. "We're getting out of here." He pushed himself against her body, into her arms, trembling from head to toe. "It'll be okay," she repeated, squeezing him tight in her arms.

"Come on Christopher." Finicky was staring at Christopher with wide eyes, her mouth ajar. The stare sent a shiver down Lilly's spine. Her stare anticipatory and Lilly could feel how her bones tensed. "I know it's been a downright nightmare, but we'll get away. It's all over now."

The last child in line stepped onto the bus and Lilly looked at Finicky. She seemed rather calm, and her eyes looked different, her right eye at least. Looked like a dark spot had formed in the corner of her pupil. Lilly had to force her eyes away from staring at the dark spot. Thought that if she stared for too long, she'd fall right in.

"We need to go, and we need to go now."

Lilly nodded, took Christopher by the hand, and led him reluctantly onto the bus. "Do you know how to drive this thing?"

Finicky was behind them. She shut the door when Lilly and Christopher squeezed themselves into the front seat. Finicky sat behind the wheel. "Yes, I've driven them before." She put the bus in gear. "Hold on everyone."

The bus leapt forward and stopped with a jolt and a collective scream and hush from the passengers. Finicky ground the gears. "Sorry," she said, "My fault." And the bus jumped forward, racing through the parking lot.

29

2:56 AM
Back in the Ballroom
Tyler

He couldn't be certain, but he was sure the man with the baseball cap was James Reilly. The Dark Lord coughed, choking on his own blood. Tyler watched as smoke slithered into his ears and nose and mouth.

Another loud sonic boom rattled the ballroom. Cassandra behind Tyler, her arms under his, helping him up. "Come on," she said. "We have to go."

Tyler lifted to his feet, staring at the baseball cap guy who did nothing more than stare at Tyler. The Dark Lord was choking and when Tyler looked at him, his face was different. He seemed human.

"Ah detective Mills," said the clown Jigglyspot, holding a red cane. Tyler noticed the clowns surrounding them. Scanned the ballroom and all the masters lying dead on the blood-soaked ground. A few clowns too. Noticed the colossal clown was standing behind them. Jigglyspot was standing over the Dark Lord. He took his hand, crouching beside him. "It's okay detective, our time in this life has come to an end." The Dark Lord Mills stared wild-eyed at Jigglyspot.

"Are the children safe?" he asked through a garbled guffaw of blood.

"Yes," Cassandra replied. "I saw them leave."

Baseball cap guy said, "Good, then they got on the bus. They should be far away by now."

Seemed to Tyler that everyone paused and looked at the baseball cap guy.

Mills stuttered, "My wife? My daughter?"

Jigglyspot took a knee beside Mills. "You will see them soon enough, detective." Put his hand on John's forehead. "Sleep now John. Let the afterlife take you. You've done well."

Tears in the detective's eyes. He let out one last stuttering cough and gurgle before his eyes closed.

"Goodbye detective. Take care of Kera, please," said Jigglyspot. He arched his back, standing up, staring at the baseball cap guy. "Helmsley?" He shook his head. "I've been looking all over for you."

"Helmsley?" said Tyler.

Helmsley baseball cap guy Reilly looked at Jigglyspot, shaking his head. "Not Helmsley, Reilly. James Reilly. And you, ya son of a bitch, are a sick fuck. What did you do to this guy Helmsley? His brain was like pea soup when I got in. Just before his light went out too, but I got stuck in his brain. It took a long time to get a clear thought going, so I hid for a while." He rolled his eyes while shaking his head. "Now that was a lesson in patience if there ever was one."

Tyler said, "So you are Reilly?"

Reilly Helmsley looked at him, nodding. "Yes Tyler. I had to make sure you wouldn't offer my heart. It was the moment of your redemption. See, I told you something was coming."

"A warning would have been nice. Fucking spiders crawling out of people, demonic rituals, pedophiles, cannibals. I mean, really Reilly, a little warning next time, please."

Reilly laughed. "You wouldn't have believed me if I told you."

Another loud sonic boom and everyone in the room shook.

Jigglyspot said as he looked around the room. "We need to go."

"Besides, I couldn't," continued Reilly. "Some strange cosmic law prevented me from telling you the truth. I had to allow you to decide on your own. Free will type of shit. But Pam and the others, Tyler, I have to tell you." He was shaking his head. "They've been against you since the beginning. Pam called the police on you, Tyler. They arrived minutes after you left that morning. They're on to you too, but that's beside the point. The cops when they arrived, I was still alive, and I was given a choice..." He paused, seemed as if he were looking for answers, his brow scrunched, eyes staring into the far reaches of thought and revelation. "By God, I think. I could have lived, but God showed me the life I would lead, and I didn't want it. You killing me really put things into perspective. How much of an ass I've always been and the torture I would have caused to so many people working for that West guy. I couldn't do it, so I decided to become a ghost and start over in some other life, but I had to help you first because it wasn't fair. Those things Pam told you I did to her never happened, Tyler. It was all a sham. Don't get me wrong, I bagged that bitch hard and then she tried to blackmail me into using my parents to launch her career and when I refused, she lied to you about what happened. She's been working for the Dark Lord and the Goddess since birth. She's always been on their side. Part of some ancient demonic rivalry or something like that. Anyway, it's over now, but you still need to be careful. That West guy's fucking insane and he'll come looking for you. You're too valuable for him not to."

Jigglyspot asked, "Is West here?"

Another sonic boom.

"Yes. At least he was here. His limo is no longer outside, so I assume he's gone." Reilly looked across the ballroom, then to Cassandra. "Do you have those matches?"

Cassandra pushed her hand into her cloak pocket and emerged with the box of matches. "Yes."

"Good," said Reilly. "You need to get out of here. There's only minutes left and I've got to blow this building before…"

BOOOM!

The ballroom shook.

Jigglyspot completed Reilly's statement. "Before the Goddess and Dark Lord come through the vortex." He looked at Tyler and Cassandra.

Cassandra handed Reilly the matches as Jigglyspot walked away. Tyler still watching Reilly. He couldn't take his eyes off him.

Jigglyspot hollered, "Come, my clowns. It is time for us to leave." He knelt beside Kera's body.

Cassandra said, "What are you doing?"

"Relax, my lady, I only mean to rescue some friends."

When he rose to his feet, Tyler could see he was holding Kera's tentacles. They seemed frightened and angry and rushed into his front shirt pocket. He slammed his cane on the marble. "Clowns gather around. We leave now. No mop bucket in the universe can clean this place after it blows." And his clowns did just that, circling around Jigglyspot, who eyeballed Tyler and Cassandra through their bodies. "And I suggest the two of you leave as soon as possible. The sonic boom that'll happen when this place blows will be catastrophic. And..." He paused, glaring at them. "West will request for you to be found. Probably by me too." He smiled. His smeared, ruined makeup cracked across his face. "I suggest you do all you can to not be found." He twisted the top on his cane and a slithering grey smoke circled him and his clowns, enveloping them. When the smoke dissipated, they were gone.

Tyler said to Reilly, "Are you sure you want to do this?"

Reilly laughed. "Of course, this is my redemption." And he smiled. "Take off Tyler. Run and hide. I'll wait as long as I can before lighting this match." He raised the match to his eyes.

"You're my hero Reilly," said Tyler.

Cassandra was tugging on his shirt.

"I know," said Reilly with a smile. "Now GO!" he hollered as another sonic boom shook the room. Part of the wall cracked and crashed to the floor.

"Come on," screamed Cassandra. "It's falling apart."

Tyler heard a growl erupt beyond the walls, followed by another sonic boom and more walls crumbling. He took off running with Cassandra. Through the hallway into the dining room and out the front door, down the stairs and into the empty parking lot. Running. Running. Running. Heavy breath.

"Keep running!" Tyler hollered.

30

2:59 AM
Through the Vortex
Sharon

She made it through the vortex into the ballroom on top of the stairs. Sharon felt weak and weary as she stumbled down the steps. Thought that someone else was in charge of her body, trying to take over in a hurried panic. She saw a man with a baseball cap standing in the center of the room within a throng of dead bodies around him. A box in his hand, in the other a match.

"Well Goddess, good to see you here."

Sharon froze, watching the man, and felt something inside her screaming. She could feel it swarming inside her stomach, yipping to get out. Sharon heard a growl erupt in the back of her throat that she was certain did not come from her. She'd never been so frightened, and she tried to push the growl back. Felt her face wince and contract. Her stomach boiling with rage and heat, and she coughed blood and green bile from her throat.

"That's nasty," said baseball cap man.

Sharon collapsed to her knees, felt blood and vomit on her lips and chin. She looked at the man, said, "Please... help me."

To which the man responded, "I am," and struck the match on the back of the box.

Part VII
The After Party

1

7:30 PM
August 9, 2019
Los Angeles, CA
Lilly

She set the dinner table. Lilly used candles this time because she thought it would be a pleasant touch. Beyond her windows, the sun was setting with a glorious orange and pink horizon. Lilly struck a match and lit the candle in the center of the table. She used her best china, wanting everything to be perfect. Lilly watched the match, the flame fluttering in the wind before she blew it out, watching the smoke rise and dissipate in midair.

"Christopher," she called, but when she looked to the stairs, he was already walking down, dressed pristine, his hair combed back and gelled to perfection. He was wearing his suit, the same suit he'd worn to his father's funeral. Lilly thought it was miraculous how his cheek had healed so quickly from Kevin's burn, but her eye remained swollen and shut and all her wounds refused to heal. Deformed, that's what Lilly believed. Deformed for the rest of her days.

"Is everything set out perfectly?" He took the last step down, holding the bannister, staring at Lilly, whose hands trembled in his presence.

"Yes," Lilly said. "Where is Sam?"

Christopher crossed the room. "Getting ready. He'll be down in a minute." He was staring at Lilly as he walked to the table. "You look ravishing."

Lilly felt her face blush. She was wearing a cocktail dress, all black with gems across the neckline. Her hair raised above the shoulders. She never had her hair so short, but Christopher insisted. He preferred short hair.

"Thank you. You look amazing too."

Christopher never responded, his eyes on the fork beside the plate at the head of the table. "This fork is dirty. Get a new one."

Lilly cleared her throat. "So sorry." She took the fork to the kitchen when the doorbell rang.

Christopher said, "That must be her. I'll get it."

Lilly didn't respond. She took a fork from a drawer and checked it for cleanliness when she heard the door open. Christopher was making small talk and when Lilly heard the woman's voice, her heart skipped a few beats. Christopher was showing her the office they'd renovated a few weeks ago. No longer was it Lilly's office for blogging efforts. Now the room served a new purpose for ritual and indoctrination.

She saw Sam on the bottom step when she returned to the dining room. He looked like he was trembling. Lilly placed the new fork on the table, setting it down perfectly.

"Come Sam. Sit down. Dinner is just about ready."

Sam did as he was told. Lilly knew that if he didn't, Christopher would scold and punish him, and she was relieved Sam didn't put up a fuss and fight. She watched as he took his seat. Lilly tried to listen to what Christopher was telling their guest, but Lilly had no comprehension of the language they were using. They were speaking in tongues, a common occurrence with Christopher these days. All those late-night phone calls he'd been receiving were always in the same language. She could hear their footsteps tapping the tile floor as they walked to the dining room. Lilly's heart skipped a few more beats.

"Good evening Ms. Finicky," said Lilly when she noticed the extra guest beside Finicky. Jenny wore a floral dress, her hair braided in pigtails. "You look so beautiful, Jenny. I didn't know you were coming." Lilly passed a nervous stare over Finicky.

"Well, I couldn't leave her out of tonight's festivities. And her father was all too eager to get her out of the house," said Finicky.

She gestured to the seat across the table. "Sit, Jenny. Have something to eat."

Jenny looked at Ms. Finicky-she was also trembling-then went to the seat beside Lilly and sat down, taking her napkin from the table and folding it across her lap.

"Good," said Finicky. "Don't look so nervous Jenny, you've been through this before." She looked at Lilly. "Where do you want me to sit?"

Lilly forced a smile across her lips. "Christopher sits at the head of the table. Ms. Finicky can sit on his right side." Her voice was shaky, her tone nervous.

"Oh wonderful," said Finicky.

"Thank you, Lilly," said Christopher as he took his seat. Finicky waited for him to sit before sitting herself. Lilly went to the kitchen.

"What masterpiece have you prepared for us tonight, Lilly?" asked Finicky as she placed her napkin over her lap.

"It's delightful," said Lilly. "A rare meat made just for the occasion."

"Wonderful," said Finicky.

Lilly looked over as Christopher and Ms. Finicky began talking in tongues again. Sam and Jenny sat motionless, staring forward as they talked. Lilly took the tray of meat and potatoes off the counter and walked to the table. She served Christopher first, as was customary these days. Some nights, she and Sam had to wait for him to finish his meal before they could eat. Christopher enjoyed it when all their attention was on him.

"Thank you, Lilly." Christopher never looked at her, holding his glass between his fingers, staring at the red liquid Lilly had poured earlier that evening. He took a sip, then placed the glass gently on the table.

"You're welcome. Enjoy your dinner."

And when she turned to Ms. Finicky her hand shook, and she dropped the serving spoon.

"What could be wrong?" Christopher scolded. "Your hand giving you problems now?"

Lilly picked up the spoon. She laughed nervously. "Nothing at all," she said. She retrieved a new spoon from the kitchen and returned to serve Ms. Finicky.

"Seriously Lilly," said Finicky, staring at Lilly with a watchful and skeptical stare. "You're as nervous as a long-tailed cat in a room full of rocking chairs." And she laughed. Christopher laughed too. "Spit it out Lilly. What's gotten into you?"

"It's nothing," Lilly blurted. "It's just that…"

"Oh, c'mon lady," said Christopher. "Say what it is."

Lilly felt fear constrict her throat and stifle her voice. She pursed her lips and swallowed. Scooped a portion of rare meat off the serving tray, and, as she served Finicky, her trembling lips uttered, "It's just that I never noticed that you and Christopher have the same birthmark." Lilly tried not to look at them, knowing they were both looking at her. "I've never seen two people with the same image of a goat on their neck."

2

8:00 PM
Somewhere in Mexico
Tyler

Tyler burst through the door of their rented room. Streams of sweat across his soot covered and tanned face.

"Cassie," he called. Tyler dropped his backpack on the green tattered bedspread. Everything about the room screamed low life. From the decades old rug someone had decided was better than a linoleum floor to the chest of drawers with two missing drawers to the dollar store painting with a crack in the glass of an old fisherman and a boy sitting in a rowboat and the cracked paint turned yellow from decades of cigarette smoke.

"In here," Cassie called from the bathroom.

"Perfect." Tyler went to the bathroom, opening the door. Cassie stood in front of the mirror in a towel, her skin moist from the shower. "I think I found it," he said in a hurried, although excited tone. "It's an old map I found in a box at the library. So strange," he said. "It's as if it was left there for me to find."

Cassie scrunched her brow. "That's a little farfetched, don't you think?"

"C'mon Cassie, this is how things are found, little breadcrumbs left over the years that lead to the castle."

"Or ballroom," Cassie blurted.

"Or ballroom," Tyler repeated. "Come, take a look." Tyler went to the bed, unzipped his backpack, and retrieved a map, spreading it out on the bed. Cassie walked up next to him, and Tyler pointed to the map. "They've been looking in the wrong place." The map showed a string of islands off the coast of Mexico. He pointed to the larger island. "This is where they're looking. The same island that's been on the news. But see…" He pointed to a smaller island to the east of the larger one. "See how it's dotted red? Makes sense, doesn't it? Everyone knows about the larger island, so why would they keep everyone there? It's this small island where the breeding is taking place, off the coast and off the radar." He reached into his backpack again, retrieved a second map, and spread it out over the first. It was an exact replica, with one exception. "See, the little island isn't on this map. It's only on the older one, before someone needed to make the island invisible."

Cassie rolled her tongue inside her mouth, nodding.

"Makes sense right?" Tyler said, hoping for approval from Cassie.

"You did well, Tyler. I think you got it."

"Yes," said Tyler triumphantly.

"So, what do we do now?"

Tyler sat on the bed. "Simple," he said,

"We find the island."

3

Under the cover of the early morning darkness
August 10, 2019
New York City
Jigglyspot

The cane's smoke slithered across Jigglyspot. He clutched the plastic bag in his fist. The contents were heavy, and he used all his strength to pull it through the vortex into the jail cell. Jigglyspot arrived in the cell through the concrete wall. The body he was dragging came through and he slid it across the room when MysterE shot up from his cell cot.

"Ah, Jiggs. You scared the shit outta me."

Jiggly stretched his back, standing tall. "A good scare keeps us on our toes, MysterE."

MysterE shook his head. "That it does," he said and stood up.

Jigglyspot bent down, resting his cane on the floor. "Help me pull the body out," he said, unzipping the bag from the head to the toes.

"Holy shit does that look like me. Fuckin weird."

"Truth be told. It took the surgeon days to get your face right. Longer to find the perfect body style and blood type."

MysterE was rubbing his stubbly chin and nodding. "Spot on work. I'll have to applaud the surgeon when I see him." He looked at Jigglyspot. "What do you need me to do?"

"Pull the bag down. I'll hold the body."

"Okay," said MysterE and they did just that, pulled the body out of the bag. "What should I do with this?" he asked, crumbling the bag in his hands.

Jigglyspot looked at him. "Keep it. We'll bring it with us." He looked through the cell bars, the hall dark and quiet. "Where are the guards?"

MysterE said, "Ah, sleeping." And he laughed. "At least, pretending to sleep."

"Good," said Jiggly, and he used all his strength to pull the body closer to the bed, propping up the back and head against the bedpost. He took the bed sheet and tied it around the neck, then tied the other end to the bedpost, pulling the knot as tight as his little hands could manage. He looked at MysterE. "See that? It's perfect."

"Think they'll figure it out?"

Jiggly shrugged. "Doesn't matter. Humans, treat em like mushrooms…"

"Feed em shit and keep em in the dark."

"Exactly." Jiggly bent over and grabbed his cane off the floor. "Are you ready to go?"

Hesitation from MysterE. "Do I really have to go to Xibalba? There's so many planets I can go to. Why Xibalba? It's so big and there's so many countries. I may get lost in the sauce."

Jigglyspot looked at him with a noxious stare. "It's what West wants. But there's no need to be concerned, MysterE. You'll be a king in Xibalba. Plus, West wants you to take up arms against the Dark Lord and Emmanuelle. Seems they're up to their shenanigans again. They never stop those two."

"Never will." MysterE clucked his tongue and nodded.

"Are you ready?"

Kept nodding and after a moment he said, "Yeah." Then a moment later, "Yeah, let's do this."

Jigglyspot smiled as he tapped his cane on the ground. Two taps and then he twisted the cap, left, then right, then left again, and smoke slithered from the cane surrounding him and MysterE when the portal opened on the wall where Jiggly had entered the cell. On the other side of the portal was hell and damnation. Xibalba waited for them with screams and screeches and fires erupting from lakes of lava. Jigglyspot and MysterE walked towards hell.

"One last step, MysterE, and we're home. Both of us free from bondage. You a king and me a free bird." And he smiled, feeling his makeup crinkle close to his eyes. MysterE tossed the body bag into hell. They watched as the plastic disintegrated.

MysterE said, "That's great, Jiggs. And it's all because Kera helped Mr. West keep his hold. That's awesome. What do you think you'll do now?"

"I'm not sure. I've never had freedom before, but I will say one thing is certain."

"What's that, Jiggs?" MysterE was staring into Xibalba.

"Well, I'm definitely not staying around this planet. West is in a fury. It's only a matter of time until he unleashes holy hell on earth. And he's got the plan to do it too. Mass hysteria and fear are his best ally and he's got a plan to recondition the population, dumb them down and get them walking in a straight line. A straight line into subjugation. I'd rather be on another star when that happens. A good vacation sounds just about right."

"Got it. Well, with all that's been going on lately, it's only a matter of time until the humans realize the truth. I'll tell you what, though, that conspiracy theory excuse is the perfect deflection. Glad the CIA came up with the term. When was that? Like, sixty years ago?" And he laughed out loud. "Fuckin' brilliant move, too. Works like a charm. You can bring them into one of our ceremonies and they still wouldn't believe it. I mean, what do you have to do, hit people over the head with a pedophilia ring that reaches to the highest of highs in political and entertainment society to make them see the truth? Too funny, right? If you think about it, with all the sex trades and trafficking going on in the world, you'd think such a story would really slap em across the face."

Jiggly laughed too. "Zero intellect remember? It's our greatest asset."

"Yeah, but you know why they're like that, Jiggs. Eventually, the frequency surrounding the planet will be gone, and then Mr. West will have a real problem. Everyone else on the planet, too. It's inevitable. He's got to unleash complete subjugation before then. I mean, how long can the one percent keep the rest of the population under their thumb once the truth is revealed? Not long, that's for sure."

"It's been thousands of years, MysterE. I think we can hold it a little longer. Plus, that's something West wants to avoid. It's a war is what it is, even at the most subliminal level, and the more knowledge he has over them, the better for his cause."

MysterE thought for a long while before he said, "Jigglyspot and the Zero Intellect," as he nodded and rubbed his stubble chin. "Great title for a movie."

"Indeed," said Jiggly. "But I'm more of a book guy myself." They stared into the vastness of Xibalba in silent contemplation, and Jigglyspot knew he would not see his friend for a very long time. "You know, MysterE, now that this ordeal is over, there's just one thing I've been dying to do."

"What would that be, Jiggs?" MysterE nervously stepped across the threshold into Xibalba. "What do you need?"

"Ahh," complained Jiggly, closing the door on his friend as the smoke returned to his cane. He knew MysterE could hear him; he was still that close. "After all this," he said, "I could use a good extraction."

Wondering About Mr. West

Read the horror novel, *Golem.*
You'll definitely find out who Mr. West is.

https://pdalleva.com/product/golem

More From PD Alleva

<u>Horror and Dark Fiction</u>

Golem
Presenting the Marriage of Kelli-Anne & Gerri Denemer
Twisted Tales of Deceit

<u>Sci-Fi/Fantasy</u>

The Dark Veil Series: The Rose Vol 1
The Dark Veil Series: The Rose Vol 2

<u>Literary</u>

A Billion Tiny Moments in Time…
Indifference

About the Author

I write books, that's what I do. Horror, scifi, thrillers, fantasy, and sometimes a literary gem. Good ones, crazy ones, fun books, entertaining books, terrifying books that are absolutely insane, books with depth and thrills, and stories that rip out the heart of humanity and tosses it on a slab to be feasted on. Yeah, that's what I do, I write books. Any questions?

My current projects include: the Pulp Fiction, Sci-Fi/Fantasy series, *The Dark Veil: The Rose Vol. III*; the horror thriller novella series, *Girl on a Mission*; the supernatural thriller series, *The Hypnotist*; and a follow up to *Jigglyspot and the Zero Intellect*, tentatively titled *The Sleepy Hollow Incident*.

Your Free book is waiting. Join the PD newsletter to stay up to date on all things PD, including, giveaways, sales, new books, and just a lot of awesome. Plus, you'll receive a free digital copy of *Twisted Tales of Deceit*. Join the newsletter at **https://pdalleva.com**